"If it is pleasure you are looking for, I assure you, I will give you far more pleasure than the baron could ever attempt to give you."

"You will . . . ?" Elizabeth snapped her mouth shut. She did not need to finish the question. The seductive look in the marquis's eyes explained his meaning all too clearly. A shiver coursed through Elizabeth. Surely it was one of righteous indignation. "I-I cannot believe . . . you w-would not dare to talk about . . . a thing like that!"

"Why not?" he asked, stepping closer. "We are speaking of marriage, are we not? You question my credentials as a candidate to replace your baron. I think it is only fair I be permitted to present the . . . benefits of a marriage with me. Not only is my wealth greater than the baron's, but I assure you, so is my experience and knowledge of how to . . . make a woman happy."

Elizabeth gasped. "Y-you odious, atrocious man. Cannot you understand? I care not for your low, scandalous 'experience.' "

"Do not be so swift to say that," the marquis said, his voice low as he reached out and pulled Elizabeth into his arms, his lips crushing hers in a demanding kiss.

An abrupt, alien shiver shot through Elizabeth and instead of escaping, she discovered herself moving closer to the marquis . . .

—from "The Rake Objects," by Cindy Holbrook

LOOK FOR THESE REGENCY ROMANCES

SCANDAL'S DAUGHTER   (0-8217-5273-1, $4.50)
by Carola Dunn

A DANGEROUS AFFAIR   (0-8217-5294-4, $4.50)
by Mona Gedney

A SUMMER COURTSHIP   (0-8217-5358-4, $4.50)
by Valerie King

TIME'S TAPESTRY   (0-8217-5381-9, $4.99)
by Joan Overfield

LADY STEPHANIE   (0-8217-5341-X, $4.50)
by Jeanne Savery

SEDUCTIVE AND SCANDALOUS

Alana Clayton

Cindy Holbrook

Martha Kirkland

Marcy Stewart

Zebra Books
Kensington Publishing Corp.
http://www.zebrabooks.com

ZEBRA BOOKS are published by

Kensington Publishing Corp.
850 Third Avenue
New York, NY 10022

First Printing: August, 1997
10 9 8 7 6 5 4 3 2 1

Printed in the United States of America

CONTENTS

Rutherford's Return

by
Alana Clayton

"Nicholas. Nich-o-las."

The Voice was softly persuasive, coaxing him out of the dark pit into which he had fallen.

"Nicholas, it's time to go. Come now, you'll feel much better if you'll just open your eyes and follow me."

The Voice was so compelling it convinced Nicholas it knew what it was talking about. He struggled to lift his heavy lids, shifting a bit in the process. The pain struck him anew, the force driving the breath from his body and causing him to groan aloud.

"Now, now, Nicholas, don't give up. This is just a minor inconvenience. I've arranged for you to be more comfortable. Now try again."

Nicholas was not easily duped, but something told him he could trust the Voice. Once again, he slowly lifted his lids, peering out until he saw a narrow splinter of light cracking the darkness.

"That's right," encouraged the Voice. *"In just a moment, you'll be able to stand, then we can get on with it."*

"Get on with what?" he croaked out between dry lips.

"Why, to take you to a place where you'll be free of pain and worry forever. A place of light, and joy, and eternal happiness. What more could a person want?"

Nicholas was still a bit sluggish, and his mind moved slowly, mulling over the Voice's invitation. Although it sounded like an excellent offer, something seemed to be missing.

"What about my family and friends? my horses?"

"Your passing will cause them some sense of loss at first,

but they'll adjust. None of them will suffer any physical want; you've left them well taken care of," the Voice assured him.

"But I don't have an heir," said Nicholas, suddenly regretting all those sweet young women he had passed by so he could enjoy just one more year of freedom.

"Your cousin will be happy to step into your shoes."

"George?" Nicholas snorted in disgust, then was sorry when the pain struck again. "George couldn't even *find* my shoes, let alone wear them. He has no sense of responsibility, and would bankrupt the estate in record time, destroying everyone connected with it. The tenants would be ignored, and the farms would go to ruin. How could you even suggest George could take my place?"

"Sorry. I didn't know you were so sensitive about the issue. Most people are so happy to get this far that they don't question the consequences."

"Well, I'm not most people," objected Nicholas. "And now that I think of it, how did I get here?"

"You have an enemy, but don't worry, you won't meet him here."

"But I want to meet him. I need to find out why he did this to me, and settle our differences." Nicholas clenched his fists, thinking he would welcome a chance to even the score.

"Impossible, Nicholas," the Voice replied sternly. *"And this is no time to be contemplating worldly revenge. You must make up your mind now. Either step through into the light or return to your world of darkness and pain."*

"Is this all a poor joke?" asked Nicholas, suddenly suspicious. "Lady Jersey has sworn she'd get me to Almack's one way or another. If I step through, will I face stale cake, bitter lemonade, and a flock of giggling girls?"

"I assure you, Nicholas, this is exactly what it seems. It will be some time before Lady Jersey is invited through this particular door."

Nicholas thought the Voice was a high stickler indeed.

"Well, Nicholas, time is growing short." From its tone, Nicho-

las surmised that if the Voice had a foot, it would be tapping impatiently.

Nicholas was sorely tempted to take the easy way and follow the Voice. But, despite the freedom from pain, and the feeling of peace that surrounded him, he stood firm and did not approach the light. Now that he thought on it, there were things he had left undone, actions he had regretted, but had done nothing about because he assumed he had time enough to right them. Most of all, he needed to know who hated him enough to kill him.

"As much as I'd like to accept your offer, I must refuse."

"Refuse, do you? Be aware that if you return, your life cannot continue as it has," warned the Voice.

"What do you mean?" asked Nicholas, wondering what penance the voice would demand.

"At times you have been less than charitable to those around you. While I don't expect you to become a contender for sainthood, I would expect you to be more aware of situations where you have the power to improve conditions."

"Such as?" asked Nicholas.

"There are many people in your country who lack jobs, who are going without food, clothing, and shelter. Children are suffering. Set an example by doing what you can to help.

"And need is not limited to the poor. The rich suffer too, although in different ways. Use your experience to influence those who would benefit from guidance."

The Voice fell silent, and Nicholas wondered whether it was conceiving a more difficult atonement.

"One more thing . . ."

"Oh, no," groaned Nicholas silently, expecting the worst.

". . . improvement begins at home."

"I agree," he said, relieved that their thoughts coincided. "I'll need some time to set my own life in order, as you suggested, then I'll begin to deal with the other problems."

"Beware of a hasty decision, Nicholas. I don't expect you to save the world, but if your efforts aren't performed in good

faith, you won't get a second chance. And you'll be facing some-one quite different if that happens."

"I don't know how successful I'll be," he said solemnly, "but I won't fail for lack of trying."

The Voice sighed, and a slight sun-sweetened breeze ruffled Nicholas's hair. *"Are you certain?"*

"I am."

The Voice was silent for a moment. *"Then, if you insist, I know just the place for you to begin making amends."*

The portal began closing, the light narrowing until Nicholas was in complete darkness again. The pain returned in increasingly severe waves and, as the darkness swallowed him, he seriously doubted the wisdom of his decision.

This was an ill-conceived plan, admitted Vanessa Truesdale as she made her way through the press of bodies. She had known it all along, but had been fooling herself; unwilling to let go of her last hope until a half hour ago when she arrived at the Cyprian's Ball.

The ballroom was crowded with courtesans displaying their wares in low-cut, flimsy gowns that left little to the imagination. They were there in hopes of catching the attention of a gentleman who would set them up in a comfortable house, and furnish them with all the necessities of life.

The men in attendance did not hesitate to gaze, touch and sample what was being offered. Vanessa thought she should have listened to Rosie when she said that this was not the place for her. No matter how dire her straits, nor how great the rewards of attracting a rich protector, Vanessa could not cast her lures and accept the rough suggestions which had been made to her that night.

Once outside on the flagstone terrace, she removed her mask, allowing the night air to rest cool and refreshing on her heated cheeks, and stepped down onto the path leading through the garden. Lights dimly showed the way, but were spaced so as to ensure complete privacy to the couples disappearing into the arbors of darkness.

Vanessa avoided the amorous pairs and strolled slowly down the path. She drew in a deep breath of fresh air, a delightful relief from the cloying, perfume-laden atmosphere of the ballroom.

Her tenacity in searching out the garden and entering it puzzled Vanessa. The darkness held more danger for a lone female than the overcrowded ballroom, yet she was drawn to the shadowy paths. It was an absurd thought, but it was as if a voice in her head had guided her through the throng of revelers, out the door, across the flagstones and down the path.

This is foolish, thought Vanessa, stopping, determined to turn back, until a voice again nudged at the edges of her mind, telling her to continue. She smiled wryly, reflecting that the strain of the past months was taking its toll. She took only a few more steps before tripping over an object in the path. Regaining her balance, she turned to see what had caused her near fall.

No. It could not be. She leaned closer and saw that, indeed, it was what she had first thought: a gentleman's dancing slipper, attached to a leg sticking out from behind a bush.

Vanessa stood frozen for a moment; she could not leave him, but she was afraid of what she would find if she looked closer. Chiding herself not to be so missish, she pushed aside the leaves and knelt beside the figure on the ground.

The man was lying on his side with his back to her, and she could see no apparent injury from that angle; perhaps it was no more than too much drink. Vanessa shook him gently and spoke, urging him to wake up. When he did not answer, she pulled on his shoulder and he rolled over onto his back. Vanessa's breath caught in her throat; she drew back her hand as if she had been burnt and rose to her feet, staring in disbelief. It was the Marquess of Rutherford: the very man responsible for her present plight.

As much as she hated him, Vanessa knew she could not leave him where he was. Gathering up her skirts, she hurried back up the path toward the terrace. When she reached the steps, she saw a man leaning against the stone balustrade smoking.

"I need help," she called out breathlessly. "Lord Rutherford is injured, and I cannot awaken him."

"Rutherford?" exclaimed the man, dropping his cigar. "Take me to him," he commanded, leaping down the steps.

Vanessa led the way until they reached the marquess. A large dark stain had spread across the snowy expanse of his shirt.

"Go back to the house, send footmen with something to carry him on. Hurry, there's not a minute to lose. We must stop the bleeding."

Vanessa turned and once again rushed toward the house. She instructed a footman concerning what was needed, then slipped unobtrusively away.

Nicholas awakened from his nightmare only to find that the pain was reality. Someone was sitting nearby, but he wasn't able to distinguish who it was. "Where am I?" he rasped out, wondering if the Voice would answer him.

"You're at home," came the reply, and Nicholas recognized the deep rumble of his friend, Colin, Viscount Atwood. "You've been shot," he explained, calm now that the danger to Nicholas's life was past.

Nicholas was struggling to set his mind in order. "When?"

"Some days ago. The bullet went clear through, but you lost a lot of blood and ended up with a fever that lasted several days. The doctor says it'll take a fortnight or two before you regain your strength, but there should be no lasting problems."

Nicholas remained silent a moment, searching his memory for remnants of what had brought him to this level, but he could dredge nothing up. "What happened?"

"No one knows. Do you remember going to the Cyprian's Ball?"

"I remember nothing."

"We went together. Thought it would be a change from the

polite drawing rooms, and it was." Colin grinned. "A particularly alluring creature attached herself to your arm and after a short time you went for a stroll in the gardens."

"Who was the woman?"

"I don't know, she had a mask on that covered her face. All I could see was that she had red hair, and particularly fine physical attributes."

"Go ahead," instructed Nick.

"There's not much more. Not long after you left, I went out on the terrace for a smoke. I had no sooner lit my cigar than a woman came running up, saying you needed help. I followed her and found you lying in the bushes."

Nicholas didn't mention the Voice to Colin. It would just be put down to ramblings brought on by the fever, and he wasn't certain it wouldn't be the truth.

"I sent the woman for help," Colin continued. "With the assistance of some footmen, we got you back to the house. Fortunately, there was a doctor at the ball; he tended the wound and we brought you home as gently as possible."

"Did you question the woman about what happened?"

"She was gone by the time I went to look for her. Nobody remembers seeing her. The footman she asked for help hadn't paid that much attention either."

"Dammit!" said Nick, slapping his hand on the bed, then grunted with the pain the movement caused.

"Take it easy," warned Colin. "You aren't well yet."

"I need to know who she is. She's the only one who can tell me what happened."

"You didn't get her name?" asked Colin.

"I don't remember," said Nick, gritting his teeth in frustration.

"Don't worry about it and it may come back," suggested Colin. "Although, when we found you, I remember looking at her and thinking she looked familiar," he said pensively. He thought for a moment, then shook his head. "No, I was too foxed, I just can't place her."

"Keep trying," prodded Nicholas. "It's important I find her. Someone out there wants me dead, and when they find out I'm not, they might decide to make another attempt."

"Could be nothing more than a robbery gone wrong," mused Colin.

The Voice had admitted that Nicholas had an enemy, but the marquess couldn't disclose that information to Colin without telling him the whole story. And he didn't think his friend would believe his tale about a portal of light and a bodiless voice inviting him to step through into heavenly bliss.

"I might think so if it had happened on the street, but not in a private garden. No, someone has a grudge against me, and I'm determined to find out who and why before it's too late."

Vanessa sat in her shabby drawing room, looking out into the even more dreary street. It had been four weeks since the Cyprian's Ball, and if it weren't for her friend Anne Wiloughby, she would think it all a bad dream.

Lady Anne was one of the few friends who had remained loyal when the rest of the *ton* had turned its back on her. She had pleaded with Vanessa to come riding with her, and to attend the events she sponsored; however, Vanessa had refused, knowing her presence could only harm Anne.

Despite Vanessa's numerous rejections, Anne continued visiting, bringing her all the tidbits of gossip about a society in which she was no longer welcome. It was Anne who had brought her the news that the Marquess of Rutherford had been shot and was in grave condition.

Vanessa's emotions were mixed. She could not wish for anyone's demise, yet she could not bring herself to pray for the man who had ruined her.

Vanessa's ambition had been modest: she had hoped to engage a respectable gentleman's attention and make a home for herself and her brother. At one time there had been several men who were on the verge of offering for her, but when the gossip started they had quickly disappeared.

After her downfall, Vanessa had left her aunt's comfortable home and had rented rooms in this dilapidated house, where worn furniture sat upon threadbare carpets, in a neighborhood just a step above complete poverty.

She had a small income from her father which served to keep a roof over their heads and food on the table, but not much more. She and Rosie, her long-time abigail, could continue to live frugally, but she had a brother to think of.

Justin needed a good education if he was to make his way in the world. Vanessa had dipped deep into her scant funds to send him to school, but she could not continue to stretch the small amount she received quarterly to cover the expense.

Despite Rosie's objections she had sought work, but had not been successful. It seemed that being raised a gently-bred lady was a detriment when looking for a position. At wit's end, she conceived the idea of finding a protector rich enough to provide for all of them. She had heard stories of jewels lavished on mistresses, and thought she could sell them to finance Justin's education.

Of course, it would have meant cutting off contact with her brother, for it would ruin his chances if her position were known, but Vanessa was willing to make any sacrifice for Justin. Her reputation did not matter, for she was already ruined in the eyes of society.

But Vanessa's venture into the world of the fashionably impure was over before it began, and she was back to where she had started. She looked out onto the street, steaming from an afternoon shower, and wondered again what she could do.

Nicholas swore silently at the effort it took for him to walk across the library and ease himself into a chair near Colin.

"Good to see you up and about," remarked Colin.

"I'm as weak as a kitten," grumbled Nicholas.

"Be patient, Nick; it'll take a little time to regain your strength."

"I don't have time," he complained, moving restlessly in his chair. "I need to find out who's trying to kill me before he's successful."

"Have you remembered anything about that night yet?"

"Yes, I can remember going to the ball, meeting the woman and going out into the garden. I remember reaching up to remove her mask, but then everything goes dark."

"That's probably when you were shot," judged Colin.

"Tell me again about that night, Colin; maybe you'll remember something new."

Colin repeated his story and they took it apart, piece by piece, looking for a clue that would help them solve the mystery.

"You say when you were bending over me, you thought the woman looked familiar."

"She did, but the light was dim and, as I said, I'd had a lot to drink."

"But if she had on a mask, how could you tell any more than you could in the ballroom?"

An astonished expression crossed Colin's face. "She wasn't wearing a mask," he exclaimed, in hushed surprise. He jumped to his feet and repeated, "By George, she wasn't wearing a mask! I can't believe I forgot; it must have been the liquor," he said pacing in front of Nicholas.

"Calm down, Colin, and stay still. You're making me dizzy."

"Sorry," replied Colin, taking his seat again. "I'm just amazed I didn't think of it until now. When we reached you, I remember looking across at her and thinking she didn't look at all like I thought she would. Her features were finer and, now that I think of it, her voice seemed different."

"Would you recognize her again?" asked Nicholas.

Colin's brow wrinkled with lines of concentration. "I don't know. I think so, but remember it was dark, and I was foxed."

The two sat in silence, deliberating on their most recent discovery.

"Wait," said Colin. Excitement lit his face again, and he leaned forward. "The mask. It was lying on the ground beside you; I picked it up and stuck it in my pocket."

"Do you still have it?"

"I don't know. Robert usually keeps everything he finds in my pockets. If he has it, I'll bring it round."

The mask, when Colin brought it to Nicholas, was disappointing. It was plain white, with no distinguishing decoration or marks, and seemed particularly fragile as Nicholas held it in his hands. It certainly did not look like something a courtesan would wear to attract a protector.

"I don't know, Colin. I seem to remember the woman who accompanied me into the garden wore something more elaborate."

"Maybe you found someone in the garden who suited you better," joked Colin, hoping to bring a smile to his friend's face.

"Maybe," murmured Nicholas, stroking the silk mask. "Colin, you must help me find her. She may have seen who shot me."

"I'll do what I can."

"Circulate among the ladybirds; see if any will admit being in the garden with me that night."

Colin grinned rakishly. "It will be a difficult chore, but I'll do it. Harriet Wilson's should be a good place to begin. I'll go there tonight. And what will you be doing while I'm suffering the charms of the Wanton Spirits?"

Nicholas held up the mask. "I'll be tracking down the shop that sold this. Perhaps they'll remember who bought it."

It had sounded easy, reflected Nicholas, as he climbed down from his carriage once again. But there were more shops that sold masks than he had imagined. Since the mask was a simple one, he had started at the modest shops whose wares did not extend to the more elaborate, bejeweled masks.

The morning had barely begun and he was already tired. He had been pushing himself these past few days, fueled by a sense of urgency that he must without delay find the woman who had saved him.

The shop that he stepped into carried an unpretentious selection of merchandise for ladies who had little to spend. He did not expect to even find that masks were sold here, but he could not afford to risk missing one shop in his search.

A gray-haired woman dressed in black bombazine worked behind the counter straightening a selection of somber-colored ribbons. She shifted her attention to Nicholas as he approached.

"May I help you, my lord?"

"Perhaps. Do you sell masks?"

She gave him a mischievous smile, which drew a corresponding one from him. "You are too late, my lord. I sold my one and only mask some weeks ago. And a great bargain it was too."

"And why is that, ma'am?"

"Why it had been here longer than I have. I was so happy to get rid of it, I almost gave it away."

"Would it have looked like this?" asked Nicholas, pulling the mask from his pocket.

The woman took it from Nicholas and examined it more closely. "The exact one," she said in surprise.

Nicholas's heart beat faster; despite all odds, he had found the right shop. "Do you remember who bought it?"

"If you had sold only one mask in years, wouldn't you?" She handed the scrap of silk back to him and began sorting ribbons again.

Nicholas could barely contain his impatience. "Could you give me her name and direction?"

The woman looked over her spectacles at him again. "I see no reason to give out the young lady's name, even though you do appear presentable."

Nicholas gritted his teeth and gripped his walking stick until his knuckles turned white. "Very commendable of you, ma'am, but I assure you I mean the young lady no harm." He reached into his pocket, pulling out more coins than the shopkeeper probably saw in a fortnight. "In fact, there will be a reward for her and anyone else who can help me clear up a matter of importance."

The woman stared at the coins on the counter, clearly torn between loyalty for her customer and the money.

"On my honor, I mean her no harm," swore Nicholas, sensing her indecision. "I merely intend to ask her a few questions about an incident she may have observed."

"I hope you're being truthful, my lord, for she's a real lady fallen on hard times."

"Then my visit should be more than welcome," he said encouragingly.

Having reached her decision, the shopkeeper took a deep breath and straightened her shoulders. "Her name is Miss Vanessa Truesdale. She lives just a short way down the street," she said, and went on to give him directions. "You'll know it by the steps being swept and the knocker polished. She's a proud one and keeps to proprieties, no matter what her surroundings."

"Thank you, ma'am. You've done both Miss Truesdale and me a great service." Tipping his hat, he turned and hurried from the shop.

The shopkeeper's directions were accurate and it wasn't long before Nicholas was stepping down in front of Miss Truesdale's house. Although it was much better kept than the others, it was far below what any reputable courtesan would inhabit. Miss Truesdale's visit to the Cyprian's Ball must not have been successful in attracting a protector, thought Nicholas, as he raised the door knocker.

A maid answered the door and Nicholas handed her his card with a request to see her mistress. The woman took his card, leaving him to wait on the step. It was only a moment before she returned.

"Miss Truesdale is not receiving today, my lord."

Nicholas could not believe it. He had never been refused entrance, and certainly not from a doxy of Miss Truesdale's level. Most women in her position would welcome a visit from the Marquess of Rutherford. It would certainly raise her status, and might attract interest from other gentlemen who were looking for a *chère amie* to fill their nights.

"When will I be able to see her?" he asked, before the door could close completely.

"I cannot say, my lord," and the door closed solidly in his face.

Nicholas raised his fist, ready to hammer down the door if necessary. Suddenly he stopped, arm raised. He could have sworn he heard a Voice murmur, *"That just won't do."* However, the street was nearly empty, with no one near enough to be heard. Nicholas hesitated a moment, then glanced quickly upward. No, it couldn't be. The Voice had been just a dream. Nevertheless he lowered his arm and made his way back to the carriage, ignoring the *"Well done"* that drifted down to his ears.

"You mean you found the woman and left without even talking to her?" Colin was incredulous. He must still be weak from his wound, Colin thought. The Nicholas of old would not have left until he had accomplished what he had set out to do.

"I didn't want to alarm the lady if she wasn't the right one. I decided that you should first see Miss Truesdale and determine whether she's the woman from the garden. If she is, then I'll approach her again."

"And if she won't see you, why do you think she'll see me?"

"I don't expect you to call," explained Nicholas. "You can wait outside her house. She must go out sometime, then you'll be able to see her."

"I'm to lurk outside a woman's house? Just how long do you think I'll be able to sit in my carriage in that area without drawing attention?"

"Then don't take your carriage; don't dress in the height of fashion, blend in."

Colin was aghast, certain that his friend had taken leave of his senses. "You want me to wear rags and sit amongst the rubbish so that I can identify this woman? Wouldn't it be easier to knock at her door?" he asked, brushing an invisible bit of lint from his immaculate coat sleeve.

"As I told you," Nicholas said patiently, "I've already tried that and it didn't work. Look on it as an adventure."

"Surely you could find a cleaner adventure than this for me," grumbled Colin. "All right, all right," he said, raising his hands in defeat, "I'll do it."

"Thank you, my friend. I'll be forever indebted to you."

It was two days before Colin caught a glimpse of the elusive Miss Truesdale. She came to the door, drew in a few deep breaths of air and carried on a brief conversation with the maid who was sweeping the steps. Colin was close enough to be certain that Miss Truesdale was indeed the woman from the Cyprian's Ball.

"Now that you know she's the right one, what do you plan on doing?"

Colin's question was a good one; one that Nicholas had contemplated for the past several days while waiting for confirmation of Miss Truesdale's identity.

"I've had my man of affairs begin investigating Miss Truesdale. Once I find out about her, perhaps I'll discover a way to convince her to listen to me."

"You mean bribe her," corrected Colin.

Nicholas smiled. "If you wish to look at it that way—then, yes, bribe her. It's the most efficient way."

* * *

"Well, Bradford, what have you found out?" Nicholas settled himself more comfortably in his chair and waited for his man of affairs to report on his inquiries.

Bradford drew a sheet of paper from his pocket, cleared his throat, then began. "Miss Truesdale is a female of little means, my lord. She lives alone with a maid who has been with her since childhood. She has one brother who is currently away at school. Up until two years ago, she was living with her aunt and went into society with more than moderate success. Although she had no dowry to speak of, several gentlemen were seriously interested in offering for her. Then something unfortunate happened." He stopped, cleared his throat again, and glanced at Nicholas.

"Go ahead," said Nicholas. "What was this ill-fated incident?"

"She was compromised, my lord."

"How was she compromised?" probed Nicholas, his curiosity aroused.

Bradford appeared surprised at the question. "It seems she and a gentleman were seen together at an inn."

"I see," said Nicholas, pondering the information. He wasn't surprised at Bradford's answer. After all, the woman had been at the Cyprian's Ball. Nicholas might even be acquainted with her companion. "Did you discover who the man was?"

Bradford seemed overcome with embarrassment. His face turned a deep red, and he would not meet Nicholas's gaze. When he spoke, his voice mirrored his confusion. "Why, it was you, my lord."

A *"tut-tut"* sounded from above, but Nicholas was too shocked to acknowledge the Voice that always seemed to be there when he least needed it.

Bradford's answer had brought Nicholas to his feet. "Me? I don't even know the woman, and now you tell me I have compromised her?"

"I'm only passing along what is common knowledge, my lord."

"Well, it isn't common knowledge to me! I have never even seen the woman, let alone spent time with her at an inn. You must be mistaken."

"No, my lord. I have talked to more than one person who has told me the same story."

"Then why didn't I know about it? Word of a scandal has not reached my ears."

"This was two years ago, my lord," Bradford explained patiently, "and you have been out of the country since then."

Nicholas paced to the window and stared out into the small garden at the rear of the house. "Thank you, Bradford. You've done an excellent job in such a short time."

Relieved to be let off so easily, Bradford quickly left the marquess alone.

Nicholas called on Miss Truesdale three days the next week, and each time the maid advised him she was not receiving. So he resorted to the same scheme that he had suggested to Colin. He waited outside her home until he saw her leave. Then he stationed himself near her front door so that she would have no option but to pass by him.

An hour later, she walked swiftly down the street toward him, carrying several books. A literary lightskirt, Nicholas thought to himself, what a novel idea. He allowed her to draw near before stepping into her path.

Vanessa stopped abruptly, uttering a gasp as recognition dawned. Pulling aside her skirts as if to avoid dirtying them, she began to edge around him, but Nicholas was not going to allow her to escape so easily.

Stepping in front of her, he said, "Miss Truesdale, I'm the Marquess of Rutherford, I've been attempting to see you for days. You must allow me a few moments of your time."

"I must? You overrate your importance, my lord. There's no reason for me to allow you even one moment of my time. Now, if you will excuse me." Again, she moved to step around him, and again he blocked her way.

"Must I call for help, my lord?"

"And who will answer?" he asked, looking around the street. The people who were near did not appear to be the kind who would go up against a man of the marquess's standing.

"I thought I had made it abundantly clear that I have no desire to see you or speak to you. Now please allow me to pass."

"Miss Truesdale, I draw no great pleasure in alarming you, but you've left me no choice. It's urgent that I speak with you; my life may rest in your hands."

Vanessa looked at him as if he had grown two heads. "Oh, come now, my lord. That's doing it up a bit too brown, isn't it? And even if it is true, why should I help you?" Color had bloomed in her cheeks, and fire lit her eyes. "Not long ago, *my* life rested in *your* hands, and you made no move to help. The fact that I am in this situation is the direct result of your callousness, but I observe that you are not suffering one whit."

"That isn't what brought me to you, Miss Truesdale. I didn't know anything about your being compromised, or my alleged involvement, until a few days ago. And while I'll grant you it's something we need to discuss, staying alive is foremost in my mind."

Vanessa gave him a look of total disbelief, tightened her hold on the books, and made ready to force her way past him.

"A pact, Miss Truesdale. Give me five minutes of your time. If at the end of five minutes you want me to leave, I will go and never approach you again. Believe me when I say my life could depend on it."

He watched her consider his bargain, and prayed that if she agreed he would be persuasive enough to convince her to help him.

Vanessa weighed Lord Rutherford's proposal. She had no desire to spend even five minutes with this man who disguised himself as a gentleman. But if she didn't, he might continue following her about, which would be even more of an embarrassment.

"Five minutes then, my lord. And you shall leave upon my request."

He stepped aside allowing her to pass. "On my word of honor."

For all that it's worth, thought Vanessa, as she opened the door.

The furnishings in the parlor were shabby, but clean. The aroma of beeswax and lemon lingered on the air, no doubt used to bring the scarred furniture to as high a gloss as was possible. A small vase of flowers stood on a table, their brightness looking out of place in such a drab setting. Miss Truesdale was evidently a woman who did her best under the worst circumstances, and he had to admire her for that.

His thoughts were cut short as Vanessa entered the room. She had removed her bonnet and spencer. Nicholas observed that she was far more attractive than he first thought.

Her hair was either light brown or dark blond, perhaps a mixture of both. Whichever it was, she wore it in a simple style that set off the fine lines of her face. Her eyes were green, and at the moment as cool as an icy mountain stream.

She was of average height and, although her figure was slight, it was pleasing. She moved gracefully across the room and took a seat, settling her skirts around her.

Nicholas wondered why she was living in such a fashion. With her looks and demeanor surely many men would like to make her life easier. Her presence at the Cyprian's Ball indicated that she was experienced, yet she exuded an air of innocence that could fool even him if he had not known the difference. It was a mixture that few men could resist.

If he had not needed her help, he would be tempted to make her an offer himself. He had not had time to set up a mistress since his return, and she appealed to him. But he could not afford to shatter the fragile truce that lay between them; she was the only link to the person who had attempted to murder him.

"You are extremely silent after insisting on talking to me, my lord. And may I remind you that you have only five minutes."

"Before my five minutes begin, Miss Truesdale, would you relate the events that ruined your reputation? I know it might be painful, but I was just advised of this rumor a few days ago. I've been out of the country until recently and wasn't aware of what had gone on. Would you tell me the details?"

Vanessa again gazed at him with an air of disbelief. "I see no sense in repeating what is over and done with, but if it will get you out of my house sooner . . ."

"It is not over and done with in my eyes, Miss Truesdale, it has only begun. Please," he implored.

Vanessa clasped her hands tightly in her lap. "If you insist," she said, anything to be rid of him. "As you know, it was two years ago. At that time my brother and I were living with my aunt. We have no other close family, and I had decided it was time to marry so that we could have a real home. Several acceptable gentlemen were on the point of offering for me, and my future seemed secure.

"Then I came down with a summer cold. It was nothing serious, just enough to keep me at home for several days, but when I returned to the drawing rooms, I was given the cut direct. I was totally bewildered until my friend, Lady Anne Wiloughby, explained what had happened.

"Over the past several days an *on-dit* had circulated. It seems that you and I had been seen rendezvousing at a country inn."

"But that's impossible," said Nicholas, breaking into her narrative. "I didn't even know you."

"That's true, but it did me no good to deny the affair; gossip had already been taken as truth. When it was clear my reputation was ruined beyond repair, I was forced to remove myself and my brother from my aunt's home. She had two daughters who were ready for their come-out, and my unsavory reputation would have ruined their chances in the *ton*.

"I have a small income, but with my brother going to school, these lodgings were all I could afford. Rosie, my maid, has been with me since I was a child. Even though I begged her to find a better position, she stayed with me. That is the end of my story, my lord, and I think your five minutes are up."

"No, this time was for our mutual problem. My five minutes will begin after we settle this issue."

"There is nothing to settle, my lord. It has been done a long time now."

"Let me be the judge of that, Miss Truesdale. Although you may not think much of me, I have never been accused of ruining a young lady's reputation. I knew nothing of what you've just told me. If I had, I would have answered the gossip at once. You may be right, it could be too late, but I'll do everything I can to straighten out the mistake.

"Can you tell me the exact date that our meeting was supposed to have occurred? I left for the Continent about that time and there's a possibility I wasn't even in the country. If that's the case then the rumor can easily be proven entirely false."

So sincere was Lord Rutherford that Vanessa was almost convinced of his desire to help her. But the marquess wanted something from her and, from what she knew of his reputation, he would do anything to achieve his goal. She tamped down the bit of hope that struggled to live in her heart, and proceeded to answer his question. "It was in May, but I don't remember the exact date. I've been trying to forget it."

"I understand your reaction, Miss Truesdale, but is there any way that you can determine the day?"

Vanessa had no inclination to do anything the marquess asked, but if there was a possibility it would help her, and indirectly aid her brother, she felt obligated to assist.

"I kept a journal, my lord, but it is packed away."

"Will you look for it, Miss Truesdale?"

"I can't believe it will do any good, Lord Rutherford. I only know that it will bring back a flood of memories I'd rather forget."

"But if it's instrumental in clearing your name, it would be worth it," he cajoled.

"All right, I'll look," she said grudgingly.

"How long do you think it will take to find the date?" His voice was eager, and his expression earnest.

"I don't know, my lord," she did not tell him the journal was still at her aunt's house and that she had no wish to pass through that door again.

"May I call again in a week's time to check on your progress?" he asked.

Vanessa did not want him in her house again, but she had agreed to the scheme, so she had no choice. "Of course."

"Good. Now there's something else I want to discuss with you. This is where my five minutes begin." Nicholas drew a deep breath, wondering how she would react when she realized he knew what she had become even though it was through no fault of her own.

"Miss Truesdale, it's my belief that you were at a certain ball some weeks ago."

Vanessa's cheeks felt uncomfortably hot. She focused on her hands folded in her lap, unable to meet Lord Rutherford's gaze. She had just complained about being accused of meeting privately with him, and now he knew she had attended the Cyprian's Ball.

"I don't mean to embarrass you, but what you saw may save my life."

Vanessa remained silent; she could not answer, could not admit the depths to which she had sunk.

"I was at the ball, and I went into the garden with a woman; was that woman you, Miss Truesdale?"

Vanessa struggled to remain calm. "My lord, what are you suggesting? You say you are going to clear my name, then suggest we had a tryst in a garden?"

"I'm sorry if I insult you, but someone shot me while I was

in the garden. My friend, Viscount Atwood, was on the terrace when a woman ran up to him and told him I was injured. He followed her and found me lying in the bushes. The woman went to get additional help and never returned."

"I'm sorry for your injury, my lord, but I see no way that I can assist you."

"Now that I've met you, I don't think it was you who went into the garden with me, but I do think you are the woman who found me. You see, you dropped your mask," he revealed, pulling the piece of white satin from his pocket.

Vanessa paled, but she retained her poise. "You're mistaken, my lord."

"I'm not judging you, Miss Truesdale. Many women in your position have been driven to do things they would normally not do in order to survive."

"I have done nothing to be ashamed of, my lord," she said, although the thought of attending the ball burned into her conscience.

"I believe you. But if you *were* at the ball, for whatever reason, and if you *were* that woman, you can help me. I need to know who is attempting to kill me and why, so I can save myself."

Vanessa thought over the events that happened in the garden. She had neither seen nor heard anything that would aid the marquess in finding out who shot him. "I know nothing that can help you, Lord Rutherford. That you can believe."

"You know that Viscount Atwood, the gentleman you approached for help, can identify you as the woman in the garden."

"No matter what the viscount says, it will not affect my answer whatsoever," she replied stubbornly.

"Miss Truesdale . . ."

"We have nothing more to discuss, my lord, and I believe your five minutes expired some time ago. Rosie will show you to the door."

A moment later he was outside her house, swearing that Miss

Truesdale had not seen the last of him yet. She had promised to search for the date of their alleged tryst, and he would use that excuse to keep himself in her life.

But clearing her of the gossip from two years ago might not redeem her reputation. If she had been one of the Wanton Spirits during the past two years, there would be nothing he could do to return her to respectability. If that were the case, he could always follow his inclination and offer her his protection. He could see that she would want for nothing.

A subtle, *"Ahem,"* sounded from above, and Nicholas looked up in annoyance.

"All right. All right. I know I promised to mend my ways. I won't take advantage of a situation for which I was partly responsible, even though it was without my knowledge." He thought a moment. "I'll arrange for Miss Truesdale to receive a quarterly allowance. I'll have my man say it was an investment her father made that he just discovered. Will that suffice?"

"It will do very well, Nicholas. I'm happy to see my belief in you is justified."

Anne Wiloughby visited Vanessa at least once a week even at the height of the Season. The day after Lord Rutherford's call, she arrived at the door with a bouquet of blossoms cut from her own garden.

"I know how much you love flowers and thought these might lift your spirits."

"Thank you so much, Anne; they're lovely. One day I hope to have a garden of my own," she replied, although she knew it was a futile dream.

When they went into the parlor, Anne immediately spied the roses. "I see you already have an arrangement. What beautiful roses."

"Yours are much more appreciated," said Vanessa, blushing slightly under her friend's gaze.

"Don't tell me you have an admirer," teased Anne.

Vanessa's blush deepened. "Far from it. Lord Rutherford sent them."

Anne's mouth dropped open. "The Marquess of Rutherford is sending you roses?" she asked, once she regained her voice. "The man who has brought you to this?" She waved her hand around the room.

"The very same," said Vanessa, looking anywhere else but at her friend.

"What can you be thinking? And where did you meet him? You told me you didn't even know the man."

"I didn't. A short time before the rumors started my aunt pointed him out to me at the Blackburns's ball, but we had never actually met until he turned up on my doorstep a few mornings ago."

"And I suppose you just invited him in, offered him tea, and talked about the weather?"

"No, of course not. I refused him time and time again. But he's a persistent man. He waited outside and caught me as I was on my way home from the bookstore. I was forced to speak to him before he would allow me to pass."

"The blackguard! Why didn't you call for help?"

Vanessa smiled. "I threatened to do so, but he pointed out to me—and rightly so—that there was no one to come to my aid."

Anne rose and paced the small room. "I can't believe he allowed you to bear the brunt of a lie without doing anything to stop it, and then has the audacity to call on you," Anne fumed. "I will have my father intercede and advise him to leave you alone."

"No, Anne, I don't want your father, or anyone else, drawn into this."

Anne's expression was one of bewilderment when she faced Vanessa. "But you can't mean to go on seeing him; it will only confirm the rumors."

"You know as well as I do that whether I see Lord Rutherford every day, or never face the man again, will not make one bit of difference in my status. I am ruined in the eyes of the *ton* and will remain so."

"But what did he want?"

"He told me he hadn't known about my plight until a few days ago. He wanted to help." Vanessa laughed. "As if anyone could."

"I know he's been traveling for the past several years," said Anne. "And perhaps he didn't know what happened to you, but that doesn't excuse him. Someone had to start those rumors; if it wasn't Lord Rutherford, who was it?"

"That's what he vows he will find out, but I can't trust him and I can't allow myself to hope. There's a possibility he was already out of the country at the time. If so, it will prove I am innocent, but I doubt it will redeem me in society's eyes. Once a person is accused, the transgression is seldom forgotten."

"Despite what you say, there is hope," said Anne, her eyes bright with excitement. "I'll do everything I can to help."

"I could ask for no better friend than you," said Vanessa, reaching out for Anne's hand.

"What are you going to do next?"

"Find the date that our alleged assignation occurred. It will be in my journal. But, at that time, my life didn't hold anything I wanted to write about, so I packed it away. There wasn't room here for all my belongings, so my aunt allowed me to store some trunks in her attic. It will be difficult for me to face her. Not that I'm ashamed," she said quickly, "but I'm angry and hurt that she didn't stand behind me when all of this started, and has made no attempt to contact me since then."

"You are perfectly right," Anne declared. "It isn't much of an aunt who won't help her niece and nephew. When you go there, hold your head high and apologize for nothing. I'll go with you, if you wish. When the truth comes out, she's the one who will be in disgrace."

"Thank you, Anne. I don't know how I can ever thank you for your support."

"You don't owe me thanks, but I would like to help in clearing your name. And afterward, I'll make sure you receive an invitation to every event the Season has to offer."

"That's a large order," said Vanessa laughing. "I never received that many when I was in the *ton's* good graces."

"But now everyone will vie for your presence."

Vanessa became sober again. "There's something else the marquess wanted," she said. "He thinks I might know something about who shot him. I told him I didn't, but he doesn't seem to believe me."

"How strange," murmured Anne. "Does he believe you hired someone to kill him because of what he did to you?"

"Surely not," exclaimed Vanessa. She was shocked; she had thought Nicholas had been asking whether she had seen anyone with a pistol running away, not that he suspected her of being responsible. If that were the case, he would not find her so easy to approach again.

"So your mystery woman couldn't help you," remarked Colin, sipping a well-aged brandy from Nicholas's excellent cellar.

"I don't know for certain whether she could not or would not," admitted Nicholas. He hesitated, then decided it would be unfair to keep anything from his friend, since Colin was devoting a great deal of his time to helping Nicholas.

"There's something I haven't told you about Miss Truesdale," he said slowly.

Colin looked up, catching Nicholas's eye. He knew Nicholas had a weakness for ladies in distress. "Don't tell me you've taken a fancy to her and have offered to set her up as your mistress?" he asked with a knowing grin.

Nicholas frowned. He did not like Colin to speak about Miss Truesdale so slightingly, even though his thoughts had followed the same course a short time before. "I had to force myself into her house, and I can assure you the atmosphere was not favorable for romance."

Colin laughed at his expression. "Rejection is a new experience for you, my friend. Perhaps you'll be more humble. Now, what is it that you haven't told me?"

"You know I asked Bradford to look into Miss Truesdale's past?"

Colin nodded, and Nicholas went on to relate what he had learned about the woman who had saved his life. When he was finished, Colin whistled.

"You are in a coil, aren't you?"

"I am," agreed Nicholas. "Bradford found no other hint of scandal attached to her name. She is not known to have been any man's fancy piece, so perhaps her presence at the Cyprian's Ball was just curiosity."

Colin gazed at him in disbelief. "You actually believe that?"

"It's possible," maintained Nicholas. "At any rate she hasn't had a protector before and doesn't have one now. Her manner is that of a lady, and I believe that despite her unfavorable circumstances that she has retained her integrity.

"It took some time, but I finally talked her into telling me about the events that compromised her. She was convincing, and I tend to believe her."

Colin snorted. "You'd believe any pretty woman who needed rescuing."

"She certainly didn't want to be saved by me," Nicholas replied ruefully. "I had to force her to promise she'd look into the date of our alleged meeting, but that was all I got out of her.

"Miss Truesdale wouldn't even admit she had been at the ball. She's convinced she knows nothing that will help me, but she might be wrong. I must persuade her to tell me what happened."

"Did it ever occur to you that it's highly unusual for the woman who blames you for her ruin to conveniently show up when you've been shot and left for dead?" asked Colin.

"You think Miss Truesdale shot me?"

"Or hired someone to and perhaps wanted to see your death

with her own eyes. From what you say, she's suffered greatly, and it wouldn't be unnatural to crave revenge."

"It isn't possible; she's too much a lady."

"So was the Countess of Stoneleigh," said Colin, speaking of an event that had happened five years earlier. "But she put a bullet into her husband when she found he had two mistresses."

"That's an entirely different situation."

"Is it? When a woman is angry at a man . . ." Colin sipped his brandy, closed his eyes and rested his head against the back of the chair, allowing Nicholas time to think about what he had suggested. Nicholas might be right, and Miss Truesdale could be blameless in his shooting, but if there was the slightest chance she had sought retaliation against the marquess, then Nicholas could not let his guard down when around her. "Then if Miss Truesdale wasn't the woman who went into the garden with you, it's likely she didn't see anything but your body after you had been shot."

"I know, but there's a small chance she saw something or someone which she considers unimportant. I can't take the chance of missing even a small clue. We've been over and over the people who might wish me harm, and haven't come up with a good suspect yet."

"You're fooling yourself, Nick. There are plenty of people with reason to wish you dead. You've stolen women right off the arms of many men; you've collected more gambling vowels than any other man I know; even your cousin, George, must be held suspect. He's your heir and I hear he doesn't have a feather to fly with."

"You make it sound as if there are a legion of men lined up to take a shot at me."

"All you need is one," replied Colin, emptying his glass. "Let's make a list of the most obvious and have them checked out. We can see if they were in town the night of ball. That might narrow it down some."

* * *

While Colin investigated the people on the list, Nicholas began his campaign to soften Miss Truesdale's attitude toward him. He sent her flowers, picturing their blooms brightening the shabby parlor. He called each morning, inviting her out for a drive, but each time Rosie turned him away with the message that Miss Truesdale had nothing new to tell him. Eventually, his persistence paid off, and one morning he was invited in.

Vanessa rose to meet him when he entered the parlor. "I wanted to thank you for the beautiful flowers." The roses he had sent the day before occupied a small round table, their aroma lending a delicate scent to the air.

"A lady should always be surrounded by flowers," he remarked, more convinced than ever that her refinement was a true reflection of her character. She could be nothing less than what she seemed, and the devil to those who said otherwise.

"But I am not considered a lady any longer." She spoke firmly, not asking for sympathy.

"Those in society are fools; you could never be anything else."

She looked up to determine his sincerity and smiled. "Thank you, my lord. It's refreshing to hear those words."

"Even though I'm the one accused of ruining you?" he asked.

"Yes. I've thought about this hard and long, and I have determined that there must be a flaw in me, that ultimately I must be to blame for what happened."

"How can you say that?" he burst out. "You're the victim of a vicious attack against your character. You didn't ask for it and you certainly didn't do anything to deserve it."

Vanessa lifted her chin in a determined fashion. "If my character had been what it should have been, then nothing could have hurt me no matter who was involved. The gossip would have been seen for what it was: a totally false accusation. But I must have displayed something that made people believe the worst."

"That isn't true. There is nothing in your character that deserves what you have suffered," he said, indignant that she should think so.

"How can you judge? You don't even know me," she replied evenly.

"I know what I see," replied Nicholas. "And from what I have heard, you led an unexceptionable life until the gossip began."

Vanessa shook her head in denial. "There had to be something," she said in a bemused manner before looking up at him. "You should be happy. I've hated you for so long, but now I'm absolving you of any fault in the whole affair. Even if you or some of your friends had a part in spreading the tale, there had to be a reason that everyone was willing to believe it."

"Many people are eager to believe anything that will cast shame on those who least deserve it. It's called jealousy, Miss Truesdale, and you had best remember it if you intend to live in this world for long."

"There was no reason for jealousy, my lord. I was merely a young woman of no means hoping for the interest of an acceptable gentleman. I wasn't looking for titles and fortune. I only wanted a home and family. Surely that couldn't raise anger in anyone."

Nicholas took Vanessa by the hand and led her to a mirror on the wall. He stood behind her, his strong hands gripping her shoulders, positioning her so she could see her reflection. He stared at her a moment before speaking, attempting to ignore the uncertainty that had crept into his mind since his discussion with Colin. Surely this woman couldn't be guilty of plotting his murder. He thrust aside the thoughts and spoke.

"I don't know what you see, but I see a lovely young woman. I'm sure that two years ago, you were just as appealing and that many men admired you. That is enough for jealousy, enough for gossip and bitterness."

Vanessa met his eyes in the mirror and saw the sincerity there. Two years of virtual isolation had almost broken her. Lord

Rutherford's kindness began to thaw the cold emptiness inhabiting her body.

"I believe I would like to take a carriage ride after all, my lord."

"You've made a wise choice, my dear."

As soon as Vanessa collected her bonnet and spencer, they were on their way out of the dingy streets into the bright, clean air of the countryside. Vanessa had not wanted to drive in any of the parks where she might meet some of her old acquaintances. Nicholas agreed, for the moment, but secretly vowed they would drive in Hyde Park soon.

Vanessa closed her eyes and breathed in the pure, sweet air.

"Are you enjoying yourself, Miss Truesdale?"

"Oh, yes," she replied, her eyes sparkling. "It's been so long since I've been driving, and with such excellent cattle," she added, admiring the bays that drew the curricle.

"Would you like to take a turn," he offered, then thought himself daft, for he never let anyone handle the ribbons but himself.

"No, thank you, my lord, I've never driven."

"We must change that," he heard himself say, and again wondered at his sanity.

"Have you found your journal yet?" he asked, after they had traveled a short distance in silence.

"I must admit I haven't looked." She glanced sideways at him from under the brim of her straw bonnet. "It's at my aunt's house, and I'm loath to stir up all the memories from back then. They've dulled some now, and I can get through most days without the past causing me too much pain."

He slowed the horses to a walk, allowing them to cool down. "I'm sorry to cause you distress, but there's no other way to go about this."

"What if I rake up the past and nothing comes of it? What then?" Misery thinned her voice and weighed down her shoulders until they drooped beneath the load. "You can go back to your life without a qualm, but I'll be left to live through that dreadful time again."

"I promise, you won't suffer alone again." He might be mad, but he could already envision the future if he could not restore her reputation. She would not be forced to go to another Cyprian's Ball to find a protector. He would buy her a house in the country, away from London's smoke. There would be a stable with riding and carriage horses for her use. There would also be a garden full of roses, and she would be there, amidst all the blossoms when he would visit.

His daydream was interrupted by a loud, *"You promised,"* echoing down from above.

Nicholas glanced quickly at Miss Truesdale. She sat quietly staring at a nearby meadow sprinkled with wildflowers; evidently she had heard nothing. He shook his head. First he was dreaming fairy tales, and now he was hearing the Voice again. What a difference near-death, an interfering voice, and a few short weeks could make in a man's life.

But if Colin was right, his daydream could turn into another nightmare, for any day now Vanessa might be waiting with a bullet for his heart instead of roses.

If anyone in Vanessa's neighborhood had cared to spy on her, they would have observed her joining Lord Rutherford in his curricle quite often in the days to follow.

She melted quickly in the warmth of his charm, continually reminding herself that it meant nothing. Even though she had forgiven him, she repeated to herself that he had played a part in her ruin no matter how blameless. But the reminders did not work as well as they once had done, and she found herself anticipating their next encounter.

Nicholas was more charmed by Vanessa with each visit. He abhorred seeing her in her present straits, but knew that the time was not right to offer help.

"Have you visited your aunt yet?" he asked one afternoon as they drove toward the outskirts of town.

"No, but a friend of mine has offered to accompany me, and we plan to go this afternoon. I'm not looking forward to it at all," she said with a grimace.

"I'm sorry to cause you more pain, but if I'm to help, it must be done," he urged gently.

"I know, and I promise to have it for you tomorrow."

Anne arrived that afternoon in her carriage, and they were soon on their way to Vanessa's aunt's house. Vanessa had worried for nothing, for she did not even see her aunt or any other member of her family. The butler led them to the attic where her trunks had been stored. After a short search, Vanessa unearthed the journal, and they quickly left the silent town house.

Nicholas approached the small house with a brisk stride the next day. During their short relationship, he had found that Vanessa was scrupulously honest, and he was confident she would keep her word about visiting her aunt. He was hoping her search for the journal had proved successful, and that she would know the date of the rendezvous by now.

When he left a half hour later, he was smiling. His visit had been a success.

"Colin, do you remember the date we left England?" Nicholas and his friend had just finished dinner and were enjoying a cigar with their port.

Colin blew a circle of smoke toward the ceiling. "Of course, May 28th."

"How can you remember that particular date without checking?" asked Nicholas skeptically.

Colin gave a short bark of laughter. "Because it was my

mother's birthday and, if I had forgotten, I would still be hearing about it."

"And do you remember what we were doing the day before? My memory is a little fuzzy."

"As well it should be. We had celebrated our departure until dawn and were to meet again that evening. That afternoon, I went to visit my mother with a suitable gift, while you—you scoundrel—had an assignation planned with a lady whose name you wouldn't reveal."

He looked at Nicholas, the puzzlement in his eyes clearing. "That was the afternoon in question, wasn't it? The day you were accused of meeting Miss Truesdale."

"It is," agreed Nicholas. "But it wasn't Miss Truesdale I met. She was unknown to me at the time." He paused, wondering whether to tell Colin the whole of it, then realized that he owed the truth to his friend who had helped him unceasingly through the past days.

"The woman I met was Susan Dalton," he revealed.

Colin whistled softly. "Victor Dalton's wife?"

Nicholas nodded. "The same. I haven't seen her since my return, but I intend to remedy that as soon as possible. She may hold the key to this whole bumblebroth."

"You're spending too much time on Miss Truesdale's dilemma," complained Colin. "In the meantime, you're neglecting our list of potential murderers." He whipped out a sheet of paper and his quizzing glass.

"I think you're enjoying this too much," accused Nicholas.

"Not at all; I'm taking the whole thing seriously, but it is more interesting than our usual occupations." Colin applied the glass to his eye and peered at the paper. "Let's start with Andrew Hendricks."

"Young Hendricks? The Earl of Stafford's son? Why do you have his name on the list?" asked Nicholas in astonishment.

"Young Hendricks, as you call him, is all of five and twenty. You carry enough of his vowels that he would be locked away for his remaining days if his father found out."

"I have no intention of telling his father that Andrew's a failure at gambling and doesn't have the sense to quit. I'm holding Hendricks's vowels for his own good. He knows that as long as he stays away from gambling, he's safe."

Colin looked at him in disbelief. "What better reason for a young man to want to see you dead?" Shaking his head he again stared down at the paper. "However, I have noted here that Hendricks was at his father's country estate on the night in question. No doubt, to curry favor with the earl and ask for an increase in his quarterly allotment."

Nicholas poured them another glass of port. "Who's next?" he asked indifferently.

"Lord Sewell. He's lost quite a bit to you, and he was in town on the night of the Cyprian's Ball," commented Colin.

"He's rich enough to lose any amount he chooses," contributed Nicholas. "You can cross him off the list unless he has another reason for wanting me dead."

"None that I know of," said Colin, again studying the list. "This goes back a way, but there are Watson and Garrison. At different times, you've snatched a pretty bit of muslin from right beneath their noses."

"As I remember," volunteered Nicholas, "they were angry at the time, but I was able to make it up to them."

"Ah. And that night has become a legend," said Colin grinning.

"Anyone else?"

"I have others on my list, but I haven't received any information on them yet. It may take a few more days."

"Good," said Nicholas draining his glass. "Tomorrow we'll begin attending every entertainment the Season has to offer until our paths accidentally cross Lady Dalton's."

"It might be safer to curtail your activities until we have a better idea of who wants you dead."

Nicholas gave an ungentlemanly snort. "I will not lock myself away like a frightened child. I'm sure whoever's after me would find it vastly amusing to imagine me cowering in my home. Further, he would know exactly where to find me."

Once Nicholas had made up his mind, urging him to reconsider would be a waste of breath, so Colin turned his thoughts in another direction. "I wonder why he hasn't tried again? You've given him plenty of opportunities."

"Pure cowardice," spit out Nicholas. "He needs a distinct advantage—preferably to find me alone and with my back to him—before he takes another shot. But I don't intend to give him that benefit again."

The Harringtons's ball was in full swing when Nicholas and Colin arrived the next evening. The rooms were crowded to the point that Nicholas could not distinguish one face from another; the ball was a success.

Nicholas and Colin had attended a Venetian breakfast, an art exhibit, and had ridden in the park that day, but had not met Lady Dalton at any of them. Nicholas wasn't discouraged. There were many entertainments going on during the Season and she could have attended any of them, or she could have chosen to remain at home to rest until the evening's festivities began.

Nicholas remembered that Lady Harrington was a particular friend of Susan's, and he was fairly certain that she would be somewhere in the crowd. The two men separated to search for Lady Dalton amidst the throng, promising to meet back at the door in an hour's time if neither was successful.

It took Nicholas almost the complete hour to find Viscountess Dalton in the last place he expected to see her. When they were acquainted, Susan had danced every set with a different gentleman. Now, she was sitting in one of the gilt-backed chairs, fanning herself in the heat of the room, looking lovely but a bit more matronly than he remembered.

"Lady Dalton," he murmured, bending over her hand. "It has been some time since I've had the pleasure of seeing you."

She looked flustered, and fanned herself even more determinedly. "Yes, it has, my lord. I'm relieved to see you've returned safely."

"Thank you. I'm sorry to say, I found the Continent far safer than England," he observed blandly.

She struggled to regain her composure, but her conversation remained stilted. "Yes, I heard about your injury, and am happy to see you up and about."

Nicholas gave a brief nod, finally releasing her hand. "May I have the pleasure of this dance, my lady?"

Lady Dalton continued wielding her fan. "It is extremely warm, my lord, not conducive to a country dance," she answered, as the sprightly music began.

He would not let her get away with such a weak excuse. "Then let me escort you to the terrace. The night air will have you comfortable in no time."

"Thank you, my lord, but I . . ."

Nicholas leaned close to her, his voice meant only for her ears. "If you aren't free, then perhaps I will seek out Lord Dalton and reminisce about our common experiences. Or perhaps we can discuss the merits of various inns."

"Entirely unacceptable," breathed an exasperated Voice from above, which Nicholas totally ignored. Too much rested on what Susan Dalton knew for him to remain a gentleman.

"Lady Dalton," he said, offering his arm to the woman who had gone deadly pale.

She stood and placed a trembling hand on his arm. "Thank you, Lord Rutherford. A breath of fresh air would be welcome."

Nicholas had to admire her composure in light of the threat he had used. He led her out a French door onto the terrace. "I'm sorry for that scene inside," he apologized, "but I needed to speak to you immediately."

"You could have called at my home where we would have had more privacy," she shot back.

"And would you have been at home for me?" he asked.

She was silent, turning her back on him to stare out into the night.

He allowed her to pout for a short time before getting down to the reason he was there. "Susan, tell me what happened the last time I saw you."

"What do you mean? You were there. You know what happened," she said without turning to face him.

"I mean what happened after we parted that afternoon?" he clarified.

"I went home," she answered shortly. "This is the first time I've seen you since then, so I assume you left for France as you intended."

"Yes, I did go to the Continent, but I've heard rumors which are disturbing."

Susan uttered a ripple of weak laughter. "There are always rumors, Nicholas. You, of all people, should know that."

"I do, but seldom am I involved in one of which I'm unaware. Particularly one where I am the cause of compromising an innocent young lady."

Lady Dalton's skirt rustled as she made an agitated movement. Nicholas took a firm hold on her elbow to keep her at his side until they had finished.

"Susan, in the past, you prided yourself on knowing every whisper of an *on-dit* that passed through the *ton*. Don't tell me you didn't hear anything of an assignation I was supposed to have had with a Miss Vanessa Truesdale," he demanded.

Lady Dalton attempted to tug her arm from his hold, but his grip did not weaken. "Oh, all right. I did hear about it, but you were already gone. What was I supposed to do?"

"Perhaps you could have done something to stop the rumor. You knew it was you, not Miss Truesdale, who was seen at the inn."

"I barely knew the woman. It would have been highly suspect if I had defended her."

"And, of course, you could not admit it was you?"

"Are you mad? If I had it would have meant the end of my marriage. Victor was already suspicious that I had taken a lover. If he had found out the truth, he would have banished me to the country forever, if not divorced me outright," she said, her voice verging on the edge of hysteria.

"So you allowed an innocent woman to bear the brunt of your guilt," Nicholas concluded.

"Don't become righteous with me," she said viciously. "It was your guilt too, and I didn't see you here defending her virtue."

"I only found out about it a few days ago. If I had known at the time it happened, I would have returned to squelch the rumors."

Susan gave a bitter laugh. "And how many would have believed you? Your denial would have only made matters worse. The only way your Miss Truesdale could have been redeemed would have been if you had married her. And you certainly weren't ready to be leg-shackled, were you?"

Nicholas had no answer, for what she said was true. His hold loosened and Susan pulled her arm from his grasp.

"I couldn't chance saying anything, Nicholas. After you left, I realized that my marriage was more important to me than I had believed, and I wanted to right what was wrong with it. I changed my ways. I'm a devoted wife to Victor now; we even have a child." Her voice was pleading for understanding.

"It still isn't right, Susan, that another should suffer for what we did."

"Since when have you become so pure?" she demanded indignantly.

"Since I have seen a young woman living in poverty, barely able to keep a roof over her head and food on her table. A young woman struggling to remain a lady in spite of everything being against her. We're the cause of Miss Truesdale being in that situation, Susan, and we owe her something."

"We can send her money," remarked Susan after a moment's thought.

"Money will help make her life more comfortable, but it will do nothing to restore her spirit and her reputation," said Nicholas. "To begin with, she was a woman of modest means. She and her brother had no family other than an aunt. She was near to contracting a marriage which would have given her and her brother a home when the gossip began circulating. She lost her suitors, and was forced to leave the safety of her aunt's home. But more than that, she lost her good name, and that is extremely important to her."

"I cannot reinstate her to the good graces of the *ton*," Susan retorted sarcastically.

"Perhaps, if the two of us work together, we can," he suggested.

"I will send her money, but I will have nothing more to do with it," she declared. "Now, I must go. People will be wondering what we're doing out here so long. There's no reason to risk my own marriage and reputation because of Miss Truesdale." She turned away from him and stalked across the terrace to the French doors.

Nicholas stood for a time on the terrace. Susan's attitude did not surprise him. Any other woman in her position would probably feel the same way and, before he had been shot, so might he have. But since his near-death, he had discovered he had a conscience, one that would not let him forget a petite woman with tremendous fortitude and sad green eyes.

"You won't believe what I've found," remarked Colin as soon as he crossed the threshold the next morning.

"Sit down and have some breakfast," invited Nicholas. "You'll impart the news better on a full stomach."

Colin filled his plate and took a seat across from Nicholas. "I've investigated everyone on our list," he said, buttering a muffin. "And guess who had the best motive and opportunity to kill you?"

"My tailor. He absolutely abhorred the material I selected for one of my coats," Nicholas remarked in a falsetto.

"You're not taking this seriously," accused Colin.

"I am," countered Nicholas. "Ignore my bad jokes, Colin. I

suppose I'm attempting to lessen the intensity of the situation; it's difficult to think that anyone I know would want to kill me. Go ahead, tell me our prime suspect."

"Your cousin, George," pronounced Colin.

Nicholas choked on his buttered eggs. "George?" he repeated, after he had collected himself. "The George who practically swoons at the sight of a rare slab of beef?"

Colin nodded. "The very one. He has strong motivation. I've found his pockets are to let, and he's in debt to everyone in town. He's squandered what money he has and is living on his expectations, which aren't much since you're young, healthy, and have plenty of time to marry and have an heir."

"Unless I'm shot down in my prime," Nicholas said, his tone ironic.

"Just so," agreed Colin. "And listen to this. Lately, he's been whispering it about to his creditors that you contracted a rare disease while on the Continent and are not expected to live long."

"What! The insolent puppy! By the time I'm through with him, he'll wish he had never heard of me." Nicholas threw his napkin on the table and began to rise.

Colin held up a restraining hand. "There's one more thing."

"What more could there be?" asked Nicholas, sinking back into his chair.

"Not only was George in town on the night in question, but I have it on good authority that he attended the Cyprian's Ball."

Nicholas had an engagement to drive with Vanessa, and even the news of his cousin's perfidy, or suspicion of Vanessa herself, would not stop him from keeping the appointment.

"Were you acquainted with Lady Susan Dalton?" It was hours later, and Nicholas and Vanessa had left the carriage and were strolling across a short stretch of grass toward a pond that shimmered in the afternoon sun.

"We had met at various functions, but I didn't know her well," answered Vanessa. "Why do you ask?"

"No particular reason. I met her the other night, and wondered if she had been a friend of yours."

Vanessa opened her reticule and reached inside. Nicholas stiffened. Was she reaching for a pistol?

Vanessa pulled out a lace-edged handkerchief.

A girlish giggle drifted down from above, making Nicholas feel like a fool. He hadn't known the Voice had a sense of humor.

"Evidently no one was a true friend of mine, except Anne," answered Vanessa, unaware that anything out of the ordinary had taken place.

Nicholas stopped and pulled her around to face him. "Well, I am your friend now," he said, feeling foolish that he had ever doubted her. He lifted a hand and stroked his finger down her cheek until he reached her chin, tipping it up. "And if anyone bothers you in any way he will answer to me."

His lips touched hers for only a moment, not even a real kiss, but enough for him to feel a tingle of awareness rush through him. It was far different from the physical impulses that usually ruled his body when he was attracted to a woman. He had to remind himself that he was not seriously drawn to Vanessa. She was a woman who had been through a difficult time because of him, and he felt compelled to right the wrong. It was also possible that she had information that might help save his life. That was all; the rest was nothing more than a physical reaction to a lovely young woman.

"I should not have allowed you to talk me into this," grumbled Nicholas, the next day. "Vanessa will never forgive me for not warning her you would be with me."

Colin's eyebrows rose at the familiar address Nicholas had used, but he did not mention it. "If you had told her, she would probably have made an excuse not to receive us. I prefer to surprise the lady; I can judge her better."

"There's no need for you to appraise Miss Truesdale's character. There's nothing wrong with it."

"Nick, you're so besotted by the woman you'd probably pull the trigger yourself if it would bring a smile to her face."

"That isn't true," denied Nicholas, trying not to think of his reaction to kissing Vanessa.

"It is; you're just too stubborn to admit it. Whether you like it or not, I'm not going to allow you to be killed because you're blinded by love."

"I'm not in love with the woman. She has information I need, and I feel I owe her something for what she's suffered."

"We'll soon see," replied Colin smugly as they drew up in front of Vanessa's house.

When the two men were shown into the parlor, they saw that Vanessa was not alone.

"My lord, I didn't expect you this morning." Vanessa's face was flushed and she spoke nervously.

"I apologize for stopping by unannounced, but it was an impulse. I hope you don't mind."

"No, of course not. Come in; we were just going to have tea. This is my friend, Lady Anne Wiloughby."

"Lady Anne," said Nicholas, bowing slightly from the waist. "And may I present Viscount Atwood."

Colin saluted both ladies' hands, and murmured all the polite greetings. His attention lingered on Anne and he chose a seat near hers.

"I have heard of your unfortunate accident, my lord. I hope you're feeling well now," remarked Anne.

"Just a little soreness now and again, Lady Anne, but nothing that is not expected," replied Nicholas.

"However, it was not an accident, I fear," volunteered Colin. "Someone wanted him dead."

"This isn't something to discuss with ladies," warned Nicholas.

"Oh, no, my lord. You have no idea how boring our lives are with nothing to speak of except fashion and stale gossip." Anne looked at him, a humorous glint shining in her eyes. "An attempted murder will certainly liven up the conversation."

"Then we must certainly do all we can to put some excitement into your life," said Colin.

"Colin . . . ," began Nicholas.

Turning his entire attention to Lady Anne, Colin related the facts of the shooting—without mentioning where it had taken place—and ended by explaining that they were searching for the guilty party.

"But how could you possibly find out who did it?" asked Anne. "There must have been quite a crowd at the Cyprian's Ball—and was it was not a masked one?"

Her question took Colin totally by surprise. A lady did not so much as acknowledge that Birds of Paradise even existed.

Anne laughed at his expression. "My dear Lord Atwood, if you expect me to accept the ridiculous position that ladies should ignore everything that is unpleasant or deemed inappropriate, then you will be vastly disappointed. My father raised me differently, and I am well able to support myself, so I don't need to act missish in order to trap a husband."

Nicholas gave a short bark of laughter. "It serves you right, Colin. Now answer the lady."

"We're looking for people who have a strong motive to want Lord Rutherford dead," said Colin. "Then we check to see where they were the night in question. If they were in the vicinity or if their whereabouts are unknown at the time, they are added to our list of suspects."

"But couldn't there be someone with a grievance against Lord Rutherford who is not known to you?"

"There's a possibility, but slim."

"And have you found anyone who was both at the ball and carried a grudge against Lord Rutherford?"

Colin hesitated momentarily before replying. "Only two so far, and both have good reason to take a shot at him."

Nicholas cleared his throat.

"Both of them believe they have good reason," corrected Colin.

The conversation veered into safer channels and time slipped by before they realized it.

"I must go," said Anne, suddenly realizing the hour had grown late. "Perhaps you would care to ride with me and we could continue our discussion," she said to Colin, her eyes measuring the close conversation in which Vanessa and the marquess were engrossed.

Colin followed her gaze, but was not happy with what he saw. He still had grave doubts about Vanessa's innocence in the shooting of Nicholas. Perhaps she did not pull the trigger, and perhaps she did not have the funds to hire it done, but she could have certainly charmed someone into doing it for her. And although he found Lady Anne delightfully engaging, and looked forward to spending more time with her, he did not like to leave Nicholas alone with Miss Truesdale. But Nick had already spent numerous hours with her; perhaps the danger was over and her hatred toward him had cooled.

Colin turned to Anne, who was awaiting his answer. "I would be delighted to accompany you," he said sincerely.

The couple bade Nicholas and Vanessa good-bye, Anne promising to visit again two days hence.

The parlor was quiet after Anne and Colin left. Nicholas watched Vanessa staring at her folded hands, and wondered what was going through her mind. She was better at hiding her feelings than most, which was a distinct disadvantage to him.

They were sitting on a settee, and he stretched his arm along the back, gently touching the silkiness of her hair. "What is it, Vanessa? You are unaccustomedly quiet."

"I did not really believe it before."

"Believe what?" he asked, still distracted by the feel of her hair between his fingers.

"That you suspect me of attempting to kill you," she said, her voice emotionless.

His hand stilled on the dark blond strands.

"You believe I was at the ball. You found I had good reason to hate you, so you've decided I am capable of shooting you."

"Vanessa—"

"No, don't interrupt. I might lose my courage. I trust this will go no further; Anne doesn't even know. It's true; I was at the Cyprian's Ball that evening" she confessed. "I found you in the garden, and went for help.

"It was a great shock to see you. I had no idea that you were back in England, and certainly did not expect to find you lying in the bushes. As soon as I saw you were well taken care of, I left. I'm sure you can understand I couldn't afford to be seen."

"Why not? Isn't that why you were there? To be seen, admired, and to collect offers?" The thought made Nicholas unaccountably irritated.

"Yes. No. I mean that's why I went. I was desperate. I had looked everywhere for work, but no one would have me for one reason or another. The Cyprian's Ball was my last chance. I had heard stories; I thought if I could find someone rich enough, I could send my brother to the best schools, and Rosie and I could live better. I never really understood what being a . . . a mistress meant until I got to the ball and those men started pawing me."

Nicholas's hand tightened on the back of the settee.

"Oh, Rosie had tried to keep me from going by telling me what would happen, but I thought I could just close my mind to it and get on for Justin's sake. It just didn't seem real until I actually faced those men." She clasped her hands tighter and gave a slight shudder.

"You may be interested to know, I was a failure in that also."

Nicholas released the breath he hadn't realized he had been holding, and visibly relaxed; his hand once again toyed with the strands of her hair.

"You mean you have not . . . ?" he asked, his voice trailing off.

Her face turned deep pink. She shook her head, "No."

"Not ever?"

"No," she whispered, keeping her eyes downcast.

The vision of a cozy little house in the country with a rose garden disappeared from Nicholas's mind. It was strange, but he wasn't too disappointed after all.

"I'm sure you won't believe me, but I did not shoot you. I tripped over you when I was walking down the path; that's all."

"How embarrassing. I've never met a young lady while lying on my back in a garden," he remarked, attempting to bring a smile to her face. "Did you see anyone?"

"No. I couldn't get you to wake up, so I ran back to the ballroom. Lord Atwood was on the terrace, although I didn't know who he was at the time. I showed him where you were, then went for additional help. As soon as I had done that, I left the ball."

"Vanessa, is there anyone you know who might want to get back at me for what I have done, or supposedly done, to you?"

"I'm alone except for Justin and Rosie: one's too old and the other is too young. My aunt and her family gave no thought that I might be innocent of the rumor. They only wanted to wash their hands of me and forget I existed; and they did so admirably."

Nicholas silently cursed the woman's desertion of her niece; and hoped someday he'd get the chance to tell her to her face what he thought of her family loyalty.

"Not everyone feels the same way, Vanessa." He reached out and turned her face toward him, catching her gaze and holding it as he slowly leaned toward her, covering her lips with his. She sat unresisting, but stiff, and he pulled away until he could look directly into the green pools of her eyes. "If I had known, I would have protected you then," he whispered. "And I promise I will do so now." He could have sworn her eyes filled with tears before she melted into his arms, raising her lips to his.

* * *

"So you're convinced Miss Truesdale could not have contrived to kill you?" said Colin.

Nicholas guided his curricle around a wagon that was blocking part of the street. "I can't imagine it," he stated firmly.

"After talking with Lady Anne, I tend to agree with you."

"You found Lady Anne . . . interesting . . . didn't you?" asked Nicholas, a satisfied smile on his face.

"She's lovely, intelligent, and not missish at all," said Colin, unable to hide his approval.

"And it seemed she found you pleasing too," judged Nicholas.

"She promised me the first set and the dinner dance tonight at Grafton's ball."

His voice was eager and Nicholas was glad his friend had an interest in Lady Anne. Colin had long ago given up hope that he could find a lady to spend his life with. He had been putting off the inevitable society marriage as long as he could. Now it looked as if he might have found a true companion after all.

"Congratulations."

"There's no need to wish me happy," Colin said gruffly. "At least, not yet. Now, back to our problem," he continued, deftly changing the subject. "If Miss Truesdale isn't involved, that leaves George."

"I still can't believe George could summon enough courage to kill me. And if his pockets are to let, how could he afford to hire someone?"

"Perhaps on expectation," suggested Colin. "That's how he's living. He tells someone he'll pay as soon as you're dead and he has inherited."

"I suppose it's possible," mused Nicholas.

"I know a good man. I'll have him check around, see if he can find out whether George has been up to no good recently."

"No matter what we find out, I need to do something about George. He can't be allowed to go about living off my name for the rest of his days."

"Why not? You've ignored him for as long as I've known you."

"And I've been wrong," said Nicholas. "I should have done something to help prepare him for life. His father died when George was only five, and his mother is a bird-witted woman as frivolous as they come. I don't know why I ever expected anything from him under those circumstances."

"That doesn't give him an excuse for murder," argued Colin.

"No, it doesn't, but it might not have happened if I had paid some attention to him."

"What do you plan to do?"

"I have a small estate called Three Oaks. It isn't far from Cambridge, and has an excellent overseer. I'm going to give George a chance to prove himself. I'll propose to send him to Three Oaks and let him learn the responsibility of a landowner, with all that it entails. If he makes a success of it, I'll arrange for him to buy the estate from its income."

"Why not just give it to him?" suggested Colin.

"Because he wouldn't learn a thing. He would end up coming back to London and living his old life until he lost everything again. By making him stay at the estate and overseeing its operations, he will appreciate the effort it takes to make money, and perhaps not be so free in throwing away what he's earned. By the time Three Oaks belongs to him in its entirety, I'm wagering that he will be mature and accepting of responsibility; perhaps even married with children."

Colin laughed at the thought. "That should settle him down, if anything will."

"I'm counting on it," said Nicholas.

Colin spoke cautiously. "I don't know whether you're aware of it, but you've changed since the shooting."

Nicholas looked at him askance. "For the better I hope."

"I'm certain many people think so. You've been more tolerant, and have gone out of your way to help people."

"Get used to it, my friend, for I intend to do more as soon as this muddle is straightened out."

"I hope I'm never shot; I couldn't afford the philanthropic consequences," Colin remarked with a straight face.

Nicholas chose to ignore his observation.

"Are you sure about this, Colin?" asked Nicholas, pacing the floor of his library.

"Positive. I've talked to dozens of people, even my own mother. They all say it was their impression that the rumor about you and Miss Truesdale originated with Lord and Lady Dalton."

"She lied to me." Nicholas slammed his fist into his palm. "Dammit, she lied to me. I talked to Susan at length and she never once mentioned spreading the gossip. She's a good actress, I'll give her that," he said bitterly. "But she won't get away with it. I'll get to the bottom of this if it means ruining her marriage in the process."

"Oh, no," moaned the Voice.

"Be quiet," Nicholas demanded between gritted teeth.

"I didn't say a word," said Colin, looking at his friend oddly.

It was several nights later that Nicholas met Lady Dalton at the Vauxhall Gardens. It was a simple matter to take her arm and disappear onto one of the walkways that crossed the grounds. Nicholas guided Susan down one of the smaller walks until they reached a wooded area that was private.

"Are you insane? Why are you dragging me into the woods?" Susan demanded.

"Because I intend to get some straight answers from you, my lady. You weren't quite truthful with me about Miss Truesdale. I have it on good word that the rumors about the lady came from you and your husband."

"Nonsense. Why would I want to ruin the chit? She was nothing to me; I barely knew her."

"More the reason for you not to care about her fate. Now

tell me the truth, Susan, or Viscount Dalton will know about us before he leaves the garden tonight."

Susan's voice was cautious. "What will you do if I tell you the truth and it isn't to your liking?"

"I don't know, but could anything be any worse than what I've already threatened?"

"I don't suppose so," she sighed. "You must understand that I was desperate . . . I . . ."

"Tell me, Susan, just tell me what happened," he demanded.

She drew in a deep breath before beginning. "The next day— the day after we had met at the inn—Victor came home from his club. He was furious. Lord Farnsley, a friend of his, told him a rumor was circulating that I had been seen at an inn with you. He wanted Victor to hear it from him rather than overhear it in a public place. Victor had been ready to call out whoever was spreading the tale, but Lord Farnsley said that he hadn't been able to trace it back to one particular person, that it was general knowledge.

"Victor demanded to know if it was true. I couldn't confess, so I lied. Victor knew as well as anyone about my proclivity for gossip; I always knew the latest *on-dit*. So I told him Vanessa Truesdale had confided that she admired you tremendously, and had vowed to wed you if it meant being caught in a compromising situation to force the marriage. Victor was more than willing to believe it was Miss Truesdale, not I, who had been seen with you."

"Why, in God's name, did you choose Miss Truesdale?" Nicholas demanded. "There are plenty of women in the *ton* who would positively gloat if their names were linked with mine."

"Don't raise your voice to me," snapped Susan, a bit of her spirit asserting itself. "I'll tell you why. She's similar to me in build; with the brimmed bonnet I was wearing that day it would have been impossible to get a good look at my face. I was hoping the person who saw me would accept they had made a mistake.

"She was also the least likely to be able to fight the gossip. I knew she had no family to speak of to stand behind her. And I was right; when the gossip started, no one questioned it."

"I can't believe you would ruin a life so easily," he said, staring at this woman with whom he had shared the most intimate of experiences.

"It was to save mine!" she nearly shouted; then took several moments to pull her emotions under control so that she could continue. "I was so close to losing Victor before I realized how much he meant to me. I had to lie, don't you see?" she pleaded, her voice hoarse and trembling.

"Victor was so relieved that I was innocent, and he wanted everyone to know that it wasn't me. She spoke freely of the relationship between you and Miss Truesdale, and I could do nothing but confirm it. It didn't take long for the rumor to spread through the drawing rooms, but by that time you had already left London and Miss Truesdale was left to face the ostracism alone."

"Did you ever give a thought to what had happened to her?" Nicholas asked.

"I tried not to. It was enough that I had lied. Whatever you think, it wasn't easy for me."

"But you did it, didn't you? You sacrificed Vanessa for your failings. A woman who had never done you a disservice; a woman who only had the ill luck to resemble you." He made a harsh sound of disgust and turned from her.

"What are you going to do?" she asked weakly.

"I don't know; I need to consider the best way out of this without making it worse. However, if you think to bring additional harm to Miss Truesdale with more lies, forget it. I'll do my worst if I hear one word of scandal fall from your lips."

Nicholas arrived at Vanessa's home as early as was acceptable the next morning. Lately, it seemed his days never really began until he saw her smile.

The flowers he had sent yesterday were arranged in an artful bouquet on the small round table. Their fragrance permeated the room, and he was thankful she would at least accept these to help soften her surroundings.

A noise sounded behind him and he turned to see her enter through the parlor door. She smiled and came swiftly to his side offering her hand. He lifted it and pressed his lips to the softness of her skin. She attempted to reclaim it, but he held tight, imprisoning it between his.

"I missed seeing you yesterday," he said, his eyes never leaving her face.

"I received your flowers," she said, nodding toward the bouquet.

"I would rather have delivered them myself."

She freed her hand from his and seated herself. "I know that you feel responsible for my misfortune, Lord Rutherford, but it isn't necessary that you devote every day to me," she said, her eyes downcast.

"Please call me Nicholas. I think we know one another well enough by now."

She blushed, no doubt remembering their last kiss.

Nicholas was encouraged by her reaction. "Do you think I call every day only because I feel guilt for your situation? Is it so unlikely that I enjoy your company?"

Vanessa laughed. "My lord, I am sure a gentleman of your stamp can find far more interesting entertainment than visiting here," she said, motioning around the room.

"None that I can think of at the moment," he answered quickly.

She smiled at him, a rosy blush rising to her cheeks. Nicholas came to stand in front of her.

"I have something to tell you, my dear. Something I'm not sure you'll want to hear."

Vanessa's hand went to her chest as if to quell the pounding of her heart. "What is it, my lord?" Her voice was wispy with uncertainty.

"It's nothing to be afraid of," he answered instantly to set her at ease. "What I bring is old news to everyone but us."

"You've learned something about the gossip?"

"I have, and you deserve to know the truth." Nicholas began the story. He stumbled several times when he told of his assignation with Susan, but the telling became easier after that. By the time that he finished, Vanessa was sitting pale and silent, her hands gripped in her lap. He moved to her side and took her icy hands in his, sharing his warmth with her.

"I hope you will find it in your heart to forgive me." He studied her face intently while she considered her answer.

"I have already said I no longer hold a grudge against you, my lord. I believe you knew nothing about the rumors until you returned to England, and when you found out about it, you at least did something. But that . . . that . . . woman," Vanessa said, her voice rising in intensity. "Who does she think she is that she can ruin another's life without a second thought?" Vanessa turned to Nicholas, her eyes blazing. "I have never been a violent person, but I believe that I could strike a fatal blow if she were here now."

"I can only imagine how you feel, and I can't blame you," replied Nicholas. "But that wouldn't help."

"And sitting here, meekly accepting what she has done, will?"

"No, but let me try to repair the damage before you tear off to exact revenge." He smiled at her, coaxing her away from anger. His thumb caressed her lower lip, pushing first at one side, then the other, until a smile formed. She gave a small shriek of surprise as he lifted her onto his lap.

"My lord," she murmured just before his lips covered hers.

"My dear," he replied, resting his head against hers, breathing in her fragrance, thinking it the sweetest scent he had ever experienced.

"It does not matter that you found the source of the gossip from two years ago, for I fear I am truly compromised now," she said, not sounding at all unhappy.

"Nonsense. There is no one here to see us, and two years ago did not happen, so you are as pure as any young lady should be."

Vanessa was disappointed with his reply; it seemed he wanted nothing more than to clear her name and free his conscience. "I don't see any way to prove that to society at large," she said, forgetting the daydreams in which she had indulged over the past few days.

"Let me worry about that. I promised to do my best to make everything right. Now there is something more important," he said, turning her face toward his and claiming her lips once more. She felt light as a feather on his lap, but the warmth of womanly curves in his arms proved she was of more substance.

She responded eagerly to his kiss, and an unfamiliar feeling crept through him. He wanted her, that was true; but more than that, he wanted to shelter her from all the ugliness in the world. He had always thought he would find his true love at one of the glittering balls for which the Season was famous, not in a rundown section of London. He smiled as he released Vanessa's lips, and trailed kisses along her jawline then to the pulse pounding in her throat. Life was strange, he thought.

"It certainly is," agreed the Voice.

Involved as he was, Nicholas did not hear it.

Lord Rutherford guided his bays through the crowded London street. His thoughts were absorbed by Vanessa. He remembered her softness and fragrance just as if she were seated beside him. He wanted her for his wife, and it didn't matter to him whether her name was cleared.

Her marriage to the man who had allegedly compromised her would make her acceptable again. But he strongly suspected that without the proving of her innocence, it would do him little good to ask her to be his wife. She would think he was doing it out of responsibility, not love.

He viewed his upcoming visit with Lady Dalton with distaste.

He did not enjoy bullying the woman, but he could not see Susan volunteering to help Vanessa.

Susan was extremely nervous when she greeted Nicholas in her drawing room. She waved the servants away and shut the door behind them. "Now what do you want that won't wait until we meet one evening?"

"I want your help in clearing Miss Truesdale's reputation."

"Miss Truesdale! Miss Truesdale! I'm sick of hearing that woman's name," burst out Susan.

"And I'm sure she wishes she had never heard yours," Nicholas replied angrily.

Susan paced across the room. "I told you before, there's nothing I can do," she said, turning to him.

"You mean there's nothing you will do, don't you? You could do a lot if you cared to. You could tell your husband the truth, then retract the lies you told about Miss Truesdale two years ago."

"How can you ask that of me?" Susan appealed, her hands outstretched. "I told you before it would ruin my marriage. After nearly losing Victor, I realized I loved my husband more than anything. I've been faithful to him; we have a child, and you want me to risk losing all that for Miss Truesdale."

"She deserves her life back as much as you do," argued Nicholas. "Even more so, because she did nothing to warrant losing it. She's already lost two years of it, along with marriage and a home of her own. How can you deny her what you have; what is every person's right to have?"

Susan moved across the floor until she was standing directly in front of Nicholas. Tears filled her eyes, and Nicholas felt a twinge of pity for her in spite of the anguish she had caused Vanessa.

"Nicholas, please. I implore you; do not ask more of me. Life would not be worth living if I lost Victor." Her hands grasped his coat lapels and she buried her face in his cravat, trembling in misery.

At that moment, the door opened and Lord Dalton stepped into the room. "It didn't take you long to begin again, did it?" he asked, looking at the couple standing closely together.

Susan jerked away from Nicholas at the sound of her husband's voice. "It isn't what you think, Victor," she said anxiously, rushing toward him.

Viscount Dalton held up his hand, effectively stopping her from moving closer. "Don't try to play me for a fool, Susan. It worked two years ago, but it won't work again."

Susan sank down upon a settee, and buried her face in her hands.

Viscount Dalton turned his attention to Lord Rutherford. "It's too bad the light was so poor at the Cyprian's Ball that I missed my mark," he said pulling off his gloves and holding them in one hand.

"It was you who shot me?" asked Nicholas, astonished at Dalton's indifferent admission to such a spineless action.

"The very one," he acknowledged casually. "You see, I wanted to believe my wife's story of mistaken identity two years ago, but I did some checking and found out that it was indeed Susan, not Miss Truesdale, who was with you on the afternoon in question. Since you had already left England and I could not demand satisfaction, I decided I would continue as if I believed Susan's story. You see, I loved my wife and didn't want to lose her," he continued, while Susan sobbed softly.

Nicholas couldn't believe what he was hearing. "You mean both of you let an innocent young woman suffer when she had done nothing?"

"It couldn't be helped," Dalton replied casually.

"The devil, it couldn't," exclaimed Nicholas. "It would only have taken a few words in the right ears."

"I suppose we were both too busy living a lie," said Dalton. "Then the child came along and the lie became truth. We were happier than we had been since we married, and I didn't want anything to intrude."

"But it did," stated Nicholas.

"Yes, it did," Dalton agreed. "You came back and I found that however much I had tried to ignore it, the thought of you being with Susan had been eating away at me. I became furious, unreasonable with the overwhelming desire for revenge. I had been drinking heavily that night, and I followed you to the ball and into the garden; a perfect place for murder. It was easy; you were totally involved with the woman, but the light was dim. That and the liquor must have caused me to misjudge my aim."

"For which I am grateful."

"I realize it was a cowardly act," said Dalton, gripping his gloves in his hand. "So I am now demanding satisfaction on the dueling field."

"Oh, no. Not again," the Voice groaned.

Nicholas shot an annoyed glance upward before holding up his hand to ward off the viscount's glove. "Lord Dalton, I have been much too near death once, and I don't want to experience it again."

"Good thinking," remarked the Voice with relief.

"Are you a coward?" asked Dalton.

"Let me finish," said Nicholas, as much to the Voice as to the viscount. "If a duel is the only way, then so be it; but I have some stipulations."

"That isn't the way a duel is handled," objected Dalton.

"Absolutely not," agreed the Voice.

"Will you keep out of this," mumbled Nicholas.

"What did you say?" asked Dalton.

"I said, 'I want something out of this.' This is not a usual duel, Dalton. Not only are you demanding satisfaction, but so am I—for Miss Truesdale. She is the innocent one in all this upheaval, and all of us owe her something. If I win, you and Lady Dalton must agree to undo the harm you've done."

"What a splendid idea," said the Voice, seemingly surprised at his ingeniousness.

Nicholas flinched, but was determined to ignore the interruptions until this discussion was over.

"How can we do that?" said Susan, sniffling.

"You must convince the *ton* that you were mistaken two years ago. That it wasn't Miss Truesdale you saw with me; it was someone else. You now remember that Miss Truesdale was at home with a cold."

"We will never be believed."

"Yes you will, for I will confirm what you say. And I'll make sure that Miss Truesdale's aunt will verify that her niece was at home the entire time."

"I'll agree," replied Dalton. "Even if you lose, I'll do what I can. I'm not completely without sympathy for the young lady; she didn't deserve what happened to her. If my efforts fail, I'll see that she never wants for anything."

"That isn't necessary, I'll provide for her myself," declared Nicholas.

Dalton raised his eyebrows, but didn't comment. There were more important things to discuss. But before he could mention seconds, Susan was clinging to his arm.

"Please, Victor, don't face Rutherford, I beg you."

"Afraid I'll kill your lover, my sweet?" His expression was scornful, and his voice cynical, as he stared down at her.

"No, it's you I don't want to lose." She observed his unyielding look of disbelief and quickly explained. "I know you're a superior shot, but anything could happen, and if you were killed I wouldn't want to live. Then what would happen to little Victor? He would have no mother or father to rely on."

"Don't be foolish, Susan. Nothing's going to happen to me, and if it did you'd be free to marry Rutherford."

"But I don't want Rutherford. I don't want anyone but you," she cried, tears streaming down her face. "I've been faithful since that unfortunate day, and I loved you even then." Dalton looked skeptical, so she continued. "I was only trying to gain your attention by appearing attractive to other men. I thought you would notice me more then."

"You've always been the most beautiful woman in the world to me," Dalton declared, softening slightly. "You didn't need to go to such extremes to gain my attention. I saw you surrounded by men who were far more handsome and dashing than I, and thought you regretted your choice for a husband."

"Never! Not once," she objected strongly. "I'm so sorry for making you think so, Victor. Please forgive me. And now that we've found one another again, I beg you, don't put your life at stake. If not for my sake, then consider your son."

The viscount gave Rutherford another long look. Then with an apologetic smile, he shrugged, and tossed his gloves on the settee. Pulling his wife into his arms, he murmured, "Only for you, my sweet, only for you."

Nicholas stared out the window, giving the couple a few moments of privacy.

"Sorry, Rutherford."

Nicholas turned toward the couple who were standing together, Victor's arm around Susan, her head on his shoulder.

"That's quite all right," he replied, relieved there would be no duel, no chance of reliving his trip to the darkness where only one sliver of light offered sanctuary.

"Oh, come now. It wasn't that bad," complained the Voice indignantly.

Nicholas frowned and glanced upward. "How would you know?"

"I beg your pardon?" said the viscount

"I said, 'I'm glad you finally know,' " Nicholas responded quickly.

Victor nodded, accepting his answer. "It seems we owe you and Miss Truesdale more than an apology. I don't know how to make up for the last two years that the young lady has suffered through."

"I intend to take care of it," said Nicholas.

"Like that, is it?" said the viscount.

Nicholas smiled for the first time since he had entered the room. "I hope so."

"Well, then we'll concentrate on restoring the young lady's good name," promised Victor. "We'll attend every event we can and explain the situation to the biggest gossips. The *on-dit* will spread quickly, I guarantee that. I can go to the men's clubs and Susan can call on every important hostess."

"Tell them I returned from the Continent and heard about the gossip, and I was appalled that a respectable young woman had been slandered without cause," instructed Nicholas. "Mention that the woman I had been with was not Miss Truesdale, but a lightskirt I had met the night before. Let them know that I intend to make sure that Miss Truesdale's spotless reputation is restored."

"Do you think it will work?" asked Susan, a frown of genuine concern on her face.

"It's the truth. The three of us will shove it down their collective throats. Then, after Miss Truesdale becomes my marchioness, no one will dare give her the cut direct."

As Nicholas strode from the room, he heard Victor murmuring to his wife. "When all this is settled, I think we should embark on a long, pleasurable trip, my love."

"It sounds like a lovely idea," replied Susan.

Nicholas hoped his future turned out as well as the viscount's.

Nicholas knocked at Vanessa's door and waited impatiently until Rosie appeared. He found Vanessa in the parlor reading, and stood a moment enjoying her quiet beauty.

"I have good news for you," he said.

Startled, she lifted her face to his. "It would be most welcome, my lord."

"I've talked to Susan and Victor Dalton. She confessed everything and he has forgiven her."

"I cannot believe he would pardon her behavior so easily," she commented.

"Love can do wondrous things," he said with a slight smile. "We had a long discussion, and they're willing to help clear your name."

Vanessa gave a sharp gasp, and hope lightened her face. "Don't tell me this if it isn't true."

"Never, my dear. The three of us will circulate and spread the story that it wasn't you who was with me that afternoon."

"But will your account be accepted?"

"Of course. After all, the Daltons began the rumor and I am one of the participants. There is nothing else they can do but believe it; or at least pretend to do so."

"If it is only pretense, I can still be ignored in many different ways."

"Not if you're my wife," he said gently.

"Your wife?" she repeated slowly, as her disbelieving senses grasped the meaning of his words. "That isn't necessary, my lord. You do not owe your life to me."

"And if I want to give it to you? No, perhaps I should say I want to exchange it with yours. To share our lives as one for the rest of our lives. What do you say, Vanessa? Will you marry me?"

"Perhaps you should wait and see whether I become respectable again."

"Bah! Do you think that bothers me one whit? I love you. I don't want you to return to the *ton* as an available lady. I want you pledged to me before anyone else gets a chance."

"I can't believe that there will be a long line of gentlemen waiting for my return," she replied laughing. "But, remember there are Justin and Rosie."

"I wouldn't have you without them," he teased.

She grew serious, and gazed deeply into his eyes. Nicholas held her gaze, hoping she would see his love for her reflected there.

Suddenly she smiled. "I've given you every chance to back out, so I accept."

Nicholas drew her into his arms, letting his kiss show her the depth of his passion.

As they embraced, the Voice said, *"Well done."*

Vanessa lifted her head as if to listen, and said, "It's almost as if heaven sighed its approval."

"Perhaps it did," Nicholas replied with a smile and a swift wink upward.

"Someday," Vanessa thought, "I'll tell him how a voice led me to him that evening in the garden."

Nicholas pulled her closer. One day, when the time was right, he would tell her of the Voice, and how it had brought him the love of his life.

The Rake Objects?

by
Cindy Holbrook

One

Pale morning light filtered into the Red Boar Inn's finest room. Betty woke slowly. With a smile of feline satisfaction, she stretched. Her muscles ached with the warmth of a long, arduous night of lovemaking. Smiling, she rolled over to the wondrous man who lay sprawled beside her, his one arm still outstretched and draped around her.

She leaned over and kissed his broad, furred chest. "Good morning, milord," she whispered in a sleep-husky voice.

"Hm," his lordship murmured, without opening his eyes, though the slightest smile tipped his sculptured lips. "Let me sleep, wench."

"But it is morning, milord," Betty said with a pout as she placed another kiss upon his chest and squirmed her body close. "The cock crowed hours ago."

"What!" The man's eyes snapped open. Brilliant, but decidedly hazed green eyes stared at her. "Blast and bedamn!" He jerked up so swiftly, that Betty, in the process of kissing him, accidentally bit her lip. She yelped and he groaned as he rolled out of the bed and stood. He promptly swayed. "Damn, I drank too much."

"Only four bottles, milord," Betty said, her injury quickly forgotten as she sat up to gaze at the magnificent body of the Marquis of Lyton. Broad-shouldered, slim-hipped, and all of six feet two, he was a sight to make a girl's heart jump. Betty's heart did jump, as well as every other nerve in her body. "Won't you come back to bed, milord?"

"Do not tempt me, sweetheart," his lordship said, snatching his clothes from the floor. "I have no time. 'Tis late, far too late." He bent to pull on his pantaloons, only to lose his balance and stumble forward. "God, my head!" Betty giggled, and then laughed as he proceeded to hop about madly. "Wretch, do not laugh at your betters," he said, though his voice was warm, and his eyes teasing.

Betty felt no fear as she would have with any other nobleman. She had already discovered that the marquis was anything but high-in-the-instep. She giggled all the more, thinking of the night before. "Yes, milord. You *are* my better . . ." She pushed back the corner of sheet still covering her. "An I would, ye'd come and show me again.

"Sweetings," growled the marquis, now ramming his muscled arms into his lawn shirt. "Do not make it any harder for me."

Betty's gaze fell to his nether region and she chuckled. "If ye come back to bed, I'll take care of that for ye, milord."

"I can't," the marquis said, shaking his head. "I have a bride waiting for me."

"What?" Betty gasped, her gaze flying to his face in shock.

"She'll be at the altar within the hour if I'm not mistaken," he said, grabbing up his satchel. "Damn, I should have brought my valet."

"Y-you are . . . getting m-married?" Betty's eyes widened. "Gore!"

"My thoughts exactly," the marquis said, for once his tone grim. He pulled out his purse and drew out some coins. He walked over to Betty, and with a lightning movement, leaned down to kiss her, even as his let the gold coins shower into her lap.

"Milord," gasped Betty, looking down at the amount of coins laying about her. "So much!"

"You've been a fine and sweet solace to a man who is about

to commit the greatest folly known to man," the marquis said. He grinned. "I've committed many a folly, but this will be the worst by far. Now give me one last kiss for courage and then I must be gone."

"Oh, yes," Betty said, reaching to kiss him passionately.

He returned her kiss with a vehemence and then growling, pulled away. "Blast and damn Richard, anyhow," he said, striding towards the door. "I wish to God he'd have just let me die." Stopping, he looked back and winked. "Good-bye, sweetings. Think kindly of me."

"I will, milord," Betty said. A twinge of envy shot through her. "Your bride is a lucky woman, she is."

The slightest, sardonic smile tipped the marquis's lips. "I wonder if she'll think the same." His laughter was deep and low as he left the room.

Betty stared after him, even after the door shut. Sighing, she glanced down at the coins. 'Twas robbery. She should have paid him instead. The marquis was the finest nobleman she had ever met in her life. It had been a rare pleasure "pleasuring" him, and she'd not forget it for a long time to come. She shook her head, envy rising within her once more. That lady he was marrying had to be the most blessed woman alive.

"You are beautiful, Elizabeth," Miss Heathering murmured, blinking back foolish tears as she gazed at her beloved charge. "Y-your dress is perfect." Void of frills and furbelows, the stark lines of Elizabeth's wedding gown only enhanced the woman's cool, blond beauty.

"Thank you," Elizabeth said, her voice calm, as she gazed into the looking glass and twitched a satin fold into place.

"You look like a princess," her younger sister Jasmine said. She gave a girlish sigh. "Truly you do."

Miss Heathering bit her lip. "I only wish y-you were not marrying that man."

"We have been all through this, Matty," Elizabeth said to her childhood governess. "If I do not marry him, our family will be ruined."

"But does it have to be to *that* man?" Matty persisted. "He . . . he simply isn't good enough for you."

"Not good enough for me?" Elizabeth asked, her delicate brows arching. "How can you say that?"

"He isn't," Matty said, lifting her chin with defiance.

"I think he's wicked," Jasmine said. "He acts proper and fine, but I think he's wicked."

"You are imagining things, dearest," Elizabeth said, laughing.

"No, I'm not," Jasmine said, her face darkening. "He's forever telling me I do not act like a proper young lady, and that if he had the schooling of me, he'd . . ."

"Elizabeth," Mrs. Hampton's voice called out. The worthy matron promptly entered the room. It was easy to see where Elizabeth had gained her blond beauty, though Mrs. Hampton's looks were faded, and unlike her daughter, she twitched with nervousness. "Do hurry. It is past time. Everyone is waiting." She wrung her hands. "Oh, I do hope everything will go well."

Elizabeth turned and walked to her mother, clasping her hands. "It will, Mother, do not fret."

"I can't help it," Mrs. Hampton said. "It is so very important that . . . that all goes well."

"It will, Mother. I promise you," Elizabeth said.

"Oh, Elizabeth," her mother said, sighing. "You've turned into such a good girl. You've been such a support since . . . since . . ." Her mother's face twisted.

"I know," Elizabeth said. "Now don't worry. Why don't you go and make sure Father is ready?"

"Oh, yes," Mrs. Hampton said. Fluttering and twittering, she left the room.

"It's not *that* important," Jasmine said, her tone stout.

Elizabeth turned, her gaze steady. "Yes, it is."

"You shouldn't have to sacrifice yourself like this," Matty said, shaking her head.

"Yes, I do," Elizabeth said. "We will never recover from . . ."

she halted and then said, "from out past debts unless I marry."
A flush rose to her checks and she laughed. "Besides, 'tis no
sacrifice. This is exactly the kind of marriage I desire." Suddenly Elizabeth's eyes turned warm and the oddest, gamin smile
crossed her lips. She reached out her hands towards Matty and
Jasmine. "Now come you two maudlinds, wish me the best of
luck."

"Oh, I do, dear," Matty cried, hastening over to clasp the
offered hand. "I do."

"Me, too," young Jasmine said, though her voice sounded
gruff.

"Very well then, let us go," Elizabeth said. She turned, and
with her satin skirts rustling, left the room.

Matty looked at Jasmine. "It is too late now."

"Yes," Jasmine said, her lower lip trembling. "I-I thought
perhaps . . ." She stopped. "Well, you know."

"Yes, I know," Matty said, sighing. "We tried at least."

Both fell silent. With faces as grim as if they were treading
to the guillotine, they turned and followed Elizabeth from the
room.

Elizabeth stood before the Reverend Milton, her future husband upon her one side, and her father upon the other. She
glanced at her groom, whose cool hand held hers. A strange,
nervous bubble rose within her throat. She sternly ignored it.
Matty and Jasmine were ridiculous. Here was a good man who
would make a fine husband. He would save the family fortunes,
yes. But of even more importance, Elizabeth could be confident
he would never be a philanderer, or drinker, or lose his fortune
upon the card tables as her brother Richard had lost her family's.
She was not sacrificing herself one wit. She was not!

Elizabeth turned her gaze back to the Reverend Milton,
whose balding head was buried deep within the book he held.
He must need spectacles, she thought inconsequentially. She
swallowed hard. The nervous bubble within her refused to be

vanquished. Indeed, it seemed to be expanding to swell through her whole chest. It shortened her breath mightily.

"Is there anyone present," the Reverend Milton's monotonous voice droned onward, "who has just reason why this man and woman may not be joined in holy matrimony? If so, let him speak . . ." A commotion sounded from behind. It sounded as if a late-comer had arrived. ". . . or forever hold his peace."

"I object!" a deep male voice said, quite loudly. Elizabeth gasped and blinked. Her gasp seemed to be echoed and magnified from the audience behind her. She looked hastily to her bridegroom. The Baron Van Etton's brown eyes mirrored equal astonishment.

"As there is no one . . ." The good reverend's voice gurgled to a halt. His head popped up from the book, befuddlement stamped across his features. "What! What is that?"

"I said, I object," the male voice spoke once again.

"Wh-ho?" Elizabeth asked, fully spinning. She started back. A tall, raven-haired man, one she had never seen before in her life, stood firmly planted within the center of the aisle. His entire image was raffish. His wrinkled coat hung awry upon him, his cravat dangled loosely about his neck, and a dark stubble shadowed his firm chin. Elizabeth frowned in disapproval.

Her frown turned to open-mouthed astonishment when the stranger looked at her with piercing, green eyes and said in a passionate, and unfortunately resonating, voice, "Elizabeth, do not do this. I cannot allow it. Please, my dearest love . . ."

The nervous bubble within Elizabeth exploded and she wheezed. "My d-dearest love . . . ?"

"Yes, sweetheart, I have finally come," he said, a twinkle sparking in his eyes. "Did you think I wouldn't?"

The man, whoever he was, clearly laughed at her. Indignation welled within Elizabeth. She lifted her chin and glared at him. "Of course I didn't think you would come! Why should I? I don't even know you!"

"How can you say that, darling?" the stranger asked, sounding pained. "After all that we've shared together!"

Elizabeth heard her mother's cry in the distance, and the sudden rumble of the crowd, but she would not turn her gaze away from the taunting eyes of the stranger. Her own eyes narrowed. "And just what did we share together?"

"Do you really want me to say it here?" the man asked, his voice lowering to an assumed, but very embarrassing, intimacy.

Complete stranger this man might be, but every instinct clamored within Elizabeth, warning her she'd not relish hearing what he might say. "No! I don't!" She spun quickly to the baron, whose face was washed to parchment, and whose eyes stared at her as if she had bit him. "Edgar, I swear, I do not know this man. I do not know what he talks about, but we never shared anything together, I promise you."

"Y-you d-didn't?" the baron stammered.

"Of course, I didn't," Elizabeth snapped. She drew in her breath. "Edgar, I swear it. I do not even know this man."

"Darling," the stranger said. "Do not deny me. I love you."

"Love me?" Elizabeth gasped, spinning to gape at the man. "You cannot love me."

His green eyes sparkled and he said, "Oh, but I do. I know I should have said it before this, but I was confused. Mad!"

"That I can well believe," Elizabeth said. "I do hope your warden isn't far behind."

The man appeared to choke slightly, but he shook his head. "No, if I'm crazed, it is crazed with love for you. Can you truly forget what we shared together?"

"I most certainly can!" Elizabeth said, infuriated by the man's histrionics.

"My daughter," the Reverend Milton gasped.

Elizabeth expelled a frustrated breath. "I can forget it, Reverend, because we never shared anything. Nothing happened between us. Nothing!"

"What happened between us cannot be called nothing," the stranger said, his voice dipping low. "It was everything, Elizabeth, everything."

"Oh, dear," Mrs. Hampton moaned. "What have you done, Elizabeth?"

Stunned, Elizabeth turned to look at her mother, who gazed at her with tearing eyes. "I . . ."

"Yes, damn it, what have you done!" roared Mr. Hampton.

Elizabeth spun to her father next. His bluff features were suffused in purple. "I . . ."

"Yes, what *have* you done, Miss Hampton?" the Baron Van Etton asked.

"I . . ." Elizabeth began again and then clamped her mouth shut. Mutely, she directed her gaze back to the man who had brought this down upon her head.

An anger seemed to flash through the stranger's eyes. "Would you really marry that jackass, Lizzy?"

An odd quiver ran through Elizabeth. No one, but no one, had ever called her Lizzy except her brother Richard, and he was long gone from her life. The unsettling name upon his lips prompted Elizabeth to retort waspishly, "Yes, I would!" More gasps and shouts arose. Elizabeth shook her head to clear it. "I mean . . ." she drew in her breath. Turning to the baron, she pinned a pleading look upon him. "Edgar, you must believe me. I do not know this man. Nor why he lies so. But he does. 'Tis all a lie."

"The heart does not lie," the stranger's voice murmured.

"Oh, shut up!" Elizabeth ground out.

"Elizabeth!" her mother cried.

Ire flared higher within Elizabeth. She looked at Edgar. "My lord, throw this man out! I do not know him. I swear I do not."

Edgar gazed at her, a picture of indecision "Do you not, Elizabeth?"

She reached out an appealing hand. "I do not, my lord. Truly I do not."

Edgar studied her a moment and then he looked to the stranger. "Sir, I do not know who you are . . ."

"Permit me introduce myself," the stranger said, flourishing a bow. "I am Marcus Tremain, the Marquis of Lyton, at your service." He cast Elizabeth a shockingly seductive look. "As I was at my dear Lizzy's."

The entire church broke into pandemonium. It didn't half match the feelings rocketing through Elizabeth. The Marquis of Lyton was known to everyone. Or at least, his reputation was. He imbued the name "rake" with a meaning that far surpassed the common mortal term.

"Oh, God," Elizabeth breathed.

"Oh, no," Mrs. Hampton wheezed.

"Be damn!" Mr. Hampton cried.

"Rake Tremain?" the Reverend Milton asked, his voice rising as he shoved forward to ogle the man with what could only be considered unholy eagerness. Then he turned to Elizabeth, bending towards *her* with a look of condemnation. "My child, you are in the house of God. Do not perjure yourself. Can you tell me that you do not know the Marquis of Lyton?"

"I know *of* him," Elizabeth said, lifting her chin. "Who does not? He is infamous as a libertine."

"Elizabeth!" Mrs. Hampton cried. "Your language!"

"Well, he is!" Elizabeth persisted. "Everyone has heard the stories. But I have never met the man personally, I vow it."

The marquis's smile widened. "Lizzy, Lizzy, there is no need to lie."

"Don't call me Lizzy," Elizabeth said, clenching her fists. She could not fathom why Rake Tremain had come to interrupt her wedding, but a tingle of fear raced down her spine, as if someone had trounced on her grave. She looked hastily to the baron. "Edgar, you must believe me. I do not know this man."

"Then why is he here?" the baron asked.

"Because . . ." Elizabeth tried desperately to think of a plausible reason. "Perhaps it is for a wager. Yes! That must be it. He is a betting man. It must be for a wager."

Edgar's look was grim. "How could he do it as a wager if he does not know you and has never met you before?"

"I don't know," Elizabeth said, shaking her head. She turned towards the marquis, who now watched her with an appraising look, very much that of a hunter planning to take his prey down. "Why are you doing this?"

Something flickered in his eyes and Elizabeth knew he was about to tell another outrageous whisker. Just why in heaven's name couldn't anyone else see that? "Because dearest, I cannot permit you to marry this man. I love you."

"You do not!" Elizabeth retorted, enraged. "You wouldn't know what love is, I am sure!"

A sternness entered his eyes. "You cannot marry this man simply for his money."

Elizabeth reared back as if he had slapped her. Mrs. Hampton moaned and Mr. Hampton began to bluster. The baron, alas, was silent. Elizabeth glared at the marquis with loathing. "I am not marrying him just for his money."

"Yes, you are," the marquis said, his eyes narrowing. "But there is no need. I will gladly lay my hand and fortune at your lovely feet."

Elizabeth clenched her teeth. "I'd rather have your dead body at my feet. Now leave, sirrah! This hoax you play is cruel."

"No, 'tis you who are cruel," the marquis said, walking closer. "How can you deny that night of wild passion and abandonment we shared?"

Once again bedlam broke out, the shouts loud enough to lift the church's roof. Elizabeth unaccountably flushed hot to her very toes. "There was no night of wild passion and abandonment, you cad." Hearing her bridegroom's sputters, even through the din, Elizabeth turned, clamping a desperate hand upon the baron's arm. "Edgar, you must believe me! Never, never would I . . . I sleep with a man like him." She cast a venomous look at the marquis. "I'd rather sleep with a snake."

"Yes," the marquis laughed. " 'Tis what you called me. Your wicked serpent of love!" He winked at the baron. "I vow, she enjoyed my 'serpent' many times that night."

"Good God!" the baron wheezed out.

"I didn't," Elizabeth cried, paling. "You lie, you fiend. You know there was never such a night!"

"Oh, but there was," the marquis said, his smile disgustingly smug.

Elizabeth drew in her breath, forcing herself to calm down. Whatever perverse, insane game this man played, she must beat him at it. She must! "Then where and when was it?" He raised his brow and Elizabeth tasted sweet triumph. "Ha! You know you cannot say, because we never did meet."

"Yes, I can," he retorted, his grin evil. "It was at my hunting box in Andover seven months ago."

Elizabeth stared at him, mouth unhinged. She snapped it shut quickly. "No!"

"It was a cold, wintry night," the fiend persisted. "You were on your way to visit your Aunt Dorinda."

"Oh Lord," Mrs. Hampton wailed, her hand flying to her chest. "I never suspected."

"A wheel to your carriage broke," the marquis said. "I assisted you and gave you shelter at my lodge."

"Is this true, Elizabeth?" Edgar asked, his voice rolling like a judgment from the Almighty.

Elizabeth spun to him. "No, Edgar, 'twas not how he said it was. I did go to my Aunt Dorinda seven months ago and the wheel on our carriage did break. How he knows of the story, I cannot say. But I never met him. I swear, I went to an inn that night. It was all quite proper, it was!"

"Truly?" the baron asked.

"Truly," Elizabeth said. "And I have a witness to prove it! My maid Matilda . . ." Elizabeth wheezed to a halt. They had been forced to let the maid go three months ago, as well as most of the serving staff. She looked at the marquis with new respect. He was not a man, but a demon. "H-how could you know?"

"Because it happened," the marquis said.

"You lie," Elizabeth said.

"Do I?" he asked, his face showing supreme confidence.

"Yes, you do," Elizabeth said. She'd not be beat by such as he. Drawing up her dignity like a cloak about her, Elizabeth turned her attentions to her one chance. She looked to the baron, her gaze honest and sincere. "Edgar, you have courted me these past six months. You know I would never do anything so scandalous and improper. You know it?"

"I had always thought so," Edgar said, his voice hesitant.

"You know me as a woman of honor," Elizabeth said, lifting her head proudly. "And you are a man of honor. Will you believe this man, this man whose reputation is one of ill-repute, over me?"

"I do not know," Edgar said, looking torn.

A disillusioned pain knifed through Elizabeth, but she pressed onward regardless. She softened her voice. "Edgar, we will have a fine and honorable marriage. We will. Unless you permit this stranger, this libertine, to destroy it. I promise to be your faithful and . . . and loving wife. This man talks, no . . . this *stranger* talks, but I promise."

"Lizzy," the marquis said lowly. "Do not persist. You will go for a fall."

"You are an honorable man, Edgar," Elizabeth said, her attention steady upon the baron. "You have promised to marry me. Will you break our troth? Will you become a lesser man because Rake Tremain chooses to play a hoax on me . . . no, on you!"

"Well . . ." Edgar said, puffing out his chest.

Elizabeth sensed victory once again. She had found the right path. Edgar existed on pride and pride alone. "Do not let him tarnish your honor, Edgar. You are too fine of man to permit this to happen."

"Lizzy, stop," the marquis said, a warning within his voice. "Don't make me do it."

"Edgar?" Elizabeth asked, allowing an appealing, melting look to enter her eyes. "Please. I do not know how he learned of my travels to my aunt, but it should not matter if you have faith in me . . . as I do in you."

Edgar swallowed. Finally, he nodded. "I-I believe you."

Satisfaction engulfed Elizabeth. "Thank you, Edgar. Thank you!"

"If that night did not happen, Lizzy," the marquis said. "Then how do I know of your birthmark?"

Elizabeth's satisfaction evaporated. She gasped and looked at the marquis. "What?"

He smiled, but kindly, like a sympathetic executioner before bringing down the ax. "Strawberry it is . . ."

"No," Elizabeth murmured, shaking her head in dread.

"And shaped like a diamond I declare."

"N-no," Elizabeth murmured again.

"It is upon your . . ."

"Oh no!" Mrs. Hampton cried, her wail high and keening. "He knows! It is true!" She threw up her hands, gasped, and then toppled to the ground in a dead faint.

Elizabeth stared at her fallen mother, stunned. Her fate had just been sealed. The proof was the din that arose from the onlookers, a noise that surpassed raising the roof and moved promptly into raising the dead. Elizabeth, feeling the executioner's ax firmly implanted into her neck, tore her gaze from her fallen mother to look numbly at the marquis.

Their gazes held a moment. Almost as a concession, the marquis said, "No, I shall not say where, but if you marry her, Edgar, you will discover it for yourself. It is located in the most charming place, I assure you."

"What?" the baron gurgled. He turned a blueing face to Elizabeth. "Madame, y-you have deceived me. I shall not take a harlot to wed." With a jerk of his priggish, pompous head, the Baron Van Etton stormed down the aisle and out of the church.

"Repent, my child," the Reverend Milton cried, waving his book. "Repent of your sins."

Wild fury ripped through Elizabeth. "Oh, I'll repent!" she stalked directly up to the marquis, drew her left arm back and plowed a balled fist directly into his chest.

Everyone shrieked, except the marquis. He rocked slightly back and then laughed, reaching out his arms to her. "That's my Lizzy!"

"I am not your Lizzy, blast you," Elizabeth cried and slapped at those encroaching arms. He clamped them about her regardless, and Elizabeth wheezed as he jerked her too him, all but lifting her from the ground. "Let me go!"

"This is the spitfire I know," the marquis said, laughing all the more. He bent, and before Elizabeth could fathom what he was about, hoisted her over his shoulder. Flushing from the sheer indignity, as well as the blood rushing to her overturned head, Elizabeth pounded upon his back, cursing with unladylike vehemence. "Excuse me, ladies and gentlemen," the marquis said, "I must have a word with my gentle, turtledove."

"You will not," Elizabeth cried, squirming and wiggling as the marquis turned and strode down the aisle toward the exiting doors.

"Please do not leave, Reverend," the marquis called over his shoulder as he walked through those doors. No matter how Elizabeth fought, he did not release her, but carried her into a small room, apparently the Reverend's study, and closed the door.

"Let me go!" Elizabeth cried, thwacking his back for emphasis.

"Certainly," the marquis said. He walked over, bent down and dumped her upon an old sofa. "Now we can talk."

"Talk!" Elizabeth wheezed, attempting to catch her breath as she dragged herself to a sitting position. "We have nothing to talk about!"

"Yes, we do," the marquis said, standing over her with a grim look upon his face.

Elizabeth suddenly realized how imposing the man was. An odd quiver ran through her. "Are you mad?" she asked. It was not a rhetorical question. She desired to know the answer most heartily.

"No," the marquis said, shaking his head. " 'Tis not I who am mad."

"Then why . . . why have you done this?" Elizabeth asked.

He ran a hand across his unshaved chin and his green eyes turned rueful. "Because your infernal brother has requested it of me."

Elizabeth froze, undefined emotions whirling through her. "Richard?"

"Yes," the marquis said. "Richard."

"I-impossible," Elizabeth said.

"Why is it impossible?" the marquis asked.

"Because . . . because . . ." Elizabeth halted, and drew in a breath. "Because I have not seen him in three years. Our family . . ."

"I know," the man said, his eyes narrowing. "Your family has disowned him. But he has not disowned you. He heard of your impending marriage to the baron and wrote to me requesting that I ensure you did not marry the popinjay."

"But how did he know?" Elizabeth asked, stunned.

The marquis's eyes turned enigmatic. "Suffice it to say, he knew. He did not wish you to sacrifice yourself to the baron."

Elizabeth stared at him a moment, assimilating his words. Then a bitter laugh choked her. "He did not want me to sacrifice myself? That is rich. He does not wish me to sacrifice myself when 'tis he who . . . who," she halted, a pain squeezing her words into silence.

"Who ran your family into the ground," the marquis said, nodding. "I did not know him in those days, but he has told me of why your family cast him off. I believe he has repented of his ways since then."

"Repented!" Elizabeth cried, hotly. "He cannot have repented if he sent you t-to do this. I-I cannot believe he . . . he told all those things." She flushed hot.

The marquis shook his head. "I wouldn't have mentioned the birthmark, but you forced me to do so."

"I did not!" Elizabeth said. "How could I have known that . . . that you knew of it . . . or would even dare to mention it."

He shrugged. "I used it as the last resort, I assure you. You were almost succeeding in talking that blockhead Van Etton around. He would have married you."

"Yes," Elizabeth said, bitterness black within her. "He would have married me. How dreadful!"

"Yes, it would have been," the marquis said. "Richard says you would never have been happy with a man such as the baron."

"He's wrong. I would have been extremely happy," Elizabeth said, her chin lifting. "The baron is a fine and honorable man."

"He is a self-consequential prig," the marquis returned. "Who'd ask you to be naught but a pattern card of respectability." His tone softened. "That's not you, Lizzy."

Elizabeth stared at the man, stunned. He said it as if he knew her, as if he were truly a friend of long standing. Elizabeth shook herself. "Yes, it is me! And my name is Elizabeth!" She pushed herself up from the sofa, hastily putting a distance between herself and this stranger who looked at her with such knowing eyes. "I suppose that Richard told you something different." She crossed her arms and swung around to confront him. "Well, he is mistaken. He has not seen me these past three years. I have changed." Her gaze hardened. "I am not the child Richard remembers. And whether he wishes to believe it or not, the simple truth is that I want to marry the baron."

The marquis nodded. "Of course you do. Your family will be up the river tick otherwise. But you need not marry the baron." He seemed to straighten and he said with a stiffness. "I am to marry you instead."

Elizabeth felt as if she had been punched in the stomach. "Wh-what?"

"I said," the marquis repeated, his gaze level, "I will marry you instead."

Elizabeth gaped at him. "Y-you will m-marry me instead?"

"Yes," he said. A rueful grin curved his lips. "Your dear brother, who loves you regardless of what you think, has requested me not only to stop the wedding, but to take care of you." He sighed and shook his head. "I own, if his letter had come earlier from India . . ."

"India?" Elizabeth asked, despite herself. "Is that where he is?"

"Yes, that is where he is, or was," the marquis said. "And that is what has caused this coil. If he were here, I would not have to be. Or even, as I said, if his letter had arrived earlier than it did, I would have been able to make different arrangements for you. But since it did not, there are no other options."

"No other options?" Elizabeth asked, her voice weak. "You are quite confused. Me marrying you is not an option. It is preposterous. I do not know why you even thought it an option, or why you would marry me just to please my brother, but I do not care. I will not marry you. Ever!"

The marquis stiffened, his face registering actual surprise. "I beg your pardon?"

"I said, I will not marry you," Elizabeth said. " 'Tis an insult that you thought I might."

"An insult?" the marquis asked, his dark brows snapping down.

"Yes," Elizabeth said, her tone frigid. "An insult of the highest degree."

He studied her a moment and then he laughed. "All right, I deserved that. I own I caused you an extreme amount of discomfort, and my entrance was not as graceful as it could have been . . ."

"Indeed," Elizabeth said.

"And, yes, it took some time for me to grow accustomed to the notion, myself," he said, smiling. His eyes warmed. "Though now I believe, I shall be pleased to marry you."

"Would you?" Elizabeth cooed. "Well, I will not be pleased to marry you. Despite your protestations, you must be insane. That or the most conceited coxcomb alive."

The warmth left his eyes. "I do not think it insane, or conceited, to believe that my suit would be far more advantageous than the baron's. My estates are far grander than his, as is my title." His eyes narrowed. "You are not going to try and tell me this was a love match. I'll not believe it."

"No," Elizabeth said, gritting her teeth. "It was not a love match, but I respected the baron. It would have been a pleasure to marry such a fine and upstanding man."

"A pleasure?" She saw a muscle jump along the marquis's

jaw. His green eyes darkened. "You use the word pleasure in the same sentence with Van Etton? Faith, you are naïve. If it is pleasure you are looking for, I assure you, I will give you far more pleasure than the baron could ever attempt to give you."

"You will . . . ?" Elizabeth snapped her mouth shut. She did not need to finish the question. The seductive look in the marquis's eyes explained his meaning all too clearly. A shiver coursed through her. Surely it was one of righteous indignation. "I-I cannot believe . . . you w-would dare to talk about . . . about a thing like that!"

"Why not?" he asked, stepping closer. "We are speaking of marriage, are we not? You question my credentials as a candidate to replace your baron. I think it only fair I be permitted to present the . . . benefits of a marriage with me. Not only is my wealth greater than the baron's, but I assure you, so is my experience and knowledge of how to . . . make a woman happy."

Elizabeth gasped. "Y-you odious, atrocious man. Cannot you understand? I care not for your low, scandalous *experience.*"

"Do not be so swift to say that," the marquis said, his voice low. In a lightning attack, he reached out and hauled Elizabeth up against him. His lips came down to crush hers in a demanding kiss. Elizabeth tried to jerk away, but he held her firm. She stiffened, determined not to give the beast the satisfaction of an undignified fight.

Her ploy seemed neither to shame nor discomfort him, for he did not release her. His lips softened, however, and slid to just tease at the corner of her mouth. His arms, that had been iron bands, loosened, and his hands slowly roamed the curve of her back; their heat felt even through the cool silk of her wedding dress.

An abrupt, alien shiver shot through Elizabeth and she gasped. His lips brushed along her lower lip, and the slightest, frustrated sound escaped Elizabeth as those lips moved away, rather than meeting hers as she suddenly desired.

"Softly now," he whispered, his lips moving to her ear. An exquisite sensation shook her as he nipped at her earlobe. Another tremble thrilled through her as his hands slid to caress her sides, his thumbs just lightly brushing under the curve of her breasts. She should step away, her mind shouted. She should escape!

Instead of escaping, Elizabeth discovered herself moving closer. His gentle teasing touch was simply not enough. It only stirred an overpowering need within her to press her strangely heated body against the firmness and strength of his.

" 'Twill be good, Lizzy," the marquis said, his voice soft, as seductive as his hands. "This marriage of ours."

"No," Elizabeth said, her voice a hoarse whisper.

"No?" He chuckled, his lips grazing hers again. "Are you sure, Lizzy?" he asked, before taking her lips with a new fierceness. This time Elizabeth did not fight the passion, but moaning, met it. His hands pulled her yielding body to him roughly, and then he was lifting her. Elizabeth, afire with a new, wild heat neither cared nor noticed.

He carried her to the sofa, and lowered her down to it. She sighed when he followed atop her. It was as if desire itself encompassed her, the friction of hard sinew against her soft curves, the trill of branding lips covering her mouth, the shiver of large hands caressing her body. Elizabeth, far past thought, lost herself in that desire. She twisted and moved to align with his body, demanded the very breath of his kiss, arched to the command of his touch.

"Lord, Lizzy," the marquis groaned, tearing his lips away from her mouth, to trace them along her cheek and to the curve of her neck. She only moaned, and turned her head to allow those lips a clear path. She trembled as his hand came to her bodice, tugging it aside, his lips discovering an even surer course.

"What in God's name!" Elizabeth's father's voice roared.

Elizabeth gasped. Marcus raised his head. For a moment his green eyes, dark with passion gazed at her. "We must finish this later," he said, his voice warm. Elizabeth blinked. Finish *this* later? Reality broadsided her, dispelling the crazed desire from just a moment before. He chuckled and rolled swiftly from her to stand.

"Elizabeth!" her mother's voice shrieked.

"Father and Mother?" Elizabeth asked. She sat up, feeling dazed and confused. Then a scorching flush covered her. Not only did her mother and father stand in the doorway with mouths ajar, but so did Matty and Jasmine.

"How could you?" Mrs. Hampton gasped, wringing her hands.

"I didn't," Elizabeth said quickly, and rather stupidly. "I mean . . ."

"You don't have to tell us what you mean," her father roared.

"But you can," Jasmine said, her eyes sparkling, "if you want to."

The marquis laughed. "You are Jasmine, aren't you?"

Jasmine dipped a quick curtsy. "Yes, my lord."

"Call me Marcus," he said, "little sister."

"Famous!" Jasmine clapped her hands together. "So you really are going to marry my sister."

"No," Elizabeth cried, shaking her head. "No! He is not going to marry me." She turned stunned eyes to Marcus as she realized his fell purpose. One which only moments ago she had desired with her entire being. "You-you were going t-to s-seduce me . . ."

His eyes sparkled. "No, just persuade you."

"You . . . you . . ." Elizabeth sputtered.

"We *are* going to be married," Marcus said, his voice firm.

"Never," Elizabeth cried, jumping up. She stumbled, unaware that her skirts had become twisted while upon the sofa. "Never!" She bent over to swat the folds into place. Another chorus of exclamations arose, and Elizabeth glanced up. Everyone was staring disconcertingly at her chest. Only then did she notice her neckline was awry, frightfully awry. "I'll never marry you!" Elizabeth tugged at her bodice viciously. The fine material ripped. She let out an enraged cry and slapped her hand over her chest for what meager semblance of modesty she could garner. The marquis laughed and she shot him a fulminating glare.

"But Elizabeth, look at you . . . ," Mrs. Hampton wailed.

"I'd rather not," Elizabeth said, gritting her teeth.

"Dearest, y-you must marry him!" Mrs. Hampton persisted. " 'Tis clear you have . . ."

"I don't care what I have!" Elizabeth said, lifting her chin. "I'll not marry a low, dishonorable rake and libertine."

Marcus stiffened and his gaze raked her in clear insult. "It appears to me it is you who lack honor in this situation. To kiss me and . . ."

"Get out!" Elizabeth shouted, stamping her foot. "Get out, before I scream."

"Very well," Marcus said, his tone crisp. "But like it or not, madame, we will be married." He stalked towards Elizabeth's family. "Let us leave my delicate bride to regain her calm."

Elizabeth, her chest heaving and her eyes tearing, stood as stiffly in control as she could while Marcus herded her objecting family from the room. The minute the door closed, she sank to the floor and sat there, her mind in a whirl.

Had any woman ever experienced such a frightful wedding day as this one? To have an honorable groom walk out the door, and a dishonorable one walk in and take his place? A dishonorable groom who had well nigh succeeded in having the honeymoon even before the wedding, at that.

Elizabeth flushed. The man was not a man. He was Satan himself. 'Twas clear he had the power to make a woman turn wanton within his arms, but Elizabeth swore to herself, he'd never have that chance again. She was a woman with spirit and intelligence as well. Indeed, her flesh had proven itself to be weak, but her spirit would never submit. She would never marry that devil, for surely that would be the road to perdition.

Elizabeth nodded her head in grim determination. Then she burst into tears.

Two

Marcus alighted from his horse before the millinery shop. His smile was tight and grim. Miss Heathering had not failed him. The Hamptons's old coach was in front of the shop and with luck the Hampton ladies were within. More importantly, Elizabeth Hampton would be within. The woman had escaped him for an entire month. She had sent his letters back unopened, thrown out his flowers, and refused to see him. Faith, as a foe she was more agile than the French he had fought.

No longer would he play this cat and mouse game. He jerked open the shop's door and entered. He halted, immediately sensing a tension. Elizabeth, as well as Miss Heathering and Jasmine, stood at the counter, with their backs turned towards him. Another short, matronly woman stood behind the counter. Her face was cold and her voice frigid as she said, "I'm sorry, Miss Hampton, but your family no longer has credit with this establishment. You are already six months behind upon payment of past debts."

"You have carried other customers past six months, Mrs. Cartwright," Elizabeth's voice sounded calm and dignified. "I do not understand . . ."

"Those customers," Mrs. Cartwright interrupted, "I expect *will* pay."

"I see," Elizabeth said.

"Furthermore," Mrs. Cartwright said, her head tilting to a

self-righteous angle, "it matters not if you could pay. I do not sell to . . . women such as you."

"Blast and damn, what the devil do you mean?" Marcus exclaimed, striding forward. The ladies started and turned towards him. He stopped suddenly as he saw Elizabeth's face. It was extremely pale, and her eyes showed a strain and fear.

She stiffened and nodded. "My lord."

Marcus remained frozen, staring at her. The woman had lost weight. He knew women's figures to a nicety, since he enjoyed them to a nicety, and Elizabeth Hampton had lost at least ten pounds. That within a month. What in blazes was she trying to do? Kill herself?

Marcus shook himself and dragged his gaze away from Elizabeth. He looked at Mrs. Cartwright and lifted a haughty brow. "I asked you, my good woman, what do you mean you will not sell to Miss Hampton?"

"You know exactly what I mean," Mrs. Cartwright said, lifting her chin. Rage shot through Marcus and he glared at her. She flushed and said more humbly, "M-my lord."

" 'Tis all right, my lord," Elizabeth said, her voice devoid of emotion. "This is not a concern of yours." She turned back and nodded to the proprietress. "We shall take our business elsewhere. Good day, Mrs. Cartwright." Her back ramrod straight, Elizabeth turned, and without a glance towards anyone, walked out of the store.

"Old cat," Jasmine said. She made a face at Mrs. Cartwright and then dashed after Elizabeth.

"Indeed," Miss Heathering said, jerking a stiff nod at Mrs. Cartwright and walking out of the shop as well.

"I'll deal with you later, madame," Marcus said in a thunderous tone. Then he strode from the shop. "Elizabeth!" he called out, overtaking her. "Wait!"

"Wait for what, my lord?" Elizabeth asked, turning upon him. Marcus halted, stunned by the burning rage within her eyes. "Wait, so that I may be further humiliated?"

Her anger fueled an equal one within Marcus. "You should

never have let that woman talk to you in that fashion. She has no right . . ."

"She has every right," Elizabeth said, her voice low. "She thinks I am your . . . your doxy."

"No matter what she thinks," Marcus said. "Her behavior should not be tolerated."

The spark of anger suddenly disappeared from Elizabeth's eyes. A weariness replaced it. "Do not concern yourself, my lord. I am quite accustomed to it."

"What?" Marcus asked.

" 'Tis a small village, my lord," Elizabeth said. "These people are hardworking and God-fearing. They do not accept loose and immoral behavior. Their disrespect falls not only upon the ones who enjoy that behavior, but on those who associate with them as well . . . like their relatives."

"Or their wives," Marcus said, finally understanding.

"Just so, my lord," Elizabeth said. The coldest look to date entered her eyes, which Marcus had thought would have been impossible. "I have suffered it because of my brother when he lived here, but I will not suffer it for anyone else."

"Did you truly suffer it, Lizzy?" Marcus asked, his eyes narrowing. "Or did you just submit to it?"

"I do not know what you mean," Elizabeth said, her chin lifting.

"Yes you do," Marcus said, his jaw clenching. "The only right these people have to treat you like this is the right you have given them. They are small-minded and provincial and you should have told them to go to hell long ago. If not for your sake, for Richard's sake."

"For Richard's sake?" she asked, her laugh bitter.

"Yes," Marcus said. "If you loved him."

"I did love him!" Elizabeth said, pain crossing her face.

"Then no matter what he had done," Marcus said, "you should have sided with him and told the rest of these self-righteous prigs to go to the devil where they belong, rather than submitting to them and turning into the perfect image of what they want."

"I . . ." Elizabeth began and then halted. She lifted her head. "You do not know my life, nor . . ." once again she stopped. She gave a small, dismissing jerk of her head. "Good-bye, my lord."

"No," Marcus said, his tone dangerous. *"Au revoir."*

" 'Tis good-bye," Elizabeth said, her tone just as dangerous. She spun and strode towards the coach.

"Good-bye," Matty whispered and followed Elizabeth directly.

"Au revoir, Marcus," Jasmine whispered instead, her eyes twinkling before she turned and skipped towards the coach.

Marcus smiled at that. The smile faded, however as he watched the old coach trundle away. Confound it anyway. Why had he rounded upon Elizabeth that way? Perhaps because of his anger at seeing a woman who was totally innocent, submit herself to the condemnation of this provincial, narrow-minded little town. Perhaps, because no matter what he had said, he damned Richard for doing it to her. He damned himself as well for doing it again to her. Right or wrong, Elizabeth was killing herself, and in more ways than one. The physical weight she had lost was but the outer sign.

A determination entered him. Will she or nill she, Elizabeth Hampton was going to live, and live fully. He'd take her from this blasted town. He'd take her from the whole damn world, if he had to, and they would settle it. She apparently would rather die than wed him, but he'd not give her that option. He smiled grimly. She thought him a dishonorable rake. She would discover that truth to the last degree.

Elizabeth sat upon the bed in her room. A book lay in her lap, but her gaze was unfocused and she did not see one word on the written page. She was going mad. That devil, Rake Tremain, was driving her there, and driving her there fast. She'd managed to escape him for an entire month, only to meet him in the millinery store. A heat flashed through her. At least that meeting proved she had a tight to her insanity.

The minute she had seen Marcus Tremain, she realized what she had sought to escape was indeed not an illusion, but the truth. She desired the scoundrel, desired him in every fiber of her body. She had told herself over and over again, that what had happened on her wedding day had been a strange accident, brought on by nerves, or confusion, or a fever of the brain. Yet when she had turned and seen the marquis again, she had once more been struck by a compelling desire, and with it, a fear.

She groaned. She must never permit the marquis to discover her weakness, for surely he would use it against her, just as he had done on her wedding day. She could never marry him. She had survived one rake and bounder in her life, she could not another.

For once, she permitted herself to think of Richard. Marcus had dared question her love for her brother. A bitterness clamped her chest. She had not only loved her brother, she had worshipped him. From little on up, they had been a team, to the torment of their mother and father. Richard had taught her to fish and ride, and even fight battles with sticks. Mrs. Hampton would decry Elizabeth's hoyden ways and send her to the schoolroom to sew samplers with fine mottoes upon them about good girls and ladies. Richard would always contrive a way to come and save her. Then they would go adventuring, to steal apples from Farmer Tendal, and swim in the hidden pond, and imagine they were pirates, or kings and queens of great domains.

Richard had been dashing in her youthful eyes. Then he had grown to the age to go up to London and things had changed. He no longer seemed dashing. He became a man about town, playing cards, chasing women, and carousing. Richard was the only son, and for two years Mr. Hampton had denied him nothing, neither the family resources or support. Elizabeth hadn't either. Marcus presumed she had deserted Richard back then. She hadn't. She'd held her head up high as the small village gossiped about Richard's duels, scandalous affairs, and infamous bets.

Then one evening, on one of his rare visits home, Richard and Mr. Hampton had a dreadful fight and Mr. Hampton spoke the words to change the family's entire world. He disowned Richard and would never recognize him again. Richard had accepted the decree with angry calm. He'd come to Elizabeth to kiss her good-bye. His last words were "I'm sorry, Lizzy, but always remember I love you."

That was three years ago. For a young girl of sixteen, it felt as if her heart had been ripped out. Richard had abandoned her and left her with a grieving, torn family. There was no longer a reason to hold her head up high. Nor could she. Without her love for Richard to blind her, she could finally see what the wages of sin demanded and they were heavy. Word spread that Richard had fled and joined the fighting in France. Debtor after debtor came to the Hamptons's door, demanding for them to honor Richard's abandoned vowels, bills and expenses.

The family had honored those bills and Elizabeth had grown up. Richard had caused enough pain, she would not. She turned herself from the path she and Richard had dreamed of as children. No longer did she think of adventure, or being a pirate, or a queen. Rather, she had schooled herself into becoming the perfect lady, striving to regain the honor for the family which Richard had destroyed. Her marriage to the baron would have made it final. It would have reclaimed the family fortunes and settled her into a safe harbor, free from scandal. Yet Richard had brought her and her family down once again. He had sent a man, a man far too much like him, to tear the golden apple from her hands.

A knock at the door interrupted her thoughts and she looked up as it opened.

"Elizabeth?" Jasmine said as she entered.

"Yes, what is it, dear?" Elizabeth said, pinning a smile upon her face.

Jasmine flushed and looked down to the carpet. "W-would you mind taking a walk with me?"

Elizabeth recognized Jasmine's look. "What have you done wrong?"

"Nothing," Jasmine said quickly. "Only . . . only I am bored. We do not go out anymore. C-could you please take a walk with me? Th-the fresh air might do you good."

"Certainly," Elizabeth said, even though she didn't wish to go. Fresh air would do her no good. "Only permit me to put on my cloak and we shall go."

She rose and followed Jasmine from the room.

"I cannot believe it," Elizabeth fumed, trying to right herself as the coach rocked and swayed. She found it difficult, since both her hands and feet were bound.

"You've got a wicked left there, my lady," the man across from her said. He wore the livery of a footman, the colors of Rake Tremain's footman. "You almost escaped us, you did."

"I would have," Elizabeth said, grinding her teeth. "If Jasmine hadn't tripped me." Her own sister had turned traitor to her. She had never asked exactly who had been communicating with Richard and Marcus. Foolish her. "And don't call me, my lady. I am just plain miss."

"But you will be . . ." the footman began and halted at her glare. "Ahem," he coughed and looked away.

"Correct," Elizabeth said. "I will never be 'my lady.' And most certainly not my lady Tremain."

The footman grinned. "Ye'll have to take that up with my lord . . . Miss Hampton."

Elizabeth narrowed her eyes. "I most certainly shall."

He grinned all the more. "I'm thinking you will at that." Leave it to Marcus Tremain to employ such a cheeky footman. "Now, just you lean back and rest. It will be a longish journey."

"Indeed," Elizabeth said. She closed her eyes, her mind roiling with schemes.

* * *

"Welcome, Lizzy," Marcus said as his footman ushered Elizabeth into a spacious hunting lodge. The furnishings were expensive, but comfortable and relaxed. A fire crackled in the large fireplace. A table with two chairs sat in front of it. Upon its linen cloth rested a bottle of champagne, and two crystal glasses glittered in the glow of candles. "Please forgive me. I am sorry I was unable to accompany you upon the journey, but I was busy preparing things here."

"I did not mind," Elizabeth said with complete honesty. She never doubted that if it had been Marcus accompanying her in the coach he would never have fallen asleep and she would never have been able to sneak the coach pistol into her cloak pocket. It rested heavily against her skirts, giving her a warm security. She stuck out her bound hands. "Though I do mind these."

"Of course," Marcus said, smiling. He walked to her and reached to untie the ropes.

"Best watch it, my lord," his footman said, from behind her. "She can fight like a hellion."

"I know," Marcus said, his green eyes light and measuring upon Elizabeth as he pulled the ropes from her wrists. "That's why she is here. It is time the lady and I make . . . peace," he said, his voice lowering to velvet. Elizabeth trembled. She knew what kind of peace he meant to make. "You may leave us, John."

"Yes, my lord," John said, a quiver of amusement in his voice.

They both remained silent as John departed. Marcus stepped back and walked over to the table. "Would you like a glass of champagne?"

"No, I would not," Elizabeth said, forcing a coolness to her voice, even as her emotions roiled like a volcano inside of her. "What I would like is for you to return me to my home. My family will be excessively worried."

"They'll not be concerned," Marcus said. He smiled. "Not

for your safety, that is. Jasmine will have given them your note by now."

"What note?" Elizabeth asked, her eyes narrowing.

"The note informing them you can no longer deny your passion for me and are eloping."

"What!" Elizabeth exclaimed.

"It is an excellent forgery so do not fear your parents will be confused," he said in a kindly tone. "Miss Heathering has your handwriting down to a nicety. But then, it stands to reason, since it was she who taught you your letters."

"Matty is in this as well?" Elizabeth gasped.

"Both Miss Heathering and Jasmine have your welfare at heart," Marcus said, nodding. "As do I."

"I doubt that," Elizabeth said. Anger shot through her, gratefully replacing the quivering sensations of before. "Abducting me, and bringing me here to—to . . ." she stopped short.

"To what?" Marcus asked, his lips twitching.

Elizabeth flushed and she tilted her chin up. "To rape me, I assume."

"No," Marcus said, shaking his head, his green eyes glowing. "Not to rape you."

Elizabeth raised her brows. "You brought me here to play cards, perhaps? How interesting."

"No," Marcus said and laughed. "I brought you here to . . . settle matters."

Elizabeth's heart slid to the pit of her stomach. "If you mean to make me marry you, then that will never be settled."

"I don't know," Marcus said, an infernal, seductive smile playing upon his lips. "I think that if you and I are permitted to discuss the subject, without the interruptions of others, we might be able to settle our differences." He walked towards her slowly. "We have only been alone once, and it seemed to me we were very close to coming to an agreement at that point. It is a negotiation I would like to finish this time."

Elizabeth flushed hot and cold, those memories flooding through her. She scuttled away. "Stay away from me."

"I see you remember," Marcus said, stalking her. "Take off your cloak, Lizzy."

"No," Elizabeth said, pedaling backwards. "You said you wouldn't rape me."

"I won't rape you, Lizzy," Marcus said, his voice low, and damnably confident. "Only seduce you."

His words struck Elizabeth's fear right in the heart. "No, you won't," Elizabeth said. She reached into her pocket and jerked the pistol out. "I'll shoot you if you try." She leveled the pistol upon him with both hands.

Marcus came to an abrupt halt, his eyes widening. "Where the devil did you get that?"

"From the coach while your footman wasn't looking," Elizabeth said. She pulled back the hammer with trembling fingers. "Don't think I don't know how to use this. Richard taught me."

A glint entered Marcus's eyes. "Another reason to curse Brother Richard."

"Now," Elizabeth said, shaking the gun, or actually the gun shook upon its own. "You are going to escort me back to my home."

Marcus studied her a considering moment. Then he flashed a smile and stretched out his arms in an open gesture. "Come, Lizzy. Cannot we talk about this first?"

Elizabeth's mouth fell open. Suddenly, she could not help it. She laughed. "You would even try to seduce me while I hold a pistol upon you?"

Marcus's smile turned rueful. "I own it is a challenge, even for a man of my expertise." His eyes darkened and he took the smallest step forward. "But for you, I shall try."

"Don't," Elizabeth said, backing off.

"What are you afraid of?" Marcus asked, still approaching. "You have the pistol. You can put a hole through my black heart anytime you think I come too close."

"And I will, I v-ow it," Elizabeth stammered, retreating a step to every advancing one of his. Her gaze was focused warily upon him, her nerves jangling in alarm. She never noticed the chair behind her. She gasped as she knocked against it. Her fingers convulsed in reflex. A loud blast sounded. Elizabeth screamed in shock. Marcus cursed, spinning.

"My God," Elizabeth said, throwing the deceiving pistol from her.

Marcus finished his revolution, his hand clamped high upon his right arm. "Dammit, Lizzy, I wasn't *that* close." Elizabeth stared at him, her heart lodged squarely in her throat. His face was a combination of pain and amusement. "I suppose I should be grateful you only shot me in the arm."

"Y-you sh-should be," Elizabeth said, her ears buzzing.

"How kind of you," Marcus drawled.

"N-no," Elizabeth said. A tremor racked her. "I-I truly mean it."

He frowned. "What?"

"It was an accident," Elizabeth croaked through dry vocal cords. "I-I wasn't aiming."

His brows shot down in a thunderous expression. "I thought you said you knew how to use a pistol."

Elizabeth flushed. "I-I only shot one once . . . when I was thirteen."

He stared at her. Then he barked a laugh. "Gads! You had me fooled, Lizzy." He stumbled over to the table and fell into one of the chairs, shaking his head. "I truly thought you knew how to shoot. Else I wouldn't have . . ." He stopped. He grinned, a totally unrepentant grin. "I wouldn't have tried that."

"Ar-re you all right?" Elizabeth asked.

" 'Tis but a scratch," Marcus said, shrugging. Then he winced. "I've had worse." He raked her with a concerned eye. "You aren't going to faint, are you?"

"Of course not," Elizabeth said, her words a blatant lie. In truth, her knees felt rubbery, and though she was breathing now, she still felt light-headed and dizzy. She had actually shot a man!

"Come and sit down," Marcus said, his voice commanding. "Before you fall down."

"No," Elizabeth said, lifting her chin. He was the man with the injury, not she. "W-we must tend to . . . to your wound. Do you have supplies?"

"Of course, this is a hunting box," Marcus said. "They are in the kitchen. You'll have to get them. There is no one else here."

"No one?" Elizabeth asked.

He raised his brow. "One does not bring a surplus of servants to an abduction. It causes talk."

"I see," Elizabeth said, biting her lip. "What about John?"

"I told him to leave," Marcus said, his tone clipped.

"Yes, but . . ." Elizabeth said.

Marcus shifted, his eyes suddenly guarded. "I sent him upon an . . . errand."

"An errand?" Elizabeth asked stupidly.

"More like a wild goose chase," Marcus said. A sardonic humor entered his eyes. "You could say my plans backfired."

Elizabeth stared at him. A sudden giggle escaped her. Faith, she was unhinged. She hadn't giggled in years. "Y-yes, you could say that."

"Cold hearted wench," Marcus said, his tone mild.

Elizabeth stiffened, though another chuckle escaped her. She shook her head, attempting to draw her frayed thoughts back to the subject at hand. "I'll . . . I'll find the supplies."

Moving swiftly to snatch up one of the candles, Elizabeth left Marcus. Heart pounding, she cursed every moment it took her to find the kitchen, put the water on to boil, and until she found bandages, shears, and basilum powder. Piling the supplies upon a tray, Elizabeth carefully carried them back to the main room.

She halted abruptly. Marcus sat where she had left him, but now he gripped a bottle of brandy in his left hand and was pouring it with obvious difficulty into the champagne glass.

He smiled at her. "It's strictly medicinal." He chuckled. "The champagne seemed rather inappropriate for the moment."

"Of course," Elizabeth said, and bustled to the table to shove the tray upon it. She studied Marcus in concern. He appeared pale, but controlled. "Take off your jacket."

"Take off your cloak," he shot back.

"Oh, yes," Elizabeth said, and quickly untied the cloak and let it fall.

"Hard-won success," Marcus murmured. Groaning, he shrugged, attempting to take off his jacket.

"Here, let me help you," Elizabeth said, and rushed to assist him. "Can you stand?"

"Of course," Marcus said, and hauled himself to his feet. Elizabeth, biting her lip, helped him shrug out of his jacket. It was a difficult affair, and once he was stripped of his jacket, Elizabeth said quickly, "We can cut the rest off."

Marcus sighed, shaking his head. "This is not the way I planned for you to undress me this evening, but so be it." He frowned. "I'd prefer to save the vest. 'Tis one of my finest."

"Very fine," Elizabeth said. She relieved him of it and tossed it aside without consideration. "Now," she muttered, grabbing up the shears. "Sit down."

Marcus lifted a brow as he obeyed. "Mighty anxious to get at me with the shears, aren't you?"

Elizabeth snapped the shears open and shut, narrowing her eyes. "Hm. It *will* be a pleasure."

Marcus shook his head and chuckled. "One Hampton saves me and the other comes behind to kill me."

"What do you mean?" Elizabeth asked, frowning. She approached him, gingerly cutting away his sleeve.

" 'Tis a long story," Marcus said, his voice tight. "How does it look?"

Elizabeth swallowed, and leaned forward to peer at the bleeding wound. Both she and Richard had suffered many an injury as rambunctious children, and the sight of blood had never bothered her. That this was a wound caused by a pistol she had fired did bother her. "It is just a graze, thank God."

"Yes," Marcus said. He sipped from his drink with his free hand. "God smiles upon the good and wicked alike. Unlike

Miss Hampton," he muttered as Elizabeth ignored him and sponged the graze clean. They fell silent as Elizabeth then dusted and bandaged the wound.

"There," Elizabeth said, finally letting her breath out. "That should do."

"Good," Marcus said. "Now sit down and have a glass of brandy. You look like you need one."

Elizabeth shook her head, lowering herself into the chair beside him. "N-no, thank you."

"Have one," he said more sternly.

Elizabeth glared at him, indignant. She noted, however, that his color already looked better. Much better than hers, no doubt. She sighed, the fight draining from her. "Very well," she said and poured herself a brandy. She made only the slightest face as she sipped it. The taste was dreadful, but the burn as it trickled down her throat felt wonderful. She'd been so cold and numb before. She took another, heartier drink of the liquid and flushed as she caught Marcus's considering gaze upon her. Drawing in a deep breath, she asked, "What did you mean when you said one Hampton saved you?"

He shook his head, his eyes guarded. "I told you, it is a long story."

"I would like to hear it," Elizabeth said, attempting a nonchalant shrug.

Marcus smiled at her, his lids lowered. "Are you truly ready, Lizzy?"

Elizabeth stared at him a moment. No, she wasn't ready. She lifted her glass to her lips and belted down the full contents. She closed her eyes as she fought a cough. Then she forced them open, ignoring the sting of tears. "Yes. Tell me of m-my brother. Tell me of . . . Richard."

Marcus leaned back, wincing. "Richard and I met almost the same time we joined the forces." He smiled wryly. " 'Twas natural for us to become friends."

"You are much alike," Elizabeth said. At the thought she reached immediately to pour herself another brandy.

Marcus's brow rose, but he refrained from comment. He said instead, "Yes, we were both running away from the life we had created. Richard because he had finally been disowned from your family and me . . ." He shook his head. "Just because."

"No," Elizabeth said. Leaning over with the brandy bottle, she refilled his glass. "Tell me."

Marcus's gaze flickered to the glass and then returned to her. "You are a dangerous woman, Lizzy." He raised the glass and nodded to her. "Not only because you know when to shoot a man, but when to fill his glass again." He sipped from it and set it down. "I joined the army because I'd had one affair too many and had been called out by a jealous husband." Bitterness curved his lips. "Only, this time the jealous husband was my good friend. I refused to meet him."

Something, hard and cruel, twisted within Elizabeth. "I see."

"Yes, I have no doubt, you do," Marcus said, the bitterness still deep within his eyes. "It had all been a game with me at the time." He laughed. "A game I learned at my lovely, but promiscuous, mother's knee, and my father's rather jaded hand. That was until they both died in a fire. I believe my father's mistress, or my mother's lover, set it off . . . I cannot remember." He sipped from his drink and shook his head. "I was eighteen, and surely I should remember, but I do not."

Elizabeth felt a regret, an odd, ridiculous regret, for Marcus. "But it was all you knew then."

"No," Marcus said, his voice stern. "I say I learned it at my parents' knee. What I meant was that it was the life I observed as a child. But they never really raised me. It was my nanny who raised me. She believed otherwise." His gaze turned sardonic. "Faith, but she believed otherwise. Not that she was prim and proper. Far from it. But the woman . . ." He shook his head. "The woman loved me, loved me like no other."

"I am sure many women have loved you," Elizabeth said, and then bit her lip. It was a terribly catty and cruel remark.

"No," Marcus said, his smile almost gentle. "They loved me

as my mother did, and as my father did. Lightly, but as deeply as they could."

Elizabeth did not know what to say. She sipped from her brandy, staring directly at him. "Continue."

He laughed. "They say the love of a good woman can redeem a man." He quaffed his drink and set it down. "Nothing can redeem a man. Not unless he chooses to be redeemed." He looked up and smiled. "But if he chooses, then is when the love of a good woman can save him."

"What do you mean?" Elizabeth asked, feeling confused and befuddled. She insanely took another sip of brandy, as if that would help clear her head.

"I had fully intended to go out against my good friend," Marcus said. He shook his head. "Then I realized that I couldn't do it. Somehow, Nanny's teaching of justice and injustice had finally sunk into my thick skull. I could not kill the man for the dishonor I had done him. And kill him I would have been forced to do. He would not have accepted anything but a duel to the death." He sighed. "The damn fool couldn't have hit a side of the barn at five paces." He sighed. "He was even worse with foils."

"What happened then?" Elizabeth asked, tensing.

His eyes showed amusement. "Remind me if we are ever married . . ." Elizabeth emitted a trembly unladylike snort, or rather snarf, ". . . not to introduce you to my friends. They thought me crazed, at first. Then they thought me cowardly." He shrugged his shoulder. "So I left under a cloud and joined the military."

"Where you met Richard," Elizabeth said softly. She drank from the brandy, its burn soothing compared to the burn in her heart.

"Yes," Marcus said, his eyes dark. "You see your brother as nothing but a rake . . . an irresponsible, selfish man."

"I did not say that," Elizabeth objected.

"I know him as a loyal man," Marcus said, his gaze unwavering. "A man who faced danger after danger and never flinched." His lips twisted. "I'll not lie. We wanted that danger. Needed it, in fact. We had both played at all the dangers society offered us, and it wasn't enough. It was war we two fools needed to teach us."

"Teach you what?" Elizabeth asked, frowning.

Marcus laughed. "To teach us what the fine line between life and death meant. To teach us that when death comes for you, honor means nothing . . . and everything."

Elizabeth blinked, shaking her head. "Exshplain."

Marcus smiled. "Your brother is one of the best fighters I've ever known. He's fierce, in fact."

A blinding thought shot through Elizabeth's fuzzy brain. She grinned, a ridiculous glow which had nothing to do with the brandy warming her. "He became a pirate, didn't he?"

Marcus frowned at her and then shook his head, laughing. "I suppose you could put it that way. There wasn't a battle he'd refuse. Few could match him either in combat or in espionage. I never had a fear with him at my back."

Elizabeth quaffed off her drink and slammed it to the table. "He was dashing, after all!"

"Dashing?" Marcus asked, his brow rising.

Elizabeth flushed. "We always dreamed of being dashing when we were children. We were going to be great adventurers. We played we were pirates, or the most royal of kings and queens."

Marcus's eyes deepened and darkened. "Then Richard was a king, Lizzy. We had gone into a mission and I had been caught." He grimaced. "The code was obvious. We could not endanger the mission because of my stupidity. I fully expected to be executed. Your brother broke the code. He came back for me and after lying, cheating, and killing, he saved me."

"He saved you?" Elizabeth asked.

"Yes, he saved me," Marcus said. His gaze grew solemn. "He broke the code, Lizzy and he saved me. There was no honor for him in that. Not by military standards. We did not leave the military with praise and acclaim, I assure you."

"But he honored you, a friend," Elizabeth said. Suddenly the weight she had carried inside of her for years dropped from her. It was as if the tears and her loss were nothing. Richard had finally become what they had dreamed of as children.

"Richard loves you," Marcus said softly, as if he could read her mind.

Tears stung Elizabeth's eyes. "Yes."

"He talked of you often," Marcus said. "Especially on those nights before battle." His gaze softened. "I came to know you, Lizzy, as Richard knew you."

Elizabeth sighed. "You mean as he once knew me."

Marcus nodded. "Even after Miss Heathering's letters came, telling him how you had changed, how you had become so proper and cool, he would not believe it."

"I-I never knew Miss Heathering wrote to him," Elizabeth said.

"She was doing so in secret," Marcus said.

"Why d-didn't she tell me?" Elizabeth asked, hurt welling up in her. "Jasmine knew, didn't she?"

"Yes," Marcus said. "But that was by accident. Richard didn't want any of the family to know. He said he'd hurt you all enough and that the best thing to do for your sake was to disappear from your life." He shook his head. "It taxed him, I believe, but he held firm." Marcus laughed. "Well, at least until he heard you were going to marry the baron. That is when I received his letter. He was under the impression you were sacrificing yourself to save the family and since he could not arrive in time to stop it, he wanted me to do so."

Elizabeth's heart twisted as she came to a full understanding. She stared at her brandy glass. "You owe him your life."

"Yes," Marcus said.

"And you were . . . or are . . . willing to repay it by marrying me."

A moment's silence passed. "Yes."

Elizabeth released her glass and drew in a deep breath. She

lifted her gaze to meet his, determined not to flinch. "Y-you are both men of honor."

Marcus grinned. "You are drunk, Lizzy."

"Yes," Elizabeth said. "I believe I am." She reached for the bottle and poured one small dollop. She drank it swiftly and stood. "H-however, I-I release you from your debt of honor. And I release R-richard from his."

Marcus stood. "Lizzy!"

Elizabeth shook her head. "It is Elizabeth now. I no longer understand what honor is, but you are released. You need not . . . nor will you . . . marry me."

Marcus studied her a moment, a moment which caused Elizabeth to shiver. Then he nodded his head. "I won't hold you against your will, Elizabeth. Tomorrow when John returns, I will let you go home."

Elizabeth looked down. Foolishly, she felt like bursting into tears. "Th-hank you." She drew in her breath. "W-would you p-lease show me where I-I might sleep?"

"Y-yes," Marcus said, rising.

With a staggering, but dignified path, he led Elizabeth from the room, down the hall and to a bedroom. Elizabeth meandered toward the bed which she could hazily define. She threw herself down upon it, closing her eyes tightly. Those feeble, unreasonable tears still threatened. "G-good night, Marcus."

"Good night, Lizzy." Marcus's voice seemed to float all about her. "I-I am sorry."

"No, I am sorry," she sighed. The tears escaped, sliding quietly down her cheek as sleep claimed her.

Three

It was ten o'clock in the morning and Marcus sat slumped in the wing chair beside the fireplace. He looked around bleakly. The champagne bottle still sat open from the night before. So did the almost-empty brandy bottle as well as the two sticky, but drained glasses.

Last night had certainly not run the course of seduction he had planned. There had certainly been a seduction, but not on his part. 'Twas Elizabeth who had seduced him. The look upon her face when she had shot him had been a study always to be remembered. Her concern and care in patching him up also endeared him to her. It was the talking afterwards, however, which had truly seduced him. Certainly when he intended to conquer a lady, he did not sit drinking brandy with her and talking of war, and the woman's brother, and of his own asinine past.

He laid his head back against the chair and closed his eyes, sighing. What the devil was he to do with Elizabeth Hampton? They must marry, and marry posthaste, if he were to save her and her family. Yet he had promised her she could leave him. A sick feeling, which had nothing to do with the evaporating fires of last night's brandy, rose within him. He had destroyed his chances with this woman and he had a feeling he would live to regret it. He cast his gaze to the brandy bottle. Faith, but he could use a glass of the hair of the dog that bit him. He wouldn't. Instinct warned him he'd need all of the few wits he still possessed about him today.

Marcus heard voices and his eyes snapped open. He turned his head precipitously as those voices invaded the room. John stood within the entrance, as well as another man. The second man, short and portly, with a benign smile upon his lips, wore the collar of the church.

Marcus groaned and closed his eyes. "Go away, John."

"My lord?" John asked. "But I've just arrived. I have the . . ."

"Forget it," Marcus said, his jaw clenching.

"Forget it?" John asked.

"Yes, forget it," Marcus said. He opened his eyes and forced himself to a stand. "There will be no need for the Reverend."

John's eyes widened as he took in Marcus's disheveled appearance and bandaged arm. He chuckled. "Had a *hunting* accident, my lord?"

"Yes," Marcus said, casting John a baleful look. "Some fool footman permitted the lady to steal the coach pistol."

"Why, the little devil," John said, his face lacking any proper display of embarrassment. "I told you she was a fighter."

"Yes," Marcus said through gritted teeth. He turned his gaze to the stranger. "I am sorry, Reverend . . . ?"

"R-reverend T-tish-meal," the short man said, or in truth, slurred.

Marcus's eyes narrowed and he studied the man closely. Only then did he notice the distinctly bloodshot eyes, red nose and befogged air of the man. Marcus cursed. He himself may be suffering a hangover, but there could be no mistake. The good Reverend was high in his altitudes, and unlike Marcus, feeling no pain. "Good God, John, couldn't you have done better than him?"

"No, my lord," John said, grinning. "All the others were too niffy-naffy. None of them would come at such short notice, or preside over such a havey-cavey ceremony."

"C-ceremony?" a new and very weak voice asked. Marcus spun around. Elizabeth stood within the hall entrance, appearing the most woe begone waif. Her clothes were disheveled, her golden hair astray, and her complexion pale . . . extremely pale.

" 'Tis nothing, Lizzy," Marcus said quickly.

"Is thish th-the bride?" the Reverend Tishmeal asked, apparently coming out of his fog. Marcus cursed. Now was not the time.

"Br-ide?" Elizabeth asked, her voice rising to a squeak.

"N-no!" Marcus said.

The minister shook his head in clear confusion. "Excushe me. Th-thought I was I h-ere to perform a w-w-edding? C-come to s-save a p-poor, f-fallen angel." He lifted a shaking finger towards Elizabeth. "Ish sh-she the one?"

"To perform a w-edding . . . ?" Elizabeth asked, her voice strangled. Her pained gaze flew to Marcus's. "F-fallen angel?"

"Now Elizabeth . . ." Marcus started.

"You intended t-to marry m-me this m-orning?" Elizabeth asked. Marcus wisely remained silent. It mattered not, for dawning understanding, and with it the inevitable wrath, filled Elizabeth's eyes. "Y-you beast! Y-you th-thought to seduce me last night, and expected me to marry you today!"

"S-seduce?" the minister asked. His bloodshot eyes widened and he looked at John, shaking his head. "L-little late for that, ain't it? Mean, she's already with ch . . ."

"I can't believe it," Elizabeth exclaimed, her furious gaze trained upon Marcus. "J-just one night! That was all it was supposed to take, wasn't it?"

"Elizabeth . . ." Marcus said.

"You thought you'd b-bed me and this morning I'd be so enthralled that I'd . . ." she halted. It appeared she would burst. "Why y-you conniving, womanizing . . . whoremonger!"

"B-bit of a sh-rew, a-ain't she?" the Reverend whispered to John in far too loud of stage whisper. "Sh-shame she's pregnant . . ."

"Wh-what?" Elizabeth squeaked, her gaze flying to the Reverend in shock.

"I'd advise him not to m-marry her," the Reverend continued in that confidential tone. "But she's c-carrying his ch-child . . ."

Elizabeth stared at the Reverend, emitting a gurgling sound. Her gaze sought Marcus in disbelief. "H-he thinks I'm . . . ! You told him I'm . . . !" She blanched. Then she moaned and her hand flew to her stomach. "Oh, no!"

"Lizzy?" Marcus asked.

"I-I don't feel well," Elizabeth whispered, swaying.

"M-morning sickness," the little minister said with a sage nod. "That far along is she?"

"Morning sick . . ." Elizabeth wheezed. Her other hand flew to her mouth.

"Come," Marcus said, striding over to Elizabeth and wrapping a supporting arm about her. "Let me take you back to bed."

"L-leave m-me alone," Elizabeth cried, slapping at him feebly.

"Sh-hould," the little minister said. "Can't be asking her to . . ."

"Be quiet!" Marcus roared, clutching the sagging Elizabeth.

"W-won't be good for the child," the minister persisted. "Y-you c-can't expect the w-woman to be d-doing *that* now. 'Tis a sh-shrew, b-but y-you . . ."

"John," Marcus roared, striving to hold Elizabeth upright. "Get that damn ass out of here now!"

"I'm a m-man of the cloth!" the little man objected.

"I don't give a damn who you are," Marcus exploded. "Come, Lizzy!" He half propelled and half carried the trembling, gagging Elizabeth through the door and down the hall.

"I . . ." Elizabeth said, choking.

"D-don't talk," Marcus ordered and marshaled her towards the bedroom. At any moment he expected Elizabeth to finally succumb to her nausea, but she clamped her mouth shut and let him drag her into the room. His gaze fell upon the washbasin upon the bureau and he directed the suffering Elizabeth over to it.

"Wh-what?" Elizabeth asked, her voice weak.

He cupped the back of her head and ruthlessly bent it down. "Cast it up!"

"N-no," Elizabeth said, her voice tormented. "Not in front of you . . ."

She didn't finish, but was forced to employ the washbasin exactly as he had ordered. Marcus supported her with one arm, while reaching for the towel beside the basin. "Here!"

Elizabeth snatched it from him with a surprising vigor. "I-I hate you."

"I know, sweetheart," Marcus said, never doubting it. How could he? Not even he could forget his first hangover. "Are you finished?"

"I . . . hafe woufe," Elizabeth mumbled from behind the cloth.

"Yes, you've said that," Marcus said. "Why don't you lie down?" He supported a now limp and unresisting Elizabeth to the bed and assisted her into it.

Elizabeth laid down, her eyes closing. "I'm going to die."

"No, you won't," Marcus said, smiling slightly. He walked back to the bureau, pulled open the drawer and drew out another cloth. He sunk it into the wash pitcher and wet it. "You only feel like you are going to die," he said, returning to the bed and sitting down.

Elizabeth groaned as the bed moved with his weight. "But I want to die!"

"No, you don't," Marcus said. He leaned over to gently run the damp cloth across her face. That was when he noticed, even with her eyes closed, tears trickled down Elizabeth's cheek. "Ah, sweetings, don't cry. Don't!"

"Y-you told that Reverend I-I was pregnant . . ."

"I didn't," Marcus said. "John did."

"B-but you th-thought I-I would m-marry you," she said, a catch in her voice. "Y-you were g-going to s-seduce m-me in one n-night . . ."

"Hush," Marcus said, reaching to brush back her hair. "I wasn't thinking . . ."

"Yes, you were!" Elizabeth said. Suddenly her eyes snapped open and she sat up. She glared at him, tears streaming down her face, her gray eyes red rimmed, her nose even redder. "You are evil! In one night . . . you thought you'd get me, body and soul."

"No, I didn't," Marcus said. He reached out a concerned hand. "Now lie back down."

"No, you promised I could leave this morning," Elizabeth said, sniffing.

"Yes, and you may," Marcus said, feeling pressed. "But why not rest a moment?"

"Y-you'll s-seduce m-me if I stay," Elizabeth said, suspicion shimmering through her tears.

"I won't," Marcus said quickly. "I promise you, I won't. I won't ever touch you again . . ."

"I don't believe you!" Elizabeth cried, and rolled over to scramble up from the bed. "I'm leaving . . ." She blanched and swayed. Moaning, she collapsed back down upon the mattress. ". . . the minute I feel better."

"Yes, you do that," Marcus said, reaching his hands out and gently placing them on her shoulders. He exerted the lightest pressure. "Now lie back down."

"And you're not going to touch me," Elizabeth said as she fell back unresisting, directly into the curve of Marcus's shoulder.

"I promise," Marcus said, drawing her down and shifting to cradle her. "Now go to sleep."

"I'm going to sleep," Elizabeth murmured. There was a pause. "Th-hen I'm going to leave you . . ."

"Yes," Marcus murmured. "I know."

"Y-you aren't going to get me," Elizabeth said with a sniff.

"No, of course not," Marcus said in a kind voice.

"It's *my* body and soul," she said, her tone weak, but indignant.

"Indeed, it is . . ."

"W-we won't have t-to marry . . ."

"No, we won't have to," Marcus agreed.

"I'm never going to see you again, you know . . ."

"I know," Marcus said.

A long pause ensued and Marcus thought Elizabeth had lulled into sleep, but she uttered one more lonesome sigh. "I wish I could die."

Marcus started. Then he chuckled softly and pulled her more fully into his arms. " 'Twould be a shame, Lizzy." He received no answer this time. Satisfied, he closed his eyes and laid his own throbbing head against the pillow. At least Lizzy slept against his good arm.

The smile disappeared from Marcus's lips. He'd promised her so many things, every single word a lie. He wanted her and he would marry her. Worse, she had divined something he had not. He did want her body *and* soul. It was a strange, shattering thought. He didn't fight it, however, nor ask how it could have happened so swiftly. He had never been a man to lie to himself or deny the strength of his passions as others would.

He groaned. Before, however, he had always known how to satisfy those passions, but this was a new and foreign desire, a desire he had no inkling on how to surfeit. He knew how to seduce a woman to win her body, but how to seduce a woman to win her soul?

Elizabeth awoke the next morning feeling oddly refreshed, physically that was. Mentally, however, she felt embarrassed and confused. She had slept an entire day and evening away. For the better part of that day, she had slept comfortably in Marcus's arms. Only in the late afternoon had he left her. He had returned then to waken her and tell her she must eat. It had been simple eggs and toast. She'd swallowed a few bites and then he had ordered her to go to sleep once more. He'd left her and not returned. She had slept deeply, but even in that deep sleep, there was the memory of him holding her, and a terrible disappointment that he was not there to do so again.

She winced at the thought and sat up. Gratefully her head did not reel, nor did her stomach lurch. She was truly feeling better and it was due to Marcus's nursing. A flush rose to her face as an incongruous image arose in her mind of what would have happened if it had been her other fiancé who had been with her yesterday. The baron would never have nursed her so kindly. Then again, she wouldn't have drunk brandy with the baron, or sat talking about war and honor. She shook her head. It must still be the effects of the hangover, but for the life of her, she couldn't seem to remember anything she and the baron had ever truly talked about.

Elizabeth pushed that disquieting thought from her mind and rose. She glanced down at her crumpled dress and attempted to straighten it to no good purpose. Setting her chin at a tilt, she ordered herself to ignore the embarrassment. 'Twas not her fault she had but one dress, and it was ridiculous to worry about how Marcus would view her. It was far too late for that now.

She left the room and wandered through the lodge, searching out Marcus. She found him sitting before the fireplace in the main room. His gaze was upon the empty grate, his eyes solemn. Stubble darkened his face and his whole body read of weariness.

"G-good morning," Elizabeth said.

He turned his head to look at her. A sudden brilliant smile crossed his lips and his green eyes lightened. "You live."

An answering smile crossed Elizabeth's lips before she knew it. "Yes, thanks to you."

"It was nothing," he said.

Elizabeth ran a nervous hand through her hair. "I d-do not know why I-I reacted that way. I suppose I cannot drink liquor."

"It wasn't just the brandy," Marcus said. "It affected you that way because of your nerves and tension." His face became stern. "And because you haven't been eating enough."

"What do you mean?" Elizabeth asked, stunned.

"You've lost weight this last month," he said.

Elizabeth flushed. "Have I?" She walked with a feigned nonchalance over to the chair which sat across from his. "I-I didn't notice."

"I did," Marcus said. He frowned. " 'Tis my fault, I know." Elizabeth bit her tongue. For some foolish reason she wanted to tell him that it wasn't, if only to erase the look on his face. She knew it would be ridiculous and stared at him helplessly. He looked away. "You will want to leave now, no doubt."

Elizabeth started. In truth, the thought hadn't crossed her mind. She didn't know what she was thinking, but it hadn't been that. "Y-yes . . . I do."

His gaze returned to hers. "I have been thinking. I cannot repair all the damage I've caused you, but there is at least one way to mitigate this last . . . fiasco, in regards to your family. We can say that we did not elope, but rather thought better of it, and went to my aunt's in London instead."

Elizabeth swallowed. "Indeed?"

"Yes," Marcus said. "We can say you were properly chaperoned at all times." He studied her and Elizabeth found she could not meet his gaze. She heard him sigh. "I've already sent John to Aunt Sarah with the message. I am confident she will uphold me in the story"

"I see," Elizabeth said, her heart sinking. Surely it was what she wanted. She shook her head in confusion. Then why did she suddenly not want to leave? She cast a quick glance at Marcus. Why, why didn't she want to leave him?

Her gaze fell upon his bandaged arm. She drew in a quick breath. Of course! There was a perfectly good explanation for why she was feeling the way she did. Faith, after all his kindness to her she would be a cold-hearted wretch to desert him when he was still wounded. She swallowed and said, "H-how is y-your arm?"

Marcus frowned. "It will heal."

"Yes, but it pains you, doesn't it?" Elizabeth asked, looking at him intently.

"Somewhat," Marcus said.

"Do y-you intend to escort me back to my family?" Elizabeth asked.

"Of course I do," Marcus said, his face darkening. "I am not that much of a cad as to send you back alone. I'll be there to support you."

"Good," Elizabeth said with a sigh. Then she flushed. "No . . . what I mean is . . . I don't see how I can leave. N-not right now."

"What?" Marcus asked, frowning.

Elizabeth drew in her breath. "If I were to leave you, it would be I who am the cad . . . or whatever a female is called. I w-would be shockingly cruel to force you t-to travel with that arm."

Marcus's eyes flared bright, and then the light disappeared and they turned serious. "Yes. Shockingly so."

"You took care of me yesterday when I was sick," Elizabeth said, trying to calm the flutter in her stomach. "I-I cannot bring myself to be less merciful."

"In truth," Marcus said, his voice steady and his face blank. "It would be very kind of you. I own I did not look forward to traveling with this arm."

Elizabeth looked away. " 'Tis the least I can do, since it was I who shot you." She shrugged her shoulder. "If we are to tell the tale of being at your aunt's, what does it matter if it is one more day or two?" She forced herself to look back at Marcus to see his reaction. Gratefully he looked suitably solemn.

"Indeed," he said, nodding. "You know, it might even lend more credence to our story. It will also give time for John to discover a female servant to act as chaperone in the return journey to your parents."

"Yes," Elizabeth said. They gazed at each other a long moment. Elizabeth drew in her breath. "H-have you eaten this morning?"

"No," Marcus said, a slow smile crossing his face.

Elizabeth smiled back. "Only permit me to go a-and try to freshen myself. Then I will see what is in the kitchen." She stood quickly, smoothing down her skirts. Not because she knew it would help, but because she wished it would do so.

A considering look entered Marcus's eyes. "I have something I would like to show you, but you must promise me you will not fly into the boughs."

"What is it?" Elizabeth asked.

"No," Marcus said, his eyes twinkling. "You must promise first."

Elizabeth frowned. Curiosity got the best of her, however. "Oh, very well. I promise."

"All right. Come," Marcus said. Smiling, he stood and held out his hand to her. Then he frowned and let it fall. "If you will follow me."

"Yes, of course," Elizabeth said.

Silently she followed Marcus through the lodge and into another bedroom. He walked across the well-appointed room towards a large armoire which stood against its wall.

"What is it?" Elizabeth asked, excitement rising within her as she stepped behind him. He flung open the doors and Elizabeth gasped. A rainbow of colors met her eyes. Dresses of every design and material billowed from the armoire's recess. Elizabeth turned a stunned gaze upon Marcus.

"I'd thought you would need a trousseau," Marcus said, his smile crooked.

"Y-you bought these dresses for me?" Elizabeth asked, her body automatically stiffening. "Thinking that . . ."

"Odious of me, wasn't it?" Marcus asked, with a hint of amusement. "And conceited . . ."

"Yes, it was," Elizabeth said, her chin jutting out.

His eyes lightened even more. "You're doing it, Lizzy."

"Doing what?" Elizabeth snapped.

"Flying into the boughs," Marcus said. "You promised you wouldn't."

"I . . ." Elizabeth stopped. She bit her lip and then a giggle escaped her.

Marcus's eyes widened. "Was that an actual laugh?"

Elizabeth's lips quivered. "No, no it wasn't." She frowned severely. "Now if you will leave me . . . I-I shall see if one of these dresses will fit me."

Marcus barked a laugh. "You do that." He strode to the door, then turned and grinned at her. "I'll lay any odds you wish that they'll fit."

"Scandalous," Elizabeth said, attempting to appear severe.

"No," Marcus said, his green eyes glittering. "If you want that, go and look in the bureau drawer over there."

He departed swiftly, closing the door behind him. Elizabeth found herself dashing to the bureau drawer in unseemly haste. She jerked out the top drawer and froze. The finest of lace petticoats, silk-ribboned corsets, and translucent undergarments lay nestled within it. She blinked and blinked again. Then a peal of laughter escaped her. She quickly clamped one hand over her mouth to muffle another peal, even as her other hand dove into the soft materials.

A heated flush rose to her face. It would be past scandalous to wear such sensual materials against her skin, materials chosen and bought by none other than Rake Tremain. The restricting thought, however, was quickly forced aside, as the more important question replaced it. Had Marcus chosen her correct size? Elizabeth hoped, nay, even prayed, he had as she hastily stripped out of her old, rumpled dress.

Only when the silk petticoats rustled about her legs and a powder blue morning dress hugged her curves snugly, did Elizabeth let out a sigh. It was one of sublime satisfaction. The fit was perfect. Naughty and improper it might be, but there was much to be said for a man who was experienced enough to know precisely which clothes would delight a woman.

Four

Marcus rested upon a blanket and watched as Elizabeth put his horse Lightning through his paces. Faith, if he wasn't pretending to be the invalid he would love to race with her. She was an excellent horsewoman. Marcus had spent many hours training Lightning himself, but that the horse took direction so promptly from Elizabeth showed her own talents.

He shook his head. Elizabeth Hampton was proving surprising in every way. The cool, proper woman he had first met at the altar was disappearing. Magically, in her stead, came the Elizabeth Hampton whom her brother Richard had talked about all those evenings. This woman was warm and human. She had a lively mind and a sense of humor just now peeking out, like gold glinting in dirt.

He frowned. Lord, but he wanted to mine for that gold, to know the woman in every way. Amazing, like a gift from heaven, she had remained here at the lodge for four days. Four days that had been both heaven and hell. At first, he had wondered how he would create a relationship with a woman without ever touching her. Sex and passion had always been the answer to any of his dealings with women before. Yet he had promised not to touch her, and he knew if he did, this strangely idyllic time would be destroyed. She would leave him and leave him fast.

Therefore he had not touched her, but for once, had taken the time to know her. He had never imagined that learning a woman's spirit could be as sensual as learning her body. Yet with Elizabeth it was so. When she told him of a cherished dream of hers, or confessed a long-hidden hurt, it could shoot a thrill through him as much as if she had kissed him.

Yet, the physical desire was still there, and growing stronger every day. Clearly, he was still as randy a rake as ever. That was the hell of this idyllic time. He wanted the woman. He wanted to take from her and give to her every passion of the body a man and woman could share.

He shook his head and steered his thoughts from such desire. Instead, he focused upon Elizabeth as she wheeled Lightning around in the meadow and brought him under control as the horse displayed his natural spirit. He should just be satisfied with the time they had together. Neither she nor he spoke of when she would leave, or why she remained. He pretended his wound still pained him and she pretended he did not lie.

It was as if they were stealing time, time away from the world, and the people they were within that world. It would of course come to an end, but Marcus swore he would not be the one to terminate it. When Elizabeth did, then he would be forced to think what he must do. He would have to let her leave here, but he knew he would never let her go. He heard Elizabeth laugh and then she steered Lightning in his direction, bringing him to a halt close to the blanket.

"He is a beautiful animal," Elizabeth said, leaning over to pat the stallion's neck. "You have trained him to be a perfect gentleman."

"He's much better at it than me," Marcus said, grinning.

"No," Elizabeth said, a flush rising to her cheeks. "You have been a gentleman too."

Pleasure ran through Marcus, but he only laughed and said, "Hear that Lightning? You are not the only one to receive accolades." The horse at that moment shook his head and snorted, just as if he understood and objected.

" 'Tis clear he does not like to share," Elizabeth said, patting the stallion again. "I have not ridden such a wonderful horse before. He and I are becoming fast friends." Then Elizabeth frowned, concern flicking in her eyes. "How do you feel?"

"I'm fine."

"You are not bored, are you?" Elizabeth asked.

"Why would I be bored?" Marcus asked, raising his brow.

"Well, I am leaving you here to sit all by yourself while I ride."

Marcus laughed. "No, you are putting on a fine equestrian show. 'Tis a pleasure to see such an excellent horsewoman in action."

"Richard and I lived on our horses' backs when we were children," Elizabeth said. A mischievous look slipped into her eyes. "In fact, you haven't seen half of what I can do. Watch!" Laughing, she wheeled Lightning around and put him into a canter back towards the meadow.

Marcus watched as she steered Lightning into making perfect circles. Next she coaxed the large stallion to rise and paw the air, just as if he were at the Astley Theatre. Only when she brought the large animal back down and trained him into walking circles once more, but much slower, steadier circles, did the jolting premonition strike Marcus. He remembered Richard boasting of Lizzy's favorite trick.

"Good God!" Marcus muttered, springing up. He saw Elizabeth pull her foot from the stirrup and his heart rammed itself hard against his rib cage. She was going to try it. She was going to stand up in the saddle. "Lizzy, no!"

"Watch!" she called out and, even as Lightning amazingly maintained his sedate pace, she shifted in the saddle and precariously moved to stand up in it. Marcus's breath caught in his throat.

"See!" Elizabeth called out, her voice triumphant. She stretched her arms out and waved them in a graceful ballet. A slow grin crossed Marcus's face. The little witch was indeed doing it. Then Elizabeth teetered. Marcus started, even as she quickly brought herself down into a crouch. She looked as if she had gained control, but then slipped, toppling from Lightning's back.

"Lizzy," Marcus cried and dashed towards her. Lightning neighed at his shout and bolted away. Marcus paid no heed as he came to a panting halt in front of Elizabeth.

She sat upon the ground, her face dazed. "I'd forgotten how tricky dismounting was."

"Are you all right?" Marcus asked, kneeling beside her.

"Oh, yes," Elizabeth said. "My pride is more bruised than I am."

Relief swelled through Marcus, and with it anger. He clutched her shoulders and shook her. "Don't ever do that again. You could have been killed."

"But I wasn't," Elizabeth said, her tone prosaic. Then she grinned at him, actually grinned.

"Don't do it again," Marcus repeated and glared at her. Elizabeth but laughed, her eyes teasing and light. Growling, Marcus pulled her to him. He meant only to hold her close to ease his fear, lessen his frustration. Yet, without thought, his lips sought hers. Elizabeth gasped slightly, and then her lips softened and met his. Marcus groaned as he tasted her willing response. He deepened the kiss, crushing her to him.

He felt Elizabeth tremble, and his own body shook. The passion was still there, as it had been the very first day he had kissed her. He forced her back to the ground, rolling to cover her body. Heat coursed through him as he felt her beneath him, felt her curves yielding to him. His groin tightened. Images of her naked and wanting beneath him flashed through his mind, making his entire body tense and jump.

Instinctively he forced himself to seize his slipping control. He'd not be a schoolboy, coming too quickly. He could not pleasure her properly if he did. With that one thought came another more piercing one. He was planning to take Elizabeth, take her on the ground as he did any peasant girl. She was ready. He knew it. He could feel it in the response of her body beneath him, in the wildness of her kiss, and the low moan in her throat.

He could take her, and stand the chance of losing her. He was just starting to know this woman, and the little part he knew, promised him he could lose her, even after claiming her body. His own body, in fierce opposition, grew harder and harder, demanding he risk it all and let the devil take the hindmost. His one hand swept up the arch of her waist, teased the outer curve of her breast. He breathed in her scent and her gasp of pleasure.

Desire, raw and pulsing, pounded through him. God, how he needed her. His hand froze. He needed her and could lose her. With a curse crashing through his mind, he tore himself away, rolling quickly from Elizabeth. He pulled himself into a sitting position with a pained groan.

"Wh-what?" Elizabeth asked. After a moment, she sat up. Her eyes were dark, her lips passion bruised, and her face dazed.

"I am sorry, Lizzy," Marcus said, his tone brisk from trying to slow his breathing. "I apologize." She looked at him, blinking like a child who didn't understand. How he wanted to return to her and kiss that confusion away, and then satisfy the bemused need he saw within her eyes. He forced himself to look away. "I promised I wouldn't touch you and I did."

"Yes," Elizabeth said. Her voice held a note of question in it.

He looked back at her. "Are you going to leave?"

"I . . ." she stopped and closed her mouth.

Marcus drew in his breath. "I promise you. I will not ever do this again. You do not have to leave here." Her gaze was wide and helpless upon him. He forced a smile. "Truly. It only happened because . . . well, because we men often react like that when we have been frightened."

"I . . . see," Elizabeth said. She flushed a deep, deep red.

"And you most likely reacted so as well because of it," Marcus said. He'd say anything to erase the reason for her to leave. He had to make her feel safe within his presence once more.

The flush upon Elizabeth's face ebbed to a pallor. "Yes, I am sure," she said, looking away. Marcus watched her, willing her to accept it. When her gaze returned, she was the controlled and dignified Elizabeth. "Yes, that was it."

They stared at each other. His lie rested heavily between them. He suddenly wanted to speak the truth. To tell her that he wanted her, but he wanted her completely. He almost laughed. He'd managed to tear himself away from her in time. He'd not destroy it now by telling her something else which would surely make her bolt. His frustrated body complained to him once more and he sighed. "Now, I think it best you return to the lodge."

Elizabeth stiffened. "Aren't you coming with me?"

He laughed. He was not about to show her the state he was in. "No, I'm not."

"But . . ." Elizabeth began.

"Lizzy, just leave," Marcus said, more sharply then he meant to do.

"Yes, of course," Elizabeth said. She rose, her face stoic.

Marcus looked at her in appeal. "I'm sorry."

"So you have said," Elizabeth said, her voice sounding tight. Not meeting his gaze, she turned and walked away.

Marcus watched her go. Then he sighed and fell back to the ground. He gazed at the sky and the passing clouds, willing his tense body to relax.

"Marcus," he murmured, "you are a damn fool."

"What would you like to do tonight?" Marcus asked, rising from the table.

"I don't know," Elizabeth said, standing. "The meal was so particularly fine, I fear it has made me sleepy."

Marcus laughed as he moved to take up his chair at the fire-place. "Yes, John is becoming an excellent chef. He has hidden talents."

"You mean many talents," Elizabeth said, moving to take up her usual chair across from Marcus. "He cannot only abduct women, but dress a fine chicken as well."

Marcus smiled. "He is demanding a raise in wages, you know."

Elizabeth grinned. "You will give it to him, of course."

"Of course," Marcus said. "Without his services, I would be lost. I fear my cooking would not be as tasty."

"However, mine is," Elizabeth said.

"I did not abduct you to be a cook," Marcus said, shaking his head. Their eyes met at this and Elizabeth flushed. She looked away hastily. No, Marcus had not abducted her for that. In truth, she now wondered why he had abducted her. Except for that episode, three days ago in the meadow, he had proven himself to be a perfect gentleman and host. No, he was more than a perfect host. He was an intriguing, intelligent man. "Now, what would you like to do?"

Elizabeth glanced at him, and the worst possible thought crossed her mind. She'd like to go ride Lightning and fall off of him again, just so Marcus would kiss her. "What would you like to do?"

"Would you like to play chess?" Marcus asked.

Elizabeth shook her head, forcing a smile. "No, you win far too often."

"Cards?" Marcus asked, rasing his brow.

"You win at that as well," Elizabeth laughed.

"Then ducks and drakes," Marcus said and grinned. "You trounced me at that."

Elizabeth laughed. " 'Tis not to my credit that the only game I can beat you at is a child's game. Besides, I only won a few more times than you did. You win things far too often."

"But you win at the games that are important, Lizzy," Marcus said, his gaze suddenly enigmatic.

"Do I?" Elizabeth asked, forcing a light tone. Indeed, she may very well have won at the game between her and Marcus. He never tried to seduce her anymore, nor did he talk of marriage. They had fallen into an easy companionship, one that was enjoyable and compelling. Why, suddenly, was it not enough for her? Elizabeth realized Marcus's gaze still rested upon her and she forced a smile. "Why don't you read to me? I would like that very much."

"Very well," Marcus said, rising. He crossed to the shelves across the room, which held a surprising quantity of books. "What would you like to hear?"

"Shakespeare," Elizabeth said without hesitation. "You do it so well."

Marcus chuckled and pulled out a book. "My newest talent . . . reading bedtime stories." He shook his head as he crossed to take up his chair again. "This had never better get out to the gossips. It will ruin my reputation completely."

Elizabeth laughed. "But you could go upon the stage, you know."

"That would raise my reputation again," Marcus laughed and opened up the book. "I think *A Midsummer Night's Dream* will be appropriate for the evening."

"Hm, yes," Elizabeth said, and settled back. In truth, she wasn't really attending to the words as Marcus began to read. Rather, she enjoyed the timbre in his voice, and being able to watch him as he became engrossed in the play. He had an excellent style of reading, imbuing his rendition with a facile change of tone and voice. She could listen to him forever.

The thought shot a feeling of pain through her. There could be no forever. This time must come to an end. Every day she awoke with the determination of telling Marcus she would leave, and every day she held it off. What she was doing was not only improper, but unconscionable to her family as well. Lord only knew what they thought.

Yet this time was far too precious. With Marcus she had felt herself come alive again, as she hadn't been for ages. She also felt herself healing. It was as if she were suddenly emerging out of the pain and scars of the past few years. She could forgive Richard. Faith, she could forgive anyone. She felt stronger and happier. Why this was so, she could not fathom, but it was so.

A fleeting, seductive thought crossed her mind. Perhaps she could let Marcus marry her. This life could continue, and her family would also be saved. She shook her head slightly, casti-gating herself as not only a silly twit, but a dishonorable one at that. First, merely because this time was so wondrous, it did not mean it would always be so. This was a dream. Reality was that Marcus was a rake, and would always be one. Second, which was truly the greatest irony, was that now she had come to know Marcus, no matter what he had done, or what his reputation was like, he had wanted to do the honorable thing in marrying her. She could not do less. His debt was to Richard, not her.

A commotion sounded from the outside door and John en-tered the room, closing the door quickly. His expression was odd. "Excuse me, my lord."

Marcus stopped reading and looked up. "Yes, what is it, John."

"If I could interrupt you for a moment. I . . . er, there is something in the stables which requires your attention."

"In the stables?" Marcus asked, raising his brow.

"Yes," John said, nodding. "I . . . was out checking upon the horses."

"Is anything the matter with them?" Marcus asked, closing the book.

"Lightning is all right, is he not?" Elizabeth asked.

"Yes, my lad- . . . I mean, Miss Hampton," John said quickly. "He is fine. It's just that I wish for my lord to come to the stables." His gaze returned to Marcus. "Ye have a certain filly that I-I think you best see."

"I do?" Marcus asked. He frowned. "Very well." He set the book aside and rose. "If you will excuse me, Lizzy."

"I can come with you," Elizabeth said.

"No!" John exclaimed. Elizabeth's eyes widened and Marcus frowned. John cleared his throat. "I mean . . . there is no need for that, Miss Hampton."

"But . . ." Elizabeth said, looking to Marcus.

He appeared suddenly tense and wary, even though he smiled at her. "There is no reason we all must see this horse. Stay here."

"Very well," Elizabeth said, and settled back.

"I'll be back shortly," Marcus said.

Elizabeth watched the two men leave. She frowned in concern. The minutes stretched by and she waited. When even more time passed, she sighed and rose. There must truly be something wrong with the filly. She would go and offer her services.

"Now what the devil is it?" Marcus asked John as he strode towards the stables set a distance from the lodge.

"It's not what is it. It's who," John said. "You've got company."

"Never say Elizabeth's family has found us," Marcus said, stifling a curse.

"No," John said, shaking his head. "But Miss Florelle has."

"What?" Marcus exclaimed, halting. "What in blazes is Lucy doing here?"

"She's come ter see you," John said, looking vexed. "She's in a terrible way. That blighter Lord Sexton whose protection she's been under has roughed her up," he snorted. "Some protector he is."

"Damn and blast," Marcus muttered and increased his stride, John pacing close behind him. He tore open the stable door and entered. A short, buxom redhead dressed in a blazing gown of grass green stood within the night lantern's glow.

She turned and cried out, "Oh, Marcus!" Within a flash she was a clinging, sobbing bundle within Marcus's arms. "Y-you must save me."

"Hush now, Lucy," Marcus said, patting her on the shoulder. "Are you all right?" He gently pushed her away to view her better. A heavy coat of paint and powder covered her face, but the darker blue hue about her eye bespoke of a hidden bruise. Marcus raised his hand to her cheek. "Damn, Sexton."

"It . . . it was terrible, Marcus," Lucy said, tears streaming down her face. "Just terrible. I-I thought he was going to kill me."

"Hush, you are safe now," Marcus said, pulling out his handkerchief and mopping both tears and powder from her face.

"He . . . he said he would kill me," Lucy said, her green eyes widening with fright, though the tears abated. "I-I didn't know what to do. He was having my town house watched."

"Lucy," Marcus said, shaking his head. "I told you before you cannot play fast and loose with your protectors."

"Y-you never minded," Lucy said, hiccuping.

John chuckled from behind them, but Marcus ignored him. "I am not of a jealous nature. But most men do not wish to share their mistresses with other men."

"No," Lucy said, taking his handkerchief from his hand to sniff into it. "I-I wish I had never left you."

Marcus bit back a smile. 'Twas he who had left her. "Yes, but it was all for the best. If we had not parted, I've no doubt one of your other lovers would have put a ball through me."

A smile tilted across Lucy's lips. "Yes, that was Lord Terrel and Baron Reece. They were so very jealous of you." Her green gaze turned dark and sultry. "But it was you, dear Marcus, always you, who held my esteem."

"Minx," Marcus said, laughing.

"Marcus," Lucy said, reaching to grasp his lapel. "Please take me back. This whole year we've been apart I've missed you."

"Lucy, no," Marcus said, quickly clasping her hands to stay their course from around his neck.

"You were always the best," Lucy said, her lashes fluttering. "Please. I promise, I w-will be faithful. I'll not look at another man."

Marcus shook his head. "I told you your infidelities had nothing to do with it."

"I know." Lucy's lower lip pouted out. "I tried to make you jealous, but you never were."

Marcus shrugged. "As I said. I am not a jealous man."

She looked at him from lowered lids. "Then you have a mistress right now?"

"No, I do not," Marcus said. "Nor do I intend to take one."

"What?" Lucy exclaimed her eyes widening.

"Bejesus," John's voice exclaimed from behind.

Lucy stared at Marcus. "Y-you mean you ain't had any . . . ?"

"I intend to marry," Marcus said, stiffening.

"If he can get the lady," John said.

"Be quiet, John," Marcus ordered. He looked sternly at Lucy. "I am not going to take a mistress." Lucy gaped at him with such incredulity that a bitterness entered Marcus. He laughed. "I know, it's shocking, but true."

Lucy shook her head. "I don't believe you."

"Neither do I," John said.

"It doesn't matter what either of you think," Marcus said. "I am not going to take a mistress."

"Th-then I have no place to turn," Lucy said, her face crumpling. "Sexton says he will kill me. I-I have no money."

"I will give you enough money," Marcus said. "Do not worry. Take it, leave London and live quietly for a while. Sexton is mad, but his passions are fickle. He'll take another mistress. We can but hope she is not as indiscreet as you are. Once he does, you can then find another protector for yourself."

Lucy's eyes lighted. "You would do this for me?"

Marcus smiled. "Of course. Only be more careful on your next choice of protectors. John, saddle a horse, I want you to escort Lucy to wherever she wishes to go."

"Yes, my lord," John said, walking over to one of the stalls.

"Thank you, Marcus," Lucy said. She stepped closer. "Are you sure, since you are spending the blunt, you wouldn't wish to have my services as well?"

"Lucy . . ." Marcus said. He did not get any further, for Lucy quickly threw her arms around him and kissed him. Surprisingly, he felt no passion. His only thought was upon how to disengage politely.

His mental debate was interrupted as he heard a sudden gasp from behind. Since John was now over in a stall, Marcus knew it did not come from his footman. A dread shot through him.

He grabbed Lucy's shoulders and pushed her away, spinning around towards that one sound.

"Lizzy," Marcus said with a pained sigh.

Elizabeth stood within the stable door, her face pale, her eyes hurt. If only they had been angry, but they were not. "I-I am sorry to interrupt."

"You weren't," Marcus said quickly. "It's not what you are thinking."

She stiffened. "How would you know what I am thinking?"

"I know," Marcus said. "You think that . . ."

"That you are kissing a woman," Elizabeth said, her voice sounding terribly light. "Was that not what you were doing?"

"Yes, it was," Marcus said, through gritted teeth. "But I . . ."

"Who is she?" Lucy asked, her brow snapping down. "I thought you said you hadn't taken another mistress and here you've got this fancy piece right here."

"Mistress?" Elizabeth exclaimed. This time she did glare at Marcus. "You tell a minister I am pregnant, and you tell this woman I am your mistress . . ."

"Are you pregnant?" Lucy cried. She looked at Marcus with wide eyes. "It all makes sense now. She caught you proper and you've got to marry her!"

"She's not pregnant!" Marcus said.

"He's not going to marry me!" Elizabeth exclaimed. "Ever!"

"Lizzy," Marcus said, an appeal in his voice.

"Then why can't I be your mistress?" Lucy asked, stamping her foot.

"Both of you be quiet!" Marcus roared, taxed beyond his endurance.

"Do not shout at me," Elizabeth said, drawing herself up to a regal, frigid pose. "I, sirrah, do not have to tolerate such from you." She picked up her skirts and lifted her chin. "No matter what lies you tell everyone, you have no control over me and you never shall." She looked with a dignity to Lucy. "As I said before, I apologies for interrupting your . . . discussion. Forgive me. I shall leave you to continue."

Elizabeth turned, and with a calm demeanor, left the stables. Silence reigned a moment. Then Lucy looked at Marcus and said with a slight tremble in her voice. "Sh-she *is* a real lady, isn't she?"

"Yes," Marcus said, smiling.

"But wh-what's she doing here then?" Lucy asked.

"It's a long story," Marcus said.

"He abducted her," John said.

"John!" Marcus said.

"Y-you abducted a lady!" Lucy exclaimed.

"He was going to force her to marry him," John said, chuckling.

"You were . . ." Lucy stopped and stared. "You've never had to force any lady before."

"I didn't force her," Marcus said.

"No, the lady shot him before he could," John added.

"She shot you!" Lucy exclaimed.

"I wasn't going to force her," Marcus growled. "I was trying to seduce her and . . ."

Lucy's eyes widened and she giggled. "She shot you for that?"

Marcus glared at her. Then he laughed. "Yes, she did."

"Lud, she is a real lady," Lucy said. She frowned, shaking her head. "You shouldn't have abducted a real lady."

"I know," Marcus said, his breath seething out. "I assure you, I know."

"How long has she been here?" Lucy asked, her eyes narrowing.

"Seven days," Marcus said.

"Seven days?" Lucy placed her hands upon her hips. "Seven days and you two still haven't . . ."

"No, we haven't," Marcus said.

She shook her head. "Ain't no one going to believe that. I don't. She's ruined. She'll marry you."

"Not after this," Marcus said, his jaw clenching.

Lucy studied him. "Are you going to let her go?"

"No, I'm not going to let her go," Marcus said, an anger raging through him. "Ever!"

Lucy stepped back. "I-I see." She cocked her head to one side. "You wouldn't let her have any lovers if she married you, would you?"

Marcus glared at her. "No, I wouldn't."

Lucy sighed. "I'd never thought to hear that either. You love her." Marcus remained silent. A hesitancy entered her eyes. "I could go and talk to her, if you want me to."

"It wouldn't help," Marcus said. He reached out and clasped her upon the shoulder. "You're a good girl, Lucy. Now, you best leave with John. I shall draw you out a bank draft."

"Thank you," Lucy said.

Marcus nodded and turned to leave the stables.

"Marcus," Lucy called out quietly.

"Yes?" he asked, turning.

"I-I wish you the best." Her gaze was solemn.

"Thank you," Marcus said, smiling. "She is."

With that he turned and walked from the stables.

Elizabeth sat upon her bed, staring into the candle flame. The emotions roiling within her far outstripped that weakling fire in heat. Most were indefinable, but the one which shaded everything was jealousy. The moment she had seen that woman kissing Marcus, a rage like she'd never felt before had ripped through her.

A knock sounded upon the door.

"Elizabeth?" Marcus's voice called softly.

"Yes," Elizabeth asked, straightening.

"I wish to talk to you," he said.

"No," Elizabeth said. "I-I do not wish to talk."

"Then listen," Marcus said. "Lucy is not my mistress. Nor is she going to be. She once was. She came to me because she needed help."

A dry chuckle escaped Elizabeth. The way she was feeling, it wasn't only Lucy who needed help. "Yes?"

"Her last protector beat her," Marcus said.

"He did?" Elizabeth asked, feeling sympathy despite herself.

"He is the jealous sort," Marcus's voice said through the wood. "And Lucy has a tendency to be easy with her charms. Lord Sexton beat her and threatened to kill her."

"He did?" Elizabeth rose and walked to the door. Only in order to hear him better, she assured herself.

"She came to me hoping I'd become her protector again," Marcus said. "I told her she couldn't be my mistress, but that I would give her enough money to escape Lord Sexton until she could find another protector."

"I see," Elizabeth said, resting her head against the door. She desperately wanted to believe him.

"Do you believe me?" Marcus asked.

Elizabeth paused. Then she said softly, "Yes, Marcus. I do."

"She only kissed me, because . . ."

"She wanted to be your mistress," Elizabeth said.

"Yes," Marcus said. His voice sounded ragged. "I cannot change the life I had before, Lizzy. I cannot do that for you. But I promise, I did not invite her here, and I would never take her back as my mistress. I do not want another mistress."

"Y-you don't?" Elizabeth asked.

"No, I don't," Marcus's voice came back, firm and strong. "You must believe me."

Elizabeth laid her cheek to the wood and sighed. "I believe you." The only thing was, she suddenly realized she was no better than Lucy. It was she who wanted to be his mistress.

"Are you going to leave?" Marcus's voice asked.

Elizabeth closed her eyes. "No."

"Thank you," Marcus's voice came back softly. "Good night, Lizzy."

"Good night, Marcus," Elizabeth said. She stood a moment and then she walked back to her bed and sat down. She stared into the candle's flame once more. God help her, but she wanted to be Marcus's mistress. Surely it was due to the hot jealousy coursing through her from seeing another woman kiss Marcus. Yet, the demanding thought swirled through her. She wanted Marcus's kisses, she wanted him to take her to bed and satisfy this burning desire she had for him. She could not marry Marcus. Never would she marry a man who did so out of honor and debt. But could she not at least have his loving? Marcus had taken so many women to bed, why couldn't he take her to bed as well?

She caught her breath. Could she honestly be thinking of giving up her honor and virtue like this? She shook her head. What honor did she truly have left? The world already thought her Marcus's mistress. If she must live with the condemnation for the rest of her life, didn't she at least deserve to experience the act for which she was branded?

She lay down upon her bed and closed her eyes. Marcus had asked her if she would leave. A bitter smile tipped her lips. Why should she leave? She faced a bleak future once she returned to her world. Perhaps, though, she could take a little passion to warm her memories with her when she left.

Five

Elizabeth looked into her mirror and drew in a deep breath. She looked positively scandalous in the filmy nightgown and peignoir, which she had found within the drawer. Of course, she wanted to look scandalous, but it still sent embarrassed heat down to her toes. Could she really do this?

It had been a long and tense day. A day where both she and Marcus had been reserved; she secretly watching Marcus, and he just as covertly studying her. 'Twas clear he knew she hid something, but she doubted he knew it was this. He had shown surprise when she had joined him in a glass of wine at dinner. Now she wished she had downed a few more glasses, no matter Marcus's confusion.

She straightened her shoulders and lifted her chin for courage. The thought of attempting to seduce Marcus, a man famous for his experience in the art, was frightening. Yet the thought of never having him make love to her was even more frightening. Focusing upon that though, Elizabeth picked up her candle and left her room, flitting through the darkened lodge until she found Marcus's bedroom door.

She automatically raised her hand to knock and then withdrew it. She was a seductress. Surely they did not timidly knock and ask for permission to enter. Her lips firming, she reached out and twisted the knob to the door. It opened. She walked in and halted abruptly.

Marcus was just then standing beside the bed, his back turned to her. He was taking off his shirt.

"Marcus!" Elizabeth said, her voice squeaking.

Marcus spun towards her. His eyes widened. "Elizabeth?"

"No," Elizabeth said, shaking her head. "Lizzy."

His eyes darkened and he said, "What is it Lizzy? What is the matter?"

Elizabeth stared at him, not knowing what to say. Surely appearing in his room dressed like this should have told him what the matter was. He was the experienced one. "I . . ." she sucked in her breath. "I want you to make love to me." She let her breath out. Amazingly, it wasn't as difficult to say as she had expected.

"What?" Marcus asked.

Elizabeth bit her lip. For a rake, Marcus was definitely being obtuse. "I said . . . I want you to make love to me." A sudden passion and heat flared in Marcus's eyes. That look alone set Elizabeth trembling.

"Lizzy," Marcus said, striding quickly to her, his hand outstretched.

"Yes," Elizabeth whispered. She shook all the more. Now he would take her in his arms!

"Give me the candle," Marcus said, his hand clasping her wrist. "Before you drop it."

"Oh, yes," Elizabeth said, blinking. She hadn't noticed with her trembling that the candle she held tilted alarmingly, nor had she noticed the hot wax dripping to the carpet.

Marcus took the candle from her and with what seemed a painstakingly slow and precise movement crossed and set it upon the bedside table. He turned and looked at her, his face almost fierce. "Are you sure, Lizzy?"

"Yes," Elizabeth said. With quivering fingers she slipped the peignoir from her shoulders, to stand in only the translucent nightgown.

"You are beautiful," Marcus said, slowly walking towards her. "So very beautiful."

Elizabeth felt a moment of nervous fear, but then Marcus reached out and placed his hand gently to the curve of her neck. With that one touch, her fear disappeared. When Marcus bent his head and gently kissed her, Elizabeth moved into him, sliding her hands to his shoulders. It felt so right to hold him and feel his arms enfold her.

He held her lightly, ever so lightly, as if she were fragile. His kiss was a featherlight tease. As light as his hands that traced her every curve, learning the arch of her back, the swell of her hips and the line of her waist; teaching her body the sweet sensation of those hands upon her. She moaned slightly in her throat and leaned into Marcus.

As if answering her need, Marcus pulled her to him, deepening their kiss with a swift, lightning fierceness. Elizabeth gasped and shivered. It was drugging sensuality colliding with raw passion. Her heart leapt, even as heat flamed through her. She clutched tightly to Marcus, meeting his lips and marauding tongue with a wild play of her own.

Marcus growled, and swept her up into his arms. Elizabeth's fingers dug into the firm muscles of his shoulders, and she threw her head back as Marcus kissed the column of her throat. He carried her to the bed and laid her down, she still arching to feel the fever of his lips upon her skin. He did not deny her, but rolled his large body on top of her, pressing her taut one into the mattress. His hands stripped the nightgown's bodice down. It did not matter, for his lips and hands covered the cool bareness of her breasts with flaming warmth.

"Marcus," Elizabeth gasped, the shattering sensations striking to the core of her, coiling an ache deep within her.

Marcus's mouth left her breasts and came back to her lips. Elizabeth groaned and met his kiss, pressing herself into his remaining hands, desperate with desire.

"We've got to slow down, Lizzy," Marcus said, his voice a rasp.

Elizabeth heard the words, but they made no sense to her

whatsoever. Her body was so alive, her emotions for this man so demanding, she couldn't even think slow. "No."

"Oh, Lizzy," Marcus chuckled and groaned at the same time. His one hand slid down her rib cage, smoothed over her hip, and then traced the silken-clad length of her thigh. Elizabeth gasped as he brushed the nightgown up and she felt the warmth of his hand on her bare skin. She moaned as his hand moved slowly along her inner thigh, drawing closer to that private part which was aching with need. "We should wait until we are married."

"No," Elizabeth said, her eyes closing in anticipation of his hand's progress. How she needed him to touch her. "W-we don't have to marry."

Marcus's hand froze. "What?"

"W-we don't have to marry," Elizabeth sighed, her body aquiver.

"We don't!" Marcus suddenly jerked his hand back.

"What?" Elizabeth asked, her eyes snapping open.

Marcus rolled from her and sprung to a stand. He glared down at her, his eyes dark thunder. "What do you mean we don't have to get married?"

"We don't," Elizabeth said. Dazed and confused, she sat up. "I-I can be your mistress."

"My mistress?" Marcus looked at her as if she were insane.

Elizabeth flushed. "Everyone th-thinks I am already."

Marcus stared at her. Then he barked a laugh. "I can't believe it!"

"Marcus," Elizabeth said, biting her lip. Her body still tingled and demanded. "I want you."

His eyes narrowed. "You want me?"

Frustration pumped a sudden rage through Elizabeth. "Yes! I want you! You tried to seduce me that very first day! You brought me here to seduce me. Well, I'm seduced. I want you!"

"God!" Marcus said. A deep pain entered his eyes. "That is rich."

Sudden fear ripped through Elizabeth. Only then did she realize her nakedness. She quickly drew up her bodice. "Don't you want me anymore?"

"Yes, Lizzy," Marcus said, his voice harsh. "I want you."

Relief flooded through Elizabeth. Yet Marcus still did not move. "Then why won't you . . ."

"Because I want more," Marcus said.

Elizabeth swallowed hard. "M-more?"

"I don't want just your body, Elizabeth," Marcus said. "I want your love."

"Love?" Elizabeth asked. Her heart jolted.

Marcus looked at her and laughed, a sad, bitter laugh. "Yes. Stupid of me, isn't it? To think you could love a bounder like me."

"Marcus . . ." Elizabeth said, and then stopped. She didn't know what else to say.

"It's your own fault, Elizabeth," Marcus said, shaking his head. "You made it clear you wouldn't be won by passion alone. You forced me see you as more than just a woman to bed. Well, I want that woman. I want your love." He stepped back. "And I'll accept no less." He turned and walked towards the door.

"Where are you going?" Elizabeth asked, astonished.

"I'm leaving," Marcus said.

"You can't just leave!" Elizabeth gasped.

Marcus spun, his face enraged. "Yes, Lizzy, I can. Astonishing, I know. Rake Tremain walking away from a woman in his bed!"

"I didn't mean . . ." Elizabeth halted.

"Yes, you did," Marcus said. His eyes narrowed. "I want your love, Elizabeth. I want you to marry me. And I warn you, it won't be a marriage of convenience. I want it to be a marriage in every way, body and soul, Lizzy. Body and soul." Elizabeth sat, staring at him. The fire went out of his eyes and he said, "You may remain here as long as you want. John will take you home when you wish. Good-bye, Lizzy." He turned and walked out the door.

"Good-bye?" Elizabeth murmured. It was not *au revoir*. It

was good-bye. She clenched her fists together. Marcus, the premier rake, had just walked out on her. Her body was afire, and he had walked out on her.

He said he wanted her love! He wanted her body and soul! Damn and blast him! She had been ready to give him her body, and suddenly it wasn't enough. He wanted her love as well. Elizabeth kicked back the cover and scrambled from the bed, pacing across the room. Well, he couldn't have her love. She'd not fall in love with a rake. She'd not submit herself to a life of misery and scandal. She didn't want that!

She halted. Sighing, she returned to the bed and laid down in it. The scent of Marcus pervaded it. She curled up and closed her eyes. It was pathetic she knew. She was in Marcus's bed, but he wasn't there.

Marcus sat in the large library chair. He watched the flames in the fireplace dance. He sipped from a glass of brandy attempting to clear his mind of everything. It was useless. Images of Elizabeth still flashed in his mind. Three days had passed, and still his mind would not churn up anything but thoughts of Elizabeth. He was going insane. He should have just taken her that night and accepted whatever he could.

He clenched his jaw. No, he knew he couldn't have done so. For once in his life he loved; loved far too much to play the usual game of seduction and then good-bye. He did not want to tarnish either his love for Elizabeth, or Elizabeth herself, with simple sex. Yet, where did that leave him? Living in hell is where it left him. He chuckled dryly and reached for his glass.

"What is so funny?" Elizabeth's voice suddenly asked. Marcus blinked. God, now he was hearing things as well. He jerked his hand back from the brandy glass. Apparently he'd had more than enough of that. "I could stand to hear something funny."

Marcus stiffened. He turned his gaze towards the imagined voice of Elizabeth. Then he blinked. "Elizabeth?" It had to be her in the flesh. He didn't think his imagination would dream up her holding a pistol leveled upon him.

"Yes," Elizabeth said. Her gray eyes flashed with mingled mischief and passion.

Marcus tensed all the more. "Why are you here? And with a pistol no less."

"I'm sorry, Marcus," Elizabeth said, shaking her head. "But I'm abducting you."

"What?" Marcus sprung up.

Elizabeth shrugged her shoulder. "Turnabout is fair play, is it not? You abducted me. I am abducting you. We haven't finished our . . . discussion at the lodge."

"No, Lizzy," Marcus said, shaking his head. "We have finished it." He drew in his breath. "I told you what I will accept. You can shoot me now, but I'm not going to the lodge with you."

Elizabeth gazed at him steadily. She sighed and lowered the pistol. "For a rake, you are being extremely difficult."

Marcus smiled, despite himself. "Perhaps because I'm not a rake anymore. I'm just a man in love."

"And I'm a woman in love," Elizabeth said softly. "Body and soul."

Marcus's heart jumped. "Then why the pistol, Lizzy?"

Her lips twisted. "Perhaps it was my last defense."

"Then put it down, sweetheart," Marcus said. "So I can kiss you."

She smiled. "I don't need to put it down. It's not loaded."

Marcus started. He barked a laugh. Striding over he grabbed hold of the pistol and tossed it aside. That out of the way, he jerked Elizabeth into his arms and kissed her with a fierce tenderness. He drew back, growing solemn. "You don't need a defense, Lizzy. I'll do anything you want . . ." He saw her eyes flare. "After we are married, that is."

Elizabeth laughed. "I hope we marry soon, Marcus." She leaned over and kissed him. "Very soon."

* * *

Elizabeth stood before the Reverend Milton, listening to him drone on and on. She smiled slightly and peeked at Marcus. His gaze was warm and light. A bubble rose within her throat. Not from nerves, but from sheer happiness. How totally different this wedding day was from the first one. She wore the same dress as before, had invited the same people who amazingly had attended, and listened to the same ceremony.

Only this time, the groom was different and so was the wedding. She desperately loved the man whom she stood beside and he loved her. A vision of their future arose from within her heart. How very, very different it would be, compared to the cold, proper one she had planned with the baron. Yes, everything was wonderfully different.

"If there is anyone who has just reason why these two should not join in holy matrimony . . ." Reverend Milton entoned. Suddenly he halted, his face a bright red. He looked up, his embarrassed gaze skittering to Elizabeth. She smiled and looked at him as innocently as she could, stifling her laughter. He coughed and looked back down. "Hm, yes. Er . . . if there is anyone who has . . . er . . . just reason why these two . . ."

"You've said that, Reverend," Marcus said, his voice low and amused.

"Get on with it," Mr. Hampton hissed, in a far louder voice.

Reverend Milton jumped. "If there is anyone who . . ." he halted, and his eyes ran down the page. "Let him speak or forever hold his . . ."

A loud commotion sounded from behind. A deep male voice roared, "I object!"

"What?" Reverend Milton squeaked. His book dropped from his hands.

"Blast and damn!" Mr. Hampton cursed.

"Oh, no," Mrs. Hampton's wail topped the crowd's exclamations. "Not again!"

"No, not again," Elizabeth said, clenching her fists. She spun around, ready to fight anyone who dared to object to her marriage to Marcus. Suddenly her fists relaxed, and she almost crowed in delight. The tall, blond man who stood in the center of the aisle looked much older than she remembered, as well as exceedingly ragged in his travel dirt, but at least this man she knew, knew very well. "Richard!"

"Oh, no!" Mrs. Hampton cried, flinging up her hands. "Richard!" She gurgled something indistinguishable, swayed, and spiraled to the ground. Elizabeth shook her head. Her weddings didn't agree with her mother.

"Richard!" shouted Mr. Hampton. He, alas, didn't faint, but stood, gaping at his disowned son.

"Yes, Richard," Marcus said, stepping forward to place a possessive arm about Elizabeth's shoulders. Elizabeth grinned up at him. Surprisingly, Marcus did not smile as he gazed at her brother. "I'm glad you could make it to *this* wedding, but what the devil do you mean by objecting to it?"

"Yes, Richard," Jasmine cried, leaving her fallen mother and rushing over to tug on his sleeve. "You aren't supposed to object."

"Indeed," Matty said, rushing forward as well. "Don't object!"

"But I do," Richard said, shaking off Jasmine's restraining hand. He strode forward. "You don't have to do this, Marcus. Nor you, Lizzy."

"I don't?" Elizabeth asked, sliding her arm around Marcus's waist.

She felt him relax. He laughed and said, "We don't?"

"No," Richard said, his eyes fierce. "I didn't expect you to marry Elizabeth, Marcus! You know I didn't."

"I'm sorry," Marcus said, his voice amused. "But you did write that I should take care of her."

"Yes, but not marry her, blast it!" Richard exclaimed.

"I guess I misread your instructions," Marcus murmured. "Since you weren't here to take care of it, I improvised."

"Improvised?" Richard asked, his voice outraged.

"Marriage did seem to be the best way to take care of Lizzy," Marcus said, his tone apologetic.

"You don't have to marry her," Richard said, his jaw clearly clenched. "I'm home now and I'm rich!"

"Rich?" Mr. Hampton exclaimed.

"Yes, Father," Richard said, turning to look at him. "I'm rich and I intend to repay you for every debt."

"I'll not take it!" roared Mr. Hampton.

"Excuse me," Marcus said, his tone firm. "You may settle your differences later, but we have a wedding to proceed with at this moment."

"No," Mr. Hampton said, his face pugnacious. "I'll not remain if he is here."

Elizabeth turned to frown at her father. She drew in a breath then, realizing where her loyalties lay. "Then do not remain. You have disowned Richard, but I have not." She looked warmly at Richard. "He is my brother, and I am happy that he is here."

"Well!" Mr. Hampton blustered. "If that is the way you feel. You two were always disobedient, unruly children." Jerking his head for emphasis, he stormed down the aisle and slammed out of the doors. Elizabeth watched, musing that it was but one more pompous, self-righteous man to desert her upon her wedding day.

"Don't worry," Jasmine said. "He'll come around."

Elizabeth shrugged. Her gaze then fell upon her mother and she laughed. "But Mother hasn't yet."

Jasmine giggled. "Hopefully she won't until after the ceremony."

"But there is no need for a ceremony," Richard said. "I tell you. That is why I am here." He looked to Marcus. "Neither of you need do this. I can take care of Lizzy now."

"No, Richard," Marcus said, a thread of laughter in his voice. "I don't think you can take care of Lizzy the way *I* intend to take care of her. It would be quite indecent."

Richard stiffened and his eyes blazed. "What!"

Elizabeth stifled her own laughter. She feigned a teary voice. "It's too late, Richard. Much too late. Marcus has . . . already seen my birthmark."

Richard started back, clearly stunned. Surprisingly, none in the pews expressed shock. Elizabeth noticed Mrs. Cartwright nodding her head up and down vehemently. Richard's face turned thunderous. "Damn you, Marcus. I can't believe it. She's my sister, for God's sake!"

"I'm sorry, I couldn't resist," Marcus said, smiling. In his truly atrocious and audacious way, Marcus withdrew his arm from Elizabeth and stepping back, patted her on her derriere. The onlookers did exclaim at this. Elizabeth stiffened. "It is charming."

"My son!" the Reverend Milton exclaimed. "You are in a house of God."

"Oh, but that is n- . . ." Jasmine objected.

"Jasmine," Elizabeth said quickly, staring at her sister. "Be quiet. You are in a house of God."

Jasmine's eyes widened and then she fell silent. Elizabeth glanced at Matty. Matty's eyes were bright and she clearly bit her lip. Elizabeth then looked at Richard. A slow smile crossed his face. "I see." He winked at Elizabeth. "Well, if he's already seen that . . ."

Elizabeth grinned. Richard may have told Marcus far too many things about her, but at least he had withheld the intimate secret of her birthmark's exact location. A sudden thought flashed through Elizabeth's mind. If she had persisted in challenging Marcus upon her first wedding day, if she had demanded he tell her where her birthmark actually lay, she could have exposed him as a fraud. In truth, she would not be standing here today. Elizabeth shook herself, and cast off the frightening thought. Smiling, she walked up to Richard. "You see, we *must* get married."

Richard reached out and pulled her to him for an enthusiastic hug. "Little minx," he whispered into her ear.

"Well," she whispered back. "You shouldn't have sent him if you hadn't planned on this."

"No, I suppose not," Richard said. He laughed. "I sent him

to save you from the baron. Now it looks like you are going to save him instead."

"We'll save each other," Elizabeth laughed.

"At least there will be some surprises on the wedding night," Richard said.

"I'm sure," Elizabeth said. "And I'm looking forward to them all."

"Lizzy!" Richard hooted.

"Excuse me," Marcus said, walking up to them. "If you are done mauling my bride, Richard, I would like to proceed with our wedding."

Richard laughed and released Elizabeth. "Proceed by all means . . . Brother."

"I will," Marcus said, grinning as he reached out and clasped Elizabeth's hand. "Do me a favor, Richard, and guard my back."

"Don't I always?" Richard said with a slight bow. He turned and strolled to the back doors. He lodged his broad shoulders against them. "Should I shoot anyone who objects?"

Marcus looked at Elizabeth pointedly. "No, we've had enough of pistols."

"Yes, we have," Elizabeth murmured, smiling wickedly at him.

Marcus chuckled and led her firmly back to the altar. "We are ready, Reverend."

The Reverend Milton gaped a moment. Then he nodded and stooped to pick up his book. He leafed through the pages. With a shaky finger, he pointed to the line. "If anyone . . ." He jumped and swallowed. "Er, no. We are past that part."

"We most certainly are," Marcus said.

"Indeed," Elizabeth giggled.

The Reverend Milton cast them a harried look. He then buried his head in the book and proceeded to finish the wedding ceremony with little pomp, and great haste. He sighed in relief when both spoke their vows. Not only was there no need for pistols, but he could feel satisfied that this couple, who were both surely past redemption, at least now had the sanction of the holy bonds of matrimony.

Nodding his head, he gave the groom permission to kiss the bride. He immediately regretted that unwitting favor, and his face turned a scorching red when the groom took his bride into his arms and kissed her with a blatant passion, one which the bride returned just as fully. He wasn't certain even marriage sanctioned such. Nor was it appropriate for the uproarious laughter and applause of the bride's family, those who remained and were conscious, that was.

Indeed, neither of Elizabeth Hampton's weddings had been appropriate. Reverend Milton sighed and sent up a pray of thanksgiving to the Almighty, nevertheless. Scandalous and improper as it might be, it was clear he'd never have to perform another wedding ceremony for the lady ever again.

THE NOTORIOUS
MR. FREEMONT

by
Martha Kirkland

One

"Remember, Delia," Mrs. Feona Glenn cautioned, pulling her shawl across her daily expanding abdomen, "the members of a vicar's family are like Caesar's wife. They must, at all times, behave in a manner that is above reproach!"

"I shall not forget," replied the recipient of that self-righteous admonition, a slender young woman with honey blond curls and lively green eyes. "Now, please," she said, saluting her sister-in-law's pale cheek, "go back inside, for though the sun says April, the breeze still speaks of March, and a woman in your condition should be sitting by a cozy fire."

After kissing each of her three small nephews, Delia gave her brother a hug and allowed him to help her into the handsome maroon traveling chaise waiting in the lane that ran in front of the vicarage. Settling against the plush gray squabs, she smiled at the owner of the carriage, a pleasingly plump matron of middle years.

"Of all the shabby-genteel nonsense I ever heard," Lady Wilding said, addressing herself to the small, pug-faced puppy who sat beside her, his stubby tail wagging in anticipation of the trip that was to begin momentarily, "that one wins the prize. Above reproach indeed! I should like to know where that peahen, Feona Glenn, thinks I am taking our dear Delia. To some bacchanal?"

Since the question was not addressed to her, Delia made no reply. Wisdom prompted her to keep her thoughts to herself, for even at this, the last minute, with her portmanteau secured in the boot and the horses pawing the earth in eagerness to begin the journey, Feona might still find some excuse to prevent her husband's younger sister from accompanying Lady Wilding to Wiltshire.

"Actually," Delia said, once the coachman had cracked his whip above the heads of the well-matched team, and the chaise had left behind the modest cottage that was the Newton-Leyes vicarage, "my sister-in-law believes I am accompanying you to Lacock to support you in your hour of need."

Lady Wilding lifted her carefully arched eyebrows, understandably surprised. "My hour of need?"

"Yes, ma'am. With your poor uncle expected to breathe his last at any moment, you would not wish to make the six-hour journey alone."

"Breathe his last? Wherever did you get such a preposterous notion? My uncle is amazingly healthy. In fact, he—"

Noting the blush on her young friend's face, her ladyship paused. "Oh. Now I see how it is. Feona would approve of a death-bed visit, but not a pleasure trip with a friend."

When Delia said nothing, Lady Wilding let the subject rest. "Your ruse notwithstanding," she added, "I must tell you that even though Lord Hazelton turned eighty on his last birthday, from all I can surmise, he will most likely live to be a hundred."

"I sincerely hope he may!"

"Of course you do. Otherwise, what is the point of your traveling all the way to Wiltshire to ask him for employment."

"Very true, ma'am. With Feona breeding again, my brother needs to augment his income by taking in student borders. To do so, however, he needs the fourth bedchamber, which I now occupy."

Delia let that excuse suffice, for she was loath to reveal, even to Lady Wilding, all her reasons for wishing to leave the vicarage. Money was, of course, a prime consideration, but there was also the matter of Delia's growing discontent at living her life as a poor relation. No matter how kindly treated—and no one could doubt the genuine affection Feona had for her husband's younger sister—to spend one's life in another woman's home, obliged to observe another woman's rules, must be unpalatable to any female.

Employment was Delia's only option, for at twenty-three years of age, and with no money to bring to a prospective husband, marriage was out of the question. Unfortunately, she had been educated by her father—a scholar of early Greek and Roman antiquities—and as a result, she lacked proficiency in those subjects needed to allow her to hire out as a governess or to teach at a female academy.

It was upon learning from Lady Wilding that her uncle, Lord Hazelton—the noted archaeologist—was retiring from field work to write his memoirs, that the idea first came to Delia that she was perfectly suited to be his assistant. She read both Greek and Latin, she had a wide knowledge of antiquities, and as her father was used to say, she wrote a very neat hand.

"Uncle Barringford will not be easy to approach," Lady Wilding said, bringing Delia's thoughts back to her traveling companion, "even though he and your father were known to one another. Both a wealthy peer and a celebrated archaeologist, Uncle is constantly besieged by people wanting something from him. As a result, he does not go much in company. Furthermore, since he remained a bachelor his entire life, he has always pleased himself in every particular. Or so I hear."

"So you hear?"

"Yes. Although I have exchanged correspondence with him from time to time, I have not seen him in a decade." She held up her hand as if to forestall an expected interruption. "And before you read me a lecture upon family loyalty, my dear, allow me to say that we are not all as devoted to our relatives as you are."

Recognizing the thinly veiled sarcasm, Delia chose to keep her own counsel, well aware of her friend's views upon what she called Delia's unpaid servitude.

"On the occasion of the last visit paid to Uncle Barringford by my sisters and myself," Lady Wilding continued, "he refused to see us. Not that I blame him overmuch, for the visit was got up by my sister, Frances, for the sole purpose of introducing her son to our uncle's notice."

"That would be Mr. Basil Venton?"

"Yes. The scheme did not succeed, however. Uncle Barringford simply instructed his butler to tell us that he had no time for tea parties and gossip, so he would thank us to take ourselves elsewhere. Of course, Frances continued to make an annual pest of herself, dragging her reluctant son in her wake, but I chose to honor our uncle's wishes."

"Until now," Delia said, the softly worded phrase a polite question.

Mildred Wilding drew off the Clarence blue kid gloves that perfectly matched her traveling dress and she studied her plump, beringed fingers. "According to the letter I received yesterday, my uncle wishes to see all his relatives to settle a matter pertaining to his will."

After removing her stylish, low-crowned bonnet, her ladyship fluffed up the still-brown curls that showed beneath her lace cap. "It is understandable," she said, her tongue in her cheek, "that you would misunderstand me and think my uncle was gravely ill."

"No need to wrap it up in clean linen, ma'am. I lied to my sister-in-law."

"And who would wonder at it? I have known Feona Glenn these past dozen years, and if she even suspected that this little trip might afford you a means of leaving your brother's care, she would have found some excuse to keep you at home."

The observation being unanswerable, Delia kept her thoughts to herself. It was true that Feona's pride did not allow her to own that her husband's sister was a drain on their finances, but it was equally true that Delia disliked deceiving her.

For the past eight years, Delia had lived under Feona and Caleb's roof, eaten from their table, depended upon them for the very clothes upon her back. When her father died unexpectedly, leaving Delia without so much as a shilling to defray the cost of her support, it was her brother and her sister-in-law who took her in. They gave her a home, sharing their earthly goods with her without the least show of resentment, and for this—if for nothing else—Delia owed them a very real debt of gratitude.

As if divining her friend's thoughts, Lady Wilding reached over and patted the young lady's hand. "Your loyalty does you credit, my dear, but if you must justify your little deception, pray think what pleasure you are giving me by accompanying me to Lacock."

"But Feona will—"

"Will have to realize that you are no longer a child. She is far too strict in her notions. It never does to hold young people on too tight a lead. They want firm guidance, of course, but that guidance should be tempered with kindness and an appreciation for the fact that we are not all fashioned from the same mold."

Delia schooled her twitching lips. "I collect, ma'am, that you obtained this vast store of parenting wisdom while rearing your own children."

Lady Wilding gathered the puppy in her arms, addressing the white-coated pug as if it understood her every word. "Delia is a saucy minx, Tasha, for she knows you are my only child. But," she continued, this time speaking directly to the young lady, "everything need not be learned firsthand. I have never fallen beneath the wheels of a carriage, but I know with a certainty that I should dislike the experience."

Chuckling, Delia said, "Your point is well taken, ma'am. If you will, pray tell me how you arrived at your more permissive approach to child rearing?"

"By observing the actions of others. Especially those of my oldest sister, Mrs. Freemont."

Her ladyship's lip curled slightly in distaste. "Beatrice was never a bright woman, but I might have forgiven her that. After all, my middle sister is not particularly needle-witted, yet I tolerate her. What I could not condone in Bea was her cowardice. She lacked the rumgumption to say boo to a goose, and as a result, she allowed her husband—as exacting a man as I ever met—to turn their only son, a sweet, obliging boy into an angry, rebellious young man. The kind of young man who eventually fulfilled his father's prophesy of debauchery by—"

Lady Wilding stopped abruptly, raising her hand to her plump bosom, obviously embarrassed at having introduced the subject. "I should not have spoken of him."

"Your sister's husband?"

"No, no, my dear. Freemont died scarce six months after my sister's passing. It is their son, Lawrence, to whom I refer. He ran away from home shortly after his fifteenth birthday. The gossips would have it that his going was the result of an incident with one of the serving girls."

Delia leaned forward, interested in spite of her brother's sermon only the day before concerning the evils of gossip. "You cannot mean that young Mr. Freemont is a black sheep?"

"I am afraid I mean just that. But please, I pray you, remember there are usually two sides to every story. And by all means, do not speak of poor Lawrence once we arrive at Hazelton Hall. Lady Venton's sensibilities, don't you know. Any reference to our nephew sends Frances into a fit of the vapors."

"You may rest easy on that head, ma'am, for I promise you, your nephew's name shall never pass my lips."

The journey was accomplished with only one long stop, and that for a nuncheon at a rambling old inn called The King's Fowler; therefore, the coach reached Lacock by midafternoon. After passing through the town, with its broad high street and its numerous smaller streets, each sporting a jumble of stone inns, red-brick shops, and timbered, wattle and daub cottages, the travelers soon found themselves approaching the ornate iron entrance gates of Hazelton Hall.

Never before having visited such an elegant establishment, and not certain the opportunity would ever come her way again,

Delia allowed herself a moment to enjoy the symmetry of the building.

Constructed in the days of the great Queen Elizabeth, the mansion was shaped to represent Her Majesty's initial. Along the front of the house, long windows were paired at intervals on both of the two main floors, and repeated in smaller proportions on the attic level. It was a handsome edifice, for time had mellowed the harsh red of the brick to a rose that was at once inviting and pleasing to the eye.

The coachman reined in the team before an impressive stone portico, and while the ladies were handed down, the heavy oak door was flung open by a footman in dark blue livery. Beside the young servant stood His Lordship's butler, an ancient so stooped over he seemed in a perpetual bow.

"Welcome, m'lady."

"Good heavens, Garrick! Are you still alive?"

"As you see, m'lady."

"Well, good for you." She motioned toward Delia. "This is Miss Glenn, who was good enough to come along to keep me company."

"Miss," the butler greeted, apparently not at all disconcerted by the arrival of an unexpected guest.

"Is my uncle receiving, Garrick?"

"No, milady. His Lordship is keeping to his rooms today, but I shall apprise him of your arrival. For now, Lady Venton is in the blue withdrawing room, where a tea tray was taken in only moments ago."

"Good man. No," she said when the old servant made as if to lead the way, "we can announce ourselves."

After handing the pug to the startled footman, and issuing instructions as to the animal's need for immediate exercise, Lady Wilding swept through the handsome pink-marbled vestibule. Preceding Delia through a hall whose decorations consisted entirely of medieval armor and battle-axes, she did not stop until they reached the door to the blue drawing room.

The rather formal apartment, with its long windows facing

onto the front lawn and its French windows giving a glimpse of a formal garden to the east, was occupied by only one person, a painfully thin, pallid-faced woman some eight years older than Lady Wilding. Recognizing Lady Venton, Delia curtsied.

"Sister!" the lady cried upon spying the newcomers. "Thank heaven you are come at last. And, Delia, my dear. Always nice to see you. I trust the Reverend and Mrs. Glenn are well?"

While Delia nodded, Lady Wilding bent to press her cheek against that of her sister. The older lady had not risen from the blue brocade slipper chair she occupied, choosing instead to conserve her strength. To her left was a mahogany drum table bearing a small silver case fitted out with a myriad of vials and apothecaries' bottles—an accoutrement never far from Her Ladyship's side—and as she spoke, she reached over to fetch a thin blue bottle of sal volatile.

"Sister," she said, taking a dainty sniff of the pungent salts, "how relieved I am that you are come in time, for my nerves are vastly overset. It is our uncle. That insolent butler will not let me see him, no matter what I say to convince him of my sincerity, and I am persuaded the old gentleman is fading fast."

Mildred Wilding gasped. "Are you telling me that Uncle is ill?"

"Ill? Sister, the man is eighty years old. He *must* be ill."

Lady Wilding gave it as her opinion that there was no *must* about it. "Depend upon it, Frances, he is abovestairs lost in one of those books of his on ancient civilizations, caring little that you and I have arrived. You know how he has always disliked having the family descend upon him."

"But he sent for us!"

As if suddenly recalling the nature of that summons, Lady Venton lowered her voice, choosing to abandon her worry for the old gentleman's health in favor of a more interesting topic. "My letter said something about his will."

"As did mine."

Frances Venton sighed contentedly. "Since the estate is unentailed, I presume Uncle has finally decided who is to be his heir. Naturally, he wishes to inform the fortunate recipient as soon as may be."

"If that thought pleases you, Frances, by all means continue to delude yourself."

"Delude? Sister, whatever can you mean?"

Ignoring the question, Lady Wilding removed her bonnet and gloves, and disposed herself upon a lyre-back settee, then she motioned for Delia to sit in the ebony and gilt armchair beside the teapoy, where she might dispense the cups and pass the silver filigree cake basket. "It is quite possible," she continued finally, "that our uncle has brought us here for no other purpose than to advise us of his decision so he may send us packing forever, no richer than before we came."

"Easy for you to be so flippant, sister. You with your two thousand a year. My brother-in-law, may he rest in peace, left you well provided for. Since my husband is never beforehand with the world, I cannot afford to whistle a fortune down the wind. Furthermore, if our uncle has not seen fit to name my poor Basil as his heir, I do not know what will become of the lad."

Mildred Wilding was accustomed to Lady Venton's habit of referring to her sister's jointure as a fortune, while denigrating her own pin money as scarce enough to keep the duns from her door, but she had never supposed that Frances expected her son to be the sole recipient of their uncle's fortune.

"Has it occurred to you, Fanny, that our uncle may well have left his money to some worthy cause? You would be wise not to pin too much hope upon Basil's chances. To do so is to court certain disappointment."

Lady Venton puffed up like a wood pigeon, her gaunt bosom heaving with insult. "I do not see that! I do not see that at all, for Basil is more than worthy to step into his uncle's shoes. And who has more right to our uncle's estate than his own grand-nephew? No one. No one has a nearer claim than my own dear son."

"I do not speak of rights, Frances. What is the point? If there

was any justice in the world, you and I would be considered the
properest claimants. After all, *we* are Uncle Barringford's
nieces. The children of his only sister. What *right* is there in
passing over an entire generation of females in preference for
a male?"

Having given her sister something to think about, Lady Wilding ruined the effect by adding, "Besides, if memory serves
me, I believe Uncle had Garrick bar the door the last time you
brought your son to visit him. Such a reception does not inspire
one to think that he holds your son in any great affection."

Sensing Lady Venton's rising indignation, Delia circum-
vented the explosion by asking about the lady's husband. "Is
Sir George with you, ma'am?"

"As though I would travel alone! Surely you must appreciate
how the journey from Sussex to Wiltshire taxes my delicate
constitution."

"Of course she does," Lady Wilding answered blandly, accepting a cup of tea from Delia. "We are all well acquainted
with your constitution, Frances." Without giving her sister time
to take further offense, she added, "So where is your husband
now?"

The lady dismissed the question with a wave of her lace handkerchief. "You know Venton when he comes to Wiltshire. He
is always to be found out of doors, a gun in his hands, shooting
whatever may offer him sport." Brightening, the older lady continued, "But I am pleased to inform you that Basil accompanied
us, so his uncle could see for himself what a fine, handsome
gentleman his nephew has become."

"Very wise," Mildred Wilding said, though to Delia's ears,
Her Ladyship's voice lacked conviction.

More than a little embarrassed to be privy to such an intimate
family discussion, Delia searched for something to direct the
conversation toward a less volatile subject. "I look forward to
meeting Mr. Venton," she said. "I do not believe he has ever
accompanied you when you visited Newton-Leyes."

"No, he has not," his mother agreed. "But the introductions

will have to be deferred for now, for my son, too, is out of doors."

"Oh? Does he share Sir George's love of hunting?"

"Not at all," the lady said, shuddering at the thought. "My son is a poet. A gentleman of sensitivity, he abhors all forms of sport. He goes out merely to commune with nature."

"An excellent employment," Lady Wilding said. "Delia, I am convinced that you must be wishing for a bit of exercise after being cooped up the better part of the day. Why do you not take a turn in the garden while my sister and I have a comfortable coze?"

Happy to seize this chance for escape, Delia stood quickly, catching up the plain green bonnet and the woolen pelisse she had worn over her carriage dress. "A wonderful idea, ma'am. I should like to view the garden before the light fades."

Hurrying to the French windows, Delia let herself out onto a low terrace where stone steps led down to the central most of three narrow gravel avenues. Bordered by beech hedges, the walks fanned out in goose-feet that stretched to the end of the long garden, coming to a stop at a wrought-iron arbor covered with thick, woody grapevines. A statue of some sort stood beneath the arbor. Due to the fading light, Delia could not make out the nature of the statue, so she determined upon that as her destination.

It being only the second week in April, spring had not come in earnest, but Delia breathed deeply of the clean, crisp air, enjoying the promise of softer weather. For the moment, it was enough that the snows had melted, revealing the sprays of black-thorn, their white blossoms spread along the hedgerows, while the twigs of the horse chestnuts bore large, toffee-brown sticky buds.

Above the arbor, quite near the statue, a bird lit among the still-bare vines. Brown with a lovely sky blue throat, the little bird uttered the haunting call of the cuckoo, causing Delia to smile at this first, true harbinger of spring.

"Hello!" she said once the song was finished. "I cannot tell

you how glad I am to see you, my friend. Such a handsome
fellow must always merit an enthusiastic welcome, but after this
long, dreary winter, depend upon it, sir, your return has been
eagerly awaited."

"Well, now," said a deep, masculine voice, "you are very
kind, madam. Believe me, I should have returned even sooner
had I known I would receive such a gratifyingly warm reception."

Stunned into silence, Delia watched as the statue emerged
from the shade of the arbor and made her a most courtly bow.

"Sir," she gasped. "I . . . I was talking to the cuckoo."

"Cruel, ma'am," he said, "to recant just when I let myself
hope that there was one among the company who would not be
unhappy to see me."

Though Delia was momentarily disconcerted, her face growing uncomfortably warm, she recovered her composure quickly
enough once it occurred to her that the statue-come-to-life could
be none other than Mr. Basil Venton. Had she not been told
only minutes ago that he was somewhere on the grounds?

She knew Mr. Venton only by hearsay, but nothing she had
heard of him had prepared her for the truth—neither his
mother's glowing description, nor the disparaging remarks made
by Lady Wilding's husband, who had always referred to his
wife's nephew as "That demmed man-milliner." Expecting to
encounter a slender young man of medium height, dressed in
the latest fashion, Delia was surprised to discover a very different sort of gentleman.

If he *was* a gentleman.

Tall and broad-shouldered, he was dressed in a well-cut coat
of mulberry superfine, a cream and silver marcella waistcoat,
and gray pantaloons, yet there was none of the dandy about his
appearance. His shirt points were not nearly high enough to be
all the crack; he wore not a single fob, stickpin, or ring; and
his coffee brown hair was brushed straight back, in a style that
suited his angular face but not the dictates of fashion.

In addition to this sartorial casualness were added thick, almost straight eyebrows, eyes too dark a blue to be universally admired, and a wide, rather satirical smile that pulled to the left, depriving the man of any claim whatsoever to classical masculine beauty.

And yet, there was something about that smile that drew a response from Delia. Against her own inclination, she felt a tug at the corners of her mouth.

"There, now," he said, "that is much better. Now I need no longer be jealous of the cuckoo."

Delia chuckled. She could not help herself, for the man had an easy relaxed way about him that was as infectious as it was outrageous. Unbidden, the thought came to her that he must be a favorite with the London ladies. Recalling what Lady Venton had said about Basil being the most logical heir to Lord Hazelton's fortune, Delia could only imagine what the addition of an inheritance would do for his popularity. If she knew anything of the world, it would need only wealth to make him the most sought-after gentleman in town.

Just as she had scrutinized him, now he studied her. While his gaze traveled slowly from her head down to the toes of her kid boots and back up again, Delia's breath caught in her throat, for she felt almost as if he had touched her with more than his glance.

Swallowing, she said, "Sir, I collect you must be wondering who I am."

"No, ma'am. At the moment, I was thinking only how fortunate I am. It must have been years since a lady referred to me as . . ." he paused a moment, and a devilish light shown in his eyes. "I believe you said, 'a handsome fellow.' "

"Sir! I told you I was speaking to the cuckoo."

"You cannot mean that *everything* you said was for that bird?"

Delia could not contain her laughter. "Your aunt told me you were a poet, sir. She did not, however, warn me that you were also a rogue."

"She should have done," he said softly, lifting his eyebrows in a manner that made Delia wonder if her lungs had ceased to function. "But have no fear, for I do not doubt she will correct the oversight directly once she sees me."

Not certain how she should answer this remark, Delia offered him her hand. "My name is Delia Glenn. I live in Newton-Leyes, and I have come to Wiltshire with your aunt."

"Aunt Mildred?"

"Why, yes," she answered. "Is she not your only aunt?"

"Actually, I have another, but for the moment let us table the discussion of my relatives." He still held her hand, and now he placed his other one over it. "You are shivering," he said.

Suddenly conscious of the disappearance of the sun and the drop in temperature, she eased her fingers free of his grasp. Surprisingly, his were not the smooth hands of a gentleman. On the contrary, they were work-roughened, and at their touch, warmth had tingled its way up Delia's arm.

"Let us go back inside," he said, "and save the stroll through my uncle's garden for a warmer day."

Taking her assent for granted, he began walking back toward the terrace. When they neared the French windows, he stepped forward and opened them for her.

"Is that you, Basil?" Lady Venton called.

"And me," Delia said, stepping inside the room and looking toward Lady Wilding, who was busy selecting a macaroon from the cake basket.

The gentleman closed the windows behind him, then he came forward, smiling broadly at both Their Ladyships who stared at him, their mouths agape. Mildred Wilding was the first to react, dropping the filigree basket and scattering cakes and cookies all over the blue and gold Axminster carpet.

As for Frances Venton, her wan face grew even paler than usual. "You!" she screamed, clamping her trembling hand over her heart as if that organ threatened to vacate its present abode. "What effrontery! How dare you come here!"

The gentleman made both ladies very proper bows, as though they had greeted him warmly. "And a good day to you, aunts," he said. "I am fine, I thank you for asking. And what of you two ladies? I hope I find you well."

Realizing that something was very wrong, though not at all certain what, Delia drew herself up to her full five feet, five inches, and though the height was not particularly impressive when compared to the gentleman's six feet plus, at least he gave his attention back to her.

"Sir," she said. "Who are you?"

He made her a perfectly unexceptional bow, and yet, there was a light in his eyes that rendered the gesture a mockery. "I, madam, am Lawrence Freemont. The proverbial bad penny."

Two

Lawrence paused at the door to Lord Hazelton's bedchamber and looked back at the robust old gentleman with the lion's mane of white hair and the equally impressive mustache. His Lordship sat in a wing chair drawn up near the fireplace, but should anyone believe him infirm, they had only to notice the decanter of brandy on the table at his elbow, the cigar held firmly between his fingers, and the open book resting on his lap, all waiting to be enjoyed.

"I shall return later, Uncle Barry, on the chance that you might like a hand or two of cribbage before bedtime."

"What's this?" the gentleman asked. "Crying craven so soon, my boy?"

Laughing, Lawrence said, "You may be right, Uncle. But who would not turn coward when faced with the prospect of dinner with such an array of guests? The majority of whom are too closely related to consider manners a requirement for felicitous dining, and all of whom believe me the devil incarnate."

"All? Even the young lady who talks to the birds in my garden?"

"No," he said softly. "Not her."

Lawrence recalled Miss Delia Glenn as she had looked when he first saw her. He had thought he was alone in the garden, and suddenly, there in the fading afternoon light stood a young lady. Dressed quite plainly, she wore her honey-colored hair caught up at the crown of her head in a style that just missed being puritanical, its severity softened only by the riot of curls that escaped their rigid confines to frame her face and neck. Looks to the contrary, however, she was no puritan.

True, she gave the appearance of serenity, almost docility, but Lawrence was not fooled. A man need observe her for only a moment to detect the vibrancy of her personality.

Totally without embarrassment, she had addressed the lone cuckoo that lit in the grapevines above the arbor. With a smile as sweet and artless as any Lawrence had ever seen, she paid the wild creature compliments and welcomed it home, and for just a moment, Lawrence had envied the little bird.

"A handsome gel, is she?" Lord Hazelton asked, recalling him to the present.

"There is something more of animation than real beauty, Uncle, though she is pleasingly slender, with soft, honey blond hair, and eyes as green as the leaves of the early sweet violet."

"By Jove, my boy, she sounds a vision. I shall be obliged to quit my room and go down to see this paragon for myself."

"Good for you, sir. I am persuaded your relatives will be pleased to have your company."

While the old gentleman muttered something about curst nuisances, Lawrence lifted his hand in farewell and exited the room, happy to be gone before Delia Glenn's name could be brought up again. For some reason, he did not wish to discuss the young lady, not even with Uncle Barry, who had been his friend and mentor for as long as he could remember.

"Good evening, sir."

Called from his musings by the very object of that reverie, Lawrence looked up to see Delia coming from the guest wing, her destination the central staircase that led to the ground-floor rooms. She wore a dinner dress of rose-colored sarcenet, and over the low corsage she had chosen to fasten a modest lace fichu, but even that chaste item could not hide the appealing feminine curves beneath the dress.

"So," he said, "you are still speaking to me. I had wondered if my aunts would manage to frighten you away."

Though she blushed prettily, the color complementing her clear, satiny complexion, Lawrence surmised that it was not so much embarrassment that stained her cheeks as the fact that he had guessed correctly, where his aunts were concerned.

"I am not so easily frightened, sir."

"Just embarrassed by my plain speaking. Forgive me, ma'am, for I have no manners at all. Any that I once had have been eroded like the pyramids, victims of time and the desert winds."

"The pyramids?" she asked, her voice hushed as if with awe. "Have you seen the pyramids, Mr. Freemont?"

"I have. As a matter of fact, I, like the cuckoo, am only just returned from Africa."

"How marvelous. Were you there on holiday?"

"Actually," he said, putting his hand beneath her elbow and leading her down the steps and toward the blue drawing room where the family convened before dinner, "I have been in Egypt for the past three years, part of an archaeological team."

From the look of admiration that lit her eyes, he might have just informed her that he was one of the gods come down from Olympus. "Are you a scientist, Mr. Freemont? Like Lord Hazelton?"

"Nothing so exalted, ma'am. I am merely an adventurer, working with other foreign adventurers, all of us in a race against the local grave robbers to see who can be first to unearth the glories of the past."

"If you would not find it a dead bore, sir, would you tell me some of what you have seen?"

"Are you quite certain, ma'am, that it is not *you* who would find it a bore?"

To his surprise, she shook her head rather vehemently, dislodging a curl that fell against her cheek, making Lawrence all too aware of the soft, touchable quality of her skin.

Unconcernedly placing the errant tress behind her ear, she said, "Anything you could tell me about your travels, Mr. Freemont, I should find fascinating. Only last week, I read an article about Mr. Thomas Young, the noted physicist who is attempting to decipher the hieroglyphics on the Rosetta Stone. Are you, perhaps, acquainted with that gentleman?"

"No, ma'am, I am not. But," he added when she appeared disappointed, "I have seen the stone itself."

This piece of information obviously rendered her speechless, for she said not another word until they reached the drawing room. Discovering that they were the first to arrive, and concerned that Delia might feel uncomfortable without a chaperone, Lawrence walked over to the far side of the room where a fire blazed in the hearth. "Are you afraid to be alone with me?" he asked quietly. "If so, I can—"

"Afraid? Not at all," she replied calmly, disposing herself upon the blue slipper chair. "Should I be?"

"Without a doubt."

Relaxing, Lawrence leaned his shoulder against the white marble mantel. "Did my aunt not warn you about me? Surely she told you that I was not to be trusted."

"I prefer to judge for myself, sir."

"Even when the person is a confessed adventurer?"

"Even then. Besides," she added, looking down at her bare fingers, "unlike the pharaohs, I have no jewelry to steal."

He lowered his voice. "Some things are more valuable than jewels, Miss Glenn. For instance, a man of my reputation might try to steal a kiss."

Delia knew he was teasing her. She knew also that her sister-in-law would say she should give him the set down he so richly deserved. Unfortunately, her rebellious lips would not cooperate; they kept threatening to turn up at the corners. Lawrence must have seen the betraying smile, for one of his thick, straight eyebrows lifted in a mischievous manner.

"Of course," he said, "now that the subject has been introduced, I should probably go ahead and kiss you, so we could have done with it. End the suspense, as it were."

Delia could not suppress the gurgle of laughter that escaped her throat. "I pray you, sir, do not think I am unappreciative of your kind offer, but I think I should much rather spend our time together hearing about the Rosetta Stone."

He put his hand over his heart, as if wounded. "But, ma'am, I assure you I am a very good kisser. Been practicing for years, don't you know. When I was but a lad of fourteen, I was taught the proper technique by one of the milkmaids on this very estate, and since that time, I—"

"Taught?" This time Delia did not even try to contain her laughter. "Must one be taught to kiss, sir? I had always assumed it was one of those acts that came quite naturally."

"Not a bit of it! I assure you, 'tis as much an art as painting or dancing, and one needs a master instructor. Or, as in my case, an instructress."

"And you, I suppose, are just such a master?"

"Modesty," he said, buffing his fingernails against the lapel of his coat, then extending his arm to study the effect, "forbids my answering that question."

"Modesty? Ha! I wonder you dare utter the word."

"And I wonder, ma'am, that you are content to whistle this learning opportunity down the wind."

"I suppose such a lack of perspicacity on my part defies understanding. But there it is."

Her would-be instructor *tsk-tsked*. "You know this means you shall be obliged to settle hereafter for only the most loutish kind of kisses."

"I shall try, sir, to accept my fate with a modicum of dignity."

He sighed dramatically. "I cannot credit such willingness to tolerate mediocrity, not in a female of your spirit."

When he said this last, he pinned her with those dark blue eyes, holding her gaze with his own. "This is your final opportunity," he murmured. "Refuse me again, and I shall be obliged to rescind my offer."

Lost in the depth of his eyes, Delia found herself wondering how it would feel to have Lawrence Freemont's lips pressed against hers. Since the very thought caused a rush of warmth to engulf her, it was just as well that Mr. Basil Venton chose that moment to enter the room.

Stopping just inside the doorway, the newcomer raised his quizzing glass and eyed his cousin as though examining an insect. "So. It is true. You are here."

"As you see," Lawrence replied, that satirical smile in evidence once again. "Does it surprise you, Venton, to discover that our uncle has chosen to include me in this, his one and only family gathering?"

"Surprise?" Basil flared his nostrils as if he smelled something unpleasant. "I should rather say that I am astounded."

Delia stared at the gentleman who dared goad his older, and much more physically fit, cousin. Only a year or two older than her own twenty-three years, Mr. Basil Venton was every inch the town dandy. From his pale locks—carefully pomaded and combed forward in a Brutus—to the golden yellow waistcoat and knee breeches—both of which owed much to a judicious use of buckram padding—he was a pink of the *ton*.

"I collect, cousin, that you have come here after all this time in hopes of discovering if you can convince my uncle to make you his heir. If that is the case, allow me to inform you that even though you are senior to me in years, you would do well not to suppose that gives you any—"

"Venton," Lawrence said, interrupting the younger man's thinly veiled threat, "allow me to make you known to Miss Glenn, a friend of our aunt's."

The slender gentleman wheeled around quickly, surprise writ plainly upon his arrogant face. "What the dev—"

"Miss Glenn," Lawrence said, "may I present Mr. Venton?"

Bowing with all the aplomb of a man of fashion, Basil Venton begged Delia's pardon for not having seen her the moment he entered the room.

"Mr. Venton," she said, wishing for the second time in as many hours that she had not been privy to such personal revelations, "how do you do?"

"Tolerable, madam. But perhaps I should ask how you do."

His gray eyes narrowed speculatively. "If the truth be known, I cannot believe my aunt would be happy to hear that her companion was discovered alone in the drawing room with a man of my cousin's ilk."

Lawrence's languid manner disappeared on the instant, and as he straightened away from the mantel, his hands clenched into fists. "You have now passed the bounds of what is acceptable behavior, Venton, and I'll warn you only once to keep a civil—"

"Mr. Venton," Delia interrupted, hoping to avert an unpleasantness, "I thank you for your concern, but I assure you it is misplaced. My father was a man of education and refinement, and using him as an example, I am more than capable of recognizing a gentleman when I see one."

Looking directly at Lawrence, she continued, "Mr. Freemont, I believe you would have liked my father."

As he returned her look, his dark blue eyes were unreadable. "Miss Glenn," Lawrence said quietly, "I like him already."

Dinner was a totally unpleasant affair. While Sir George Venton ignored the entire company, interested only in stuffing food into his mouth and tossing back glasses of wine, his wife and son pointedly snubbed Lawrence Freemont. Lady Wilding was not so much rude as unusually quiet, leaving it to Delia to introduce such topics as might be agreeable to all those present. As a result, any resemblance to polite table conversation was pure coincidence.

When the interminable meal finally ended, Lawrence excused himself to the ladies and disappeared. He did not return later when the tea tray was brought in, nor was he in evidence at any time during the next two days. Not until Thursday did Delia encounter him again.

That morning, as on the two preceding it, she sat alone in a cheerful little room fitted out with yellow and white chintz chairs and a table that would seat no more than six people.

Though a buffet breakfast was served each day, apparently none of the other guests cared to partake of the meal. As for Delia, she was an early riser, and accustomed to breaking her fast with something more substantial than a cup of chocolate.

Also, she kept hoping she might encounter Lord Hazelton in those early hours when a personal conversation would be possible.

Losing faith in the likelihood of an accidental encounter, she had written a letter to the old gentleman, introducing herself and informing him that she sought employment as his assistant. It he did not come down to breakfast that morning, Delia was prepared to give the letter to the butler to deliver to His Lordship's chamber.

The two-page missive lay beside her plate. While she stirred cream into a cup of coffee, she heard the door being opened. Crossing her fingers for luck, she turned to see who was joining her at this early hour. It was Lawrence Freemont.

Dressed in a Devonshire brown coat and drab pantaloons, he was even more handsome than Delia remembered. Obviously he had just come in from out of doors, for his hair was slightly windblown, and the pleasant scent of fresh air clung to him.

"Miss Glenn," Lawrence said, "I was told you might be in here."

Not expecting to see him, and more than a little flustered at his having sought her out, she made much of pressing her napkin to her lips before she finally spoke. "You wished to see me?"

"Actually, there is something I believe *you* might wish to see. If you have nothing pressing planned for the morning, I should like to show you a horse."

Though not a true fancier of horseflesh, Delia was quite agreeable to a stroll to the stables. In fact, the thought of spending time with Mr. Lawrence Freemont caused an unmistakable flutter in the region of her heart. "I shall get my wrap," she said, rising from the table.

"There is no need to abandon your breakfast, ma'am. I assure you, the excursion can wait until you are finished with your meal."

Mentally consigning to the garbage pail the basted eggs and kippers she had only just placed upon her plate, Delia declared herself replete and more than ready for the out of doors. "I shall join you in five minutes, sir."

As good as her word, she met him at the foot of the grand staircase within the allotted time. She had changed her kid slippers for walking boots, and over her arm she carried a pelerine fashioned of bronze kerseymere, the chocolate brown braid on the hip-length cape matched by the ribbons of her shallow-brimmed capote.

Turning at the sound of her footfalls, Lawrence smiled up at her. It was a wicked smile, and Delia tried valiantly not to respond to it.

"If I were a betting man," he said, snapping shut a chased gold timepiece and returning it to his pocket, "I would now be poorer by several pounds."

"Say no more, sir, for I am beginning to know your character a little, and I perceive an insult hovering about, just waiting to be tossed my way."

"Acquit me, for I was on the verge of paying you a compliment. I did not believe there was a female living who actually adhered to the precepts of punctuality."

"And this is your idea of a compliment? To malign my entire sex?"

He took the pelerine from her arm and draped it across her shoulders; then he turned her so he could fasten the chocolate brown frogs that held it fast. "If it is compliments you want, madam, allow me to tell you what this bronze does to your eyes."

Already rendered quite breathless by the intimacy of his having fastened her cape, his strong fingers brushing against the sides of her neck, she was deprived of further air by his softly spoken words.

"There is a spot along the banks of the Nile," he said, "where one may stand and watch the sun disappear into the Valley of the Kings. At that particular place, the Nile is rather nondescript, but for one brief, exquisite moment, with the sun's blazing red, gold, and orange reflected on the surface of the water, the ancient river is turned to a bronzed emerald.

"A gem," he added softly, "not unlike your eyes at this minute."

Bronzed emeralds.

Delia licked her suddenly dry lips. "I . . . I hope I shall be warm enough."

Taking her change in subject in good part, Lawrence replied, "I believe you will be comfortable, for the sun is out in all its glory. If you should have need of it, however, there is a lap robe."

Because Delia was busy placing her letter in the silver salver reposing on the walnut console, the significance of a lap robe did not immediately occur to her. By the time it had penetrated her brain, the footman had opened the heavy oak door, revealing a curricle waiting beside the portico, a groom standing at the heads of a pair of matched bays.

Her voice not quite steady, Delia said, "I thought your invitation was for a walk to the stables. The Hazelton stables."

The warm smile that had softened Lawrence's angular face slowly faded. "The horse I wish to show you is not on this estate."

"But I . . ."

"If you are not comfortable riding alone with me," he said, jerking his thumb toward the curricle to indicate the small, elevated seat to the rear of the vehicle, "the groom may accompany us."

Like Caesar's wife, a vicar's family must be above reproach. Her sister-in-law's parting words rang in Delia's ears, but not for all the perfume in Arabia would she have admitted to Lawrence that she felt the need for a chaperone.

Though why she should wish to shield him for rebuff, she could not say. After all, even if one were to disregard the disreputable nature of his past, his manners were much too free. Lawrence Freemont was at best a rogue, and if his family were to be believed, at his worst he was also a libertine and a debaucher of innocent females. Knowing this, Delia was convinced she should not allow herself to talk to him, far less accept his escort off the property.

And yet, there were times in every person's life when they must decide for themselves what feelings should take precedence. In this instance, something deep inside Delia's soul told her that her trust was of prime importance to Lawrence. Far more important than her sister-in-law's notions of propriety.

Speaking softly, for his ears only, she asked, "Are you planning to renew your offer of that kissing lesson?"

The question seemed to take him by surprise, but after only a moment, his mouth pulled to the left in that sardonic smile Delia was coming to know. "I promise you, I have nothing on my agenda but horses." Then he ruined the whole by adding, "At least, for today."

Delia ignored that last statement, choosing instead to concentrate upon the first. "In that case, sir, I see no reason why the groom should not return to his duties in the stable."

"Good girl."

Without another word, Lawrence took her arm and helped her into the curricle. After offering her the lap robe, which she refused, he sprang up beside her and nodded for the groom to stand aside.

For the first mile or so, Delia gave her attention to the well-matched horses, their yellowish-tan coats made more dramatic by their black tails, manes, and lower legs, but in time she grew bored with that pastime. Soon the scenery, too, lost its appeal, as did the long, low stone wall that appeared from time to time behind the hedgerow to their right.

Since Lawrence had not introduced a topic for conversation, Delia broke the silence with the first thing that entered her mind. "Before we arrive at our destination, sir, perhaps I should warn you that I know little of horseflesh."

Her companion did not seem too distressed by this confession. In fact, the suspicion of a smile played at the corner of his mouth. "You are knowledgeable enough to enjoy the horse I wish to show you."

Distrustful of the studied blandness of his tone, Delia leaned forward, trying to see his face. As if to thwart her attempt, he very pointedly kept his eyes on the road.

"Are you teasing me?" she asked, sitting back. "Is there truly a horse?"

"There is most definitely a horse."

"Actually," she continued, trying for a blandness of her own in hopes of getting a telling reaction from him, "I find the beasts rather boring."

"I promise you," he said, his voice on the edge of laughter, "you will not find this beast boring."

"Lawrence Freemont! I knew you were teasing me."

"No, no. I am in earnest, and within five minutes, you will know all. But more than that, I will not say."

She would have taxed him further upon the subject if he had not slowed the team at just that moment. The stone wall that had played hide and seek with them for the last mile had appeared again then parted to reveal a wooden gate, and Lawrence guided the bays through the opening and up a newly graded carriageway that led to an old, gray stone manor house. Not built on the grand scale of Hazelton Hall, the edifice was handsome rather than impressive—or, rather, it would be handsome once the new roof was completed and the scaffolding removed.

Aside from the men on the roof, there were several workmen on the ground, most of them employed in taming a wide expanse of rolling lawn that had been allowed to grow wild. Stopping the curricle, Lawrence called to one of the workers who came forward, removing his cap respectfully.

"Good day to ye, sir. Miss."

"Good day," Lawrence said. "Be so good as to inform Mrs. Paxton that we are here. Tell her we will return within the hour."

Not waiting for a reply, Lawrence signaled the horses and they were off once again, following the carriageway until it became nothing but a rough path only wide enough to accommodate the curricle.

"Is this Mrs. Paxton's house?"

"No. It is mine."

"Yours? But I thought—" Delia stopped herself just in time.

"You thought I had returned to Wiltshire in hopes of inheriting my uncle's estate."

She felt the heat of embarrassment scorch her face.

"Actually," he said, his tone not the least insulted, "I came home because it was time to do so."

He paused, and Delia thought he had said all he meant to, but after a moment he continued. "For years I hated this place. I considered it the source of all my boyhood disappointment. The few times I let myself think of it, I drew pleasure from picturing the walls decayed and fallen to the ground."

"And now?"

"Now I am older, and at least a fraction wiser, and I have came to realize that brick and mortar have no power over a person's soul. At least none but that power we give it. It is that which a man carries inside him that determines his joy or sadness—call it spirit, if you wish—and only he can build or destroy that spirit. Having learned that lesson, I have chosen to come home and make repairs to both my life and my house."

Not knowing what to say to such a telling revelation, Delia remained silent.

Obviously Lawrence took her lead, for he said nothing more until the path came to an end beside a stand of towering beech trees—their smooth, silver-gray bark glistening in the morning sun. Halting the team, he jumped down and tied the ribbons to a low, still-bare branch.

"Come," he said, reaching his hands up to assist Delia, "your horse awaits."

Three

Your horse awaits.

Whatever Delia had supposed Lawrence meant, she was totally unprepared for what she saw the moment she rounded the stand of beeches. The land was composed of rolling fields already showing new greenery, and cut into one of the far hillsides was a large white horse. An unbelievably large white horse. Primitive, yet totally recognizable, the animal was fully sixty feet high and at least that wide.

"How?" she said, her voice hushed with reverence. "What I mean is, who . . ." Unable to speak coherently, she fell silent.

After a time, Lawrence answered her uncompleted questions. "This particular chalk figure is prehistoric, so I cannot tell you who made it. But I can tell you how it was done."

"You know the procedure?"

"I do. Actually, the technique is quite simple. I discovered it for myself when I was a lad."

He stretched his arm out as if to call her attention to the expanse of fields. "What you see here is nothing more than a grass cloak lying upon a chalk substructure. To draw a picture, one need only mark out the boundaries then cut away the green grass and the topsoil. The white chalk below is then revealed."

Delia sighed. "It is wonderful. Are there any more such figures?"

"Dozens. In Wiltshire, they are quite common. Of course,

several newer, larger ones were cut during the last century, but I prefer this one because it is so old."

"Even without seeing the newer ones, I share your opinion. How old is this figure? Do you know?"

He shrugged his shoulders. "Who can say. Someday scientists may devise a method for such dating, but for now, all they can do is guess. Of a certainty, this horse is thousands of years older than the pyramids of Egypt. Perhaps even tens of thousands."

At her indrawn breath, Lawrence chuckled. "Tell me, ma'am, is it as you expected? Do you find this beast boring?"

"You know I do not. He is fascinating."

She had been standing with her back to Lawrence, but now she turned, looking up into his face, her eyes alight with wonder. "This place is pure magic," she said softly. "And I thank you for sharing it with me."

As Lawrence gazed down into her delicate face, he decided he had been mistaken when he described Delia to his uncle, described her as having something more of animation than real beauty. At this moment, with her satiny skin aglow with excitement and her soft lips parted in awe, she was the most beautiful girl he had ever seen.

She had called this place magic, but Lawrence was discovering enchantment of another sort. Fascination. With scarce two inches separating them, he found himself battling an almost overwhelming desire to bend down and taste the sweet magic of those parted lips.

Perceiving the glow in Lawrence's eyes—a look even the most sheltered, unsophisticated female could not misunderstand—Delia experienced a sudden breathlessness. He wanted to kiss her. And to her dismay, she discovered within herself a yearning to be kissed. A wish to feel his lips upon hers. An aching need to feel his powerful arms locking her in an embrace, holding her against his hard chest.

Wanting his kiss with all her heart, Delia managed somehow to step back.

Heretofore she had dismissed all Lawrence's rather warmish remarks as mere teasing, certainly nothing more than the idle flirtation of a practiced rogue. Now, however, she was forced to reevaluate what was happening between them.

Of course, she had found him attractive from their first meeting. And who would not? Lawrence Freemont was tall, well built, and devilishly handsome. Furthermore, he was just the sort of ramshackle rogue no romantic miss could fail to find amusing. And she was certainly a romantic lady. Otherwise, why was her heart—normally a quite reliable organ—behaving in such an alarming manner, thumping so loudly she wondered that the sound was not echoing off the distant hills.

This will never do! It does not even bear thinking about.

Delia had come to Wiltshire seeking a job, not a flirtation. And certainly not to fall under the spell of a man who had the power to break her heart.

And break her heart he would, for if only half of what she had heard of Lawrence Freemont was true, his notorious style of life and his morals were the very antithesis of the code by which she lived. And not only her precepts, but those of her family as well. To encourage Lawrence was to laugh in the face of her brother's principles, to show ingratitude for Feona and Caleb's sustaining kindnesses. And though she might wish to leave the vicarage in search of a life of her own, she had no wish to estrange herself from all that was left of her family.

Afraid to look at Lawrence for fear she would reveal the thoughts that were playing havoc with her sanity, Delia turned and walked back toward the curricle. She felt, rather than heard, him behind her.

"If you have looked your fill," he said, his voice annoyingly calm in the face of her emotionally charged reactions, "my housekeeper, Mrs. Paxton, will be expecting us back at the house. She will have prepared a tea tray."

"Oh, but I really should return to Hazelton Hall. My absence will be remarked, and Lady Wilding will—"

"Will understand that you were too polite to disappoint an elderly lady who was looking forward to meeting you."

"But, I—"

"While you partake of the refreshments," he continued, "I have a bit of business that wants doing. I should not be much above a half hour."

Suddenly ravenously hungry, and inordinately relieved that Lawrence would be busy elsewhere, Delia agreed to the tea. Lord Hazelton might, at that very moment, be reading her letter, ready to give her an interview; if nothing else, taking tea at the manor house would give Delia some much-needed solitude in which to compose her thoughts before she returned to the hall.

"I hope you are not offended, Miss Glenn, at taking tea in the housekeeper's rooms. It's just that the manor is at sixes and sevens at the moment, what with the new roof, and workmen fixing fireboxes and hunting out dry rot in the wainscoting, and the like."

Delia sipped gratefully from the gold-rimmed china cup; then, helping herself to another sandwich, she smiled at the elderly housekeeper whose iron gray hair was only partially concealed beneath a rather youthful lace cap. "This is very nice, Mrs. Paxton. A very comfortable apartment."

The housekeeper glanced around the tiny, overstuffed room with pride, calling Delia's attention first to the indulgence of a cozy fire, then to such pieces of furniture as she thought most interesting. "That mahogany end table by your chair, I found it in the attics. And this settee," she said, patting the faded yellow brocade, "was once in Mrs. Beatrice Freemont's morning room. I took it off the carter's dray the day Mr. Lawrence Freemont sent the bulk of the furniture to the vicar to distribute among the needy."

The loquacious woman paused only long enough to take a sip of her tea. Until the new furniture arrives, this is the only comfortable room in the house. Aside from Mr. Lawrence Freemont's bedchamber, of course. Not that he would complain even if the chamber was as bad as the rest of the house, the dear man. But then, he was always such a sweet-tempered lad. And such a good baby! Never a bit of fuss or trouble."

Ignoring this forgivably biased appraisal, Delia found one thing the woman said of particular interest, that Lawrence had a bedchamber at the manor. "But surely Mr. Freemont is staying at his uncle's house. I mean, I *understood* that he was residing there."

"No, miss. He's over there all the time, right enough, but that's on account of him being so fond of the old gentleman. Thick as thieves the two of them were when Mr. Freemont was a lad. But he said he'd come home to stay, and stay he has. Though," she added, lowering her voice, "I never thought I'd live to see the day, not with him being so heartsore when he left."

"Heartsore?"

"Hurt, Miss. Fair tore the young lad's heart out, his father always expecting the worst of him the way he did, and his mother never taking his part, never mind him being her only child. But say what they would, I never believed 'twas the lad got that girl in the family way."

Delia almost choked on her tea. So, debauchery had played some part in Lawrence's expulsion from his home. For some inexplicable reason, she hoped it wasn't with the milkmaid.

"If you was to ask me," Mrs. Paxton continued, "the girl was no better than she should have been, especially once all the local lads began making eyes at her. As pretty a lass as you'd want to see, I'll own the truth to that, but she wasn't steady-like. Give her a task, and quick as you could say Bob's your uncle, she'd be off somewhere daydreaming, the dusting forgot and the beds not made."

After delivering that evaluation of the maid's character, Mrs. Paxton seemed to fall into a bit of silent reminiscing, which was a good thing, for Lawrence chose that moment to return.

"Have you enough tea there to spare me a drop, Paxie?" Picking up a cup, he held it toward the smiling housekeeper.

"Always, sir," she replied, a look of doting affection in her rheumy gray eyes.

It seemed to Delia that Lawrence looked even larger than usual in this small, cramped room, and she wondered where he would sit. To her surprise, he chose a low footstool quite near the hearth. Bending down with an athletic grace, he perched upon the footstool, leaning his broad back against the wall and stretching his long legs out in front of him with every appearance of comfort.

" 'Twas always his favorite place," Mrs. Paxton explained, noticing Delia's interest. "Time out of mind Master Lawrence would come have his tea with me, and always he'd choose that old footstool."

Not the least embarrassed by the housekeeper's reminiscences, the object of the discussion said, "It's a wise lad who learns where the best tea and muffins are to be found." Lifting his cup in salute, he added, "I missed this."

The elderly woman beamed as if she had been given an accolade. "Say what you will, sir, there's no place like—"

The platitude was interrupted by a freckle-faced young scullery maid wearing a mob cap and apron almost as big as she was. "Yer pardon, sir," she said, bobbing a quick, nervous curtsy in Lawrence's direction, "but cook be needing to ask summit of Mrs. Paxton."

Excusing herself, the housekeeper hurried away to see to the cook, and without her well-meant chatter, the room was suddenly quiet, the only sound the crackle of the fire and the occasional clink of a teacup upon a saucer. Not that Delia felt the need for conversation. Far from it.

Being alone with Lawrence in this warm, snug room was having a decidedly mesmerizing effect upon her, almost as if she were actually living one of her fantasies—the most prevalent of her daydreams, the one in which she shared a home with a mysterious, unidentified male whom she loved and who loved her in return.

Only this time the man sitting across the room from her, his eyes closed and the rock-hard lines of his body relaxed, was not some faceless, characterless persona. He was Lawrence Freemont, the man who was intruding far too often into Delia's thoughts, and having far too much influence upon the rhythm of her heart.

She was berating herself for letting his looks, his personality, his presence invade her most private fantasies when his deep, almost musical voice wove itself into her thoughts.

"There is a place in the south of Spain," he said softly, "that I should like to show you."

"Spain?" she asked, interested in spite of her resolve to distance herself from him.

"What I would show you is deep inside a cave. I came upon it quite by accident a few years ago while hiding from a band of very angry French soldiers."

Surprised to hear that he had taken part in the Peninsular War, Delia spoke before she thought. "You were in the army?"

"In a manner of speaking. Being a well-informed young lady, you probably already know that Parliament supplied money and arms to any country resisting Napoleon's troops."

"Yes. I had read that."

"For the better part of a year, it was my job to make certain those arms got to the *guerrilleros* in Spain."

"I see," she said. Of course, she did not see at all, but then, there was so much she did not know about this man.

"The cave I should like to show you," he continued, "is high in the Serranía de Ronda. In my quest for a hiding place, I had made my way into the largest of the chambers, traveling for perhaps a quarter of a mile, more often than not slipping upon the moisture-slickened stones underfoot, while the dim light of my lantern glimmered in the pools of water that collect from the constantly seeping limestone walls.

"Interested only in the very real necessity of saving my neck,

I was suddenly transfixed by the discovery of color upon the walls. Reds and yellow ochres."

Delia felt her breath catch in her throat. "Cave drawings," she breathed.

"The most exciting I have ever seen. Beautifully executed and strangely evocative, they made me feel as though the artist—surely returned to dust at least thirty thousand years ago—might yet live, that I might encounter this ancient person just around the next turn, busy telling a new story on another wall."

Delia was no less transfixed than Lawrence by his telling of what he had discovered. "What was depicted?"

"Numerous scenes. In one place horses, graceful and spirited. In another, a herd of cattle, two bulls challenging one another at the forefront, their long horns sweeping upward like menacing wings that seemed to move in the shadows cast by my lantern."

"How wonderful," Delia whispered, "not only to see something so beautiful, but to know you might be the first person to have looked upon the drawings for eons."

Lawrence nodded. "I knew you would appreciate my feelings. The depictions were amazing, of course, but what made the gooseflesh prickle its way up my spine was the feeling of shared humanity with those ancient people who, like me, had sought shelter in the cave. Sooty stains made by their fires still showed upon the walls, and I touched crude depressions worn into the rocks, depressions used to prepare and store their food, by people from perhaps as early as the Stone Age."

Lost in her vision of that beautiful, mysterious cave and its prehistoric dwellers, Delia failed to hear Mrs. Paxton enter the room. She gasped when the elderly lady touched her shoulder.

"You were a million miles away, miss. I brought fresh tea. May I fill your cup?"

Too dazed to respond, Delia smiled gratefully when Lawrence answered for her. "We cannot stay longer," he said, rising to his feet in one smooth, easy motion, "for I promised Miss Glenn I would have her back to Hazelton Hall within the hour."

As they took their leave, Lawrence leaned over and placed a kiss on the housekeeper's wrinkled cheek, then he whispered something in her ear that made her giggle like a young girl. "Go on with you, now, sir. None of your teasing. You'll have Miss Glenn thinking you'd no proper raising at all. Her with her pretty manners and polite ways, she'll not know what to make of you."

The truth of that utterance made Delia blush, for she most definitely did not know what to make of Mr. Lawrence Freemont. It was obvious that Mrs. Paxton held him in great affection, as, from all accounts, did his uncle, Lord Hazelton. Yet the rest of his family regarded him as little better than a pariah.

Which of them, she wondered, saw the real Lawrence Freemont?

As for her own opinion, after this last half hour, Delia was very much afraid that she wanted to believe he was the charming, relaxed gentleman she saw before her—the man who had been discerning enough to know she would enjoy seeing the white horse and hearing about the cave in southern Spain.

Delia was no closer to solving the riddle of Lawrence Freemont when the curricle stopped beside the stone portico of Hazelton Hall. While a groom ran to the horses' heads, Lawrence leapt down, assisted Delia, then walked her to the door. Stopping just inside the vestibule, he removed his hat, took the hand she offered, and lifted it to his lips.

"I have business in Lacock," he said, "so I will not stay, but I thank you for the pleasure of—"

"Miss!" the footman said, hurrying forward to meet her. "His Lordship has been asking for you this hour and more."

Her skin still tingling from the touch of Lawrence's warm lips upon her fingers, Delia pulled her hand free and turned to the agitated footman, her mind not as clear as it might have been. "What did you say?"

"His Lordship, miss. He be waiting for you in the book room. This way, if you please."

"Until later then," Lawrence said, bowing again and stepping back outside, pulling the massive door shut behind him. The decision made for her, Delia followed the servant down the corridor, removing her bonnet and pelerine as she walked.

"Miss Glenn, m'lord," the footman announced.

"Here," she said, shoving her things into his arms, "please see these are taken to my room."

Pausing at the door to the long, teak-paneled library with its row upon row of books, she tried in vain to bring some order to the many curls that had come loose from her coiffure.

Conscious of the significance of this meeting, and all too aware of the importance of a good first impression, Delia stood straight and tall, trying for a look that was assured, yet at the same time not too coming for a lady seeking employment. "Lord Hazelton," she said, "thank you for seeing me."

"Yes, yes. Come in," he said, putting aside the rather ponderous-looking volume he held upon his knees and rising to greet her.

Delia had been informed that His Lordship was in good health, but she was unprepared for the gentleman who stood before her. Tall and vigorous-looking, he was a lion of a man, with a thick mane of snow white hair and eyes as watchful as a predator. "Sit down," he said, the words more an order than an invitation.

Disposing herself in the brown leather wing chair that was a companion to the one her host occupied, Delia folded her hands quietly and waited for Lord Hazelton to begin the interview.

He observed her for a full two minutes before he spoke, and Delia had the distinct impression that he was testing her mettle. "So," he began finally, "your father was Zachery Glenn. I corresponded with him a number of times over the years."

"Yes, my lord. It was I who wrote out my father's letters to you. His health was not good, and I became his eyes, as well as his research assistant. A job, I shall not scruple to tell you, for which I was eminently qualified. Which is, of course, why I believe I can be of help to you in the compilation of data for your memoirs."

While she spoke, His Lordship stroked his mustache, never lifting his gaze from her face, almost as if *she* were data that needed to be studied and evaluated. Delia sat quietly, trying not to squirm while he weighed and measured her, waiting for the barrage of questions she expected to be asked regarding her education and suitability for the job. The catechism, when it finally came, was more accusation than inquiry.

"You are a handsome girl," he said. "Why are you not married and filling a nursery?"

Though Delia felt the heat of embarrassment stain her cheeks, she tried to remain calm. "Sir, you are a gentleman who has observed people the world over. Surely I do not have to tell you that females without marriage portions may be as handsome as they like and still never receive an offer for their hand."

"Fustian, my girl. 'Tis early days yet for such a pessimistic conclusion on your part."

"I choose rather to call it realism."

"Let us not quibble over words. I have no doubt there is some fellow out there right now casting sheep's eyes at you, wanting only a bit of encouragement to make you an offer."

Unbidden, the image of Lawrence Freemont flashed into Delia's mind, that sardonic smile in evidence, and though she knew no one could read her thoughts, still she felt herself blush to the very roots of her hair.

"Aha! So there is such a person."

"No, no, my lord. I assure you, there is no one."

If, at this admission, Delia experienced a sensation very like a boulder settling in her chest and weighing heavily upon her heart, she tried to conceal the fact from her interviewer. "I am at liberty to accept employment, sir, commencing at this moment and continuing for as long as my assistance is needed."

"Very well," His Lordship said rather abruptly, "I shall need some time to consider the matter."

"Of course."

"I will let you know my answer by tomorrow."

The interview obviously at an end, Delia stood, curtsied politely, and quit the room, not as hopeful as she might have been about her prospects.

It was while she climbed the broad staircase to seek the solitude of her room that she met Mr. Basil Venton descending to the ground floor. Looking every bit the town beau, with his slender person snugly encased in a puce coat totally unsuited to an afternoon in the country, he stopped just in front of her, barring her way.

"Well, Miss Glenn," he began, "I could not believe the testimony of my eyes some half hour ago when I saw my cousin's curricle tooling up the carriageway, you sitting by his side."

In no mood to banter words with this angry popinjay, Delia said, "I can see no reason for your disbelief, sir. Even in the country, a lady may take a morning ride in an open carriage without giving occasion for astonishment. In fact, such an outing is quite unexceptional."

"Not when the driver is my cousin. To ride about the countryside with him is to court disaster, and a lady cannot be too careful where her reputation is concerned."

Caesar's wife!

Recalling her sister-in-law's admonition, Delia felt an illogical desire to give Mr. Venton a smart box on the ear.

The gentleman, unaware that he stood beneath the sword of Damocles, continued his diatribe. "If you are entertaining some foolish notion that my uncle may choose to leave his fortune to Lawrence Freemont, and that my cousin will, in turn, lay that fortune at your feet, I must inform you that such hopes could prove disastrous. I speak as a friend, madam, when I tell you that my cousin has a history of ruining women then leaving them to their fate."

He leaned in very close to her, so close Delia could smell the pomade upon his pale hair. "You would do well to heed my warning."

"Sir!" she exclaimed. "Your warning is as insulting as it is inappropriate. Even if you were a friend of long standing—which you are not!—I cannot think of any justification for your speaking to me in such a warm manner. As for your libelous account of Mr. Freemont's history with females, to repeat such gossip does you more discredit than it does him.

"And now," she continued, "I give *you* warning. If you do not step aside and let me pass this instant, I shall be obliged to scream at the top of my lungs until as many of the household as may hear me come to investigate the commotion. At which time, I will leave it to you to explain to your uncle your boorish behavior toward a guest in his house."

Mr. Venton stepped aside with all haste, and once her path was clear, Delia lifted her skirts and sped up the remaining stairs and down the corridor, not stopping until she was inside her bedchamber.

Trembling from the unpleasant encounter with Basil Venton, she leaned her back against the closed door and gave voice to her anger. "It is a lie! Basil is a spiteful, jealous man, and regardless of what he and his family choose to believe, I have witnessed nothing in Lawrence's character to substantiate their claim of debauchery."

Not that it signified, for whatever the gentleman had or had not done to earn him his unsavory reputation, it was no concern of hers. *He* was no concern of hers. Lawrence Freemont meant nothing to her, and she meant nothing to him.

It was this last observation that prompted Delia to throw herself upon the bed and give herself up to an orgy of tears.

Four

Once again, Lord Hazelton did not join his relatives for dinner. However, he had sent word to each of them that he would be down for tea at nine o'clock, at which time he would discuss the matter that had brought them all to Wiltshire.

As for Delia, though she was dispirited, not to mention just a bit puffy around the eyes from the sea of tears she had shed, she had managed, somehow, to get through the interminable meal and the endless speculation as to who would get what. But she drew the line at the family gathering around the tea tray. That was another matter entirely!

His Lordship's will had nothing to do with her. Moreover, she had had just about all she could withstand of the Hazelton family and their predilection for airing their dirty linen before a stranger.

At quarter to nine, Delia claimed the headache—a time-honored excuse that would get her out of the room with the greatest degree of speed. After bidding Lady Wilding a good night, she was taking her leave of Lady Venton and Sir George when the footman opened the drawing room door and announced Mr. Lawrence Freemont.

"Aunts," Lawrence said, bowing to both ladies, only one of whom acknowledged the greeting. "Good evening, Uncle George. Basil, I collect a sennight's rustication has not left you totally bored with us provincials."

Not waiting for a reply from either gentleman, Lawrence

spared his last bow for Delia. "Miss Glenn," he said, turning upon her a look of such unholy amusement that she was unable to check her answering smile. "You were not leaving, I trust?"

Her supposed headache, along with that dispirited feeling that had blue-deviled her since her encounter with Mr. Venton on the stairs, dissolved like morning fog exposed to the warmth of the sun.

"Please stay," Lawrence said. "I am persuaded you will find my uncle's remarks vastly interesting."

Unable to resist the disarming smile he bestowed upon her, Delia disposed herself upon the lyre-back chair she had vacated only moments earlier.

Her heart was suddenly light and her pulse was noticeably quickened, and the onset of both anomalies she traced directly to Mr. Freemont's arrival. The warmth that enveloped her, as well as the feeling of renewed vigor and awareness, those she attributed directly to the sight of his tall, athletic person as he lounged nonchalantly against the mantel.

I love him!

That revelation—simple, yet powerfully unnerving—elevated the rate of her pulse to a dangerous level, one that left her feeling quite faint.

How had this happened?

When?

And most important of all, what was she to do with this unlooked for complication?

Marriage was out of the question. She was a penniless female, with nothing to recommend her but a willingness to share her heart and her life with the man she loved, and she was not so foolish as to expect any gentleman to take her under those circumstances. Even if she did receive an offer—a possibility too implausible to contemplate—how could she align herself with a man whose reputation would surely alienate her from the only family she possessed?

As for her hope of becoming Lord Hazelton's assistant, that was no longer a viable option. Even if Delia were offered the position, she would be unable to accept it. Not now. How could she remain at Hazelton Hall, only a short distance from the Freemont estate, all the while knowing herself in love with her employer's nephew? Lawrence came and went as he pleased in His Lordship's house, and to see him every day, loving him as she did, would be torment.

Impelled to look at him, she discovered that he was watching her, and she had the fancy that Lawrence knew what was going on inside her head. But what of her heart? Could he read that as well?

As if in answer to her unasked question, he straightened from the mantel and came to her, stopping just inches from her chair. His eyes, usually lit with mockery, were serious now, and in the dark blue depths was a look she could not read. "Delia," he said softly, "what has stolen the color from your cheeks? Tell me, and I will see what can be done to restore—"

"I see you are all here," Lord Hazelton said, interrupting whatever Lawrence had been about to say, and making Delia jump as if she were guilty of some reprehensible act.

She had not heard the drawing room door open. In fact, she was so overset by the startling realization that she loved Lawrence Freemont, that everyone else, save the object of her affections, had virtually disappeared from the room. Brought back to reality by His Lordship's entrance, Delia cast her eyes downward, unwilling for Lawrence, or anyone else, to read what might be revealed there.

"I shall come right to the point," Lord Hazelton announced. Instead of doing as he said, however, he paused, looking pointedly at Basil Venton and causing that young gentleman to quit with all haste the wing chair closest to the fire. After His Lordship made himself comfortable in the abandoned seat, he continued. "The subject is my will. Or, more accurately, the disposition of my estate and any resulting monies it may bring."

Ignoring the audible breaths drawn and held, the old gentleman continued. "I have decided to apprise you of my decision at this time because I will be remaining here at the hall from now on, working upon my memoirs, and I do not wish to be constantly interrupted by relatives popping in whenever they please, their object to ingratiate themselves into my favor."

Motioning toward the ancient butler who stood near the door, a small, cloth bag in either gnarled hand, he said, "Garrick holds all that could be called family jewelry. The pieces, mostly geegaws belonging to my mother and my grandmother, are not of any great worth, but because they might hold some sentimental value to my nieces, I have divided them as equitably as possible so that each woman may have her fair share."

At his master's signal, Garrick inched his way across the blue and gold carpet, presenting the bags to a smiling Lady Wilding so that she might make her choice. Once she had chosen, she drew the string eagerly and dumped the contents into her lap. A tangled mass of necklaces, bracelets, pins, and earrings spilled over her mauve satin skirt, and while she struggled to extricate a double strand of pearls, the butler took the remaining bag to Lady Venton.

"I am sure I thank you, Uncle," Frances Venton said, setting her gift, unopened, on the table beside her blue bottle of sal volatile. "But what of the estate?"

"The jewelry," Lord Hazelton replied, "is the extent of the distribution of my assets."

Persisting, the lady said, "Whom have you chosen as your heir?"

"My heir?" he said, as though the thought had never occurred to him. "Why, no one. If the title is of any consequence to either your son or Lawrence, they may petition the courts for it after my death. As for the estate, I have bequeathed it to the Royal Antiquities Society. The house is to be turned into a museum, and the monies from the land are to be used to fund field research and artifact preservation."

A general gasp sounded throughout the room.

Of the assembled party, only Lawrence Freemont appeared unmoved by his uncle's announcement. In fact, Delia would have been willing to wager a large sum of money—if she had possessed any—that the disposition of the estate came as no surprise to Lawrence.

"But . . . but, Uncle!" Lady Venton cried. "You cannot mean to give it all away. To totally disinherit your nephew."

"And why should I not?"

Lifting his bushy eyebrows, the old gentleman stared at his niece. After enduring only a few seconds of that icy stare, Frances Venton was obliged to seek solace in her smelling salts.

"If I had chosen to designate anyone as my heir, it would have been the nephew who is most like a son to me—the only one who has never asked anything of me but my friendship and an occasional bit of advice. Advice," he added, looking fondly at Lawrence, "which he ignored more often than not. However, that nephew informs me he has no need of my largesse."

"Hmph," Lady Venton said inelegantly, disbelief writ plainly upon her face. "A rogue's trick, surely."

Lord Hazelton ignored her remark.

"As for your son, Frances, why should I leave my money to that young popinjay? From all I can learn of him, he would waste little time in squandering it, spending the entire fortune indulging in the excesses of the town beau.

"No," he continued. "I think not. Much better to give the entire estate where it will do some good. Help preserve the fragile records of mankind. Educate those who come after us so that each generation need not be obliged to reinvent the wheel."

It was not to be wondered at that the Ventons quit the hall at an early hour the next day. Her Ladyship, feeling much put upon, did not take her leave of her uncle or her sister, and only because she chanced upon Delia coming from a walk about the estate grounds did she bid her farewell.

Delia, less than pleased to be the recipient of the lady's parting words, picked up the little white pug who had accompanied her on her walk, holding the exuberant animal so he would not run off in search of adventure. Though she tried to show some interest in Her Ladyship's final harangue against her uncle, pretense was the best Delia could muster. After the bitter arguments and accusations she had been forced to witness following Lord Hazelton's announcement that he was leaving his worldly goods to the Royal Antiquities Society, Delia had no interest whatsoever in anything the Ventons had to say.

Furthermore, her head was pounding from lack of sleep, and her heart was aching from the realization that by midmorning she, too, would be gone. And once she left the hall, she would never see Lawrence Freemont again. Never again see that wicked grin. Never again look into those deep blue eyes and see the devilment alight in their depths. And, worst of all, never again hear his voice.

Delia swallowed a lump that rose in her throat, the obstruction threatening to choke her at the prospect of a future without the man she loved. How could she bear to live for years and years and never experience the thrill of hearing Lawrence say he loved her? How could she sleep night after night in her chaste bed, longing for the exquisite joy of being held in his arms?

And she would not even have the opportunity to bid him farewell! As soon as Lady Wilding was dressed, they were leaving Wiltshire.

After writing a note to Lord Hazelton explaining that she could not, after all, take the position as his assistant, Delia had given the missive to the butler to deliver, then she had packed her portmanteau. Now there was nothing to do but return to Newton-Leyes and the restrictions of the vicarage—restrictions made more onerous by the knowledge that her brother needed her room and the money it would bring to help support his growing family.

" 'Tis criminal," Lady Venton said, bringing Delia's thoughts back to the present, "what my uncle has chosen to do with this estate. And I, for one, will never set foot upon it again."

Not wanting to hear more on that subject, and hoping to bring this meeting to a relatively pleasant conclusion, Delia asked the lady if she had been pleased with her share of the family jewelry.

"Mere trumpery, the lot of it. Besides, what are a few thousand pounds worth of geegaws when compared to this entire estate?"

Delia chose not to reply. Since the only jewelry she possessed was a silver locket left her by her mother, she found it difficult to summon any sympathy for Lady Venton, especially when Her Ladyship showed contempt for things worth several thousand pounds.

Thankfully, Sir George called impatiently for his wife to step lively, and Her Ladyship hurried to the carriage, leaving Delia standing in the doorway, the pug in her arms wagging his tail as if affecting a happy send-off to the departing guests.

The chaise and four, with its trio of angry, disappointed passengers, had only just pulled away from the portico when Delia was informed by one of the footmen that Lord Hazelton wished to see her.

"In the blue drawing room, miss."

Surprised at this request for a second interview, she asked, "Was my letter delivered to him?"

"Yes, miss. I gave it to His Lordship's valet myself, not half an hour ago."

Looking at the dog in her arms, the servant added, "Give the little fellow to me, if you please, and I'll see he gets back upstairs."

Not wishing to emulate Lady Venton's rudeness in leaving without a proper farewell to her host, Delia surrendered the pug; then, after removing her bonnet and pelisse and giving them to the footman as well, she went to find Lord Hazelton.

"Come in," he called, answering her soft knock upon the door.

"Good morning, sir. I hope I find you well."

His Lordship sat in the blue brocade slipper chair, and to his left, lying face-up on the mahogany drum table, was Delia's letter.

"Sit down," he said, by way of greeting.

When she complied, perching on the edge of the settee, he took the letter, gave it a cursory look, then returned it to the table. "So, Miss Glenn, you have decided not to work for me after all. May I say, I am vastly disappointed. I was looking forward to making your further acquaintance."

It needed only that to make Delia's misery complete. "Sir, I—"

"Have you told my nephew of your decision?"

"Your nephew? Mr. Fremont, do you mean?"

His Lordship's thick, snow white eyebrows met above his nose in what could only be called a scowl. "I dislike disassembling, my girl, so let us have honesty between us."

"Of . . . of course, sir."

"Did you inform Lawrence that you were leaving?"

"No, my lord."

"And why not? I should think you would feel you owed him that courtesy."

Delia found she could not meet the elderly gentleman's gaze, so she concentrated instead upon her hands, which rested in her lap, the fingers laced painfully tight.

"Is it his reputation?" Lord Hazelton asked.

She wanted to deny the suggestion, but how could she when it was partially true. Lawrence was a rogue and the black sheep of his family. Unfortunately for the sake of Delia's heart, he was also perceptive and gentle, and the very man most suited to make her happy for the rest of her life.

As if reading her mind, His Lordship muttered something beneath his breath. "I would have thought you more discerning than to believe all you hear, my girl. In fact, Lawrence told me you were a female who thought for herself."

He peered at her in a way that made Delia decidedly uncomfortable, his all-too-perceptive eyes practically peeling away at the layers of her conscience. "Was my nephew mistaken? Are you, after all, just another sheep happy to follow the flock? Are you content to let someone else dictate your principles?"

"I . . . I hope not, my lord."

As if changing the subject, Lord Hazelton mentioned his first archaeological dig. "It was in Mesopotamia, and though I was not a lad by any means, it was my first experience at field research. The team, a group of seasoned archaeologists, had been working within the original trial trenches for more than two years; unfortunately, the finds had not been as rewarding as they, or the backers, had hoped.

"When I saw something interesting some distance from the major site, and expressed my desire to investigate, my fellow-workers teased me mercilessly. Laughing among themselves, they remarked upon their greater knowledge and upon my inexperience and, so they would have it, my inability to judge."

Fascinated by the story, Delia sat forward, not wanting to miss a word. "What did you do, my lord?"

"Not content to accept another's judgment, I followed my own instincts. Even if I failed, I told myself, at least I would do so as a result of my own beliefs, and not those of someone else."

"And did you find anything?"

"I unearthed a small pottery lamp from the early Christian era and a shekel from Israel that dated from about one hundred and forty years before Christ. Not the treasure the backers hoped to see, of course, but to me they were finds beyond price; something far better than gold statues or jewel-encrusted crowns."

Delia was quick to perceive the moral of his story. "You missed your true occupation, my lord. You should have been a writer of fables. However, accepting or rejecting the judgment of others regarding Lawrence Freemont is not my only consideration."

"And what else, if I may ask, is of any significance?"

Delia shook her head. There was still her family to be considered, plus the fact that she loved Lawrence and that it would break her heart to see him every day, knowing her feelings were not returned. Of course, she was not prepared to share that particular confidence with Lawrence's uncle.

"Come, come," he said, "this is no time for missishness. If you—"

"Excuse the interruption, Uncle," Lady Wilding said, peering around the door. "I knocked, but you must not have heard." Looking at Delia, she said, " 'Tis time to leave, my dear. The carriage is at the door, and the horses are pulling against the reins, ready to go. Fetch your bonnet so that we may not keep them standing too long in the breeze."

"Yes, ma'am. I will be right with you," Delia said, rising from the settee and offering her hand to Lord Hazelton. "It was a pleasure to meet you, sir. Please accept my best wishes for success with the writing of your memoirs."

"Are you quite certain," he asked, taking her hand and holding it, "that this is what you—"

"Delia!" Lady Wilding said, looking around the room as though searching for something she had lost, "where is Tasha?"

"I gave the pug to the footman, ma'am. He said he would take the little fellow up to you."

"He did not do so."

"But that was a good twenty minutes ago. Just before I came in here to speak with His Lordship. Surely the servant gave the pup to your maid, or—"

"I tell you, he did not!"

Suddenly agitated, Her Ladyship put her hand to her plump bosom. "What if the servant set Tasha down and let him run away? Oh, dear me! The horses! They are quite restive. What if my little one should get beneath their hooves?"

Turning quickly, Mildred Wilding ran from the room, with Delia fast upon her heels, neither lady stopping until they had reached the portico and seen for themselves that the little dog was in no danger of being trampled.

A footman stood at the door, Delia's bonnet and pelisse over his arm, but he was not the same servant to whom Delia had given those items earlier.

"Where is the other footman?" she asked.

"James, do you mean, miss?"

"I mean the one to whom I gave those things. I also gave him Her Ladyship's dog."

"I'm sure I can't say where he may be, miss. As for your things, I found them draped over the newel post at the bottom of the stairs. Of the little dog, I have seen nothing."

Tears spilled down Lady Wilding's cheeks. "Where is my little one? Tasha!" she yelled. "Tasha! Come to Mama."

When there was no answering bark, the lady turned anguished eyes toward Delia. "What can have happened to him? I cannot possibly leave without my baby."

"Of course you cannot," Delia agreed. "We shall not set one foot from the premises until he is found and returned to you."

Her own misery set aside in light of her friend's distress, Delia bade the footman run to the kitchen area to ask if anyone there had seen the pug. "Meanwhile, ma'am, I shall go up to search the bedchambers."

Lifting her skirts, Delia sped up the stairs, and as she reached the top step and turned to go down the corridor, she heard Lord Hazelton call out to the coachman to return the horses to the stable. It was only later that she realized there was a note of satisfaction in the old gentleman's voice.

A thorough inspection of both her chamber and the one previously occupied by Lady Wilding yielded nothing, even though Delia searched the cupboards and got down on her hands and knees to look beneath the beds. A full quarter hour later, after she had opened the door to each chamber on the floor and whistled for the little dog, Delia went back downstairs. To her dismay, it seemed that the human inhabitants had now disappeared, for there was no sign of either His Lordship or Lady Wilding. The servants, too, seemed to have vanished.

With no one to ask what had become of her host and his niece, Delia decided to seek Lord Hazelton in the blue drawing room, where she had met with him earlier. A quick survey of that room proved unprofitable, and she was about to return to the vestibule when she noticed that the French windows leading to the side garden stood open. Thinking perhaps the little dog might have gone out to investigate the area, Delia lost no time in making her way to the terrace.

While she descended the stone steps that led down to the most central of the three narrow gravel avenues, she called the pug's name. "Tasha! Here boy. Come."

Briefly glancing beneath the hedges that bordered the walk, and finding nothing, Delia continued toward the wrought-iron arbor where she had met Lawrence that first day she arrived at Hazelton Hall. Scarcely a week later, the thick, woody grape vines that covered the arbor were showing new tendrils, and perched atop the tangled mass were two cuckoos occupied in vowing their love for one another.

"Witchet-witchet-watchat," the female uttered in rapid fashion, to which the besotted male crooned, *"Cuckoo, cuckoo, cuc-cuc-koo."*

Sparing a moment to observe the courting birds, Delia was startled, once again, to see Lawrence Freemont appear as if from nowhere. His handsome face was set in stern, almost angry lines, and he stopped some distance from her, staring at her as if not trusting himself to come closer.

"Come to bid the cuckoo farewell?" he asked. "All in all, he is a most fortunate bird, for not only do you welcome him with compliments, but you spare a minute to take your leave of him. 'Tis a courtesy I might have wished for myself, but then—"

"Lawrence," she said breathlessly, her low spirits suddenly lifted at the sight of him, "how glad I am that you are come."

If the speaker blushed at the impropriety of her unguarded utterance, not so her auditor, for that gentleman found nothing to dislike in her speech. As a matter of fact, he repaid her warm greeting by covering the distance between them in three quick strides and taking her firmly in his arms.

"How glad *I* am," he said, his countenance only slightly less reproachful, that I was not obliged to pursue you all the way to Newton-Leyes just to do this."

When his lips touched hers, the kiss held none of his apparent anger. Quite the opposite, for Delia had not known that a kiss could be so gentle. Gentle, and yet at the same time devastating, both to her senses and to her resolve to leave Wiltshire before her feelings for Lawrence resulted in a broken heart.

"How could you think of leaving me?" he asked softly. "Surely you must know that you captivated me from the first moment we met."

His words were like water to a person wandering in the desert, greedy with thirst, and Delia buried her face in his shoulder to keep him from reading in her eyes just how much she wanted to believe him, how she longed to stay with him forever, his arms around her and his lips upon her lips. It was only the recollection that he must be practiced in the art of seduction that kept her from telling him that she loved him—kept her from surrendering to the impulse to cast every scruple aside and give her heart and her future into his keeping.

Putting his hand beneath her chin, he urged her to look up at him, and when she did, he kissed her again. Appalled to discover that her very soul was responsive to his touch, she said the only thing she could think of. "Is this one of those kissing lessons you keep offering me?"

He shook his head. "I was mistaken about that. Believe me, you do not need instruction. You are a natural. Born to kiss and be kissed." Tightening his arms around her, he added, "However, I find I cannot abide the thought of anyone but me reaping the benefit of your natural ability."

"Sir," she said, trying to still the mad beating of her heart, "a gentleman would not speak of such things."

"And what," he said, a devilish light in those deep blue eyes, "gave you the idea that I was a gentleman?"

Her only answer was a soft laugh.

"Here I was thinking I needed to explain to you how I got my reputation for being a cad, and all the time you believed me to be a gentleman. The bard was correct, what fools we mortals be."

Though aware that he was teasing her, Delia put her hands upon his chest and pushed, obliging him to loosen, if not relinquish his hold upon her. "I have never believed you a cad, sir. Whatever may have happened in your past, I cannot convince myself that you are anything but a kind, compassionate man."

"Kind? Compassionate? I fear that may be doing it a bit too brown."

His mouth pulled to the left in that sardonic smile Delia was coming to adore. "I am no saint, but I do not consider myself more of a sinner than any other man. I readily confess to having done a few things in the recent past that I do not look back upon with any great degree of pride, and as for the distant past, I committed my share of boyish peccadillos. However, you may believe me when I tell you that I have never knowingly brought harm to an innocent person. Though some members of my family may choose to consider me a black sheep, I have never been guilty of debauchery."

Delia felt as if a lead weight had been lifted from her heart. "Sir, you need say no more upon the subject."

"I must, for I wish to have done with the subject forever."

"Very well. I am listening."

"The incident that convinced my father of my sinful ways, and precipitated my departure from his house, was nothing more than a naïve boy's wish to rectify an act of injustice. I suppose my cousin informed you that my disgrace had something to do with one of the serving girls employed at the manor."

Delia nodded.

"In that, at least, he was correct. The maid, discovering that she was *enceinte,* wanted to return to her home and the father of her child, a man who had been pleading with her to marry him for more than a year. Unfortunately, when my mother discovered the girl's condition, she turned her off, refusing even to give her the wages she had earned.

Lawrence's eyes grew shadowed, as if even now the memory of his parents' mean-spiritedness gave him pain. "Without funds, the girl had no way of getting home. When I heard of her plight, I gave her all the money I had, which was slightly more than five pounds, enough for her journey. In her gratitude, she threw her arms around me and kissed me. This was what my father saw and totally misinterpreted."

"The poor girl," Delia said, not doubting the truth of his story. "And poor Lawrence. Why did you not explain the whole to your family?"

"I told my uncle. His good opinion mattered to me. As for the others," he shrugged his shoulders, "they could believe what they wished."

He looked deeply into her eyes, as if he would know the secrets of her soul. "Now," he said quietly, "there is one other person whose opinion matters to me."

Breathless at the seriousness of his tone, Delia found she could hardly speak. "Me?"

"You," he replied. "Do you believe me?"

"I believe you. In fact, I never truly thought you capable of any wrongdoing."

Apparently satisfied with her answer, Lawrence pulled her close in his arms again. "There is one more question whose answer I would know. Do you trust me enough to risk your future with mine?"

Not certain he was asking what she hoped he was asking, Delia said, "How can I trust a man who would laugh at me?"

"Laugh at you? Acquit me of that, my love, for I take you very seriously."

My love. The endearment made her feel much more confident, but still she teased, "Was it not you who invited me to see a horse—a chalk horse—knowing all the while that I believed the animal in question to be flesh and blood?"

"Guilty," he murmured, slipping his hand to the side of her neck and letting his strong, warm fingers mingle with the curls at her nape, curls that refused to stay confined to her coiffure. Slowly, mesmerizingly, he traced his thumb along the soft plane of her jaw.

"And was it not you," she said, the wonder of what he was doing to her almost causing her to lose her train of thought, "who laughed at me for saying I did not care for the beasts?"

"I remember nothing," he said, placing his warm lips where his thumb had been, trailing soft, tantalizing kisses along her jaw, then across her check, stopping only when he reached the pulse in her temple. "Nothing but how adorable you looked, and how badly I wanted to take you in my arms and kiss you."

As if overcome by the memory, he bent his head and claimed her lips, kissing her until she began to lose all sense of time and place, conscious only of the man who held her close.

"Marry me," he muttered against her mouth, his breath mingling with hers.

Delia's heart was too full to allow her brain to think coherently. "Did you say *marry?*"

"Yes," Lawrence replied, kissing her again. "And I warn you, I am not above using bribery to get what I want."

Though Delia had not the least notion of refusing him, she found the idea of bribery far too tempting to ignore. But first she was obliged to move her mouth a few inches from his so that she could put two coherent thoughts together. "This bribery," she said finally, "what form would it take?"

Obviously unable to converse with her so far away, Lawrence drew her close again, resting his chin against her forehead. "I had thought that for our wedding trip I might take you to see the land of the pharaohs. Or if you should prefer it, perhaps we might journey to Greece. I have heard there is no more romantic view on this earth than the Acropolis by moonlight."

In all truth, Delia was exactly where she wanted to be, in Lawrence Freemont's arms, but she had not yet heard the words that would make her the happiest woman in the world. "If you wish to bribe me, sir, tell me that you love me."

He crushed her to him. "How can that be a bribe, my dearest heart, when it is nothing more than the truth. I have never loved anyone as I love you. Nor, if you should refuse me, would I ever love again."

A refusal being the farthest thing from her mind, Delia wound her arms around his waist and turned her face up to his for another kiss.

"Here they are," Lady Wilding announced some minutes later, as if it were Delia and Lawrence who had been lost all along.

Her Ladyship's words were punctuated by the sharp *yip, yip* of the pug, who ran toward Delia, his stubby tail wagging as though he had not seen her for days.

"Tasha!" Delia cried, extricating herself from Lawrence's embrace and bending down to scoop the dog into her arms. "You are found."

"He was never lost," Lady Wilding informed her. "It was all a ruse. A trick played by my uncle to force us to remain at Hazelton Hall until Lawrence could be sent for."

With the heat of embarrassment warming her cheeks, Delia handed over the pug to his mistress. "You are not vexed with His Lordship, I hope."

"Why, no, my dear. Why should I be? After all, Lawrence is my favorite nephew."

At this, Mr. Freemont threw back his head and laughed. "Faint praise, Aunt, especially when one takes into account that your only *other* nephew is Basil Venton."

"Just so," said the lady.

Not bothering to take her leave of them, Lady Wilding made her way back toward the house. When she reached the stone steps of the terrace, she turned and called to Lawrence. "Nephew?"

"Yes, Aunt."

"Not for a king's ransom would I be as prudish as Delia's sister-in-law, but Feona put the girl in my care, so I stand *in loco parentis,* as it were. That being the case, perhaps I should remind Delia of Feona's admonition that a vicar's family, like Caesar's wife, must be above reproach."

"Your point is well taken, Aunt. We will be in directly."

"I give you exactly three minutes," amended the self-appointed chaperone, "then I expect to see Delia in the drawing room."

Since time was of the essence, Delia and Lawrence decided

not to waste even a second of it. When he opened his arms, she walked into them as though she had been doing so all her life.

"At last," he said, fitting her body close against his.

"At last," she agreed, lifting her face for his kiss.

A HALO
FOR MR. DEVLIN

by
Marcy Stewart

*Dedicated to the Friends of the Library
in Dayton, Tenn.*

Someone was in his room.

Grant Devlin slitted his eyes, his lean frame tightening with immediate wakefulness. The figure searching through his bag was unrecognizable in the darkness. Keeping his vision centered upon the intruder, Grant slowly lowered his hand to the left boot beside his bed, fingered the pocket within it, and grasped the cool handle of his stiletto.

The invader turned a hooded face toward him. Grant froze, wondering if the scoundrel had detected his movement. Whatever the cause, the thief began to creep toward the bed. Grant barely restrained his grin. The fellow was playing into his hands. When the bulky shadow drew near, he sprang.

Unexpectedly, his opponent buckled. He had anticipated a swung fist at the least, not this passive resistance, and the force of his leap carried him downward with the intruder. Nevertheless, he brought his blade threateningly close to the villain's neck. But as his battle-fogged brain returned to sensibility, he realized he straddled not a thief to be subdued, but a panting, writhing mass of skirts and veils. He lowered his dagger and flung back the dark netting hiding the woman's face. He could not believe whom he saw beneath.

"Lady DuBarry?"

"Quiet," whispered his captive, her enticing face registering alarm and anger in turns. "The innkeeper will hear you."

"The innkeeper?" he repeated with indignation, though he obligingly lowered his voice to a heavy whisper. "You should have thought of him before stealing into my room in the middle of the night. Why are you here?"

Lowering her lashes, she squirmed beneath him for an instant, then grew still. When she looked at him next, her eyes were seductive in the dim light of the room, her fingers laden with promise as they stroked his bare chest.

"If you are determined to continue in this manner, Grant, perhaps you will carry me to the bed before my back breaks. After all, 'tis what I offered you this afternoon. Perhaps you have reconsidered?"

"Now, Margaret," Grant chided with a wry smile as he clasped her fingers and pulled her upward with him, "surely you don't expect me to believe you risked all for a midnight tryst."

"You underestimate yourself, my dear," she answered, gazing longingly at his lips.

He stepped backward, reaching for the shirt he'd draped over the bedpost. Fortunately the unseasonable coolness of Warwickshire had prompted him to sleep in his pantaloons, and he was thankful for it.

"What I don't underestimate is your husband's fondness for duels. That beside, your claiming passion doesn't explain why you were searching my belongings." He fumbled a couple of buttons into their holes, then retreated further when Lady DuBarry drew closer. "Margaret, stop. I'm not made of ice—"

"I am glad to hear it. I was beginning to wonder if you found me unattractive."

"Impossible. But I draw the line at wives."

"Even very lonely ones?" she pouted.

"Especially them."

"Don't tell me you are a man of principle; I had greater hopes for you."

"The only principle I claim is that of self-preservation. Imagine if Lord DuBarry returned from London early and found you here. Do you want a scandalbroth? Do you want me dead?"

"I should weep forever if you were gone, but that is precisely what *has* happened, my darling. Neville returned this evening!"

He laughed. When she continued to stare at him steadily, his good humor fled. "You *were* jesting, of course."

"I am telling you the truth."

He sliced a look behind him, half expecting to see the lurking figure of the Viscount Neville DuBarry, fifteen years his senior but still in his prime, a towering bull of a man who made Grant's six feet of hard muscle appear boyish. A man known for his fighting skills, whether it be fisticuffs, pistols or swords; a man renowned for his jealous temperament.

"Blister me, woman! Why did you not shoot me while I slept? It would have been easier for both of us."

He rushed to his bag and set it upon the dresser, throwing toiletry items within. He was irked to see her teeth gleam whitely in the darkness; *she* could afford to be amused.

"Neville doesn't know I'm here. However . . ."

He paused expectantly. She adopted a coy, beseeching manner he was coming to recognize; her head tilting to one side and her body swaying slightly, reminding him of a child seeking a treat. He didn't doubt her pose often gained what she sought, but he hadn't liked it that afternoon, and he liked it even less now.

"However," she continued in a girlish voice, "he did ask to see my emerald pendant."

Now it was Grant's turn to cut the darkness with an alabaster grin. "Ah, the necklace. At last we discover the true reason for your visit."

"You know you shouldn't have taken it," she scolded prettily.

"*Taken* it? You make it sound as if I stole it."

"Well, in a manner you did. I am an innocent when it comes to cards—"

Grant snorted. "Stop, Margaret. You will slay me with laughter before your husband has his opportunity." He hurried to the corner and tossed an untidy heap of discarded clothes into his portmanteau.

"How ungallant you are," she bit, dropping all pretense at seduction. "You were much more charming today, but now I realize that was because you knew you could fleece me of my husband's most precious gift to me."

"You're making my winning the stones seem like a plot. I didn't know the dashed thing existed until you wagered it."

"Yes, and I didn't know you made a profession of cards until my friend Millicent told me. You remember, she was arriving just as you left? She recognized you as the one who caused Lord Tambry's ruin."

Grant's mouth tightened into a thin line. "Lord Tambry's avarice caused his ruin, not I." He seized his jacket from the back of a chair and put it on with a hurried lack of care.

"You are suggesting I caused the loss of my necklace in the same manner, but I didn't know when I invited you that we would spend half our day gambling. I had other hopes, or I would not have extended the invitation"

"Nor would I have accepted it had you told me what was in your overheated little brain. If you recall, you said I would be one of a small party of neighbors."

"All of which you planned to pluck like a hawk among chickens."

He grunted. "If that is how you like to categorize your friends . . ."

"Oh!" she growled, curling her hands into fists and stamping her slipper. "You are the most maddening creature I have ever met!"

"Careful. Remember the innkeeper's ears."

"You are no gentleman!"

"I've never claimed to be."

"It's a good thing you haven't. My husband once spoke of you. He said that when one is born on the wrong side of the blanket, even an earl's blood cannot purify the peasant strain. I should have believed him!"

Grant paused only an instant at this familiar blow, then jerked the strap tight across his bag and grabbed its handle. Leveling the lady a hard stare, he brushed past her to seize the pillow from his bed. He pulled a small kidskin pouch from the interior

of the pillowcase, bounced it in his hand, and slipped it into his
pocket. At that moment, an uproar of thundering hooves and
men's voices could be heard outside the inn.

For the space of two heartbeats, Grant and Margaret exchanged alarmed stares. When heavy blows sounded on the
front door, they dashed to the window.

"Neville!" she said in deathly tones, the color draining from
her skin.

"Could there be any doubt?" he muttered. "Your husband
doesn't trust you as much as you think. But was it necessary
to bring an army with him?"

Grant had a clear view of the three large men crowding behind Lord DuBarry, though the front door was several rooms
aside and well beneath his bedchamber on the first floor. He
could not see the men's facial expressions, but their stances
conveyed extreme ire.

"Oh, what shall I do?" she begged. "He will slay me."

If that is so, imagine what he will do to me, Grant thought,
glaring at her. But the fright swimming in her eyes stilled the
words. Though she had brought this disaster upon both of them,
laying blame served no purpose.

The innkeeper could be heard on the stair now, yelling for
quiet, assuring the visitors he was coming, that they were wak-
ing the entire establishment.

"Is there a back stair?" she asked desperately.

"No," he replied with surety. One of the first things he
checked in every new abode was alternate exits. "The only way
out is this window. When the host allows them in, we'll make
the jump."

Margaret looked from him to the two-storey drop beneath
the glass. He did not think it possible for her face to grow more
pale, but it did.

"I cannot jump from this window."

"You don't have any choice, Margaret, unless you want your
husband to find you here." Tears began to spill down her cheeks.
"I'll go first and catch you," he added in kinder tones. "We'll

fetch my horse from the stable, and I'll return you home before they discover us."

"My mount is hidden in a copse a stone's throw from the inn," she choked. "But a fall such as this . . . I'll break something."

"Better a turned ankle than a sliced throat."

After an instant's silence, she shook her head. "No. I can't. I—I'm afraid of heights."

He could hear the innkeeper throwing back the locks. Below them, Lord DuBarry and his henchmen entered the building. Heated voices filtered upstairs.

"Do as you please, then," he said in exasperation. "I'm going."

She made a pleading little sound. Making a sudden decision, he pulled the pouch from his pocket and loosened its leather strings. Other than the flashing green stones set in gold, there were only a few coins remaining. He sighed in resignation as he passed her the necklace.

"There. At least you will have a reason for being here. If I'm gone, there will be less chance of his misinterpreting things."

Her eyes widened with relief. "Yes, do you go now. I have thought of an explanation." She dashed him a surprisingly regretful look, then kissed his cheek. Before he had time to reshuffle his senses, she whispered, "Forgive me."

She then put her hands to the shoulder of her gown, ripped downward and shrieked, "Help! He is attacking me! Someone, please!"

Grant's jaw dropped. "You she-devil!"

"You had best hurry," she warned. Then, louder: "Help!"

Heavy boots rattled the stairs. Grant lifted the sash, threw his bag to the ground, spared her a final look of resentment, and plunged through the window.

Daylight found Grant well away from the inn. Had he not stolen a lift on the back of a carriage making its slow and stealthy way through the night with its load of whisky bottles hidden in the straw, he might have lost more than a night's sleep and a healthy installment on his dream.

He certainly could not have outrun the viscount on foot, not with the damage he'd done his knee in the drop from the inn's window. He'd been unable to retrieve his horse, thanks to Lord DuBarry's posting a man at the stable. Grant had contemplated fighting the fellow for his roan, but he'd dismissed the idea; he could hardly walk.

There was one thing he'd not lost, he told himself as he rounded a well-wooded stretch of road, and that was his low estimate of humanity—and womankind in particular. It did not require being raised as the solitary mongrel among three legitimate heirs to form his view, either, though those humbling years had left their imprint.

Thinking of his half-brothers made him smile grimly. How pleased they would be to see him hobbling along this country lane with his bag thrown over one shoulder. It was exactly the kind of future they predicted for him.

Around the next curve, he spotted a posting house and quickened his pace. In his pocket he had enough coins for a hearty breakfast and perhaps a small wager that might yield a seat on the mail coach he saw pulling into the yard, if fortune smiled.

As he neared the establishment, two hostlers rushed to change the horses. A man, three women and a lad exited the conveyance and approached the inn, pausing at the door to attend a young woman dressed all in black. Whatever she said detained the passengers a mere instant; only the older male hesitated long enough to search his pockets and drop a coin into a leather bag she carried, prompting a smile that dazzled Grant even at this distance. After the man disappeared inside, the lady in black removed the coin and examined it. The sudden droop in her posture screamed dejection so loudly that Grant fought himself not to laugh.

The poor chit; she must have fallen on hard times. Her gown was far too short for fashion; its hem, which was no hem at all but a thready cessation of material, barely grazed her ankles. In truth, the reprehensible dress did not fit her in any manner. The bodice, for an example, stretched to painful-looking tightness across a healthy bosom. It was the one feature of shabbiness he could not regret.

She did not seem cognizant of his appraisal. At his approach, bottomless brown orbs sparked with renewed eagerness; she straightened her shoulders and looked him squarely in the eye.

"Would you care to make a contribution for the mission, sir?" she asked in a clear, low voice.

He hesitated. Her elocution instantly drew him back to firelit drawing rooms, petits fours, and mirrorlike tea services presided over by ladies in silk. She wore a dark hat and veil that hid her hair and a portion of forehead, but the smooth, creamy skin of her face and ungloved hands spoke of expensive lotions and a life untouched by scrubbing dishes or clothes. As he studied her, she widened a beautiful pair of lips over perfect teeth, displaying the absolute self-assuredness of a pampered and well-nourished puppy. There was an air of freshness about her, innocence even, inasmuch as any woman could possess that quality. How had she fallen to begging? It could be interesting to find out.

"And what mission might that be, miss?" he asked at last, giving her a lazy smile that seldom failed to cause a reaction in a female. This one, however, appeared unmoved.

"What mission?" Her gaze raked the inn's yard with intensity, as if she hoped to find an answer in the patchy grass. A scruffy-looking dog raced past the coach chasing a butterfly. One of the hostlers threw a rock at the animal, causing it to howl. "Bao," she said with sudden illumination. "Bao-Bao."

"I beg pardon?" Watching the movement of her sparkling eyes, he had almost forgotten his question; now he worried at her childish mimicry of the dog. What a waste of beauty if she was mad.

"The mission is called Bao-Bao," she explained in tones that said he should know that already.

For the first time since he had gone to bed last evening, laughter returned to his bones. "And you are a missionary to this place?"

She wrinkled her nose, a disarming gesture in a perfectly proportioned face. "Can you not see by my clothes that I have dressed from the mission barrel?"

With approval he noted how neatly she parried the question. "And where is this . . . Bao-Bao?"

"Where?" Her glance began to drift again. "Why, Africa, of course."

"Indeed? Oh, yes; it's the small country below the Cape of Good Hope, if memory serves."

"I think it may be," she said faintly.

"Except that would be off the coast, wouldn't it?"

"It is an island," she said after a moment's pondering.

"Would that be where they grow the baobab trees?" he persisted, enjoying her discomfiture immensely. Geography had been one of many subjects in which he excelled his brothers. Throughout his interminable boyhood, he'd imagined extensive travels away from them.

"Baobab trees?" she echoed in undisguised mystification.

"Yes, you know of them, surely. Their fruit is called monkey bread, and the natives employ it in the preparation of cooling drinks. The leaves, I am told, are used for fever and dysentery, and the bark makes a strong fiber."

"What a useful-sounding tree," she said, her expression full of wonder. "I—I've never actually been to Bao-Bao; I am only collecting donations in preparation to going there."

"You've asked the wrong person for contributions, I'm sorry to say. Mayhaps you've noticed I have no horse. Almost everything I own in the world is in this bag."

"Oh, I see." Her disappointment rapidly gave way to concern. "If you are hungry, I have a few shillings. I'm going inside now; I'll share my breakfast with you."

For one surprising moment, shame rushed through him for baiting her so. He was not used to generosity from females;

perhaps she was a genuine reformer. But no, something was amiss here, and he wanted to discover the secret.

"And what will you use to pay for our breakfast—coins pinched from the mission's fund?"

He was made further ashamed by her look of dismay. "I have aught else or I would not." Brightening, she added, "But even missionaries must eat."

He was beginning to suspect that nothing would dampen this one's spirits for long. "If I am lucky, I'll share my breakfast with *you*," he promised, and opening the door, nodded for her to precede him. She did so, but not without giving him a questioning look.

The interior of the inn did not pretend elegance. Within a few paces of the door squatted a scarred, unornamented desk, presently unmanned. To the immediate right was a beamed chamber containing an enormous, smoking fireplace and rough tables and chairs; the occupants of the coach and a few other strangers sat at more than half of them, talking in sleepy voices as they ate. As Grant made to follow the young lady into the dining area, a tiny old man, bent and knotted as a stunted tree, scurried from the corridor beside the stair waving his arms forbiddingly.

" 'Ere, 'ere," he whined, "I told ye to be off. No beggars 'lowed in my place."

"But I have enough for breakfast now," the girl protested.

"Eh? Begged or stolen from my customers, no doubt. Be off wi' ye, troublesome baggage!"

"Do I hear rightly?" Grant asked in a menacing voice, surprised at how much the little man ruffled him. "You are refusing to serve this lady and myself?"

"She was alone, so she ain't no lady," the innkeeper replied crossly, the lines in his forehead deepening. "But I didn't say nutthink about ye."

"The lady is with me."

"Is she now?" The old man's lips pursed sourly. "Then ye

just be some kind o' gypsy, farmin' out yer skirt to do yer beggin' fer ye."

"Watch your tongue, old man," Grant spat.

The girl moaned suddenly and collapsed against Grant's shoulder, drawing the attention of the diners. Alarmed, Grant moved quickly to support her. Her head lolled against his chest and tilted upward; in that instant she astonished and delighted him with a glimpse of mischievous eyes.

"I am so very hungry," she said, her words weak but loud enough to be heard at the tables. "Why, oh why, will you not give us a crust of bread? Here is my coin. If you cannot soften your heart for me, won't you at least consider the fate of the mission? Please, sir."

"The mission is in Bao-Bao, you know," Grant added for good measure.

"I care naught for heathens I'll never see," replied the ancient, but a glance at his other customers, one or two of whom were frowning, forced him to add grudgingly, "Oh, verra well. Go re in."

"You are too kind," said the young lady, recovering sufficiently to walk toward an empty table near the window.

In the act of following her, Grant had his attention snagged by several notices nailed to the anteroom's wall. One lithograph caught his particular interest, for he recalled seeing another like it at last evening's inn. The poster promised five thousand pounds for the return of one Brittania Rutland, daughter of Sir Clyde Rutland of Kent. It went on to describe her as a comely young lady possessing brown eyes and brown hair. She had last been seen at her betrothal ball the week before, wearing a bronze silk ballgown.

His gaze drifted from the poster to the lady in black, who was watching him with expectant cheerfulness from her sunny corner. What were the odds? he wondered. She was more than comely. He could not see her hair, but her brows were dark and she certainly had the correct eye color.

No, it was not possible. Even if she were running from an

undesired wedding, why would a wealthy heiress attire herself
so poorly? Besides, such gifts did not come to him; he'd always
had to scrabble for every crumb.

But—*five thousand pounds*. The chance was worth pursuing.
At the very least, he must discover the shade of her hair. When
he joined her at the table, his smile radiated hope.

"Have you done stagework before, miss?" he asked. "You
have the instincts of an actress."

She looked pleased. "Do I, truly? I've often wondered what
that profession would be like." Running one finger idly across
the table's surface, she gave her worn sleeves a discreet tug, as
if suddenly becoming aware of their inadequacies, then dropped
her hands to her lap. "But Father wouldn't hear of it. Besides,
I was only partly acting a moment ago. I *am* weak from hunger."

"Fortunately, you don't look weak. I can't abide whey-faced
females."

"Can you not? I'm certain if your whey-faced acquaintances
were told of your prejudice, they would pinch bruises into their
cheeks to please you."

His smile faded. Had this pert pretender dared to scold him,
or was she being flirtatious? But no, her rascally grin robbed
her words of sting or lures. He found himself responding in
kind.

"Do you realize I don't even know your name? Forgive my
rudeness in not introducing myself. I am Grant Devlin from
Surrey."

She bowed her head politely. "You are a long way from home,
sir. Are you journeying south, then?"

"No," he said before he could stop himself, hardly noting in
this reminder of recent disaster that she had neglected to give
her name. He'd determined to avoid the London direction in
case Lord DuBarry took it in mind to defend his wife's dubious
honor. Surely the viscount would think Grant meant to return
to his rooms in London, or even to his father's estate in Surrey,
where greater opportunities existed to ply his vocation.

But now Grant wanted only to follow this mysterious, happy

child, even if it were to the DuBarry estate itself. Five thousand pounds would travel a long way in softening the loss of Margaret's trinket.

"In which direction are *you* bound?" he asked.

A dreamy expression settled across her features. "I go to Scotland."

He feigned a small gasp. "What an extraordinary coincidence. I, too, am headed for that wild country, miss, or Mrs. . . . ?"

"I am called Mary," she said with an uncomfortable glance. "Miss Mary Smith."

"Mary Smith?" He could not hide his disbelief at so common a name.

She hesitated. "Jones, I mean."

His lips twitched. She might be a natural actress, but she was a terrible liar. He knew all women told untruths but accounted her ineptitude to her credit. It suggested she did not make a habit of it.

"You are Mary Jones, then," he pronounced in apparent confusion.

"No," she said, fluttering a hand dismissively. "Smith-Jones."

"You are . . . Mary Smith-Jones?"

"Yes, now you have it. Oh, excellent; Mr. Tavis is bringing us a loaf of bread and a platter of eggs. You must cut your slices first, Mr. Devlin, before I gobble the entire thing myself."

"More is forthcoming, Miss Mary Smith-Jones. Don't forget I intend to pay." To the grumpy innkeeper he added, "Bring a rasher of bacon, and coffee, too." When the host huffed away, Grant returned his attention to her. "Now, let us see if I understand what you have told me. You are going to Bao-Bao by way of Scotland. What an intriguing route."

"Oh. Well, I am still collecting funds, you see."

"Perhaps you travel to join a relative, or . . ."

"Um, yes. I have many relatives."

"Generous ones, I imagine, for you to journey so far to them, and all by yourself, too. Tell me, what think they of this path you've chosen?"

"The path I have—oh. They are happy for me, naturally."

"Are they? Now that surprises me. I should guess they'd find it wrenching to say good-bye to a beautiful young lady like yourself, especially in the light of all the deprivations and danger you will face."

"Oh, well," she replied in a muffled voice, then rolled her eyes and pointed to her mouth as she finished chewing a large mouthful of bread. Swallowing, she continued, "They are all very devout."

"Calvinists, are they?"

"Um, some of them."

"That would explain Scotland, then."

When Mr. Tavis returned with their coffee and bacon, Grant forced his mind from sparring with his delectable companion to the necessary consideration of winning a seat aboard the coach. But what if she did not own a ticket? He put the question to her.

"I intend to catch the next mail," she admitted. "There seems a goodly amount of traffic here."

"And you hope to find a more generous donor than you've discovered so far this morning."

"Surely there will be *someone*," she agreed with enthusiasm.

"Well, Miss Smith-Jones, what would you say to my purchasing our tickets on the coach that waits outside?"

Sparks danced into her eyes. His spirits lightened at her childlike merriment. What an engaging sprite she was.

"But you are nearly penniless, you said."

"Only for the moment, or I am more useless than I need be."

He turned his chair to greater advantage in seeing the room's occupants. At one of the tables, a trio of men was occupied at cards, but there was no time for a game now. Unfortunately, most of the travelers looked to possess little more than he presently did, and he'd never knowingly tricked anyone of their last farthing—not if it meant they would go hungry.

For a moment the image of Lord Tambry's devastated face flitted through his mind's eye. He banished it. The old man had long been an acquaintance of his father's and knew of Grant's reputation. Whatever had happened to the marquess, he'd brought on himself.

Across the room, Mr. Tavis leaned against the wall in what looked to be a rare moment of idleness. Perhaps drawn by Grant's speculative regard, the host met his gaze with a frown. The little man had already proved himself to be a curmudgeon. There was no conscience to be lost there. The time had arrived for Grant to employ the trick he used for his most desperate moments.

"Whatever happens next," he whispered to his companion, "do not become alarmed."

With a startled look, she assured him she would not. He winked, began to search his pockets with growing distress, and finally stood, bringing his bag to the table and plundering through it. In a trice, Mr. Tavis was upon them.

" 'Ere, wot's wrong? Don' tell me ye canna pay for yer food, or I'll call in me men to beat it out o' ye!"

"I've been robbed," Grant declared. "It must have been that smithy yesterday. I sold him my horse, and I thought he put the money in my bag, but—"

"Think I'm fallin' fer that? Just wait until Big Jess get 'is 'ands on ye. *Then* we'll see wot *we* find in that bag o' yourn."

Grant scanned the interested faces of the customers, cupped his hand over his left eye and said plaintively, "You wouldn't harm a veteran of the Peninsula, would you? It's not my fault people take advantage of me. You'd be surprised how often it happens, once they realize I've lost the sight in one eye."

Mr. Tavis peered at him, then straightened irritably. "Fie on ye! There ain't nutthink wrong with yer eyes."

"Tell that to the Frog who shot me in the head." Grant brushed back lock of hair from his temple. "See this scar? The bullet is still lodged in my skull. The surgeon said it was too dangerously placed to remove."

To Grant's satisfaction, several gasps could be heard. An older lady at the nearest table pressed her fingers to her lips. Miss Smith-Jones watched him with utter absorption. She did well to do so; she could learn from him.

"That little 'ole could be from anythin', ye charlatan, and clappin' yer 'and o'er yerself don't make me ferget wot I seen before. No blind man's peepers move like that."

Slowly, Grant lowered his arm. "My eye does move naturally, doesn't it? I've worked hard to make it do so."

"Faugh and faugh again! I'm callin' Big Jess." Mr. Tavis began to move away.

"Of course, in times of stress it doesn't work as well," Grant said, forcing his left eye to wander at will. It was a thing he'd practiced since childhood, having learned the serving girls found it vastly entertaining.

"Look at his eye!" shouted the lad seated with the women. He immediately crossed and uncrossed his own. "Can't do it! It must be the truth!"

"Poor soul," commiserated the plump woman sitting beside him.

"Ye gullibles," Mr. Tavis threw at them. "I seen better at the fair."

"Now you are upsetting me," Grant said, folding his arms across his chest. While he stared indignantly with his right eye, his left rolled upward and disappeared beneath a fluttering eyelid, revealing only a milky slit.

"Saints preserve us!" cried the woman.

"Gor!" added the boy admiringly.

From the corner of his open eye, Grant noted that Miss Smith-Jones looked stricken. In spite of his warning, she appeared to be falling for his spiel. He felt a moment's doubt. Could a young woman involved in an unsacred impersonation be so naïve? Surely it did not mean she was truly a missionary.

"Tricks," Mr. Tavis pronounced with a downturning of his mouth.

One of the gentlemen sitting at cards scraped back his chair shouting, "Here now, Tavis, don't plague the fellow; let him have his meal. He served his country!"

"Easy for ye to say," declared the host. "Ain't comin' out o' yer pocket, is it?"

"Please, don't disturb Mr. Tavis," Grant commanded the room. "He has right of it; my disability is not his problem. However, there is a thing I can do that will prove the truth of my claim—but no, Mr. Tavis wouldn't be interested in wagering his word against mine."

"I'll tell ye wot I'm interested in—yer payin' up, that's wot."

"What is it you do, sir?" breathed the boy. "Tell us!"

Grant looked hesitant. "Well—it is only that I've learned to throw cards into a hat at five paces. I know it sounds easy, but if you've ever closed one eye and tried such a thing, you've seen how difficult it can be."

"But not fer a one-eyed jack," disputed the host. "Used to it, ye are."

"Oh," said Grant with a raising of his brows. "Then you do believe me."

Despite protesting that the gypsy-man had probably practiced for years with both eyes blindfolded for such an opportunity as this, Mr. Tavis found himself netted by his customers, who began pounding the tables, whistling, and shouting insults. Within moments, a top hat was placed on an empty table in the center of the room, and a deck of cards supplied by the cardplayers. The patrons moved to either side to see better, and Grant strode off five generous paces. For each man, makeshift blindfolds were devised from handkerchiefs folded over one eye and anchored in place by strips of leather tied behind their heads.

Mr. Tavis went first. After five tries, not one card lay upon the table, let alone inside the hat. Grant managed to land four, with the fifth teetering upon the brim.

"He's won the meal!" gloated a bald man near the fireplace. "I can die in peace; I've lived to see Tavis bested!"

The innkeeper shook his head angrily and stomped toward the kitchen.

"Here, Mr. Tavis," Grant called after him. "Why not try again? A day's labor in your stable against a ticket on the coach."

"Bah!" replied the host, who slammed the door behind him.

"I'll try it, but I've only a shilling," the lad said. "I want your boots if I win."

"Waste your fa-di-la money, you will," said the plump lady before Grant could respond.

"But, Ma, it's mine to spend. Pa said so."

Grant rather liked the boy, but he paused a mere moment before bowing to the woman. "Only by your leave, dear lady."

At this unexpected gallantry, she shook with giggles, her generous middle rocking the table. "Learn the hard way then, Curtis."

It was only the beginning for Grant. In the ten minutes remaining before the coachman called forth the passengers, he won enough to send himself and the new acquaintance he hoped would add significantly to his fortune through the next two counties.

When he presented her ticket, however, she did not exhibit the gratitude and admiration he'd been expecting. She thanked him nicely enough, but her unaccustomed solemnity disquieted him.

"You are not truly blind in one eye, are you?" she whispered as they made their way to the coach.

He gave her a deep look that flushed confusion into her cheeks.

"We all play our little games, don't we, Miss Mary Smith-Jones?" he replied.

The lady known as Miss Smith-Jones took her place in the coach and schooled herself to make no reaction when Mr. Devlin sat beside her—unnecessarily closely, too, she thought. She could not like the strange tumble of emotions that had overcome her during the past hour and now threatened the settling of the best meal she'd enjoyed in four days. She had been happy since making her decision after months of debate, and certain she'd made the correct one. But after meeting Mr. Devlin, all of her old doubts were returning in force, and a few new ones as well.

Under cover of a thick veil of lashes, she studied him again. It was something she had been unable to prevent herself from doing since setting eyes upon him in the inn's yard. The unknown cause of this fascination was a prime source of her distress. Certainly he was attractive—quite stunningly so—but it could not be that which caused her senses to sharpen painfully, not now. How amusing that the thought should enter her head!

He made her burn with curiosity. Surely that was all it was; that and the limp, which had first softened her toward him. Moreover, the blatant flaws in his character were stimulating a hideous self-examination. Nurse Vonnie would have said God sent him for this purpose, and perhaps He had. Nurse was always looking for ways to improve behavior, though, and possibly a too-early assessment of the stranger's origins would be a mistake.

Mr. Devlin possessed the darkest hair she had ever seen on an Englishman, and his eyes were an extraordinary green, like a new leaf in spring. But the color was not half so arresting as the expressiveness of them; one moment they communicated sincerity, the next, cynicism. He was quick to laugh, so that she often wondered if he mocked her; then a raw, aching look would sweep across his features, flashing a vulnerability that drew her like a beacon.

She should not be analyzing him in such detail, not in the light of the decision she had made. Nurse would grin her gap-toothed smile and accuse her of throwing her heart away again. The old woman often declared she bestowed her allegiances and trust too easily, as if affection could ever be wasted.

But all of that was moot, anyway—fodder for the most riotous laughter. Once it would not have been, but it most certainly was now.

No, she was not attracted to Mr. Devlin's magnetic presence; on the contrary, she found it repelling that a handsome man of charm and ability, obviously raised as a gentleman, could fall so low as to gamble and trick harmless working people and children with lies. He would do better to find genteel employment.

This in turn made her doubt the nobility of her own deception. It had seemed the sunniest lark when she and Sally, the vicar's daughter, had exchanged gowns, especially considering the reason. But watching Mr. Devlin made her wonder. Was she any better than he?

It was not the first time in her life she had behaved falsely, though naturally she had never enacted anything this drastic. As the coach lurched into numbing motion, countless childhood and adolescent escapades began to play through her mind. She had once simulated a violent illness through the use of crushed berries (to stain her cheeks into a fevered flushedness and smashed peas (it did not bear thinking about how these were used) which served to excuse her from a full two weeks of a detested tutor's prattle before she was unmasked.

Other events had been worse. The head groom had been livid after she tacked a pair of wooden wings to her mare's finest leather saddle; she had wanted to convince Aaron, the neighbor's son to the west, that animals had souls and Biscuit was an angel. After one unfortunate dinner party, Father sentenced her to a week's confinement for draping her floured body in a bedsheet and pretending to be a statue in the garden—and this in spite of the vicar's amusement.

There were many such incidents. Often and often she had been accused of causing her mother's gray hairs; and at this moment, far from home, she felt twinges of guilt awakening. Did that mean she was finally attaining maturity and would become a staid lady hereafter? Surely not. Doubtless she was homesick.

If only she did not find Mr. Devlin so upsetting, she would feel better. He had shown her generosity and good humor in the brief while she had known him, but his cheerful larceny disappointed her far more than it should. There could be no other explanation but that she was growing disappointed in herself.

In the midst of her contemplation, he became aware of her regard and smiled mischievously. Quickly she averted her eyes and vowed to notice him no more.

Grant was pleased to see that only two of the former occupants of the mail coach were continuing north with them: the man who had given Miss Smith-Jones a meagre contribution, a Mr. Abner Craven as he introduced himself; and Mrs. Heath, a widow of middle years with a face as sharply alert as a hunter at point. Even so, the conveyance felt crowded; not so much because of Mr. Craven's pungent, unwashed state nor the widow's astonishingly large knees which kept knocking gongs of pain into Grant's injured one—"So sorry," she said often, "all my height's in me legs and always has been since I grew backteeth"—but moreso from the young lady's steadily growing silence. Her little corner beside him throbbed with tension, palpable as a gathering storm. Although their acquaintance was brief, her melancholy seemed so uncharacteristic that he felt quite disturbed and would have questioned her had Mrs. Heath not been so quick.

"I think it's admirable that a young lady like you is a missionary to the Bahbuhs," said that lady after a long monologue about her travels to visit her nine sisters, all of whom she declared to be scattered like marbles across the English countryside. "Of a cert those people need civilizing, as do all who don't have the good luck of being born here. But you are so *young*. What does your mamma say? I'm guessing she'd rather you marry and give her grandchildren."

Miss Smith-Jones cleared her throat and stared fixedly at a point between Mr. Craven and Mrs. Heath. "I believe she would prefer I marry," she said.

"As I thought. Had any of me girls gone off to tend savages, I'd of drowned me head in the washbucket. What's behind it, Miss Smith-Jones?" The woman gave an exaggerated wink and stared pointedly at Grant. "You got a feller over in Bahbuh, or is this fine gentleman going with you?"

"Oh, my goodness, no," Miss Smith-Jones fired.

"It's Bao-Bao," Grant corrected simultaneously, adding with a caressing look for his seat-mate, "and the lady and I have only just met."

"Of course you have," returned Mrs. Heath with a knowing smile. "I see all now; yes, I do." She leaned forward confidingly, grinding Grant's knee so fiercely he barely restrained himself from a yelp of agony. "You're off to Gretna Green, aren't you, loves?"

"No!" shouted the young lady, looking back and forth between Grant and the woman, her eyes round with consternation. "You have misunderstood everything—"

"If you ain't no missionary, I wants me penny back," commented Mr. Craven. "I ain't funding no runaways, I ain't."

Miss Smith-Jones plowed through her purse. "You may have your money, sir, and gladly, though I am not running away to Gretna Green with this stranger."

"But he bought your ticket," said Mrs. Heath with the beginnings of a frown. "I saw him. You ought not to let a stranger buy you something like that. What would your mamma say?"

"I can see now I shouldn't have. It so happens that I am temporarily penniless, and I was desperate. I—I have to go on, you see."

"To Bao-Bao," Grant said helpfully.

"Yes. To . . . there."

Grant had not been so entertained since his eldest half-brother fell off his horse before a houseful of guests. Quietening a faint tugging of his conscience, he leaned back expansively, draped an arm across Miss Smith-Jones's shoulders and was further amused to see a paroxysm of alarm cross her face.

"Oh, cut line, Mary, and tell the truth. What harm can these people do us?"

"None!" assured Mrs. Heath. "None at all. I have a fondness for romance, I do." She shot a coy glance toward Mr. Craven. "Are you listening, sir? Though if you're married, forget I said a word!" When the farmer scowled and edged closer to the door, she laughed heartily.

"I don't know what he's talking about!" Miss Smith-Jones cried, twisting away from Grant's embrace. "I don't know this man!"

Mrs. Heath tsked. "A lovers' quarrel already. Many's ahead, I can assure you. Am I right, Mr. Craven?"

This last apparently thawed the farmer. "Yes, ma'am. If fights was corn, I'd be a rich man."

"Why won't you people listen to me? He is a stranger, I tell you!"

"Mary, Mary," Grant soothed. He could no more stop himself than he could halt a storm with a feather. "There is no point to this masquerade. You're becoming overheated. Why don't you remove your hat and veil and relax?"

"Do, love," Mrs. Heath encouraged. "You'll feel better."

Grant watched with interest as the helpless rage in Miss Smith-Jones's expression changed to calculation.

"Tell me the color of my hair," she said in tones of triumph. "Then I'll remove my hat."

"Why, Mary," he said sadly, though in truth he was hard put to keep from laughing.

"You cannot, can you? Would a man who intended to marry me not know something so obvious as my hair color?"

"Why must you persist in continuing this charade, my darling?"

"Tell Mrs. Heath and Mr. Craven if you know me so well."

"You'd as better," said the farmer. "If you doesn't guess it, I'll twist that knee of yours ye keep whinin' about."

"Very well, I'll play. You hair is brown."

Startlement crossed the young lady's expression, then comprehension. "How stupid I am. You can see my eyebrows."

Mrs. Heath laughed until she became breathless. "You two are better than a puppet show! Far better!"

Miss Smith-Jones remained broodingly silent until the coach stopped at a tavern for the noon meal. As soon as she descended from the carriage—after brushing aside Grant's elegantly proffered assistance—she walked briskly toward the establishment, her chin set at a defiant angle. Grant shadowed her. After two or three unsuccessful, evasive maneuvers, she planted her slippers in the bare earth and glared snapping eyes at him.

"Stop following me, or I will—I will—"

Grant gestured expectantly, smiling encouragement. "Will what, Miss Smith-Jones? Do continue; I find your every word fascinating."

"Oh! If only my father were here, he would—"

"You seem unable to complete a sentence, my dear. Mayhaps we should go inside and away from the sun where you can think better. Let us take a little table, and you can tell me all about your father. I want to know everything about you."

Her brows descended. "Why are you doing this to me?"

"Doing what? If you mean, taking an interest in you, why shouldn't I show my concern for your high calling? I behave thus with all the missionaries in my acquaintance."

A number which, having met you, Miss Brittania Rutland I hope, totals exactly zero, he told her silently. He did not bother to hide the skepticism from his expression. Amusing she may be, but she was as deceptive as every other wench he'd known. If one day he chanced upon an honest female, the surprise would kill him.

"If you pretended to be betrothed to every missionary in your acquaintance," she returned with a quaver in her voice, "you'd be thrown into a madhouse."

Her button eyes began to fill. Tears were always alarming, but he was unpleasantly shocked at how hers disturbed him.

"Now, Mary, surely you understand I did that to protect your reputation. You recall how Mrs. Craven wanted to scold you for accepting your fare from a stranger. Such things aren't done by young ladies. Some gentlemen would misinterpret the acceptance of a gift of money."

She appeared to contemplate this. "Even when the recipient is a missionary?"

"If the missionary is as fetching as you."

She immediately looked down. A tiny bead of perspiration squeezed beneath her hat and trickled earthward. He could not resist blotting it with his handkerchief, an action which caused her to flinch, then smile briefly, trustingly. His handkerchief hesitated in midair; for a fraction of time, he found his fingers oddly reluctant to stray from her fair skin. Sternly he reminded himself of the deception she waged, and the moment passed.

"In truth," he continued daringly, guiding her through the tavern door, "you don't look like a missionary at all."

"What is a missionary supposed to look like?"

"Not like you."

"I imagine you think they are all old, or unfortunate spinsters."

"Something like that—the ones who aren't men."

"Then I'd advise you to widen your perception, sir. You are working from prejudice."

"Am I? You've observed many different types of missionaries, I daresay—noblemen, perhaps, or daughters of noblemen . . ."

The color that burnished her cheeks told him all he needed to know, though he advised himself to go easy. Judging from the guarded scrutiny she was giving him, she could bolt at any time.

Their disagreement had carried them to a scarred table in the corner of a smallish common room. The interior was lit by a single mullioned window and a scattering of candles on the walls. Despite the poor light, the table was clearly not clean, nor was the frail, spotty lad who came to serve them. Grant requested he wipe the tabletop, then bring them ale, bread and cheese. He hoped such fare was simple enough not to give rise to illness later.

Leaving them, the boy by necessity passed an obese, unkempt man slouching behind the establishment's long, oaken bar; the owner most likely, Grant thought. He winced to see the man cuff the younger one for no apparent reason other than ill-temper. Still frowning, Grant returned his attention to the lady sitting across from him.

"And now, Miss Smith-Jones, you were going to tell me about your father."

She seemed to have recovered from her bout with tears. The look she gave him was assessing and entirely uncooperative.

"If you are not blind in one eye as you claimed to be, how did you receive that scar on your forehead?"

Without conscious thought, he rubbed the small indentation on his temple. "I wish I could tell you the cause was a heroic one, but in actuality it was a gift from my half-brother."

She straightened with interest, but he sensed a reserve remaining. "What happened?"

"You seriously want to know? Very well, I'll tell you. Gordon and I were sword-fighting with sticks from the garden. I was winning—forgive me for casting modesty aside—"

"I have the notion modesty often finds itself so treated by you," she contributed with a reluctant smile.

"Alas, you crush me. To continue. I *was* winning when Baxter came to Gordon's defense. Baxter is my eldest half-brother, I must explain. It was Baxter who felled me with a spear thrust—wooden, of course—to the head."

"How unfair!" Her effusion of sympathy quickly subsided. "That is . . ."

"Pray do not keep me in suspense, Miss Smith-Jones. *That is . . .*"

She lowered her lashes. "If you are telling the truth."

"Why would I lie about such a thing?" He cocked his head and studied her, truly curious.

"You lied at the inn."

"There was good reason for it. You yourself are sharing in the profit of those lies, you might recall." When she frowned, he added, "Besides, the innkeeper deserved it."

"I suppose that made the deception all right. Did the young boy also deserve it?"

A wave of heat passed over him. "Is this why you've been so blue-deviled all morning? Because you think I treated that boy unfairly?"

"I can never be happy to see injustice."

"The child lost only a shilling! What did you expect me to do, pretend to lose and give him my boots?"

"He believed you were half-blind. He knew he couldn't win. I think he wanted to help you with his shilling but feared you'd be too proud to accept a gift. He sacrificed his pleasure because he pitied you."

"That is the most ridiculous thing I've ever heard. You can't know what his motives were on a moment's acquaintance. He thought he could best me, as any healthy lad his age would."

"Did you not see the kindness in his eyes?" she queried pensively. "Can you not simply *feel* it from certain people?"

He laughed, a hollow sound that echoed back to him from the cobwebbed rafters. "Kindness is an emotion of convenience. It's one of many veneers of civilization that is feigned by the bestowers, applauded by observers, and endured by its receivers."

"Surely you don't mean that." Her voice was more sad than condemning.

"You believe in kindness, Miss Smith-Jones? Allow me to explain kindness as I have observed it."

The lad returned with two mugs, and Grant swallowed from his before continuing.

"Many years ago, when my father passed by my grandfather's farm on one of his frequent journeys, it was kindness which led my mother to bring the stranger a drink from the well. It was kindness that prompted my grandfather to shoe the earl's horse, then to extend the hospitality of his house when a three-day rain set in. I won't call it kindness that caused my mother to love my father, or kindness that led him to take advantage of that love. But when my birth resulted from that liaison and caused my mother's death, it was an act of what could be called *kindness* that caused my father to take me into his household. While my father has kept his distance, I cannot tell you how *kind* his wife has been to me through the years, nor her sons. I have been raised on kindness, Miss Smith-Jones. I have spent the majority of my days among the privileged of Society while being reminded on every hand that I cannot participate in it. You can imagine my gratitude for such beneficence, such all-encompassing *kindness*."

He drained the cup, hoping to calm his hammering heart. Not since his nursery days had he spoken of his old hurt, and he could not imagine why he had done so now.

"You are very bitter," commented his companion after a lengthy silence. He glanced at her solemn face and snorted. What had he expected—sympathy? And why should he want that from her?

"Where is that lad?" he complained. "I need more ale."

The serving-boy appeared shortly afterward, backing through the hinged kitchen door carrying a large platter with several plates balanced on top. Less thirsty than he was eager to fill the silence, Grant snapped his fingers. The lad saw his gesture, nodded, and hurriedly served all the dishes excepting the bread and cheese, which he straightaway brought them.

"Sorry, sir," he said breathlessly. " 'Tis always busy when the coach comes."

"That great lout holding up the wall over there should help you," Grant said.

The boy tittered, then whispered, "That's me uncle. He owns the place. Says I got to earn me wages."

"I'd say you're doing so. Bring us a pitcher, will you? Your uncle's brew is tolerable enough after a long ride."

The lad scurried off. Still stinging from his outburst, Grant did not look at his companion but watched the boy. To his consternation, the man behind the counter slapped the child and demanded he put wings to his feet. Grant felt the cruelty could not be borne, especially with fire still raging inside him.

"Say there," he called ringingly across the room, slowly rising to his feet. "If you want to knock a fellow around, try someone big enough to look you in the eye."

He heard Miss Smith-Jones's swiftly indrawn breath. Nearby, Mrs. Heath leaned toward Mr. Craven, who sat at an adjoining table, and whispered excitedly while watching Grant. They might look impressed, but the boy himself didn't look appreciative; he gazed wildly at the customers, then eased through the door.

The owner lifted his hands defenselessly, splaying his fingers and forcing a humorless series of chuckles. "Just keeping the lad on his toes, sir, to serve you better."

"You'd do well to help him, then, not strike him senseless."

The man shrugged. "I'm not one to argue with the customers." Sweeping the room with a narrow gaze, he asked, "Anyone need anything?"

Though his tone was challenging, a small lady sitting alone inquired bravely, "A cuppa tae?"

With a resentful flash for Grant, the innkeeper barreled through the kitchen door. Somewhat deflated, Grant sat. But when he lifted his glance to Miss Smith-Jones, he was surprised to see her observing him with sparkling approval.

"That was *kind* of you," she teased.

"It was not."

"Now you are being modest. So many virtues, Mr. Devlin."

"You are a child, Miss Smith-Jones. I was not being kind or modest; I merely vented my anger on Mr. Innkeeper."

"Call it what you will, but the results are the same."

"I've made a bad matter worse. How do you think the boy's uncle will treat him once we depart?"

"Oh." After a moment, she brightened again. "But that was not your intention. You *wanted* to do him a kindness."

She could not know the web of emotions she aroused in him. He tasted every unfamiliar one. The strongest flavor was guilt.

"How do you know what I want, Miss Smith-Jones?"

She busied herself with cutting a slice of cheese from the wedge. "You are a kind man, Mr. Devlin, no matter what you say. I have a way of knowing these things. In spite of the trick you played on the people at the inn, I recognized goodness in you at once. You have proved it all morning to me, at least." She made a childish face of distaste which would have amused him if he didn't feel so singed. "Except for that brief while in the carriage when you pretended to be my betrothed. But even that turned out to be kindness disguised—you were protecting my reputation, you said."

He could not let her go on any longer. She was trying to build him into a heroic character, and he was nothing of the sort. It made him angry that she would try. While he mustn't disclose the true reason he followed her, he could not let her spin halos from smoky imaginings.

"I'm not good, Miss Smith-Jones. I am a gambler by vocation."

She blinked, then offered him a slice of cheese. He took a large bite and chewed it thoroughly while keeping his gaze locked with hers.

"I had surmised that, Mr. Devlin. I suppose you must earn your living somehow. Probably there was no opportunity to learn a vocation; such things cannot be easy for earl's sons."

He reached for her untouched tankard, questioned her with a glance and, receiving permission, drank deeply.

"I'm shallow. My lifelong ambition has been to own an estate that equals my father's in size and wealth."

She did not hesitate a fraction. "With the deprivations and

insults you've received repeatedly, it's no wonder you have such a goal. I cannot fault you for that."

"Three months ago," he parried after taking a deep breath, "I won the estate of one of my father's oldest friends. Though Cappel's Landing is in desperate need of refurbishing, it's worth a fortune. I've saved almost enough to restore it, and when I've done so, I'll retire from cards and wagers."

"There, you see? The gambling life does not agree with you. You can hardly wait to be done with it."

His brows turned downward. "Unfortunately, losing the estate ruined Lord Tambry. He's had to move his household, including a wife and daughter, to his brother's house. According to rumor, His Lordship has taken to bed and is deathly ill."

At this, Miss Smith-Jones set her cheese sandwich on the dish. She did not look at him but seemed to be studying the pattern of roses in the chipped plate.

"Hm. You've nothing to say to that, have you?" When she persisted in keeping her lashes lowered, he grew more irritated. "Why is it you hope to find virtue in me, anyway? Perhaps it's the *missionary* in you. I suppose there are no hidden truths in *you,* no deceptions, no falsehoods, nothing to make an intolerable life easier. You, I imagine, are perfect."

"I am far from perfect," she said tonelessly.

The door to the inn opened, bringing with it a flash of sunlight. Grant turned a scowling face toward the entrance. Lord DuBarry and one of his men strode inside and began to scan the occupants of the common room.

Grant's blood ceased to flow in his veins. He could not think; but he must, and quickly. The viscount's gaze had not yet found their dark corner; there was still time. Grant slipped into the chair nearest Miss Smith-Jones, in effect hiding his face from his enemies. Loverlike, he circled one arm around her chair's back and leaned his other elbow on the table. She appeared quite surprised. No doubt she would be even more surprised in a moment.

"Kiss me," he whispered.

"Pardon?" She looked as if she could not decide whether to laugh or become offended. Reading the inexplicable urgency in his expression, she tried to edge backward. His grip on her chair tightened to steel. "You are mad!"

"Miss Smith-Jones. Those men over there are searching for me. The big one would like to string his boots with my hair. I need your help—your *kindness*. Please."

Her gaze flickered uncertainly toward the doorway. There was no more time. He grabbed her. Protesting lips moved angrily beneath his. She stiffened; he drew her closer.

"Ooh," trilled Mrs. Heath from somewhere far away. "Look, Mr. Craven. Did you ever kiss anyone in a tavern? Don't blush, now; I'll never tell!"

Releasing his companion's lips for an instant, he trailed tiny kisses to her ear, cooling them with his breath, punctuating them with nearly inaudible words. "Don't fight me. If you. Regard me. At all."

He heard her sigh as if in resignation. As she did so, her body relaxed. Hesitant fingers touched the hair at the nape of his neck. He hadn't expected this much cooperation, and his gratification gave birth to a sigh of his own. Her lips, stiff as wood a moment ago, became soft, yielding, mesmerizing; he could explore them forever. The dull light in the room faded to black. The tavern and its people were no more; the vengeful men waiting to tear the limbs from his body dissipated into bad dreams distantly recalled. His universe was here to be discovered in this passionate woman who returned his kisses with innocent abandon.

A heavy hand descended upon his shoulder. Reality intruded, crushing as the expression in Lord DuBarry's eyes. The viscount ripped Grant from the chair and sent him spinning to the floor.

"Hullo, Devlin," his Lordship clipped. "I bring you tidings from my wife."

Grant offered no resistance. Impressions were moving too quickly. His focus remained upon the lady who had entranced him with tender lips and a sweet, daring spirit. He forgave her for being a liar. Doubtless she had good reason. Perhaps her father beat her. How tragic that the viscount must appear and force the enchantment from her eyes. Now horror and bewilderment marred the perfection of her face.

Lord DuBarry planted a boot on his chest. "What, have you nothing to say in return? How disappointing. I'd heard you never lack for words. Where's that touted charm of yours now—buried in the same place you left your honor?"

"What honor, milord?" inquired his compatriot in a husky voice.

"Point taken, Maurice. A by-blow has no honor, not even when his father is as exceptional as this one's."

While Grant fought to sort his reeling senses, Maurice brought a swift kick to his side. Grant only partially deflected it with his arms. Pain bolted through his body, pounding every thought from his head except survival. He grasped the bottom of the viscount's boot and shoved, unbalancing DuBarry long enough for Grant to roll sideward, then climb to his knees. Maurice kicked him again, this time to the square of his back. Grant crashed against a chair and heard screams. He hoped they weren't his own. If he didn't get to his feet soon, he'd be mush. He ordered his body to move and watched his hand reach for the table as if it had all the time in the world.

"Here, take it outside, gents!" bellowed the tavern-owner. Good. Grant had not hoped to find help from that quarter, even though concern for his furniture motivated the man, not himself. The reason didn't matter, only the result. Hadn't Miss Smith-Jones/Rutland said something of the sort about kindness? He was finding none of that here. His mind was running like a babbling brook. He must focus. But every time he tried, the pain shattered—

"Take him outside we will," His Lordship said. "And there we'll finish it."

The pair pulled him roughly to his feet and began dragging him toward the door. Though Grant's head fell forward, he was not spared the sight of patrons rising, scraping back chairs, grinning, willing to follow this unexpected entertainment outside.

Marcy Stewart

Only his mysterious lady looked less than amused. Well, that was unfair; Mrs. Heath was shrieking like a banshee.

The sunlight struck his eyes as sharply as a blow. His assailants pitched him to the ground, jarring every bone. His cheek pressed against something hard; he raised himself slightly and saw he'd fallen against a rock. He forced himself to his knees in time to watch a handsome leather glove sail to the earth beside him.

"Name your weapon," Lord DuBarry said.

Grant's lips twitched ironically as he swayed. "Cards."

He saw the blow coming and shielded his head with crossed arms. But he was not struck after all. Miss Smith-Jones had somehow inserted herself between the two men.

"I don't know what Mr. Devlin has done to you or your wife, but what you are planning is inhuman! You cannot mean to offer a challenge after hurting him so—it would be murder!"

Although Grant heartily agreed, he could not allow her to endanger herself, nor could he tolerate the scathing way in which the viscount's glance raked her from head to toe. Mustering his strength, he struggled to his feet.

"Out of my way, woman," said his Lordship, and brushed her aside with enough force to cause her to stumble. Distinct rumblings could be heard from the onlookers.

"Don't dare touch her," Grant warned in a thin voice.

"How amusing of you to make demands after what you've done. Pistols or swords—what shall it be? Choose or I'll shoot you where you stand."

Through waves of pain, Grant squinted at DuBarry and tasted the loss of hope. The viscount was an expert at shooting and fencing, and Grant possessed no more than an average skill. Fighting had never interested him; charm had served him too well. And now his life was going to end here, at this little inn near an unknown village. Of what use had been his struggles, his goals? It had all been for nothing. His gaze moved to the terrorized face of Miss Smith-Jones, and he smiled at her sadly. Precisely when existence was at its most interesting, he was to be cut off. He wanted to rail at the heavens for the injustice of it. He had done nothing wrong, nothing. What idiocy to die for it!

"I never touched your wife," he ventured, knowing it was useless but loving life too much not to try. He kept his voice low to prevent the spectators from hearing. It would not serve to cross Lady DuBarry's word publicly. Miss Smith-Jones, who hovered nearby, did hear him, and she watched nervously.

"A coward as well," the viscount said. "I've no patience with your lies. Choose."

"I spent one afternoon teaching Margaret the rules of faro and hazard only. For this you want to kill me?"

Lord DuBarry moved threateningly close, so close Grant felt his breath on his cheeks. "My wife is skilled enough to run a gaming table were she so inclined," he said between his teeth.

"*Is* she?" whispered Grant, shock coursing through him. But why should he be surprised? If he were not so sore, he might laugh.

The viscount did not think it funny. "Dare you pretend ignorance? I warrant you'll also deny cheating my emeralds from her."

"I don't cheat."

The viscount's lips twisted. "Deny it, liar; now you are delighting me. Deny that you would take advantage of a man's wife when he was gone. Deny also that you offered her a chance to win my gift back in your bedroom last night. And when she appeared there, trusting in your gentlemanly behavior, deny that you attacked her as well. I want your soul blackened with lies when I send you to meet your Maker!"

Grant stared at him dismally. Margaret had covered every point, and if there were inconsistencies in her tale, the viscount was too besotted to see them.

"I choose pistols," he said after a moment, hoping a bullet would offer a less painful exit than the blade.

His Lordship smiled without humor and turned to Maurice,

who had watched their exchange with glowering scorn. "Pistols it shall be."

As Maurice hurried to fetch the weapons, Miss Smith-Jones stirred to life and again pushed her way between the two opponents, this time flinging her arms around Grant and resting her head on his chest, almost toppling him over in her earnestness. Although Grant was touched by the gesture, he knew it could do no good and might cause her harm. He stroked her cheek with the back of his hand, then began to draw her apart from him.

"No!" she cried loudly. "You must not protect me any longer, not at the cost of your life!"

He was too startled to know how to respond to this.

"Move your woman away," commanded Lord DuBarry. "I wonder that she tolerates your faithlessness."

Maurice had brought the pistol case and opened it; he now presented it to Mr. Devlin. Even as Grant reached past Miss Smith-Jones's frantic presence to select one of the lethal beauties, she dashed the case to the ground. The crowd, which had observed all with many ribald comments and suggestions characteristic of the lowest company, gasped at this effrontery. Furious, the viscount moved as if to strike her. Grant snatched her behind him, and just as swiftly, she scrambled back.

"He was with me!" she shouted. "He spent the entire night with me, only he is too much of a gentleman to say so!"

Except for a low cry of distress from Mrs. Heath, this declaration brought an ogling silence to their audience. When Grant drew breath to protest, she touched cool fingers to his lips. "No, my darling, you mustn't deny it. This man means to kill you for something you *cannot* have done."

He could not miss the tremulous question in her expression, fleeting as it was. *"No,* I did not," he whispered to reassure her. "But you mustn't do this." Even as he said the words, a ribbon of hope wound itself around his heart. But the icy eyes of Lord DuBarry loosened it.

"Stand aside, lightskirt," he ordered, "unless you mean to do your man's fighting for him. I'd not be surprised if that's what he intends."

Weakness notwithstanding, this was too much for Grant. With the smoothness of a dream, he swung Miss Smith-Jones from harm's way and shoved the viscount squarely in the chest. DuBarry staggered back. Face contorted with rage, the viscount rushed forward, his hands knotted into fists. Grant stood his ground and blocked his opponent's right, then sunk a blow to his abdomen that doubled him over. At this, Maurice rushed forward, but a blur of motion bounded from the crowd onto his back. It was the serving boy, Grant saw with amazement. The lad clung to Maurice's neck like a monkey gone mad, hammering blows upon the sides of the man's head and tweaking his ears. Maurice roared and peeled the boy's arms away, then tossed him backward to the ground. The lad yelled. The tavern-keeper launched forward then, the force of his weight bringing Maurice to the ground. Once landed, the stout host did not seem to know what to do with his captive, so he merely sat upon him while the other made desperate but futile attempts to release himself.

All of this Grant saw within instants while keeping the wheezing viscount to the forefront of his attention. When DuBarry straightened, saw the helpless state of his ally and the cheering wildness of the assembly, he paused, bent and retrieved a pistol from the ground, then leveled it at Grant.

"I've no intention of brawling. I've come to kill you, Devlin. I'll give you a ten-count to take your weapon; then I shall shoot. Ten."

"Have you not heard anything I said?" Miss Smith-Jones cried.

"Nine," said DuBarry.

"I told you he was with me last night!"

"Eight. And who are you? Some wench who will say anything to save the man she fancies at the moment. Seven."

Grant stepped toward the remaining weapon and lifted it slowly.

"Six."

"I am not just anyone," Miss Smith-Jones pled. "I am a lady, run away from home to marry the man she loves."

"Five. You, a lady? Devlin, I compliment you on finding your match. 'Tis hard to judge who is the greater pretender between you. Four."

She drew a deep breath. "My father is Sir Clyde Rutland, baronet and owner of Bridgewater Green in Kent, and I have run away from wedding the Viscount Morris Culpepper to—to marry this man who stands before you!"

In the act of raising his weapon, Grant paused. "No more," he breathed. She was ruining herself for him. How could she? Certainly the girl was an innocent, he admitted that to himself now, but she was far from mindless. She must know what she sacrificed, though perhaps the emotion of the moment had dislodged her senses. He could not let her do this.

"Three," said Lord DuBarry hesitantly. "Culpepper, you say? I heard his bride ran off the night the engagement was to be announced." He narrowed his eyes. "You probably heard that as well. Two."

"You said you were gone when your wife supposedly came to him," she argued. "Therefore you cannot have seen him. How can you be so certain I'm not telling the truth?"

The viscount gave her a direct look. "My wife saw him."

Grant stiffened, waiting for the final number. But Brittania had edged closer, and the viscount watched her uneasily.

"But *you* did not see him," she said with confidence. "*I* did. We spent the entire night together. Your wife must have him confused with someone else."

Enough, thought Grant. Miss Rutland's reputation was shattering to pieces before his eyes. "Don't listen to her. She's lying to protect me."

DuBarry's gaze shifted from Grant to Brittania. "I have his horse in my stable."

"How do you know it's his horse? Does it have his name on it?"

"You are no one. An impostor, and an impudent one at that."

Seemingly brimming with composure now, she tilted her head. "Am I? Do you know Culpepper, sir?"

"Vaguely," admitted the viscount.

"He is a stoutly built gentleman with bristly red hair that no comb can subdue."

"Anyone might know that."

"And there is a large growth on the back of his neck. I have not seen it of course, but among the servants he is known as Wart-hog."

This description caused Grant's pistol arm to give a great lurch, and even Lord DuBarry's lips spasmed.

"We called him the Mole at Eton," he said. His gaze moved consideringly between Grant and Brittania. The weapon lowered. "Perhaps my wife was mistaken." The words might have been ripped from him.

Grant also lowered his pistol, but he said, "No. Margaret did come to my room to retrieve her jewelry. Nothing more passed between us. When she heard you arrive, she tore her dress in fear of you. I have not set eyes upon Miss Rutland before this morning."

"You see how he tries to protect me," she said softly, linking her arm in his.

"Get up, Maurice," Lord DuBarry commanded after a moment. Stepping to his horse, the viscount paused to pass a stern look at Grant. "You had best honor your promise to this lady. She saved your life."

Grant gazed into the eyes of the woman leaning against him. Past the adoring look she feigned, he saw terror, and her body trembled like chaff before a gale. For no reason he could fathom, he recalled the sweetness of her lips. His heart began to race. He had not asked for this—neither her sacrifice nor her fetching ways that called him to forget his plans and consider new ones.

"I always honor my promises," he told the viscount coldly. *Especially the ones I've made to myself.*

* * *

Later that afternoon, again trapped within the confines of the mailcoach, Brittania swallowed the lump in her throat and centered her gaze on her folded hands. She had made several attempts at conversation with her companions, all of which failed miserably. Mrs. Heath kept her skirts carefully clear of Miss Rutland's, and no society lady could lay claim to a more chilling cut direct. After Brittania had commented for the second time on the fortuitousness of the weather for traveling, Mr. Craven surprised her by patting her knee with gruff understanding, and tears sprang to her eyes at the kindness; but even so, he would not speak with her.

The hardest rejection to endure was Mr. Devlin's. At the inn, he had brushed away her offers to tend his wounds and, after a few moments spent upstairs with washbowl and towel, he descended, declaring himself good as new. Although she noted how gingerly he moved, he accepted none of her sympathy. After the briefest expression of gratitude for her self-recriminating lies, he trailed her silently into the conveyance, leaned into the corner, stretched his legs as far as the opposite seat would allow, crossed his arms and pretended to sleep.

She told herself it did not matter that she had forfeited her good name for him, and he did not appreciate it. The important thing was that he had not been killed, and her reputation was gone anyway: the first blow struck when she ran away from home, the second soon to follow. None of that mattered anyhow.

She nodded with assurance, a nod that caught the sleepy gaze of Mr. Devlin. She had no sooner returned his glance than his shifted away. He did not want her to see him looking at her, she supposed. What was wrong with him? Did he think she would insist upon his wedding her, now that she had labeled herself a loose woman for his sake? If he knew the true reason for her journey, he would relax in an instant. But she could not tell him.

Why could she not tell him? she wondered suddenly. There

was no reason to maintain silence on the matter, not now, when her true name had been disclosed. There was nothing to fear among these people; no one here would try to bundle her back to her father. And if they did, if Mrs. Heath, for an example, decided to inform someone about her, what mattered it? She could always put forth her plans at another date. Which she would do if thwarted, of course. It was not as though she were having second thoughts and *wanted* to be stopped. The very idea made her chuckle.

Thus she felt free now to speak. But given Mr. Devlin's present silence, he had no interest in her life, nor did anyone else for that matter. Or did he? Did they? There was only one way to know.

"I am running away to be married," she announced baldly.

Mrs. Heath sniffed without looking at her. "So you hope. The bull's tasted the milk now, and the chickens are into the corn. You know what comes of that."

Brittania frowned, then continued, "I don't mean I intend to marry Mr. Devlin. Today is the first day I ever saw him, as I told you before. Will you not admit it now, sir, or will you persist in letting these good people think ill of me?"

Grant no longer appeared playful as he had that morning, and he waved a hand carelessly. "She speaks truth. We don't know each other at all."

Mrs. Heath looked justifiably confused. For the first time in an hour, she met Brittania's gaze. "But—what about what you said to that lord?"

"That was only to save Mr. Devlin," Brittania said.

"Yet I saw you kissing him!"

"I asked her to do that to escape the viscount's notice," Grant said. "You saw how well it worked."

Brittania sent him a beaming smile for this effort, but he closed his eyes again. She felt as if she had been slapped.

"Cornucopia!" cried the older woman, all hauteur falling away. "Then you are still a good girl?"

"I have always tried to be," Brittania replied, knowing her parents would scream if they heard her.

"I knew it all along! But oh, lud, what will your mamma say when she finds out what you've done? Don't you know how people gossip?"

"It doesn't matter. I'm going to be married and live in Australia, or possibly America, where people don't trouble themselves over such trifles."

Mr. Devlin's eyes opened, and he made a noise of disbelief.

"What, do you think they will care who my father is on the frontier?" the young lady challenged.

"I think you're either spinning fairy tales or have no sense at all. First a missionary, then a pioneer bride. Who is the real Brittania Rutland, I wonder?"

A sudden stillness crept over her. "How did you know my name?" she asked quietly.

His eyes widened. "You told us. Don't you remember?"

"I spoke my father's name, but not mine."

"Oh, yes you did," he said with a small laugh. "How could I have known it otherwise?"

"I don't know, but I very carefully did not say *Brittania*. I did not want anyone hearing my Christian name because I don't like it."

"Why not?" asked Mrs. Heath.

"It makes me sound like a country, even if it is our own dear one. No one is named Belgium or Austria."

After an instant's pause, Mr. Devlin said, "And what of Frances and Americus?"

Apparently he would argue about anything. Or mayhap he only wished to distract her. She narrowed her eyes.

"I'm still certain I did not say my given name."

Mr. Craven had looked alert for some moments, and now he seized his opportunity. "I didn't hear ye say no Brittania, miss. Would've remembered that."

The color in Mr. Devlin's cheeks deepened. "I'm sure you said it. You must have."

Mrs. Heath clucked her tongue. "What does it matter, children? Talk of something else. I want to know who Miss Rutland's marrying, I do."

Brittania was not sure why it concerned her so much, but she was certain Mr. Devlin was lying again. Reluctantly, she moved her gaze from Grant to the older lady.

"My intended is called Seth Turner, and we are running away to Gretna Green."

Grant's lips curled. "How very pedestrian of you. I confess I liked the sound of Bao-Bao better. At least it was unique."

Irritated beyond measure, she replied, "Pray forgive me, Mr. Devlin, but I am not in the habit of arranging my life for your entertainment."

"You consider this escapade to be arranging your life? Destroying it would be more apt."

"Fortunately, I do not wait upon your opinion for my actions; and if my intended could hear you just now, I don't like to think what he would do."

"You frighten me, Miss Rutland. Your *intended* must be a staunch defender of yourself, especially considering how he has allowed you to proceed to your destination alone."

"Well, we thought it safer to travel separately," Brittania said defensively. This was not exactly true; *Seth* had thought it safer, and the subject had been a thorn between them for weeks. Being on her own had not seemed quite the thing to *her,* but he had been right about the costume—no one had bothered her; indeed, most had avoided her quite nicely, once they thought she was a missionary.

"And why should you both consider that safer, I wonder?" Grant questioned.

"My father does not approve of Seth."

"That I can guess, since you were promised to a viscount when you ran away." Grant showed his teeth in a tight smile. "You *do* remember telling everyone *that,* I hope."

"Of course I do." His air of superiority was annoying in the extreme.

"My head's a-ringin'," cried Mr. Craven, stuffing a finger in each ear. "Give over, do, ye pair o' magpies."

Grant appeared not to notice his interruption. "But here you are, a defenseless young woman traveling alone. I find it astonishing this Turner person allows it. I should not have permitted you to do so, not in a million years."

"Wouldn't you?" Warmth flowed through her, tinged with more than a little pique at Seth.

"Nor would any gentleman I know," Grant added hastily, as if fearful of giving her ideas. "Not even my brothers."

"Well, that is the dilemma, you see. Seth is not a gentleman. He was our gardener before Papa caught him kissing me and gave him the sack."

At this remark, Mr. Devlin gave her a look of such incredulous scorn that she rapidly glanced away. She found no approval in Mrs. Heath's eyes, either, nor Mr. Craven's. Brittania swallowed somberly and turned to the window.

"Headstrong, you must be," Mrs. Heath pronounced.

"Are you out of your mind?" Mr. Devlin said angrily, at the same moment.

Brittania thought her heart would burst from the injustice of his condemnation—and Mrs. Heath's, too, of course. "Of all people in this world, Mr. Devlin, I thought you would understand."

Her comment seemed to enrage him further. "You mean because I'm an earl's bastard?"

"Hie!" burst Mr. Craven. "If the carriage would stop, I'd gets meself off, I would."

"Mr. Craven, poor dear," sympathized Mrs. Heath. "You're used to quiet, as I am. A peaceful woman, 'tis how everyone describes me in Tunnelly Wells. You could hear a gnat land in me house, I tell you."

Oblivious to the older passengers, Brittania heard only the pain in Mr. Devlin's voice. "I meant no offense. It is only that I know you have felt society's injustice. It is no fault of Seth's that he was not born privileged."

Mr. Devlin did not seem at all appeased. "How good of you to be so egalitarian."

Evidently Mrs. Heath could not hide her interest in the conversation any longer, not even for Mr. Craven. "Now that I think on it, 'tis all very romantic. Mr. Turner must be a prize for you to give up all for him."

"He *is* quite marvelous," Brittania said dreamily, visualizing his windswept blond hair and the muscles that stretched his shirt in the most distracting way. Aware of Mr. Devlin's undivided, though disapproving attention, she continued with pleasurable slowness, "But I don't know that I'm giving up *everything*. Several months ago, when Papa first became aware that Seth and I loved each other, he threatened to cut me off. But when I reach twenty-five years, I have an inheritance coming from my maiden aunt; Papa cannot touch that."

"Twenty-five," Grant said. "And when will that be? Judging from the maturity of your decisions, I'd guess at least a decade."

"I am one-and-twenty," she returned in offended tones.

Grant laughed. "Four years away. And what will Mr. Marvelous do in the meantime—pitch hay and muck stables, while you scrub laundry in the river? Forgive me if my mind balks at the image."

This was too close to the mark for comfort. "No one is asking you to think about my future marriage, Mr. Devlin. Obviously you have no patience for anyone's thoughts but your own, and I can see no point in continuing this conversation any longer."

"You relieve me," he snapped.

"It is my great pleasure to do so."

His mouth, his beautifully curved mouth that she had kissed only hours ago, turned downward in a sneer. "How gracious you are."

"I endeavor to be so, even when others are not."

Although his expression spoke volumes, Mr. Devlin said nothing to this. He crossed his arms and closed his eyes, as if overcome with sudden sleep.

Eyebrows arched, Mrs. Heath pressed her lips together and

gazed meaningfully at Mr. Craven. For the first time in twenty years, the farmer winked.

Dusk had fallen by the time the mail coach pulled into the courtyard of a large inn outside Manchester. The passengers alighted and walked toward the inviting, half-timbered building with all the eagerness stiff muscles would allow. Brittania approached more slowly, watching Mr. Devlin's back with disfavor. Apparently empty pockets did not disturb him. No doubt he was in a hurry to win more shillings from the unsuspecting.

There had been no opportunity for continuing her conversation with him had she wished to do so, which she did not; although it would have been uplifting to have him admit he was wrong, that she wasn't being childish in running away to be married. But a Mrs. Sanforth and her two young children had joined the coach some hours past; and while Mr. Craven had fallen into loud snores almost instantly, Mrs. Heath and Brittania had spent their afternoon trying to appease the youngsters, in particular the squawling infant. Mr. Devlin was kept occupied by the toddler, a chubby little girl with dirty fingers who insisted on climbing into his lap, a thing he tried mightily to discourage. He had finally given up and fallen asleep soon after the child did, his head nodding against hers at every bump. Brittania had not been able to keep her eyes from the sight.

She paused now to watch the reunion of Mrs. Sanforth and her husband, who had driven a wagon to meet his family. As Mr. Sanford accepted the embrace of his older child, Brittania's gaze shifted to the light-filled windows of the inn. Mr. Devlin had not yet entered, nor had Mrs. Heath. They both appeared to be awaiting her. Brittania moved forward feeling oddly reluctant, yet intense. Perhaps it was the coolness of the early spring air or the faint scent of wildflowers from a nearby field, but something was causing the tips of her fingers to tremble with anticipation, as if her life was about to take a wild and unexpected turn.

Foolishness, all of it.

"I have remembered you are without funds for a room tonight," Mr. Devlin said when she reached him.

"You needn't trouble yourself," she told him. "I'm not your responsibility."

"I'm well aware of that. But someone must help you or God knows what will happen."

"Oh?" Her temples began to throb. "How odd that you should think so. I wonder that I did so well before meeting you."

"Doing well, were you? Then who was that starving beggar I met this morning?"

At this, Mrs. Heath cackled. "Children, children!"

Brittania was not distracted. "And I suppose you are doing better? What would you have done had I not lied for you today?"

"It's not necessary to remind me I'm in your debt," he said, his face flushing. "That's why I wanted to offer you supper and a room."

"Saints above!" declared Mrs. Heath. "What would her ma—"

"I meant her own room," Mr. Devlin explained rapidly.

"Thank you, but no," Brittania said, her blush beginning to fade. "You may have no luck at your gambling tonight. I'll stay with Mrs. Heath, if she'll have me."

"That's what I meant to suggest," the older lady said. "Though what you'll do tomorrow, I've no idea, I'm sure. Mr. Craven and I are pausing in our journeys to visit a cotton mill his nephew owns in Manchester. We arranged it at the last stop." Mrs. Heath grinned wolfishly. "It's the first of many such pauses if I has me way, youngsters. He's a widower, don't you know. You're not the only ones to find romance on a coach."

Both Grant and Brittania rapidly decried finding any such thing, much to the hilarity of Mrs. Heath, who insisted they go inside and join her and Mr. Craven.

Being penniless, Brittania felt she had little choice in the matter. Once again she mourned the necessity of leaving home in the middle of the night with only the remains of her month's allowance. It would have been so easy to save had she known how much would be needed; but having never spent her own money for meals and lodging before, she had woefully underestimated all.

As she entered the brightly lit interior, a nagging thought pushed itself into the forefront of her mind. From henceforth on, she would be counting her shillings. But love would cheer her, she comforted herself. Yet the worry persisted.

A noisy and convivial crowd filled the spacious tavern. A pretty serving-maid explained there were no private dining rooms available due to a large wedding party, then led them to a table near the center of the room. Brittania fought her way through a gamut of merriment. The tables were spaced extremely close, and from the sound and scent of things, the ale was flowing too freely. Revelers, both male and female, stared boldly at them as they passed. A giddy woman, lost in the telling of a story, flung her arms wide and slapped Brittania's middle, then looked annoyed as if it had been the young lady's fault. Brittania was seized by a sudden, unexpected nostalgia for her quiet sitting room with its tiny fireplace and firescreen embroidered by her own mother's hand.

They placed their orders. Mr. Devlin's gaze moved restlessly, then stilled. Brittania looked to see what had caught his attention. Of course, she should have known; a group of men were playing cards a few tables over—a little island of quiet amid a sea of noise. Mr. Devlin did not wait for his plate of beef to arrive. Asking them to tell the serving-maid he had moved, he made his way to the card table and was soon seated.

Why this was so disappointing, Brittania could not say. She was not even cheered by the arrival of a platter of roasted fowl and parsnips, a generous offering on the part of Mrs. Heath. While that good lady chattered loudly with Mr. Craven, Brittania chewed moodily and glanced often in Mr. Devlin's direction. He did not once look at her, and she found his abandonment disturbing. It was not that he owed her anything, but she had rather grown used to him after this long day, and it seemed he should be more considerate.

Halfway through their meal, a small group of musicians arrived and set up near the back wall. At the first sound of strings, a cheer arose, and several men rushed to push tables aside for dancing. Brittania and her companions soon found themselves on the perimeter of an impromptu dance floor that extended into the lobby. Immediately, well-dressed, boisterous couples jumped to their feet and began the steps of the gigue. The scarcity of space caused many collisions, which prompted even more hilarity. Ordinarily, the spectacle would have brought sympathetic laughter to Brittania, but she felt woefully apart and continued to eat solemnly, even over the rhythmic clapping of Mrs. Heath and foot-stomping of Mr. Craven.

Finally, even those two succumbed and joined the dance. Brittania placed her fork on the edge of her plate and stared fixedly at Mr. Devlin. He still appeared absorbed in his game, yet as she drilled him with her eyes, he did at last glance up. Instantly, he looked down, then back again, this time holding her gaze. The expression in his eyes grew more forceful. Her heart seemed to suspend its beating.

" 'Scuse me, miss," said a voice nearby. "My name is Andrew Cartegger. Would you care to dance?"

With reluctance she tore her gaze from Mr. Devlin's and saw a young man observing her with a beseeching look. He had a pleasant face and was dressed in a well-tailored tan jacket and black trousers. Still in a fog, Brittania returned her glance to Mr. Devlin, but that gentleman looked to be reabsorbed in his game. A flare of indignation brought her to her feet.

"I should be pleased," she said. "Only allow me to remove this bonnet, will you? My head is aching." She could not restrain her sigh of relief when the ugly, tight hat was gone, though she shuddered to think how mashed her hair must look. "You may call me . . . Miss Smith-Jones." There seemed no reason to spread her name further. Papa might be after her.

Mr. Cartegger expressed his delight in meeting her, then

swung her into the dance. He began to explain that he was present for the wedding of his cousin, the son of a manufacturer in Manchester, on the morrow. He appeared to be a straightforward young man, quite entertaining in the times she attended him between glances at Mr. Devlin, who satisfied her by returning those looks more and more.

Before many bouncing steps had passed, she felt a tendril of hair loosening, then saw it fall across her right shoulder. How irritating it was. Unless done by the most expert hand, her hair was too heavy to be contained by pins. Before long, another curl in back snaked past her collar. She must look the most dreadful fright. One of the other ladies was wearing her hair loose, she noticed; well, the lady was somewhat younger than herself and might be considered a girl, but perhaps no one in this rowdy crowd would condemn her for yanking free the last of the pins and shaking out her hair. It felt so *good*.

Her dancing partner had observed this transition with polite restraint, but now his eyes glowed quite alarmingly. "Ecod," he breathed. "Your hair . . ."

"Have I embarrassed you?" she worried. "It's a tangle, I know, but you cannot believe how it was killing me."

" 'Tis so long," he continued as if he didn't hear.

"Mamma doesn't like me to cut it," she explained.

"And those curls," he breathed.

"I know. It is a trial; the waves will not obey me."

"I have never seen anything so glorious in all my life."

"Oh. Well, thank you. But you really mustn't touch it, you know; I don't—"

Mr. Devlin brushed past her then and sided Mr. Cartegger. "I'll step in now, if the lady will allow," he said in tones which brooked no argument.

"Now see here, sir—"

"No, it's all right," Brittania said swiftly. "Mr. Devlin is my— escort."

"I see. I wish you had told me," said Mr. Cartegger, who bowed in disappointment and turned away.

The gigue ended then, and a waltz began. With mischief brewing in her eyes, Brittania waited. His cheeks darkening, Mr. Devlin's gaze ran along her face and the riot of waves framing it. When he embraced her for the dance, he jerked her alarmingly close. She could feel her heart hammering against his chest.

"Thank you for rescuing me," she said, her lips almost touching his shoulder. In a voice of exaggerated regret she added, "But I have caused you to leave your cards."

"Hush, impertinent child," he commanded.

She obeyed. When he brought her even closer, she did not object but closed her eyes. With a distant part of her brain, she noted the amateurish performance of the musicians, but even missed harmonies could not distract from the music she felt in the body moving against hers. She became so lost in sensation that only belatedly did she realize the masterful way in which she was being twirled from the common-room into the lobby and then outside. They were not the only couple to do so. The inn door now stood open, and several were whirling along the pavement and grass, while others made for darker areas of the courtyard for more intimate embraces. Mr. Devlin danced her toward a distant oak, seemingly intent upon privacy. Telling herself she could hardly object before learning what he wanted, she permitted him to back her against the tree.

"Do you know what you looked like in there?" he demanded heatedly.

Her lips tightened. "I suppose you are going to tell me."

"Yes, I am. No self-respecting female wears her hair down like this." He lifted a strand of her hair in demonstration, then released it in obvious distaste. "Only little girls and Cyprians. You should know that."

Angrily, she combed her fingers through her hair. "I'll tell you what I know, Mr. Devlin. You are hardly one to be instructing *me* on behavior."

"There, she's off again!" he told the oak, then tidied another wayward curl behind her ear. "The little saint, frowning on a

Marcy Stewart

man for his vocation, when she'd best watch her own actions. Did you see how that devil in there looked at you? He wanted to ravish you on the spot! And *you,* letting him touch your hair when you'd known him only seconds—"

"I did not notice *him* touching it so much as I notice *you* doing so," she said reasonably.

Caught in the act of smoothing yet another wild strand, he hesitated. The green of his eyes darkened, bringing to mind a storm-ridden sea. The noises of the night, the snatches of music drifting on the wind, faded.

She could not breathe.

Slowly he brought his other hand to her hair and stroked backwards. Threading his fingers through her curls, he snatched her to him in a kiss that stole the strength from her legs.

When he broke away, he pressed his cheek against hers, his breath coming in ragged patches that tickled her skin and delighted her soul.

What was wrong with her? She shouldn't be doing this, allowing a man almost a stranger to kiss her beneath the moon. Most of all, she shouldn't be rejoicing in his embrace with a depth of feeling she had never known before, not even with Seth, whose salty, wet kisses had once thrilled her. But now it seemed that thrill had been the threat of discovery, the excitement of defying parents whose rules had chafed since childhood.

She had promised to marry Seth, she reminded herself. Poor, forbidden Seth, whose face she could no longer recall. She closed her eyes briefly as she pressed her cheek more closely to Mr. Devlin's, loving the rough feel of his day-long growth of beard against her smooth skin. She could remain thus forever.

The thought frightened her. It meant only one thing. Her mother had repeatedly promised that when Brittania truly fell in love, she would know. That promise was part of the reason she had fled from wedding Morris, whom her father had chosen in a fit of impatience to be rid of her.

She had thought Seth offered a safe refuge from boredom;

at least he did not disgust her physically as the viscount did. But now, warm in the arms of an illegitimate ne'er-do-well, she acknowledged that love had found her at last. And the object of her love was the antithesis of everything she believed in; for underneath her rebellious exterior beat a most conservative heart.

As her thoughts raced, Grant kissed her again, seizing her so tightly to himself that she felt almost a part of him. He was not such a bad man, she assured herself. She could name countless good qualities: he liked children; he was protective of her; his nature was generous most of the time. If he did earn his living by gambling, necessity had made him do so. There were worse things in a man.

To her regret, his hold on her loosened. She could sense him searching for words. Did he mean to declare himself so soon? No one would do such a thing after knowing someone only a day, would they? Perhaps Mr. Devlin felt he must move quickly, because of Seth.

And so he should. He could not know that tomorrow was her designated day to meet the ex-gardener. And what would she answer, should this irritating, enticing man ask her that most compelling of questions? She must have more time to think; she couldn't—

"Don't marry the gardener," he murmured into her hair. "Let me take you home tomorrow."

The sudden peak in her emotions plummeted. "Take me home, Mr. Devlin? To what? An angry father who will do his best to mend things with the viscount so he can, in his own words, 'spend his declining years in daughterless peace'?"

To her rage, he laughed. "I can sympathize with his feelings."

"Oh, can you? Your actions a moment ago bear no witness to your words."

He put his hands to her cheeks and kissed her briefly, maddeningly. Even that little peck made her heart spasm, but she shook her head carelessly to demonstrate her distaste. This seemed to amuse him further.

"I wonder that your activities have not sent your father to his grave already. Listen now to reason, and allow me to help you escape the greatest mistake of your life."

"Allow you to—oh, you cannot imagine how furious you make me. Should I change my mind about marrying Seth, I wouldn't need *your* help."

"Then you are reconsidering? If I've been in the least instrumental in that—" and here he paused to trace a finger from her temple to her chin "—then I suggest I can be of even more use in assuring a safe journey home."

"Are you saying—you mean that you kissed me in order to—oh, I cannot believe you would stoop so low!"

He appeared surprised. "Why, Miss Rutland! I trust you didn't put more importance to the past few moments than was intended. Warm wine, a little bad music, a crescent moon— combine that with a day caged in a coach, and what do you expect? Any fool would succumb to the urges of spring."

"The urges of—but I thought you—" She stopped, feeling tears bubbling to the surface. She must not weep; she could not give him the satisfaction. "I thought you were a good man, but you are a monster," she whispered.

"I won't quarrel with you there," he said, his eyes suddenly coming over solemn. "I tried to tell you earlier today what I am like, but you'd have none of it. But if I am a monster, that gardener is even worse. You don't love him; your kisses tell me you don't. Go home, Brittania. Don't do something that will ruin your life forever."

She could listen no more. She squeezed past him and ran toward the inn. Dancers still spun in the lobby and the tavern room, and, half-blinded with unshed tears, she wound her way among them, searching desperately for Mrs. Heath. Finally she found the older woman at their table, sipping ale with Mr. Craven and another couple. Seeing Brittania's distress, Mrs. Heath half-rose to accompany her, but the young lady would not allow it. Attaining the number of their room, Brittania murmured apologies for her tiredness and retreated.

She was again forced to find a path through the dancers, and it seemed they deliberately blocked her at every turn. Eventually she reached the hall, but a red-faced, panting couple was resting on the bottom tread of the stairs. As the man groaned and used the rail to help himself rise, she noted something at the edge of her vision: a poster hanging behind the desk. She turned to stare at the lithograph with disbelief. *Brittania Rutland,* it said in bold letters, along with her physical description. *Reward: Five thousand pounds.*

Papa, she thought. *Oh, Papa.*

Heat spread downward through her body. She turned slowly, half expecting every eye to be fixed upon her in accusation and avarice. But no one noticed her, no one excepting Mr. Devlin, who was only now entering the inn. *He* was watching her, his frame taut and still in the doorway, his gaze riveted to hers as she glanced from the lithograph to him. He, too, looked at the notice, and there was no surprise in his expression, only comprehension, and perhaps a dollop of shame.

No wonder he'd begged her to go home. How secretly pleased she had been that he had offered to accompany her. Even when he spurned her affection moments ago, she had still thought him generous to offer that.

There should be more shame in his eyes. There should be more.

You knew, she mouthed, and saw no denial in him. Before another heartbeat passed, she raced between the protesting couple and pounded up the stairs.

"Brittania!" he called, but she did not pause until she reached her room and locked the door. He did not follow her, and it was good he did not. She rested her burning cheek against the cool door and thought, *I would not have answered him if he did.*

The night brought little sleep for Grant. Tortured by images of Brittania's face, he turned restlessly on one of the inn's best beds, rented by a night's good winnings. He had shattered her faith in him at last, but it brought him no relief. The soreness in his muscles from yesterday's thrashing was nothing compared to the ache in his soul.

An hour or so before dawn, he dressed and descended painfully to the tavern room, nodding past the innkeeper who was adding figures in a ledger at his desk in the lobby. A sleepy serving-girl brought Grant coffee and bread which he consumed by the hearth, well away from the other early-risers, mostly servants, who broke the morning's stillness with hoarse chatter.

Observing them with scowling disinterest, he tried but failed to throw off his restlessness and indecision. He must return Brittania home. There was no use going on with this charade, not now that she knew his purpose. Surely after a night's sleep she would see reason. Surely she would not make him use force. And if she did, if she still insisted on wedding the gardener, *could* he make her return to her father against her will?

He could not imagine it. Yet he couldn't allow her to destroy her life. He rested his elbow on the table and closed his eyes, tapping his fist against his forehead. What jest of fate had been responsible for this impasse? Yesterday morning at this time, he had only Lord DuBarry and the possibility of death to fear. How could the addition of one beautiful, impetuous stranger complicate life so?

Behind closed lids, he distantly noted a clatter on the stair and opened his eyes upon a berobed Mrs. Heath, her grey locks straggling loose from her nightcap, hastening toward him. Alarm clanged him to his feet.

"Mr. Devlin, Mr. Devlin! Thank God you are here! She is gone—Miss Rutland has run off during the night! Here is her note—you see she says she was to meet her beloved, her *beloved*, mind you, though Mr. Craven and I thought she had an eye for you, since no two young people can quarrel so well lest they care bricks for onest another; but something happened between you, didn't it? She was asleep when I got to bed, or so I thought, so I couldn't ask—"

"Thank you, Mrs. Heath," he said, knowing there would be no end to her questions. Crumpling the note in his fist, he surprised her by kissing her cheek before racing to the innkeeper. Demanding the hire of a horse, he overpaid him, fearing the time it would take to haggle. Mrs. Heath hovered nearby, then begged him to let her know what happened.

"You can always reach me at Tunnelly Wells!" she called as he fired up the stairs to fetch his belongings.

Setting off moments later, Grant's spirits were hopeful. The inn's sorrel was stalwart, if not fast, and biddable to the extreme. Moreover, the girl who had served him breakfast remembered seeing a young lady leave the inn at the beginning of her shift. Brittania could have no more than two hours' start on him. Her note had given a destination, too: five miles north of Manchester, at the branching of the road past a large farmhouse.

The inclusion of her direction was the most cheering prospect of all; she must have known he would see the note. Grant took it to mean she wanted him to stop her. His lips curved upward. She was half-child and half-woman, and one-hundred-percent trouble.

Unless, of course, she meant to deliberately mislead him. If so, he would never find her. His anxiety increased again, and he urged the steed faster.

Past Manchester, he began to despair. He should have found her by now, were she on foot, and she must be; she'd had no funds to hire a horse. Perhaps Brittania had found a ride, though. Pray God it was some upright farmer she'd asked, and not a libertine with an eye for an innocent lass. She could be lying in a ditch at this very moment. He swore at the thought and applied his whip to the horse's flanks.

The moments slipped past, then an hour and more. The sun was out in force, half-blinding him when the north road snaked eastward. He was certain he'd gone more than five miles beyond the city now; perhaps ten or fifteen. She had lied in the note. There was no farmhouse, no branching of the road. He had been tricked. Her feelings ran no deeper than any woman's. He'd been a fool to think she was different.

The thought had no sooner crept into his brain than he saw the road fork and, to the right of the juncture the farmhouse, a well-kept structure with a thatched roof and several outbuildings. He contemplated it, wondering if Brittania watched him from one of the windows even at that moment. Yet she had not said she was to meet the gardener here, but at the road's branching. Nevertheless, he turned the horse down the dirt lane leading to the house.

A young lass, no more than fifteen, he guessed, emerged as he approached. She was thin with wispy blond locks, but her dress was clean and her apron starched. Blinking repeatedly as she watched him, her deep blue eyes were as startling as a bird's wing flickering color.

"Saw a young lady not more than twenty minutes ago," she said in answer to his question. "Old Johnny give her a ride on his wagon and set her down a bit over there. Road narrows quick, and no wagon can turn 'round without going all the way to its ending. Thought it a strange place for her to go, I did. Nothing but an old crumbly lodge down it."

Mumbling his thanks, he urged his horse up the drive, then down the right fork. Within moments, he saw the girl had not misled him about the road. Wild-growing trees crowded both sides, at some places meeting overhead like a natural arch. Roots ruffled the surface of the pavement which soon dwindled to gravel, then deeply rutted dirt. The panting beast he rode stepped gingerly where led, but Grant realized it would only be moments before the poor creature twisted a leg. Sighing, he dismounted and tied the reins to a scraggly beech.

He groaned a little, working out his stiffness as he walked. When this was over, he promised himself a long soak in a hot bath and three days in bed. He laughed suddenly, surprised to feel a surge of fear. When this was over? It would never be over. No matter how the next moments resolved, his life would never be the same, thanks to one dusky-haired wildcat. He could not wait to get his hands on her again. He truly could not wait.

His pulse accelerated, remembering the deep pleasure of her lips. That she might now be pressing that sweet mouth to a conniving gardener's nearly left him breathless with rage.

Rounding the next bend, his heart leapt as he saw her. In the distance was the lodge the girl had told him about, and running toward Brittania was a tall, fair man with the look of a Viking about him. Grant frowned as he slipped beside a tree to watch.

So this was the kind of man she called *beloved.* He could not see the attraction himself, unless a woman were gullible enough to be enraptured by the chest of a giant and arms like tree trunks. And now the beast had the audacity to envelop her in an embrace that lifted her from the ground like a rag doll. That she seemed not as enthusiastic as the gardener did little to soothe Grant's feelings.

Brittania began to speak. The giant did not appear pleased by her words. And what was this? From the yawning doorway of the lodge, a woman came toward them. Her cotton blouse scooped low over full breasts, and her dark skirt showed little flashes of ankle as she walked, no *sauntered,* toward the couple. There was an arrogance to her approach that caused an immediate stiffness in Brittania's posture.

What goes on? he wondered, beginning to smile at this new intrigue. Brittania was not happy; even at a distance he could see that. When the Viking began pulling her toward the lodge, she balked. The woman clasped her other arm and tugged. Brittania jerked free and received a slap from the female for her effort.

Grant needed no further urging. Keeping in the shadow of the trees, he moved swiftly toward them. The Viking and gypsy were intent upon getting Brittania inside the house and paid him no notice. He was almost upon them when he heard a rustling to his left. Before he could turn halfway, something heavy descended upon the back of his neck, and he fell into blackness.

* * *

He lay at the bottom of a deep well. Sounds came and went, hollow echoing noises that bounced painfully through his head. Flashes of light broke the darkness occasionally, but nothing recognizable. He didn't mind; he had no desire to see anything that might require action on his part. But gradually he became aware of a soft noise, often repeated, that beckoned him to reluctant, crushing awareness.

"Mr. Devlin, please," begged Brittania's quavering voice. "Wake up. You must."

He groaned and opened his eyes. He could see nothing. "I'm blind," he said, his voice cracking with dryness and dismay.

"No, you are not. It is nighttime," Brittania's relieved whisper told him. "You've been unconscious since this morning. Thank God you are all right."

"Nighttime?" He tried to move. Pain radiated from his head downward. He closed his eyes briefly and clenched his teeth. "I can't move!"

"Hush!" she whispered heavily. "Of course you cannot move; you are tied hand and foot as I am." In a less irritated voice she continued, "We must be quiet or we'll wake them."

Memory stirred, bringing with it full consciousness. He was lying on a rough floor, splinters scratching his cheek. Earthy scents pricked his nose; the lodge had given shelter to more birds and animals than humans in recent years. As his eyes adjusted, the blackness was not so intense as before. He began to make out shapes: a window, a table, the half-open door, a dying fire in the yard beyond it. Brittania's voice had come from somewhere behind his head. Carefully, painfully, he inched his way around until he could see her. She loomed over him, bound to a chair. There was just sufficient light to see the flash of her angry eyes.

"Where are they?" he asked quietly.

"Outside the door by the fire, where it is warm," she replied with resentment. "The fireplace in here is blocked, Seth said, or he would have laid a fire for us."

"How considerate of him."

She paused the length of two heartbeats. "You needn't take that tone with me. No one asked you to follow."

"No? Why did you leave such explicit directions, then?"

"I left the note for Mrs. Heath, so she wouldn't worry."

"But you knew she would give it to me."

"I don't know anything about anyone," she said, her voice catching. "Except that—you—I mean, *people*, are interested only in my for—fortune."

The sudden ache in his chest overshadowed that of his head. "Don't cry, Britt. We have to keep our wits about us so that we can escape. Tell me what has been happening."

A taut silence followed. "I don't think I can. You will say you tried to warn me but I wouldn't listen."

"No, I won't. I myself have been a fool too many times to accuse someone else of it."

She paused again. "I think you have just done so, but I don't care anymore." She cleared her throat. "Seth never intended to marry me. It was all a ruse to hold me for ransom. He and his brother Claude planned it from the beginning."

"His brother?" That would account for the headache. "And the woman?"

"Talba?" The scorn in her voice would have made him laugh were he in less straitened circumstances. "She is Claude's . . . companion."

"So there are three in all?"

"Two at this moment. As soon as I delivered myself into their hands, Claude went to demand the ransom from Papa. Ten thousand pounds, in case you are wondering. Twice what you hoped to receive for me."

He could not bear the shame in her voice. "Britt . . . don't."

"Don't what? I am only speaking the truth."

He swallowed. "I won't insult you by denying the reward

prompted me to follow you at first. But that was before I knew you."

"And now that you do? Had you succeeded in taking me home, am I to believe you wouldn't have accepted the five thousand?"

Seconds spun away into silence.

"I thought not," she said in dismal tones.

"No, I was thinking," he objected.

"I believe I have your answer, if you must think so long."

"Wait a moment, be fair. I had plans. Lord Tambry's estate—"

"I am sick to death of hearing about that poor, ruined man."

"—but no, I would not have taken the money," he finished, and was shocked to know it was true. "I had rather have your good opinion."

"Oh, truly?" she challenged. "And why should you care about that?"

"Because I love you, impossible child!" he whispered heatedly, the words tearing from him like pages off his soul. He heard them with horror, but it was a horror soon dissolved by release. For the first time in memory, he felt happy.

After a moment, she said thinly, "You expect me to believe that?"

"If I were not trussed like a chicken, beautiful lady, I would convince you of it."

"I want to believe you, Mr. Devlin—Grant. But perhaps you hope to gain a greater fortune by marrying me."

The yearning in her voice hurt. She loved him, too. He had not been wrong. But his plans . . . all of his plans . . . "Marry you? Did anyone say anything about marriage, at least in the immediate future?"

"Oh. What *were* you suggesting, then?"

"Nothing so scandalous as you're thinking. Listen, my love. If your father frowns on a gardener, what will he think of an illegitimate gambler with no home?"

"He will like it that you have noble blood," she said doubtfully.

"He will be more pleased if I have an independent fortune.

Cappel's Landing needs vast expenditures to bring it to the mark. When we're free of this scrape, I'll work harder to accomplish my goal—"

"Gambling, you mean."

"I have no other way, Britt."

"If you wish to marry me, you must return Cappel's Landing to Lord Tambry."

"What?"

"I cannot build my happiness on that man's misfortune."

He felt an instant's fury, then a lightening of spirits, as though a long-held burden was lifting from him. She was forcing him to do the thing he knew to be right. He'd not had the courage alone. He had not been happy enough. But there was another consideration.

"If I do that, it will take years before we can wed."

"No, it won't. If I go home, Papa will force me to marry Morris Culpepper. I think—I think—"

"Go on, Britt. There can be no secrets between us now."

"Well, it seems dreadfully bold to say, but I see no other choice but for us to free ourselves and continue on to Gretna Green."

He felt a moment's elation, then sense returned. A moment more, and she would have him as mad as herself. "Have you learned nothing over the past few days? You can't live as I do; you deserve better."

"It will only be for a while. Don't forget my inheritance in a few years."

"Much can happen in a few years, my darling. You cannot mean to scrape out a living as I do, never knowing if the night will bring a roof over your head."

"I could endure anything so long as I was with you," she said solemnly.

A wave of tenderness swept over him. "Let's plan a way out of here. Then we'll see."

Her mischievous grin gleamed in the moonlight. "I already have a plan."

Without another word, she began to bounce the chair closer,

turning her back to him. Seconds later, she tipped over, grunting at the impact of flesh against wood. Both of them lay tensely still, waiting. When no one rushed through the door, she scooted downward until their hands met. Fingers tangled together, reaching, searching.

"I'm useless," he said. "My hands are swollen."

"It's no wonder; you've been lying there all day. Let me try."

Moments passed as she fumbled at the ropes at his wrists. At last he felt them loosen, then fall away. Blood pounded to his fingertips, making him dizzy with pain. There was no time to give in to it. He brought his hands around, flexed his fingers, pushed himself to a sitting position to loosen his feet. He cursed at his clumsy slowness, but eventually the ropes unknotted. Within seconds, he removed his left boot and the knife inside it. Immediately he turned to Brittania and carefully slashed her bonds.

Taking her in his arms, he kissed her briefly. Then, with her help, he struggled to his feet. He felt dismayed at his lack of strength. If they failed to slip away undetected, he would not be able to fight the blond giant lying outside.

Quietly he pulled Brittania toward the door, then slowly nudged it wider open. He cringed at the sound of creaking hinges. Yards away, the fire burned low inside a circle of stones. Turner, his mouth open on loud snores, lay on a blanket nearby.

Grant raised an eyebrow and whispered, "Your taste in men is not very flattering."

"I never saw him asleep before," she mouthed into his ear.

"I'm glad to hear it." He glanced into the shadows around the fire. "Where's the woman?"

"Right 'ere beside you, pointing a gun at yer 'ead," said a voice.

Grant swerved, pushing Brittania back at the same instant, as Claude's woman emerged from the corner of the house, her hand balancing a long pistol at him. She laughed at his shocked expression and walked closer.

"Drop that blade, me 'andsome," she said, gesturing with her weapon until he slowly complied. "Good thing fer me I 'ad to 'eed nature's call, weren't it?" Entirely ignoring Brittania, she spoke only to him, her gaze running along his frame with appreciation.

"Good for you, perhaps, but not so fortunate for us," replied Grant, allowing his glance to roam with equal favor. "Why is a lovely lass like you—Talba, is it?—keeping such bad company?"

She laughed loudly enough to cause Seth's snoring to pause. Keeping his eyes on her approach, Grant held his breath until the raucous sounds began again.

"Don't waste yer pretty words, me 'andsome. Me an' Claude are going to be rich, thanks to that spoilt miss shaking be'ind ye." Speaking louder, she added, "Up, Seth! Seth!"

The gardener stirred, his lids flickering open. At that instant, Talba's hand began to waver as loud noises turned her attention to the road. With torches held aloft, a party of men on horseback was approaching as fast as the pathway allowed.

Without hesitation, Grant snatched the gun from the woman's hand and pushed her aside. Turner's eyes widened. He rolled to his feet, fumbling beneath the blankets. As soon as Grant saw the glint of metal, he fired. The gardener howled and clutched his bleeding hand to his chest, his blunderbuss falling to the earth.

"Get his gun!" Grant ordered Brittania. "We'll hold them off!"

To his consternation, she ignored him and ran toward the riders. "It is not Claude!" she called over her shoulder. "It's Papa!"

Grant felt a terrible sinking in his stomach. Better had it been the gardener's brother.

The pounding of hooves lessened and stopped. Several of the men dismounted. A few of them apprehended Turner, who was trying to slink away. Two others went for Talba, and another pair came in his direction, drawing him over to face the wrath of the tall, graying man who could only be Brittania's father.

Grant had never seen anyone so full of thunder. Distantly he heard Brittania explaining and explaining, but he could make no sense of it. The tight fingers gripping either arm brought him back to attention.

"Do you think I could fail to track you, missy?" Sir Rutland was shouting. "Even had we not caught Claude Turner, you left a clear trail after telling everyone of your dallying with this—this by-blow."

"There was no dallying, sir," Grant said swiftly. "She lied about that to save me from a duel."

"Lied or fried, I have nothing to say to you, young man, no matter if I did go to school with your father. I should kill you, and no one would fault me if I did, least of all the earl. Nevertheless, I've decided to let my daughter suffer the consequences of her actions. I'll not tolerate a little surprise sullying our name nine months hence and shaming her mother. I've brought a parson and a special license. I'm giving you notice that no matter what happens in the next minutes, I'm banishing Brittania to my plantation in the West Indies until this scandal dies or I do. Now, sir, here is your choice. Do you choose my daughter, or do you choose to hang? I give you no clues as to which will be worse!"

Disbelief, then sunrise dawned on Brittania's face. "Oh, *Papa!*"

Grant shrugged free of his captors and opened his arms wide. Brittania shot into his embrace, almost tumbling him to the ground in her joy. Grant rested his cheek against her head and tried to hide his smile.

"This plantation, sir," he said. "Might it be anywhere near Bao-Bao?"

WATCH FOR THESE REGENCY ROMANCES

YOU WON'T WANT TO READ
JUST ONE—KATHERINE STONE

ROOMMATES   (0-8217-5206-5, $6.99/$7.99)
No one could have prepared Carrie for the monumental
changes she would face when she met her new circle of friends
at Stanford University. Once their lives intertwined and became
woven into the tapestry of the times, they would never be the
same.

TWINS   (0-8217-5207-3, $6.99/$7.99)
Brook and Melanie Chandler were so different, it was hard to
believe they were sisters. One was a dark, serious, ambitious
New York attorney; the other, a golden, glamourous, sophisti-
cated supermodel. But they were more than sisters—they were
twins and more alike than even they knew . . .

THE CARLTON CLUB   (0-8217-5204-9, $6.99/$7.99)
It was the place to see and be seen, the only place to be. And
for those who frequented the playground of the very rich, it
was a way of life. Mark, Kathleen, Leslie and Janet—they
worked together, played together, and loved together, all behind
exclusive gates of the *Carlton Club*.

*Available wherever paperbacks are sold, or order direct from the
Publisher. Send cover price plus 50¢ per copy for mailing and
handling to Penguin USA, P.O. Box 999, c/o Dept. 17109,
Bergenfield, NJ 07621. Residents of New York and Tennessee
must include sales tax. DO NOT SEND CASH.*